THE
HEART
OF THE
WORLD

ALSO BY AMIE KAUFMAN

The Isles of the Gods Duology

The Starbound Trilogy
(with Meagan Spooner)

The Unearthed Duology
(with Meagan Spooner)

The Other Side of the Sky Duology
(with Meagan Spooner)

The Elementals Trilogy (for children)

The World Between Blinks Duology
(with Ryan Graudin, for children)

ALSO BY AMIE KAUFMAN
AND JAY KRISTOFF

Aurora Rising (Aurora Cycle_01)

Aurora Burning (Aurora Cycle_02)

Aurora's End (Aurora Cycle_03)

Illuminae (The Illuminae Files_01)

Gemina (The Illuminae Files_02)

Obsidio (The Illuminae Files_03)

Memento (The Illuminae Files_0.5)

THE HEART OF THE WORLD

THE ISLES OF THE GODS
VOLUME 2

AMIE KAUFMAN

ALFRED A. KNOPF
NEW YORK

THIS IS A BORZOI BOOK PUBLISHED BY ALFRED A. KNOPF

This is a work of fiction. Names, characters, places, and incidents either are the product of the author's imagination or are used fictitiously. Any resemblance to actual persons, living or dead, events, or locales is entirely coincidental.

Text copyright © 2024 by LaRoux Industries Pty Ltd.
Jacket art copyright © 2024 by Aykut Aydoğdu
Map illustration copyright © 2023 by Virginia Allyn

All rights reserved. Published in the United States by Alfred A. Knopf, an imprint of Random House Children's Books, a division of Penguin Random House LLC, New York.

Knopf, Borzoi Books, and the colophon are registered trademarks of Penguin Random House LLC.

Visit us on the Web! GetUnderlined.com

Educators and librarians, for a variety of teaching tools, visit us at RHTeachersLibrarians.com

Library of Congress Cataloging-in-Publication Data is available upon request.
ISBN 978-0-593-47932-2 (trade) | ISBN 978-0-593-47934-6 (ebook) |
ISBN 978-0-593-89659-4 (intl. ed.)

The text of this book is set in 11-point Calisto MT.
Interior design by Ken Crossland

Printed in the United States of America
10 9 8 7 6 5 4 3 2 1
First Edition

Random House Children's Books supports the First Amendment and celebrates the right to read.

Penguin Random House LLC supports copyright. Copyright fuels creativity, encourages diverse voices, promotes free speech, and creates a vibrant culture. Thank you for buying an authorized edition of this book and for complying with copyright laws by not reproducing, scanning, or distributing any part in any form without permission. You are supporting writers and allowing Penguin Random House to publish books for every reader.

For Kacey

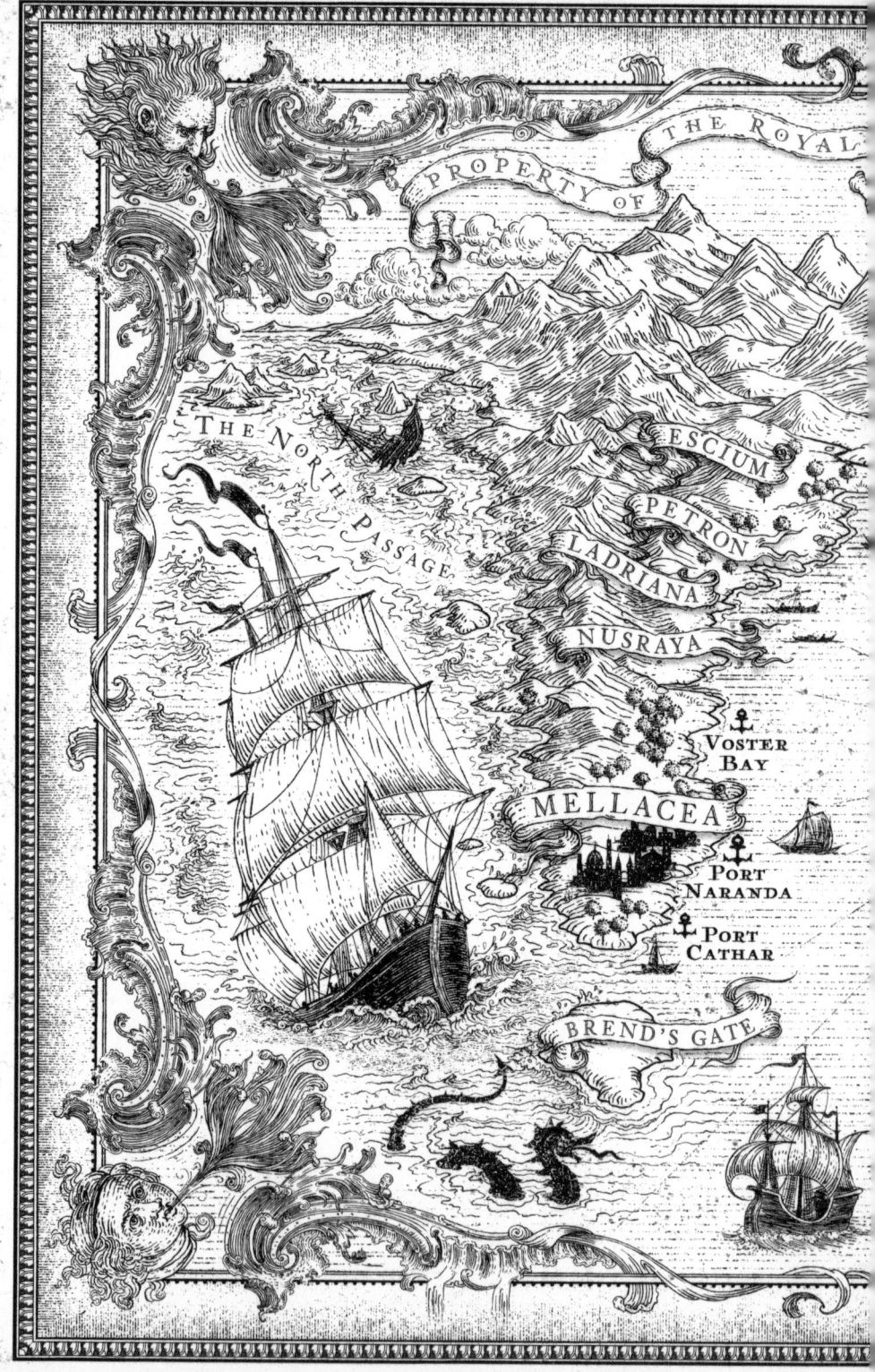

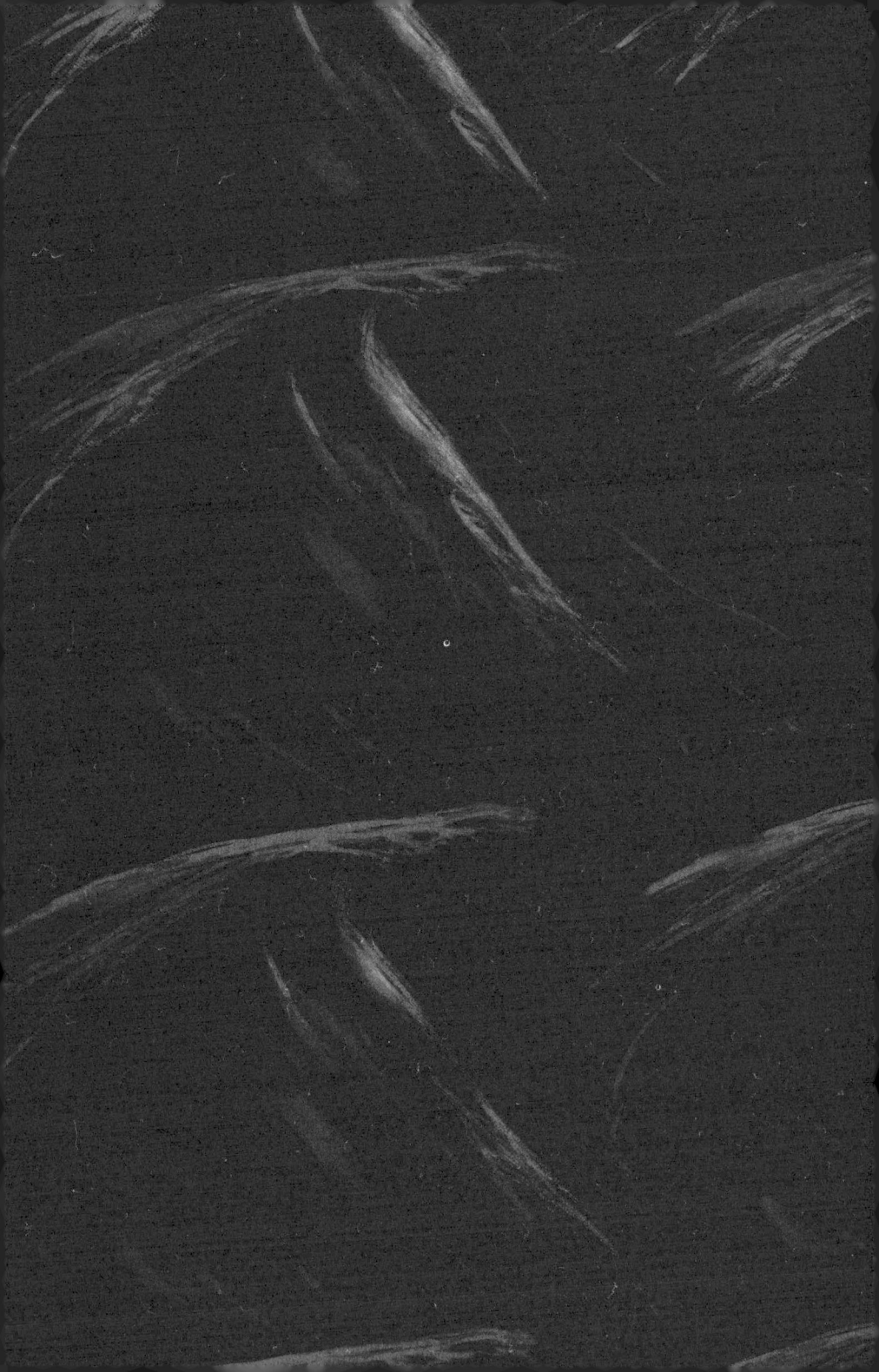

Letter from Lord Keegan Wollesley to a young scholar

You asked what happened. It's an imprecise question, but I shall do my best to answer.

Where does one begin to recount a story like this?

In the beginning there was the Mother. She created all things, and the gods were her children. They each cared for their people, until in time they grew restless, and began to war among themselves.

It was in the clash between Macean the Gambler and Barrica the Warrior that the land of Vostain was destroyed. Deprived of his followers in a single heartbeat, the laughing god Valus was no more.

So the king of Alinor, Anselm, offered such a great sacrifice, such an act of faith, that Barrica was empowered to bind Macean in sleep, and prevent him from making war. After that, the gods stepped back from our world, except for Barrica, who left the door ajar to keep watch over her sleeping brother, changing her name from Barrica the Warrior to Barrica the Sentinel.

And that's the end of the story—for five hundred years, at least.

We pick up the thread again when Prince Leander of Alinor boarded a ship to make his family's traditional pilgrimage to the Isles of the Gods, to strengthen Barrica, so she could maintain her bindings on Macean. Aboard that ship was Selly Walker, daughter of the fleet, a girl with the sea in her veins. Also aboard, your humble correspondent. I am sometimes asked if I set out as the prince's companion—the answer is no. I was en route to the Bibliotek, and unaware of the ship's change of course.

In Mellacea, faith in their sleeping god had waned over five centuries, but was now rising—the green sisters had maintained a stubborn presence, and their second-in-command, Sister Beris, was ready to awaken her god.

Her interests aligned with those of Laskia, who wished to prove to her older sister, Ruby—the leader of their gang—that she was ready for greater responsibility. Laskia intercepted and destroyed what she believed to be the prince's ship. In fact, she had found a decoy fleet, sent to distract such as her from the prince's mission.

She was accompanied by Jude Kien, once a schoolmate of Leander and myself, now a member of a Port Naranda gang. Jude's role was to identify the prince's body, but amid the carnage, his task proved impossible.

Laskia's people killed all those aboard the progress fleet and left evidence to frame the Mellacean government, hoping to prompt a war that would serve both Sister Beris's and Ruby's interests. They then came in pursuit of Selly's ship, which they had seen on the horizon, and knew to be a witness. Despite

Prince Leander's fearsome feats of magic, their pursuit was ultimately successful.

They murdered every soul aboard—or believed they had. Selly, the prince, and I survived, rigged a lifeboat, and set sail for Port Naranda in Mellacea, the only land within reach.

We intended on handing ourselves over to the Alinorish ambassador. Shortly after she met with us, however, she was assassinated—our dinghy had been discovered, and Laskia was now aware of our presence.

The assassination meant that war was inevitable, but we still hoped we could limit the damage to a conflict between humans, rather than gods. Macean was dangerously close to awakening, and we knew we had to make the sacrifice that would strengthen Barrica, at any cost.

We purchased a fishing boat, and laid in a course for the Isles of the Gods.

Upon reaching the Isle of Barrica, we discovered that Laskia had sent thugs to destroy the temple. The sacrifice was now impossible.

With Laskia close behind us, we pressed on to the Isle of the Mother in the hope of finding her temple intact. Legend has it that all gods are present in the temple of their mother, and we hoped to find Barrica's presence strong enough to receive a sacrifice.

We arrived with only moments to spare, and discovered there was no way down to the altar. Knowing a great sacrifice was called for, Leander offered his life, leaping from above. In doing so, he unexpectedly empowered Barrica enough that she was able to save him from death, making him a Messenger.

As his new power threatened to overwhelm Leander, Selly

bound herself to him as his anchor, sharing the load, and saving his life.

Laskia attempted to emulate him, and also made the leap. With her god bound in sleep, he was slow to respond, and we set sail for Kirkpool and home, believing we had witnessed her death.

We were wrong.

PART ONE

HOMECOMING

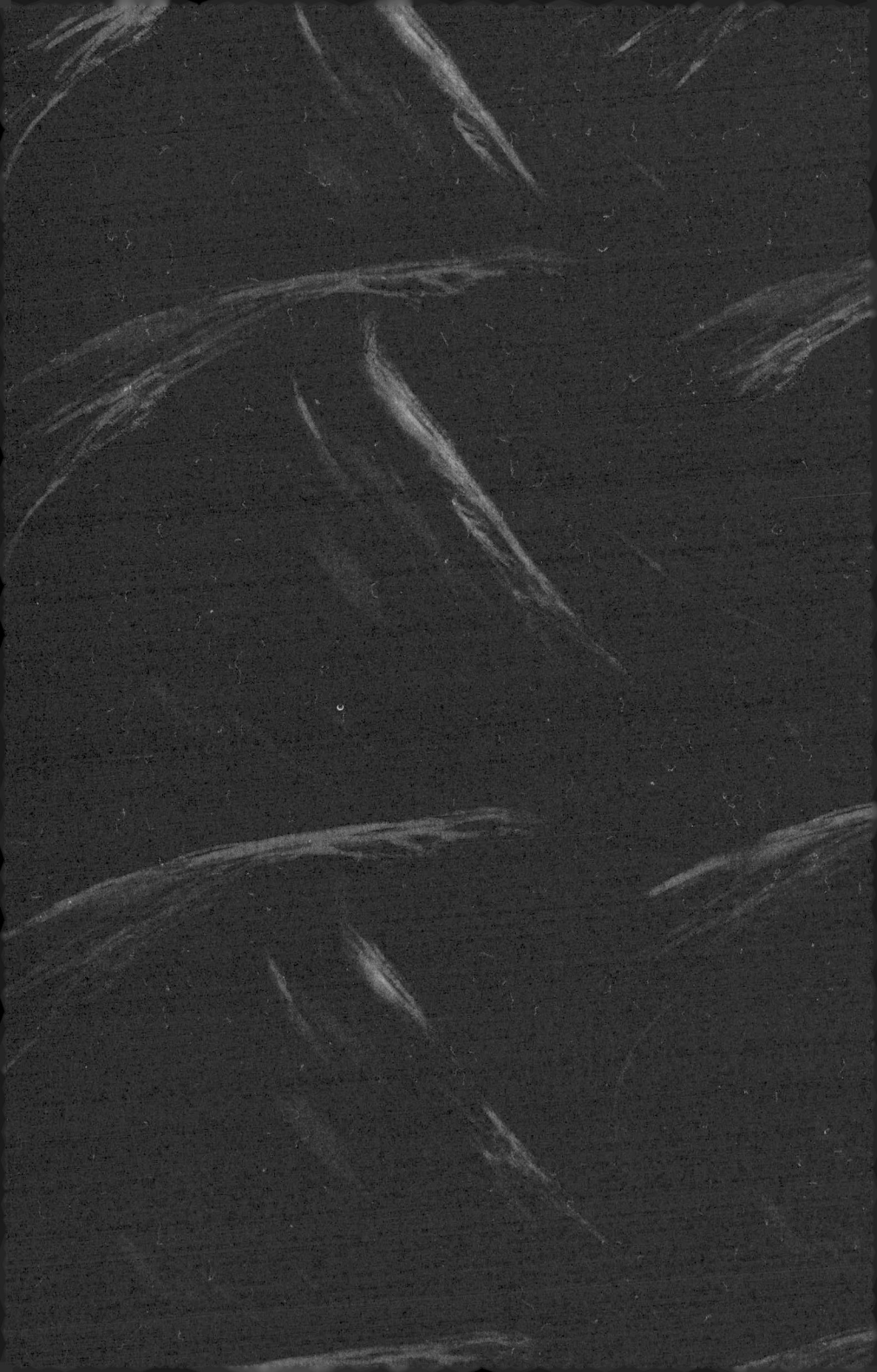

SELLY

The Docks
Kirkpool, Alinor

Everything in Kirkpool that can float, from a battleship to a bathtub, is coming to greet us. Steamships and schooners, merchants and fishing boats, they're all jostling for space in crowded harbor waters made choppy by their maneuvering.

The decks are thick with bodies, and everyone's cheering, flying sapphire-blue Alinorish flags, waving as the *Emma* makes her way in toward the golden city on the hill.

Leander stands silently at my side, gazing out across the harbor with a calm I'm desperate to break. There's no easy laugh, no wink to put me at ease, no joke about how this kind of welcoming committee is just another day in his charmed life, full of all the usual admirers. When I scan his eyes, I can read nothing in them.

Before he became a vessel for the power of his goddess, his gaze was the warm brown mahogany of a ship's timbers. Now it's the same emerald green as our magician's marks.

I know he's in there, though. I *know*.

I grip the wheel tighter and exchange a glance with Keegan as we enter the thickest part of the cheering fleet, the boats around us sitting low in the water, every one of them loaded to the point of instability. Our scholar is taking it all in solemnly.

The crowd is shouting and singing, greeting us as joyfully as if we've won a war for them. And I suppose we have.

For all of them, this moment is more than victory. And then I hear the word in their cries.

Messenger!

Somehow they know what Leander is—just as they knew he was coming. "Seven hells, Keegan, do you . . . ?"

"I hear it," he murmurs. "But how word has traveled ahead of us, I don't know."

The cries around us are of pure joy. Alinor has a Messenger, and Mellacea will be forced to cower before us. This is absolute triumph.

They don't understand that we paid for this power with their prince.

Leander shifts his weight toward me, and lifts one hand to lay it over mine where I grip the wheel. A shiver of magic goes through me, like the static before a storm, my body prickling.

It happens every time he touches me, this current of raw power. He's barely left my side since we left the Isle of the Mother—and Laskia's broken body, and Jude's broken spirit—behind.

When I sleep, Leander sits quietly with me, and when I come up on deck, he follows, never out of reach. I can tell where he is at any given moment without turning my head, feel the press of his mind against mine as clearly as if it were his fingers weaving through mine to squeeze.

"We shouldn't talk to anybody until we've seen Queen Augusta," Keegan says, walking back along the deck toward us.

"I'm not planning on giving interviews," I reply. Somehow we'd both thought we would just quietly sail back into Kirkpool, find a place to tie up, and then figure out a way into the palace. This is . . . the opposite of that.

He speaks gently. "We need to tell her *everything*, Selly. These people must not know the decoy fleet is gone, or they wouldn't be celebrating like this."

"Oh, goddess," I breathe, and for a moment, as if in response to the word, the air around me shifts the way it does before a storm, close and heavy. Barrica's nearer to us than she was before Leander became her Messenger. The words that were once a simple epithet are now . . . something else, when whispered so close to her vessel.

"Leander," I say softly. "It's getting harder to sail, the wind in here is a mess with so many boats. Can you please guide us in?"

He doesn't reply—he hasn't since it happened—but I know he can hear me.

At night, I dream of him—I see him through frosted glass, or on the other side of a jostling crowd, never quite able to reach him. And it *is* him, I know it is. I know he's not gone, even if I don't know how to reach him yet.

I wake up each morning *knowing* I was just talking to him. I remember the feel of it—the warmth of his smile, like sunlight—and seeing the whole of him, not just the ghost of him, in his gaze.

Last night, I dreamed he was at the bottom of the sea, standing on white sand, reaching up to me. I was on the surface, trying desperately to dive down to him, tremors running through my limbs, nausea pushing its way up my throat.

Time and again I'd duck underwater, trying to claw my way through the currents, my lungs burning and bursting—and every time I'd fall short, shooting back up to gasp for air, my eyes stinging with salt, my heart pounding so hard I could feel it in my temples.

He stretched his hand out to me, fingers grasping, his wide eyes pleading with me to come for him. I woke, gasping for breath and blinking back tears.

He's reaching out, trying to talk to me through my dreams from where he's hunkered down behind his barricades.

The first night of our voyage home, Keegan and I talked about the strangeness of my connection with Leander. We sat on deck, beneath an extraordinary blanket of twinkling stars, barely able to believe we'd survived the chase to the temple that day, let alone everything that came after.

"The concept of a Messenger sharing a bond with someone like this was never in the stories," Keegan said.

Leander was at my side, and though his breathing had evened out from the pained rasp it had been as we left the Temple of the Mother, he was still pressed close against me. There was nothing of my laughing, charming prince in him now. He felt more like a scared animal, sensitive to every noise, flinching at every movement.

"The stories are centuries old," I pointed out. "Who knows what details were lost?"

"Almost all of them, I'd say. Messengers always vanished from the historical record so quickly. Like fireflies, a flash before they were gone again. Something about you, about the connection between you . . . you keep him here, like an anchor."

Sensing Leander's struggle to hold himself together over the past few days, I can see why the Messengers from history disappeared so soon after they showed up. The sheer amount of power in him threatens to split him at the seams. It's all too easy to guess at the fate of the Messengers from the old stories.

The vast energy he's trying to contain fizzes between us, jumping in tiny zaps of static. Somehow I'm helping him, but apart from being close to him, I don't know what it is I'm doing.

I have to figure it out, before the magic builds inside him to unbearable levels.

If the Messengers of the past never had anchors, then maybe his fate can be different. Maybe he won't simply flicker out like a firefly's glow in the darkness.

This boy fought for me, and I fought for him, and I will *not* let him go.

The water currents shift around us to carry the *Emma* along, and I can see the glinting pinpricks of the air spirits as they press against the sails to keep them from flapping. Leander doesn't even seem to charm the spirits anymore—they just rush to do as he wishes.

Effortlessly they carry us through the fleet, the water choppy as the steamships churn it up with their propellers, the wind gusting and then lulling as we travel in and out of the shadows of sails.

As we draw closer to the dock, I can make out the individual faces of the blue-clad Queensguard, linking arms to hold back the onlookers from the place that's been cleared for us to dock. There are sailors crowded onto the decks of all the ships in prime positions nearby, craning their necks for a look at Leander.

My chest aches, and my throat tightens at the sight of them. I should be standing on the deck of the *Lizabetta*. It should be Rensa guiding us in.

Leander's grip on my hand tightens, his skin cool against mine. He senses my sadness, I know it. I lean in to press my shoulder to his, to feel the warmth of him.

Keegan starts to lower the sail as we close the distance between us and the dock, and the air spirits dance in the puffs of current left behind as the canvas folds in on itself. When the *Emma* bumps in gently against the worn timbers of the dock, there are many hands waiting to make us fast.

"Who's in charge?" I ask as a couple of Queensguard jump down to locate our mooring lines. I can hear how brittle my voice sounds.

The guards look up to the dock, where a man with a shock of blond hair stands, his handsome face slack with awe. "I, uh—" he begins, then pulls himself together and snaps a salute. "I am."

"We need to head up to the palace *right now*," I say. "In a closed carriage."

"Right away," he agrees, somehow standing even *more* upright.

"Leander." I turn my attention back to my prince and squeeze his hand. "Let's go. Come with me." In the same way that Leander taught me to cast my mind out for spirits, now I reach for his—there's the crackling sensation of power passing between us for a moment, a hint of *him,* and then it's over. He's understood, and together we cross the deck.

The Queensguard who wait for us shift their weight as they watch, uncertain. I can imagine how we must look to them, now we're up close. Hardly heroes, with our old, ragged clothes, our sunburned skin, chapped lips, shadowed eyes.

The captain offers his hand, and Keegan takes it first, climbing up to join him on the dock. I go next, gripping tightly as I scramble after him—it's a long step up from a boat as small as the *Emma.*

I see the moment the Queensguard captain notices the magician's marks on my forearm—geometric, different from any I've ever seen before, or any he's seen, I'm sure. His grip slackens for an instant, before he recovers.

They formed when I used my magic for the first time, to calm a storm near the Isles, to save Leander's life. We had no time to learn what they meant before I became my prince's anchor, holding him in place in the world.

I say nothing, but turn to offer my hand to Leander. He grips it and climbs up, agile despite his seeming obliviousness to the world around him.

The moment he sets foot on the dock, a shock wave of pure magic ripples out from us. The timbers groan a protest, and cries go up as the circle of onlookers stagger for balance.

It's like being hit by lightning. My mouth tastes of copper, my limbs are numb for an instant, then tingle unbearably, and then comes a wash of pure, righteous wrath.

Divine power bubbles up, threatening to overwhelm me and making me itch to find a weapon, *any* weapon.

The roar of the crowd has become a battle cry, and the Queensguard are reaching for their weapons without knowing where the enemy is.

This is the power of Barrica, the warrior goddess, with a Messenger standing on Alinorish soil once more.

I swing around toward Leander, but a shock runs through me as our gazes meet—his emerald eyes have changed again.

Now, I see the storm we battle every night raging in his irises. In a moment, he'll be completely consumed by the bloodlust raging around us, by the magic flowing through him.

And it will burn him up.

Without thinking I throw my arms around him, press my temple to his, and launch my mind into the space where our dreams live.

The next instant I've been transported somewhere else, and I'm lost in a sea of people. My body is buffeted this way and that, like a paper boat in a storm. Someone slams into my shoulder and spins me around, but before I can focus my gaze, the ground tilts, and I'm stumbling again.

A chorus of voices rises all around me, echoing harshly, too garbled to understand. I squint, but there's bright light coming from somewhere, and my eyes tear up, stinging.

A door slams nearby, and it's like an earthquake, the force of it rippling through the ground beneath my feet. I press my hands over my ears, and the air seems to thicken around me until it's like breathing water, though I can't find the familiar tang of sea salt on my tongue. Instead, it tastes like blood.

"Selly!" Someone's calling my name, but there are bodies coming and going, and another roar shakes us like dice in a cup. There's a sensation like water sweeping around my legs, trying to knock me off balance, but when I look down there's nothing there.

"Selly!"

I know that voice.

"Leander!" My voice cracks, and tears stream down my cheeks. "Leander, where are you?"

Then he's there. He grabs my hand and pulls me through the crowd. "This way!" he shouts over the roar, and I can only read the shape of the words on his lips.

Suddenly there's a door, and he yanks it open, bundling me through it. Together we put our shoulders against it, shoving it closed against the press of the crowd, and with a click, it locks. The sound on the other side dims to a dull buzz, and I can hear the harsh rasp of our breath.

We stand pinned in place, staring at each other. Then something between us breaks, and I throw myself into his arms. He wraps me up, his breath still ragged in my ear, and holds me tight. I can't stop myself from touching him, from making sure over and over again that he's real. I run my hand along his arm. I cup his cheek and drink in his face. I revel in the press of his fingertips against my skin. It's *him*. And he's been hiding here, a prisoner inside his own mind.

For that, I realize with sudden clarity, is where we are.

Though I've never been there, I recognize the marble floors

and painted walls of the palace, his home, his retreat. We're standing on a balcony, like the sort that overlooks a theater—I've never been on one, but I've looked up to see them from the cheap seats.

Sapphire-blue curtains frame the view out into nothingness. There are cushions piled up on the floor to make a giant nest, each embroidered with an emerald-green design that's all straight lines. Now that I'm looking around, I see the design is on everything: the wallpaper, the thick carpet beneath our feet, even carved into the wood of the balcony's railing.

Leander clutches at my arms, and when I look down, a jolt of recognition runs through me. Every embroidered line of the cushions, every pattern engraved in the wood around us, all of it . . . is *me*. It's the strange geometric lines of my magician's marks. The marks that appeared as I protected him in the storm.

"I can hear her voice, Selly." He's hoarse with exhaustion, swaying on his feet.

"Whose voice?" I ask, but I know the answer. It sits like a lead weight inside me.

"Barrica. The goddess. She's out there." With a nod of his head, he indicates a door on the other side of the balcony, opposite the one we came through.

"She wants you to let her in?"

"Yes. But the world is so loud, so bright—how can I face a *goddess*?" His eyes—still surging with Barrica's power—meet mine, full of fear. His terror staggers me, as though someone has sunk a hook between my ribs and is tugging at my heart. His fear is an ache I can hardly bear, and I lean in to rest my forehead against his.

Before either of us can say anything else, the ruckus rises to a fever pitch, the world he's kept at bay howling to be let in to swallow him whole.

"Leander, we have to go!" I shout over the din.

But he just shakes his head, his arms tightening around me. "I can't—it's all too much, too loud. The pain . . ."

The door gives a terrible, squealing groan, like a ship coming apart at the seams.

"We can't stay here," I say in his ear, trying not to jump at each splintering crack behind us. "You have to come back with me. There has to be a way out of here, Leander. Barrica bound us together—she can't have meant it just to be this."

He draws back, his green eyes meeting mine. "Selly— I don't know how."

The palace of his mind trembles, as if under attack from some terrible siege engine beyond the walls. A war machine, ready to crush the very stones of this place to dust in order to reach Leander.

Barrica.

She's fighting to be let into his mind—to be let into the world.

Deep in my gut lies the certainty that we *must not* open the door that keeps our goddess from our world. The last time the gods walked among us, they turned an entire country to dust.

I shift my arms around Leander to take hold of his shoulders, giving him the tiniest shake to get him to focus on my face. "It's either the storm or the goddess. Leander, you have to trust me."

Leander shudders and says nothing, too consumed by the effort of holding the attacking forces on either side of him at bay.

The door gives another agonized scream under the pressure of the crowds outside it, conjuring up a sudden memory of riding the *Lizabetta* through a howling gale, listening to her wail as she was battered by wind and waves—but she held.

Storms at sea are so loud, someone can shout in your ear and you won't hear them. But a ship knows how to give. Even if her timbers are groaning, and her sails are cracking, and it feels like she's going to break apart on the next wave. She's built to let the force of the storm run through her. Her captain, her crew . . . they know what to do.

I lift my head, staring at Leander, feeling a sudden, wild grin flash across my face. *I* know what to do.

In one movement I turn the handle and the door flies open. The roar of the crowd—the screams, the dissonant shouts—washes over us like waves. The blinding lights dazzle my vision. My skin stings as though grains of sand are whipping through the air like a million tiny arrows, all striking us at once.

But I tilt my head and unfocus my gaze as Leander taught me, and the roiling mass of bodies before us shifts—suddenly I see them all like spirits, just white lines, dancing lights.

I raise one hand and make a fist, grabbing the fabric of the dream and twisting. In one motion, I send them all swirling and melting into water.

Their shouts become thunder.

The flashes of light become lightning.

Their jostling becomes the wind, the waves bashing away at us.

We're at sea in a storm.

And I was *born* knowing how to sail.

I've made the game into something I can win, and as the rain begins to fall, plastering our hair flat against our heads, I smile into the storm. I show my teeth.

"Grab that line, my prince, and haul! We can sail out of here!"

SELLY

The Docks
Kirkpool, Alinor

My eyes snap open, bright light dazzling them. My whole body aches, pain shooting through my muscles as they clench and spasm. I'm locked in place—I can't see, and I can't move.

Then sound comes rushing in—shouts all around me—and I feel the rough wood of the dock against my back, and then I *remember.*

Leander. The storm.

I'm back in the real world. But is he?

I've only felt like this once before, after scrambling with my crew to see the *Lizabetta* through a freak hurricane—and even then, my battered, bruised body didn't feel this . . . *hollow.* I try to sit up and give a ragged, hoarse cry.

Then something—*someone*—blocks out the sun.

The tousled hair, the way he tilts his head, silhouetted

against the light . . . I'm half made of hope and half desperately afraid of what I'll see.

Then I blink away the tears, and it's Leander looking back at me. He's looking back at me properly, those green eyes of his full of life, full of *him*.

"Leander?" I whisper, barely audible, as if too loud a noise, too sudden an expression of the hope that's washing through me might scare him away.

His fingers tighten around mine.

"I'm here," he whispers, his voice husky as he speaks his first words in days. "You saw me through the storm."

Tears well up to blur my vision, and my body is weightless with relief.

"Easy there, sailor," he murmurs, trying for a tease, and falling desperately short.

I ignore the pain that sears my muscles as I reach up to grab him and pull him down to me. His body is warm against mine, his heart beating steadily, and all I can think is, *He's here, he's here, he's here with me.*

"Say it again," I whisper, trying to ignore the pain hammering at my temples. "Say you've come back."

"I've come back," he whispers. He looks exhausted, his eyes shadowed, strain showing in his face. But it's him—truly him.

"I was so afraid. . . ." My throat closes, and I bury my head against his shoulder, letting him hold me once more.

"Me too," he murmurs. "Me too, Selly."

And then someone clears their throat above us. "Your Highness . . ."

Leander rolls over onto his back to collapse beside me, and

we both gaze up at the deeply flustered captain of the Queensguard. He's still holding his unsheathed sword, having drawn it during the onslaught of Barrica's will before I pulled Leander into our shared dream, but he holds it loosely, uncertainly. Like a nobleman who's just been handed a hoe and told to plant a field. I guess this wasn't in any of his training manuals.

"Captain," says Leander, with a fair imitation of his usual grin. "I don't suppose you'd like to put that away?"

The man's eyes widen, and he looks down at his sword in confusion. He fumbles with it, trying to follow his prince's orders. Keegan steps cautiously around him and stoops to offer me a hand, heaving me to my feet, and then does the same for Leander. Every movement is agony—it feels like I've actually sailed through a storm, my body aching with the punishment that comes the day after you've pushed too far.

For a beat, the three of us look at each other, hardly able to believe we're standing on home soil, together.

"I suppose we'd better get to the palace," Leander says, lifting his head to gaze around the harbor, lined with his screaming subjects. "My sister is going to have many, many questions."

"We have an auto waiting," the captain ventures nervously. "And a route has been cleared."

I've never been in an auto before. There are two bench seats facing each other. Leander and I take one, and Keegan and the captain—who looks like he'd rather ride on the roof than in the presence of a prince and Messenger—take the other. The engine rumbles, and the seat vibrates beneath me.

I watch the world go by beyond the window as the auto begins to glide away from the dock and up the hill toward the palace.

And for all I've bent every effort since the Isles to getting here, suddenly I want nothing so much as to throw open the door, to tumble out and pull Leander with me. I want to run back toward the *Emma,* and the sea. I didn't take proper note of the moment I left the water behind, of the moment I stepped off my ship. Now, I feel as though I should have. Regret lances through me, quick and sharp.

Our driver carefully makes her way along the cobbled road, past the streets that branch off to either side, past the homes and shop fronts, the last, ragged flowers before winter spilling out of window boxes. There are people hanging out of every window to get a look at us, and they're cheering, waving flags. Autos and carriages have pulled over to the side of the road, their wheels up on the pavement to clear the way for us.

"How did you know we were coming?" Keegan asks, breaking the silence.

"Barrica spoke to us," the captain replies, a note of awe in his voice. "Her voice rang out in every temple. I heard it myself. She said her Messenger was coming by sea. And we all—I was there, and I can't explain it—we knew it was Prince Leander. I don't remember her saying it. I don't even remember the words she used. But we knew."

I can see his uncertainty, though he tries to hide it behind his stiff posture. I can see the questions he wants to ask trying to push their way up his throat. The Alinorish have always had signs our goddess was real—the flowers in our temples bloom year-round, and our wells refill themselves before our eyes at the spring festival. Other countries lack that proof—ours is the goddess who remained closest to our world, to keep an eye on her sleeping brother.

Still, it's one thing to see flowers bloom, and another to hear her very voice. The cheering reception waiting for us was our first clue, but it's the captain's expression that's really telling me what we're in for.

As we get farther from the port, there are barriers along the sides of the road to keep the cheering crowds back, clearing a path all the way up Royal Hill from the docks. The edges of the street are jammed with bodies, a sea of people waving little Alinorish flags, sapphire blue with the white spear to signify Barrica the Warrior. Others are throwing streamers, sapphire blue and magician's green, jostling their neighbors to see the Messenger.

Some of them are gasping and pointing, too, and it takes me a moment to understand why. Then I see it, and my gasp echoes around the inside of the auto.

As we pass each building, the flowers in the window boxes, mostly pale and limp as winter threatens, start to bloom. Their blossoms flood with color, and each of them begins to grow. Even the ones that aren't vines seem to become them, and they wind across buildings and down drainpipes, up lampposts and across shop fronts. The air fills with a gorgeous perfume, and I turn my gaze toward Leander.

"Did you do that?"

"Not on purpose," he mutters. But he doesn't ask what I'm talking about, even though he hasn't turned his head to look. I can feel the power in him buzzing against my skin where our shoulders are pressed together.

The screaming grows louder as we make our way up the hill, the flowering vines keeping pace with us, snaking from building to building and across the street like a canopy. People are holding up their children now—to see Leander or to seek his blessing, I don't know. I can't help ducking my head as the noise builds.

"You all right?" he asks quietly.

The truth is that I'd rather sail through another hurricane than deal with this, and I'm sure he can sense that, as easily as I can sense him through our bond. But I pull myself together. "You know, the last time I was on this road, I was coming down the hill. I was hitching a ride on the back of a carriage, and some fool's parade of autos was holding up traffic."

"Sounds unbearable," Leander replies, grinning.

"Well, I was about to meet a boy at the docks who was far worse, so that put it into perspective for me."

He laughs, and with a pang, I realize I can't remember the last time I heard him do that. "It'll be over soon, I promise. It's just a parade. We're nearly home, the palace is just ahead."

Just a parade.

Home. Palace.

There's a ringing in my ears I don't think has anything to do with the noise.

I always knew who Leander was, but until this moment, I'm not sure I *knew* it, in my bones, in my heart. Spirits save me.

The boy beside me is a *prince.* The things that are normal to him . . . How am I ever, ever supposed to do this?

The driver turns off the main road, and I glance at Leander, who leans in to speak to the captain over the noise of the crowd. "Where is she going?"

"The Temple of Barrica, Your Highness," he replies. "We set up the route to—that is, we assumed . . ."

"Of course," Leander says, with a tight smile.

There's a flock of clergy gathered on the front steps of the temple like seagulls waiting for a feast.

Their robes are an imitation of ancient military uniforms. They wear kilts and chest plates, but the armor is quilted metallic fabric, rather than anything that would actually stop a weapon. A few have spears, and all of them are standing at attention like soldiers.

I'm used to seeing them out the front of the temple, trying to eyeball people into attending services, or holding out dishes for donations, but this is something else. Every one of them has their gaze trained on Leander, and there's a light in their eyes . . . this is as close as they've ever come to meeting their goddess. Over the past few days it's been easy to forget where his power comes from. But these people haven't.

A man walks forward as we climb out of the auto. He's trembling as he salutes, clearly holding himself together by willpower alone. "Your Highness," he says, holding the salute, tears in his eyes. He has an open, friendly face, with golden-brown skin and thinning black hair that he's cut short.

"Father Marsen," says Leander, with a polite nod. None of his discomfort is visible yet, but I can feel it rippling through me. He keeps it from showing by turning to bring me into the conversation. "Selly, this is Father Marsen, head of the Alinorish church. Father, Selly Walker."

"Miss Walker, a pleasure." Father Marsen turns his gaze on me, a question in his eyes. He's friendly still, but clearly wondering what a saltblood's doing standing beside his prince and Messenger.

"Selly . . . anchors me," Leander says quietly, curling his hand around mine. "She's why I'm here."

"Our nation stands in your debt," Father Marsen says, turning that salute on me.

He leads us past the ranks of saluting clergy and inside the temple, the noise of the crowd cut off so abruptly as we step over the threshold that it's clearly the work of the goddess. Our footsteps echo up to the soaring ceilings. The beauty of this place isn't in intricate carvings or complicated architecture. This is a soldier's temple, and the lines are clean, simple, and straight. Each sandstone block is perfectly aligned.

Rows of pews face an unadorned altar at the front, and the only decorations are the flowers in full bloom, as if it were the height of summer, spilling from baskets on every column. That's not Leander's work—it's always been that way in Alinorish temples. A sign that Barrica had left the door ajar and could still glimpse our world.

Leander's hand is clammy in mine as we walk toward the altar, and when I glance at him, there's a strange glow to his green eyes. I can already tell this is going to be too much for him—I can feel power leaking into me through his grip, just an unpleasant sense of pins and needles, but I don't think he knows it's happening.

I cast an apologetic glance at the priest as my prince tows me ahead of everyone else, but he doesn't look annoyed—rather, he's reverently scuttling along after us.

The altar itself is a simple table, set in front of a huge stone statue of Barrica. She wears a chest plate and kilt, like her clergy, and holds up a sword and shield. When I try to study her face, I can't quite focus on it, and when I look away, I can't quite remember her stern, beautiful features.

Leander drops my hand and takes a couple of steps forward, standing alone to gaze up at the statue. I feel, rather than see, Father Marsen step up beside me.

"He is a blessing," he says quietly, studying Leander.

"I'm just glad he's alive," I reply, keeping my voice low. Leander's still dressed in the same ragged clothes he's been in for days—all three of us are—but there's a power to him that makes it hard to look away.

"You are a blessing too," Father Marsen says.

"Me?"

"Indeed. No Messenger before him has had someone like you at their side. It gives me hope that our goddess saw what was needed, and provided."

"I'm doing my best."

"You were made for him, my child."

"I feel like I should confess that I didn't go to temple a lot, growing up."

His smile takes me by surprise. "Nor did I, actually. My faith came when I was older. And yours is written on you."

"What do you mean?"

"Your marks," he says. "Look up." He lifts one hand to point, and I follow the line of his finger.

There, on Barrica's shield and down the blade of her sword, are geometric designs, straight lines and shapes exactly like the magician's marks on my arms. And then, as Father Marsen gestures, I realize they're all over the church: running down pillars, on the ends of pews. Everywhere.

"I always thought it was just decoration," he admits. "But whoever designed this place—well, the temple has been here more than five hundred years. Its architect lived when the goddess walked in our world. He must have seen the marks on Barrica with his own eyes, when this place was built."

Goose bumps rise along the back of my neck, and my whole body feels like it's tingling. I'm standing at the end of a road that's been leading to *me*, all through the centuries.

"I . . . I didn't know," I whisper, the words totally inadequate for the awe that makes me feel like my heart's trying to beat through my chest. Somewhere behind that wonder, though, is a sliver of fear. The goddess has been waiting for me. For us. What does she want from Leander and me?

"The prince is our Messenger," the priest says quietly. "But you are his shield. The mark of the goddess is on you, Selly Walker. I meant it when I said you were made for him."

I glance down at my forearms, at the lines there, unlike any I've ever seen.

Is this why they've always been those humiliating green stripes, stuck like a child's, no matter how hard I tried to master my magic? Was I never faulty, never a failure, just waiting for my purpose?

How long has the goddess's hand been on me?

I look once more at my prince, at the lines of tension in his body, the way his hands are slowly curling into fists as the power of this place pushes through his veins.

How long has her hand been on me, and what does she plan for the rest of my story?

LASKIA

The Docks
Port Naranda, Mellacea

M y body is burning from the inside out.
I need a place for this power, a way to release some of it before it destroys me. I need a lightning rod, and none of my crew are strong enough to bear it.

My god will help me. He *must* help me.

This filthy fishing boat is closing on the dock with agonizing slowness, creeping past rows of moored boats, toward the crooked cranes that mark the dockside square.

I stagger across the deck, the crew scattering before me. I reached out to one as we left the Isles, tried desperately to drain my magic into her. And then to another, and then another.

Each one died, their hearts seizing and stopping, their bodies shriveling and curling up into old age in an instant.

I couldn't speak, or I would have screamed—I just pointed toward Port Naranda, and Dasriel roared at them to sail the damn ship, with every inch of canvas raised.

Macean was in me, the Gambler's power coursing through my veins, and as the boat's timbers nearly came apart and the sails threatened to rip, I reveled in that risk. I laughed against the wind, feeling us poised on the edge of destruction, the dice thrown, waiting for them to land.

Now, I catch movement out of the corner of my eye and turn in time to spy one of the sailors scrambling over the railing of the boat and splashing into the water. He strikes out for the far dock, his panicked flailing choppy and inefficient.

I could almost reward him for his gamble.

But only almost.

Desperate for the chance to release some of this burning energy inside me, I lash out with it in the direction of the fleeing sailor.

The power slices through him—reducing him instantly to crumbling ash that floats in a grisly, spreading pool upon the tossing waves—and then it *continues,* slicing in a widening arc toward the buildings on the far side of the harbor.

With a deep, guttural groan of tortured brick and mortar, a tall apartment complex implodes upon itself, falling down into the street like a puppet with its strings cut, sending out a massive cloud of dust and ash that envelops half of the now-staring crowd gathered around the harbor.

When the roar of crumbling brickwork fades, the harbor is silent.

I draw a deep, labored breath, my skin crawling. The use of Macean's power has done nothing to vent the seething, searing pain of his presence inside me. No matter what I do, there's always too much of it, always more pouring into me.

I want to peel off my own skin to stop the air from touching it, gouge out my own eyes to stop the light. I want to huddle inside my own mind and hide, but I know that if I let myself stop before finding someone to join myself to, I'll never come back out. So every ounce of my being is directed to keeping myself here, in this world. I have to do what the prince did with that sailor girl, and find a vessel strong enough to help me control this gift.

Macean is stirring from his sleep, and I can sense his power building like a tidal wave, ready to be unleashed. If I'm to survive his coming, then he must show me how.

I make a noise, and Dasriel recovers from his shock at seeing me level half a city block with a gesture, and stumbles up to leap onto the dock as we close on it.

"Make way, you fools!" he bellows, holding his ruined hand against his chest, and the sailors throw down the gangplank as I stride toward them. The people standing near the docks shake off their frozen terror and scuttle away like ants. If they scream, I can't hear them over the roaring in my ears.

I grab for the handrail on the gangplank as I stumble, and it gives way like wet paper, twisting and crumpling under the strength of my grip.

I need to get to the temple. And I need Ruby. In the same way birds fly south without ever having done it before, I know where to go, and what must happen. My god, stirring in the depths of my psyche, tells me what I must do.

This power will consume me if I don't obey him.

JUDE

The Temple of Macean
Port Naranda, Mellacea

I watch from my hiding place by the mast as Laskia stalks down the gangplank like a beast on the prowl. Bits of the building she leveled are still settling, the dust cloud still spreading—the people in the square scatter before her now like prey.

Around me the few crew members still alive are cowering, exchanging furtive looks that wonder if they dare push off now she's gone. One of them meets my eyes, a desperate question written silently on his face. They want to sail back out of Port Naranda and run for their lives, while they still have them, but after watching the fate of the man who tried to swim away, they don't dare move. I stare back at him, my own face offering up no answers.

I'm burning with that same need, my mind racing as I try to plan my own escape. If I have to carry my mother on my back, if I have to steal a barrow and wheel her through the streets, I'm getting us out of here. We're going today. We'll head north and work our way up through the principalities. I'll beg, borrow, or steal—whatever it takes—like I should have done in the first place.

After Laskia rose at the Temple of the Mother, Dasriel and I staggered back to the ship with her, his hand shredded when his gun backfired and bound in a tourniquet. Laskia was screaming as I hauled her down the path, her arm slung around my shoulder.

I'll never forget that weird, discordant sound—it wasn't human. But then she went quiet, and it was worse.

I can hear the word in the crowd, rippling through the people scattering out of Laskia's way.

Messenger, they say, their fearful eyes never leaving her, as though they can sense the presence of their god walking among them. Their voices are a mixture of awe and hope—even after watching her murder a man for trying to run, seeing her destroy a building with a wave of her hand, their eyes are full of a desperate faith that makes me sick to my stomach.

I want to run far and fast enough that I never find out what she's capable of, though a cold, heavy dread in my gut tells me that soon enough the whole world will know.

A shadow falls over me, and I look up. Dasriel is looming above me, cradling his injured hand. His eyes are hard, his jaw and head stubbled with days of travel.

"Get up," he grunts. "Hurry."

A sick horror washes through me. "What?"

He grabs me by the scruff of the neck, catching my hair,

my shirt collar, and hauls me up. "She's heading for the temple, I'm following. You go get Ruby."

"Ruby?" I manage, choking as my collar pulls tight around my neck. "What's she going to do with her?"

"Seven hells, boy, I don't know," he replies, hauling me higher until I can get my feet under me, though he still doesn't let go. "Ruby's the only one who's ever been able to make her listen." When he releases me I stumble back, gasping for air, and he snaps the fingers of his good hand, a flame springing to life. "So you're bringing Ruby to the temple or you're burning. Your choice."

I sealed my fate with Dasriel the moment I shouted a warning to Leander, back on the Isles. The moment I saved his life, and made sure there's a Messenger of Barrica out there to counter Laskia. Dasriel doesn't care what happens to me, as long as it hurts.

His gaze is hard when it meets mine. Resignation roils in my gut, my limbs heavy.

He takes my silence for what it is: defeat. I can't do anything for my mother if I'm dead.

Dismissing me with a glance, he turns to jog after Laskia, and I follow him down the gangplank without a word.

The last time I was at the Gem Cutter was just a few days ago. Dasriel had shown up at my prize fight and dragged me here, and I was about to learn that I was being sent to murder Leander.

Just a few days and a lifetime ago.

Now, I'm battered and bruised and heaving for breath as I run past the bouncers on the front door and into the empty bar—it's abandoned at this time of morning, except for the bartender behind the counter polishing glasses.

For a wild moment my heart leaps at the idea that it could be Tom, even though he works at Ruby Red, never here.

I have to tell Tom to run. I should have thought of that.

But it's a girl with rosewood skin the same shade as the bar, a glittering red pin at her lapel. She startles, backing up and hitting the row of bottles behind her, backlit on their shelf, and they wobble and rattle with the impact. I race past the silent dance floor, past the tables with their smooth tablecloths and velvet chairs, the lights above us dimmed.

There's another woman standing guard at the door to Ruby's inner sanctum, clad in immaculate black, her red pin in her collar.

"Just a minute now—" she begins, raising one hand.

"I'm coming from Laskia," I gasp. "Let me in, *now.*"

Her eyes widen, and she pushes open the door, standing aside. I stumble through, trying to remember how to stop moving.

Ruby is sitting with Sister Beris on her dark red velvet sofa, and even at this hour of the morning she's in one of her shimmering golden dresses, her dark brown curls held back by a headband that she wears like a tiara.

Sister Beris, her skin an almost translucent white, in contrast to Ruby's rich brown, is in her usual green robes and speaking fervently. "—all feel it, a new strength, and—"

Both their heads snap up as the door rebounds against the wall with a bang, and they come to their feet.

"Jude," Ruby snaps. "What—"

I double over, bracing my hands against my knees, gasping for breath. "It's Laskia," I manage. "You have to go to the temple, she's . . ."

"She's what?" demands Sister Beris, when I trail off. "What news? Macean has been restless in his sleep. Something has changed—what has happened?"

"She's a Messenger," I hear myself say. "Laskia is the Messenger of Macean."

"What?" Ruby's brow is creased.

Sister Beris's mouth falls open. "Do you know what you're saying?" she demands. "Jude, surely—"

"I saw it," I say flatly. "She sacrificed herself. She . . . she died. I think she died, I don't know. Macean . . . raised her."

"She is at the temple?" Beris asks, her eyes lighting with a bright, gleaming hope.

I nod.

"And she requires her sister, you believe?"

"I don't know what she—yes. Yes, Sister."

Without another word, Beris grabs Ruby's wrist, starting for the door. I'm frozen in place for a moment—my brain can't keep up with the idea that someone just manhandled *Ruby*.

I hesitate as they vanish. Dasriel is with Laskia, and it would be some time before he noticed, if I didn't arrive with Ruby and the green sister.

The question is *how* much time. Enough to collect my mother, enough for us to get out of the city?

The memory of Dasriel's furious stare flashes through my mind, and I swallow hard. Even if Laskia doesn't notice I'm gone, Dasriel will.

Slowly, my feet begin to follow the others, as I curse myself for a coward.

There's already a crowd teeming around the temple as we push our way toward it. I'm staying close—if I'm not going to run, then I need Dasriel to give me points for loyalty. Perhaps it will make it easier, later.

The largest church in Port Naranda is at the juncture of several streets, like the hub of a wheel, with spokes radiating out in every direction. Half the city is fighting for a clear path to the huge building, its stonework long ago painted black to mark the slumber of the god it was built to worship.

Great stone steps lead up to it from street level, arrayed with green sisters who stand like guards, ready to fend off the masses. Towering columns rise behind them, framing a figure clutching at her head.

Ruby stops short, forcing Sister Beris, who's still trying to pull her along by her wrist, to stop and turn. Suddenly I'm seeing Laskia through their eyes, and Ruby's gasp goes through me like cold water.

Laskia hasn't changed her clothes, hasn't washed, since we were on the Isle of the Mother. Her clothes are filthy, her face a mess of dirt and sweat. She moves like an animal, stalking to the top of the steps to stare out at the crowd, her eyes bright green, glowing as if she's lit from within.

She begins to stagger down the steps, trailed by Dasriel and a short, plump woman in the robes of a green sister.

"Who's that?" I whisper, and for a moment Ruby forgets I'm her errand boy and whispers a reply.

"Sister Petra, the head of the church. Beris is her second."

Beris is ignoring us now, pushing her way once more through the crowd, shoving bodies aside as she makes for Laskia. "He is awakening!" she cries, and people nearby take up the shout. "Our god will return! First, he has come for Laskia!"

All around us, the people who have streamed in from every part of the city are lifting their hands to press their fingertips to their foreheads, their palms covering their eyes. It's the greeting of the ordinary people to the green sisters, referring to Macean—*Our god's mind awaits us, though his eyes are closed*—and now they're aiming it at Laskia.

"What's wrong with her?" Ruby whispers, her eyes never leaving her little sister.

"She's coming apart," I say slowly. "It's too much for her. Too much power. It's been getting worse."

"Her faith is strong," Sister Beris protests, looking back at us, her eyes alight. "She will serve him as he awakens!"

A large part of me is as close to praying as I've been in years—praying Laskia will simply die again, that this power will overwhelm her.

Then Laskia moans, still clutching at her head, her fingers gripping her curls and tugging on them. She reaches one hand out toward . . . toward Ruby, I realize. But the gang boss beside me doesn't move from where she stands.

We reach the bottom of the steps, and Sister Beris begins to make her way up, leaving Ruby and me behind.

Laskia stumbles down to meet us, Sister Petra and Dasriel in her wake.

As our two groups draw closer, I fall back. Perhaps as they pay attention to each other, I can fade out of view. Perhaps I can slip away. Forget waiting—a sick, exhausted fear is sitting in my gut, twisting into ice and telling me to *run.*

Then Laskia stumbles, and shrieks. Sister Petra lunges to catch her before she falls down the steps, toward the crowd, and Laskia grabs hold of the first sister, hands latching onto her forearms. There's a flash of blinding green light, and when I blink my vision clear again, Sister Petra lies at Laskia's feet. Her body is shriveled and shrunken, lost within her green robes, and as Laskia's foot catches on the fabric, Sister Petra's face and one arm crumble to dust.

A murmur goes through the crowd below—fear, wonder, an uneasy shifting as everyone mentally calculates the distance between them and the Messenger who can kill you in an instant.

This—this instant death, this lifetime of aging poured into one heartbeat—is what happened to each of the sailors when Laskia tried desperately to bind herself to them. So I know what will come next: a moment of coherency, the fire burned down low enough that for an instant, Laskia can think, can communicate.

Her head lifts like a hunting dog's, and she casts her gaze around.

"Ruby," she breathes, holding out one hand. "Ruby, my sister. You're strong enough. You can help me."

"Not a chance in the seven hells," Ruby snaps, backing up toward me, her lip curling in something between fear and revulsion. "You stay away from me!"

"Grab her!" Beris snaps, but I can't move. I want no part of this. My heart is beating out of my chest, and my legs are shaking, as if a single step to flee will send me tumbling back down the stone steps into the uncertain crowd.

Then Ruby tries to run, her body slamming into mine and knocking us both down, my bones aching and my head spinning from the impact. A moment later Dasriel is there, and as he pulls Ruby off me, she screams, clawing for purchase, grabbing at my arms to try and rip herself free. Our eyes meet—hers wide with terror, mine in shock—and then she's gone.

Dasriel dumps her in front of Laskia, and Laskia leans down, hands latching onto either side of Ruby's face. The crowd below is perfectly still now, and I feel like my jagged breathing must be carrying across their heads, through the streets of Port Naranda, the only sound anywhere.

And then Ruby starts to scream again. The sound is raw, ripped straight from her throat, and she's fighting to get away, her hands desperately trying to pry her little sister's off the sides of her face.

Dasriel just watches. Sister Beris doesn't move to help. She's never helped anyone, unless she thought it advanced her god's cause, and now she's on the verge of religious ecstasy, tears running down her cheeks.

But Ruby doesn't die. She doesn't age, she doesn't crumble. She simply screams, until she has no more voice left, and the noises she makes die down to whimpers, and then everything is still. I only know she's alive by the way she heaves for breath.

Laskia straightens and looks around, taking in the bodies crammed into the streets all around us, the green sisters arrayed on the temple steps, Dasriel watching her, me still sprawled unmoving on the stone.

The whole city, faces upturned toward her.

And slowly, she smiles.

LASKIA

The Temple of Macean
Port Naranda, Mellacea

It takes only a thought to amplify my voice so it rings out across the crowd, perfectly audible to each of the thousands of enraptured people arrayed before me.

"You sense your god," I call out, letting every ounce of my faith into my tone, letting my words echo through the streets. "I know you do. The green sisters kept the flame of our faith alight for centuries, so often alone in their churches. When all others turned away from our Macean in his slumber, the sisters were faithful, and they tended the embers when there was no one else. But now all can see the light of his fire, and it will burn brightly again."

Shopkeepers stand side by side with sailors, with bakers, with merchants and doctors and servants, with the rich and the poor and everyone in between. There is no distinction between them. Every one of them is listening to my words.

My body aches, and the light still gleams too brightly for me, and my clothes are still too rough against my body. I shift my weight and my foot scrapes across the stone step deafeningly.

But I have poured enough of my power into Ruby to buy myself a moment's ease, and she crouches by my side, waiting until I need to do so again.

So now, I will speak to my people.

"Your faith is awakening our sleeping god. He hears you, and he moves toward you. I will bring him back into our world, and he will bend all the nations of this land to his will—he will lead us to our rightful place atop the world."

I raise my hands, and it takes only another thought to illuminate myself so that I shine with the green light of the sisters' robes, glowing like a beacon for all to see. It's a relief to use this power—it rushes through me like a river in a canyon, roaring, gathering pace, always looking for a way out.

"There will be no more shortages, no more doing without. No more taking second place to the other countries of the Crescent Sea. Our god will walk among us once more!"

Their cheers are like a great wave rising up.

I can feel the pressure inside my head, as Macean bears down on my mind. The words are only half mine, and it feels as though my body, my mind, are going to break apart at the seams.

He wants to force his way through into this world, but I know that if he does, he'll break me in the process.

I draw a rasping breath, and hold off my god a little longer. I will find a way to bring him back without burning myself up, and then I will stand by his side as he rules.

"We must prepare for war!" I hear myself shout. "We must prepare to rise! Mellacea will sleep no more!"

The sound of the crowd rolls across me like thunder, and swallows me whole.

And in this moment, I am invincible.

SELLY

The Royal Palace
Kirkpool, Alinor

The three of us have been shown to a quiet room to wait for Queen Augusta. This place is like nothing I've ever seen—the walls are decorated with gilt scrollwork and the velvet wallpaper with intricate patterns that remind me of the pitch and swoop of Leander's royal magician's marks.

I'm perched on the edge of a spindly-legged sofa beside my prince, barely making contact with it. I'm painfully aware that I'm filthy, and I don't want to get the furniture dirty. I'm not sure how much longer I can keep myself upright, though—my limbs still ache with the aftermath of the magic Leander grounded through me at the docks.

My prince is sprawled beside me, his head tilted back to study the ceiling, his fingers twined through mine. We're so out of place in our rough sailors' clothes, our faces sunburned, lips chapped, hair askew, but he doesn't seem to mind.

Keegan stands opposite us, lost in his thoughts. I study his tired face, and then my gaze slides to the portrait behind him. It must be one of Leander's ancestors. She looks like him—the same mischief in her gaze, the same faint smile tugging at the corners of her mouth. And then, as I'm gazing directly at the painting, it winks at me.

I squeak, and Leander's attention snaps back to the room. He pinches the bridge of his nose as the glare of the sunlight through the windows bothers him.

Wait, how did I know that's what it was?

"The painting?" he asks, and Keegan swings around to eye the portraits on the walls with immediate suspicion.

"It moved," I whisper, well aware I sound like I've lost my mind. "It winked at me."

"It's the magic," Leander replies tiredly. "It's leaking out of me. It's why the flowers bloomed as we came up through the streets. I don't know what's going to happen next, but I think—"

Abruptly the double doors fly open with a bang, and I'm staring straight at Queen Augusta.

She looks like her brother too, but her smile isn't written on her face like Leander's. She's a tall woman with the same sandstone skin, her black hair in an intricate braid. Her long dress is Alinorish blue, the sleeves cut at the elbow to reveal her magician's marks.

She's followed by another woman who, judging by her resemblance, must be their sister, Princess Coria. Then comes a third—small, blond, and immaculately put together in a beaded rose dress, almost certainly the queen's wife, the Princess Consort Delphine.

Keegan's bowing, so I scramble up off the couch to do the

same, and then realize I should probably curtsy, attempting to switch to that halfway through. The result is a twisted kind of bob that looks like I'm buckling at the knees, and Leander comes to his feet to sling an arm around my shoulders before things get any worse.

"Leander!" the queen cries, making to move toward him, freezing as he winces. "What's wrong?"

"Your voice is too loud, and the lights are too bright," I say. And then, after a pause that goes a beat too long: "Your Majesty."

Augusta's rank isn't really what I'm worrying about right now, and in fairness, I don't think it's on her mind either. She immediately turns away from us and closes the doors behind her—quietly—shutting out the guards and gawking officials.

Princess Delphine heads straight for the curtains, and pulls at the velvet ropes that hold them apart, so they fall across the window. Princess Coria is the one who hurries toward us, then stops short with a gasp.

"Gus, his eyes are green!"

The queen turns back from closing the doors, taking in the pair of us, Leander's arm around my shoulders, every inch of us bedraggled.

She lets out a slow breath. "Are you truly a Messenger?"

"Yes," Leander says quietly. "Her power is in me, Gus. But I'm also . . ." His voice breaks, and I slide my arm around his waist and squeeze. "I'm still me," he manages, softer still. "Barely."

"I can't believe it," the queen says slowly, walking forward, and gesturing absently for us to sit.

Augusta glances at her wife, and then back to us once more.

I'm not sure who she is, in this moment—Leander's sister, who loves him, or his queen, who's just been handed the most powerful . . . what? Magician? Or weapon? Her eyes are soft as she looks at him, but her features are composed.

"And you are?" She twists to look over her shoulder at Keegan, who was doing his very best impression of a portrait.

"Keegan Wollesley, Your Majesty," he stammers, flushing. "I was a passenger on the ship Le—His Highness boarded for the Isles."

One brow lifts, and Augusta turns back toward me, waiting for my reply next. She definitely hasn't missed the way Leander and I are clinging to each other.

"Selly Walker," I say, lifting my chin. "I was a sailor aboard the *Lizabetta*."

"Was?" the queen repeats, going still.

I force myself to keep my voice even. "The ship is lost, Your Majesty."

For a long moment, all I can hear is the slow ticking of the clock in the corner.

"I think," the queen says slowly, "that you'd better tell me exactly what has happened."

LEANDER

The Royal Palace
Kirkpool, Alinor

It's surreal to be sitting here, watched by the portraits of generations past, telling my sisters a story we can barely believe ourselves.

I let Selly and Keegan do most of the talking. Their voices are rippling in my ears like chimes, and though the closed curtains help, I still feel as though every noise, every movement, is bigger than it should be. And I can feel Barrica's power filling me up once more, taking me closer to the moment I'll have no choice but to retreat back inside my mind again.

So I make the most of the time I have, and lean my shoulder against Selly's, and let their voices wash over me. I'm only drawn back to the conversation when my sister speaks my name.

"Leander?"

"Hmm?"

"You sped an entire *ship* along?" Augusta is asking. "You

moved the *Lizabetta*? You've always been the most powerful of us, but even you . . ."

"That's nothing to what he can do now," Selly says quietly. "He doesn't even need a sacrifice anymore."

"What did you sacrifice to raise a storm, and move the ship?" Augusta whispers, shaking her head against the answer some part of her knows is coming. Our eyes meet, and I see the moment she flinches. The moment she realizes that I gave the spirits something of *myself,* to conjure the wind and waves and fight to save the *Lizabetta.*

I close my eyes again as the story continues, through the sinking of the *Lizabetta,* the sailing of the *Little Lizabetta* to Port Naranda.

Neither Selly nor Keegan tells her about Jude, I notice. They don't tell her about the small moments that even now seem like only ours. Keegan's and my quiet conversation at the inn, by moonlight, in which our friendship became real. Selly's and my trip to the night market, to the nightclub, where I tried to tell her how I felt about her.

When Selly's recounting reaches the Temple of the Mother, there's silence for a moment as her voice breaks. I can feel the tears ready to spill down her cheeks as though they're my own, and I tighten my hand around hers.

"And there was no way down to the altar to make the sacrifice," I say quietly, my voice still rough with disuse. "So I leaped."

Coria's eyes are bright with unshed tears, and Delphine mutters something in Fontesquan, giving up on dignity and letting herself fold to sit on the ground. Augusta simply stares at me, measuring the words, trying them on for size. Trying to make them fit into her brain.

"And Barrica caught you?" she asks, very carefully.

I shake my head, just a fraction. "Wouldn't have been a sacrifice if I'd thought she'd do that," I murmur. "But she lifted me up, afterward. She poured her power into me. She brought me back."

"Leander, how could you—" It's Coria, always the most emotional of us, giving up and letting her tears spill down her cheeks.

"It was my fault," I say simply, and Selly practically growls beside me. "It was," I tell her. "None of it would have happened if I'd been on time. The problem was mine to solve."

"Leander," says Augusta slowly, and I can see her two selves. My sister, and my queen. Appalled, and at the same time . . . beginning to grasp the power I now hold.

Beginning to understand what I am, and what I can do.

"Your Majesty," says Keegan, from his place by the wall. "The Mellacean who was pursuing us, Laskia. She leaped too."

Augusta's eyes widen. "Please, tell me—"

Keegan shakes his head. "Her sleeping god was too weak, or too unwilling, to save her," he replies.

"But our goddess does not sleep, and Leander's faith was rewarded," Augusta says slowly. "In the old stories, Messengers were powerful enough to change the course of rivers, to flatten mountains."

For as long as they're in those stories, anyway. Which is never very long.

But none of us say that.

"Maybe I should flatten a mountain," I say, trying for a grin, and falling exhaustedly short. "I . . . I can barely control it, Gus. It's eating me alive."

"Is that what happened at the docks?" she asks, her keen eyes fixed on my face. "You lost control of the magic?"

"I'd already lost control of it, and it only got worse when I stepped onto Alinorish soil, surrounded by Barrica's worshippers. What happened at the docks was that Selly brought me back. Until this morning I was . . ."

"He was like a raw nerve," Selly says quietly. "Hiding inside his own mind from the sound, the light, the power."

"The power—*her* power—is constantly pouring into me." An uncomfortable shiver goes through me at even voicing the sensation. Or perhaps at the way Augusta repeats the word, softly, like she's tasting it.

"Power?"

"Like a tap constantly refilling a bucket. At the Temple of the Mother, when Barrica raised me, it was like . . . like I was full of lightning, and needed a way to ground it. There was so much magic in me, I thought I was going to die. And then Selly—"

"Grabbed him," Selly says firmly, right before I can say *kissed me*. I blink at her, but don't try to correct her. If I had the whole royal family staring me down—and they weren't *my* family—maybe I'd censor things too. "And his lightning grounded through me."

"And that's why I'm still alive," I say. "Selly's my anchor, when the storm tries to carry me away."

Augusta is studying us both, her expression hard to read. "I don't recall an anchor ever existing in the stories."

"I suppose Barrica's had five centuries to think it over," I reply.

"What we don't know, we'll learn," she says crisply, fully queen once more, no longer the concerned sister. "There must be something in the records about the Messengers of old. We'll set our researchers to the task, and learn how you can best wield this gift. What it means for your country, what you can actually do with it."

"Thank you," I say softly, glancing past her to Keegan. He understands my meaning without words, and inclines his head ever so slightly. *He's* the one I want in those old records. And he'll find a way in for me.

"I am grateful—Alinor is grateful—for your service," Augusta is saying to Selly. "We should get all of you cleaned up, and then we will think on the best course of action." Her eyes creep back toward me, thoughtful. I'm not used to being on the receiving end of that particular stare from my sister.

Selly simply nods, but I grew up with nobles on every side, and I can hear the subtext that she misses: *And then we'll figure out what to do with you.*

"Gus," I say quietly. "Selly will be staying with me."

"I understand—or rather, I know I can never understand—what you've been through," she replies. "I appreciate that your bond must run deep." *But,* says the faintest tilt of her head, in a language I learned to read as a child, *she is a sailor, and you cannot imagine it's appropriate for you to be clinging to each other like that.*

"Your Majesty," begins Selly. "It's not—"

"Leander is with his family now," Augusta replies, in a quelling tone. "We will see you are rewarded."

"Now, hold on," Selly begins, but my sister cuts her off.

"I understand the loss of your ship—"

"It's not—"

"And of course your crew—"

"Don't you dare bring them into—"

"Dare?" My sister's tone is like ice, and I press a hand against Selly's knee, silently asking her to stop. She casts me a sidelong look that tells me just what an effort it is, and bites her lip.

"Augusta," I say quietly, and in that moment, I let a little of my newfound power buzz through the room—both my sisters, gifted magicians, feel it, and I hear Coria's intake of breath.

Augusta's gaze hardens. She inherited the throne from our father when she was fourteen, and I was just a toddler. She had our grieving mother as a regent until she was crowned at nineteen, and she's had more than a decade since then to become the formidable queen, politician, and leader she is now.

"Augusta," I say again, softer. "I need Selly with me. She's . . . she's my copper rod in this storm. She's the only thing that's kept me alive. And she's—" She's my *what*? She just shied away from telling my sister that we kissed. "She's my friend. Who has sacrificed everything in the service of our family."

Everyone is silent for a moment, and Delphine reaches up from where she sits on the floor to take Augusta's hand. Her own lightning rod, in a way. And whatever passes between them, it causes my sister's shoulders to drop.

"Of course," she says. "Selly Walker, will you continue your service to our family? Will you remain at my brother's side?"

Selly gazes back at her, windswept and exhausted, this girl from the sea who never asked for any of this, never wanted it. For whom this room, this court, is as far from home as she could ever travel, no matter how far she sailed.

And then she looks at me. At the boy who loves her, and needs her. And I'm the one she's talking to, when she replies.

"Of course," she says simply, and the guilt goes through me like a knife.

And so, for better or for worse, Selly Walker joins the royal court.

KEEGAN

◆

The Royal Palace
Kirkpool, Alinor

I'm caught by surprise when I hear my name.

"Keegan as well," Selly is saying. "He needs to stay with us."

"What?" It's not a very queenly question, and Queen Augusta is clearly approaching the end of her tolerance. I only just avoid echoing it myself, as a strange, falling sensation swoops inside me.

"He got us this far," Selly says, with the kind of stubborn desperation that is, I would argue, *actually* what got us this far. "I don't want to risk taking him away from Leander—not when he's so clever, and he's seen everything. He—" I see the moment she latches onto an argument she knows will work, as she sits up straighter. "Keegan's a scholar, and he knows the old stories. He's the one person who knows history *and* knows what Leander's been through. He'll help Leander get control of his power."

I've learned to read the jut of Selly's chin these days, and I can see how badly she needs this. It's not about helping Leander wield this gift from the goddess—it's about not abandoning Selly to the machinations of the court.

For a moment there, I thought I could take whatever reward the queen offered me for my service, and go. Leander needs me to research his... condition, after all. I thought I'd have a chance to bolt for the Bibliotek, before my father finds out where I am.

I thought that in making it to the palace I had completed every task that could be placed in my way.

And in that moment, I could smell the old books. I could practically touch the dark wood of the shelves.

But instead, feeling like I'm lifting my whole weight from the floor by sheer strength of will, I turn away from that vision. I cannot leave my friends while they still need me.

"I wish only to serve, Your Majesty," I say quietly.

"And I need an aide," Leander says, apology in his gaze. "I need someone who knows me—who knows my capacity, and my views—and who can speak for me. The noise in my head, Gus... I can't do everything you need me to."

Princess Coria speaks up. "It would be perfectly reasonable for him to have a liaison, even as a prince," she points out. "Let alone as a Messenger."

"I need help," Leander says quietly.

"And this is the help you want?" the queen asks, glancing across at me more thoughtfully than she has so far. I fight the urge to stand up straighter—such an effort would look ridiculous in my ragged, filthy, salt-stained clothes. "We could provide you with someone well-versed in the lore, someone who could liaise with my staff—"

"There's no one better versed than Keegan," Leander replies quietly. "And no one I trust more to find out what he doesn't already know." And at that, I find I stand up straighter anyway.

"Then I must call on you too, Keegan Wollesley," the queen says solemnly. "Stay and talk with me a little longer, and we will make arrangements. Leander, go. Wash. Rest. Coria and Delphine will see you settled."

Leander shoots me a quick glance that asks if I can handle her alone, and I see the exhaustion on his face—in the shadows under his eyes, the pained twist of his mouth. So, for the second time since we entered this room, I nod to him discreetly.

Leander and Selly rise, and they leave with the princess and the queen's consort, neither of whom is required to get them settled anywhere. But the queen wishes to speak directly to me, and so they all depart.

"Well," she says quietly, as the door closes behind them. "You and I are about to get to know each other well, Mr. Wollesley."

"Ma'am," I agree, not knowing what else to say.

"My brother is clearly under the impression that you have a good brain, and a calm head," she continues. "And I rarely see him express admiration for anyone, so I'm inclined to trust his opinion."

"Thank you, ma'am," I say, feeling anything but calm and clever.

"Am I right in thinking you're engaged?" she asks, catching me off guard, so that I blink at her for a moment. "To Lady

Dastenholtz," she elaborates, as though I might need reminding of my fiancée's name.

"I . . ." Spirits save me, I *am* still engaged. It hasn't even been two weeks since I ran for it. There's every chance my father has covered the whole thing up, and nobody even knows I was missing.

"Congratulations," Augusta says firmly, leaving me in no doubt as to where she stands on the matter. "It's most convenient. You and Lady Dastenholtz are practically chaperones."

I blink at her yet again. "Ma'am?"

"For my brother and Miss Walker."

I wonder for a moment what she'd say if she'd seen Selly and her brother curled up together at an inn in Port Naranda, holding each other in a storm, bathed in holy light as they kissed in the temple. Perhaps she reads some of this on my face. Or perhaps she caught the moment Selly cut Leander off, when he was about to mention it.

"Whatever has gone before, now they are at court, and it will be different."

"Of course, ma'am."

"So, to other matters," she says, moving on briskly. "What I am about to say will sound cold, I acknowledge that. As monarch, I do not have the luxury of indulging in my emotions, not at a moment such as this."

"I understand," I say. And I do. Perhaps because I know her brother—because I know the small shifts of expression that allow those close to him to read his mood—I can see her brain working, see the way she hardens herself. Folding suddenly cold hands behind my back, I brace myself.

"I need to understand what Leander is capable of," she says quietly. "He spoke of becoming overwhelmed, of the noise in his head. But he also spoke of flattening a *mountain*. Was he serious?"

"None of us know what he can do, Your Majesty."

"I *must* know, Mr. Wollesley. And you must find out for me."

"I . . . yes, Your Majesty." My heart is beating far too fast, far too hard, pushing against my ribs, as her gaze rests on me. "May I ask what you have in mind?"

She lets out a slow breath. "We have a Messenger, and Mellacea does not. Other countries and principalities will rally around us, and back our calls for peace, if they perceive our power. We can dictate new treaty terms, Mr. Wollesley. We can ensure lasting peace."

She's right, I know that. We can use this power for good.

I want to believe that's why her eyes lit up, as she began to understand what Leander has become—what he can do. Because she wants peace.

"I understand," I say slowly. And the worst of it is, I do. If those on the decoy fleet—if the ambassador back in Port Naranda—can be the last to die, then we should use Leander's power to ensure that.

"I need to know how soon Leander can be ready to act," the queen says quietly. "What he will be able to do. How clearheaded he can be. I need to know about his stamina—what will overwhelm him."

"Do we need to know what he can truly do?" I ask carefully. "Or what we can *say* he can do? If we are aiming only to intimidate the Mellaceans into negotiations, I mean."

"I would prefer to know with certainty," she replies, her gaze ranging over the portraits around us as if asking them a question. "You will report to me on these questions as soon as you are able."

The silence stretches, my questions unspoken, but just as clear as if I'd blurted them out.

If you only want to negotiate, how does it matter what he can actually do?

Why does his stamina matter if he's only a threat?

What use could you have for flattening a mountain?

She gazes at me evenly, waiting to see if I'll ask.

"Your Majesty," I say eventually, and bow deeply, in the hope this will end the conversation. A significant part of me wishes I could just keep bending, curl into a small ball, and crouch in one place until everyone stopped noticing I was there.

What a mess this is. What a mess, in every possible way. But though it pains me to see my friends pushing aside their own desires to serve their country, letting themselves be trapped for the good of others, my usually helpful brain is refusing to supply me with a single good alternative. Or even a bad alternative.

What matters is that we avoid a war. That we play our cards so well that Mellacea backs down, and stays down for generations. And we must hope that's what our queen wants as well.

And if the price of peace is Leander clinging to his sanity, if it's Selly stranding herself away from the sea, and if it's me giving up the Bibliotek and returning to my family's embrace—to marriage, if necessary—then so be it. It's what must be done.

All I ever wanted was a quiet place and a good book.

How has that turned out to be more difficult to achieve than any quest in my favorite tales?

It's only when I look up that I realize Queen Augusta has left the room.

JUDE

*The Tenements
Port Naranda, Mellacea*

I shove my way through the crowd, grabbing at bodies and pushing them aside, fighting my way against the current as they try to get closer to the temple.

When I burst free of the mass of them, I *run,* the sounds of Ruby's raw screams still echoing in my ears.

I duck down an alleyway, past a bank, where customers and employees are fighting to get out the door and run toward Laskia, drawn by an urge they don't understand. I'm still running six blocks later, when I reach the tenements, nearly slipping on the slick cobblestones as I take the final corner.

Home.

I've got a handful of the golden dollars Laskia paid the sailors, and however far it can get Mum and me, that's how far we're running.

I pound up the stairs, lungs burning, mentally making a list of what I can fit in a bag. It'll have to be small—I'll be carrying

Mum, most likely. She's barely left her bed in months, and I'll have to keep her warm, because if she starts coughing . . .

I reach our landing, and stop short.

The front door of our apartment is wide open.

Maybe it's just Mrs. Tevner, our nosy neighbor. Maybe she's dropped by to check on Mum while I'm away.

The back of my neck is prickling, and the strangest sensation is washing through my body as I walk along what suddenly feels like an endless hallway. It's as if I'm sinking, as if I'm in the water and every part of me is slowly dissolving.

When I stop in the doorway, Mrs. Tevner's inside, as I thought. But so are half a dozen other neighbors, sitting on the sofa and on our single chair, standing in the corners.

Mrs. Tevner's lined face is tear-streaked. "Oh, Jude," she says, coming to her feet and taking me in—I'm beaten and bloodied, filthy, and somehow already sure of what she's about to say, but unable to believe it. "Oh, my boy," she whispers. "I'm so sorry."

I glance through the doorway to my mother's bedroom, and see a still form lying on the bed, carefully covered by one of our bedsheets.

Ice slowly flows through my veins, down my arms to my hands, leaving them numb, trembling. My mouth is dry, and I can't make myself breathe.

Everything I've done, every compromise I've made, every piece of my soul I've given away . . . it was all for nothing.

My mother is gone.

SELLY

The Royal Palace
Kirkpool, Alinor

The royal servants nearly have a collective fit at the idea of me sharing Leander's apartments. Torn between reverence for their Messenger and some kind of snobby panic about the fact that we're not even pretending I'm not at his side, their protests are spluttered and hissed, whispered about as subtly as a hurricane.

In the end, watching the strain on Leander's face—the way he turns on his heel and walks toward the window, gazing out at the horizon—and feeling the way he desperately tries to shut out their din, I suggest a compromise, and they take it.

They set up a little cot for me in one of his antechambers, with a door closed safely between us. A proper place for a servant, or whatever I'm supposed to be in their eyes. The cot has silk pillowcases and gold embroidery on its quilt, and there's a little table beside it with a pitcher of water, a glass, and one of the fat green candles they make at the temple, in case I want to charm any spirits on short notice.

"What's that supposed to be?" Leander demands, when the doors close behind the servants and he turns to see their handiwork.

"Peace and quiet," I say, leaning down to rumple the covers so it looks like I've slept. "I mean, assuming . . ." I trail off, my cheeks heating, deeply aware of the words *you want me to share your bed.*

Suddenly we're back in Port Naranda, lying side by side on a creaky bed, senses attuned to every movement, every breath. That night at the club, he'd asked if he could kiss me.

I'd said no. *It will only make it worse,* I said.

We thought we were parting ways the next morning. We've never discussed the fact that we woke up tangled together, clinging to each other.

I wish now with all my heart I'd had the guts to show him what he meant to me in that moment. It wouldn't have made it worse, would it? Because here we are, bound together more intimately than any two people in history—and still we haven't kissed. At least not when he's been conscious, rather than in the process of transforming into a Messenger of the goddess. Not when he looked back at me, and wanted to kiss me more than anything in the world.

Finally alone for the first time since before the Isles, we just stare at each other, neither of us knowing what to do next.

"I think I need you close, even when I'm sleeping," he says softly. "I'm sorry." The depth of sorrow in those green eyes of his breaks me a little, and I find a smile, walking forward to join him.

"Don't be. You've seen what my bunk was like. I think I can slum it here. Show me around."

So he does.

His quarters are . . . well, for a start, they're bigger than the whole of the *Lizabetta*. I was expecting a fancy bedroom, but there's a *closet* larger than my old cabin, with racks upon racks of clothes lining it, and another room, apparently for dressing in, that's packed with gold-edged mirrors.

There's his sitting room, full of gold-and-velvet furniture that screams *I'm a prince* but doesn't even whisper *I'm Leander.* There's the first antechamber, where I suppose guests are greeted by someone who decides whether they're allowed in. Then there's the second antechamber—in theory my bedroom—where the guests wait until he's ready for them.

And then there's the bathroom. I won't let anyone insult shipboard life, but even I can admit that the less said about that particular arrangement at sea, the better. Leander's bathing chamber is fitted out with white marble, and has fixtures of gold. There's a bath big enough to throw a party in—how they fill it I can't imagine—and a showerhead the size of a dinner plate. There's a mural of mermaids, all watching you while you bathe.

"There's a limit," I tell him, as we eyeball that huge shower. "You're not coming in here, my prince."

"Of course not," he says, ushering me into the bathroom with a bow, and closing the door.

And then—I can feel him there as easily as if I could see him—he leans against the other side of the bathroom door the whole time I shower. I stretch my mind out to stay pressed against his, which sort of feels like washing while remembering to keep touching the ceiling with one hand and singing a shanty. It works, though, and the feeling of washing the grime and sweat off my skin and out of my hair is *glorious*.

When I emerge, there's a feast laid out on a low table, a dozen little plates and bowls holding the kind of food that's one small piece of something on top of another small piece of something else. Fancy, but not filling—and hard to identify.

"The kitchen threw something together, in case we were hungry," Leander says as I lean down to inspect the least thrown-together meal I've ever eaten in my life.

He watches as I work my way through each of the dishes in turn, and occasionally he chimes in to name a mystery ingredient.

"You don't want even a little?" I try, waggling an ornate silver spoon at him. It feels like making jokes at a funeral, but neither of us is ready to talk about the overwhelming events of the day. "It's not bad."

"I . . . I don't think I need to eat," he says quietly.

I'm stuffing some fish inside a bread roll as he says it, and my fingers go still as I look up at him. "At all?"

Slowly, he shakes his head. A shiver goes through me, and my throat seems to close, so it's hard to get a breath.

Every living thing eats. What does it mean that he doesn't? Does Barrica nourish him in some other way? How long can that last?

I finish my meal in silence, and together, we climb into bed. I don't think he needs the covers to stay warm, either, but I want to crawl under them, so he does too.

We lie there, hands entwined, gazing at each other. Not speaking, not knowing what to say.

The bed's too soft, and I'm sinking into it, and I can't hear the creaking of the *Lizabetta*'s timbers, my lullaby as long as I can remember. With the lights out, the room's lit by the moonlight streaming in through the glass doors that lead onto the balcony. When I relax my gaze a little, I find I can watch the air spirits playing with the curtains—I left a window just a touch ajar. I couldn't stand how stuffy it is in here.

Beside me, Leander is still. I can feel the way his mind is straining—he's fighting some battle, but I can't tell what it is.

And eventually, somehow, I sleep.

A crash wakes me, and I startle, thrashing against the tangle of sheets as my eyes fly open.

It's daylight, and the room has come alive. The low table covered in my empty plates and bowls goes flying across the room, smashing into the far wall with the deafening crash of splintering wood and broken crockery. A pair of armchairs goes skittering in the other direction, and papers are raining down from somewhere.

It's as if invisible hands are tossing the furniture around, and the epicenter is our bed.

I twist around to check on Leander, and his eyes are wide but unseeing, his hands flung up to protect himself from some invisible foe, his face frozen in fear.

"Leander!"

When he doesn't respond, I press one hand to his chest, and the instant I make contact, I know it was a mistake. Power sizzles through me, every muscle in my body contracting in agony, and I'm hurled away from him. I go flying off the bed and crash to the floor still tangled up in the sheets, pain lancing through my body.

I scramble upright, and when I make it back to the edge of the bed, it's to find Leander staring at me in shock, propped up on one elbow, heaving for breath.

"Selly, what was . . ." He can barely speak, and when the open window crashes closed, he flinches as though it struck him. "What happened?"

"That's my question," I say, creeping up to perch on the edge of the bed, careful not to touch him. "Were you dreaming?"

"Yes," he says slowly, as if remembering. Then he collapses onto his back, eyes closed. "Yes. It was a dream, or something like one."

"What did you see?" I whisper.

"Barrica. Or rather, I didn't see her, but . . . she was there. You know how dreams are."

"But this was only something like a dream?" I say, icicles of dread needling at my insides.

"That's right," he admits softly. "It's not a trance, not a dream. It was the place I went where I hid in my head. And she was hammering at that door, Selly. She wants to come through, and I'm the way for her to do it."

"What do you mean?"

"I don't know. Just that if she's going to return to the world, it will be through me, somehow."

The question hangs between us, unspoken but taking up all the air in the room: *Would Leander survive being used as a doorway back to our world?*

"There were others there too," he continues. "I think they're the Messengers who came before me. I couldn't hear what they were saying—it was like we were caught in the same crowd, but you weren't there to sail us out of it. There was one . . . I'm sure it was Anselm."

The name sends a shock through me. King Anselm was the ancestor of Leander's who sacrificed himself five hundred years ago—who made Barrica strong enough to bind Macean in sleep, before she left our world forever. Or not-so-forever, perhaps. Does some part of him linger in Leander's connection to her?

"Did he say anything?" I ask.

Leander shakes his head. "He didn't have to. I know what happened. He couldn't take it—the noise, the brightness, the too-muchness of it. The magic in him burned him up. I think he's warning me about that."

"He didn't have an anchor," I murmur. "You do. I'm right here with you, Leander."

"There's so much magic, Selly," he whispers. "I don't know what to do."

"Nor do I." I straighten the pair of silk pajamas I borrowed from him, and shuffle closer to sit beside him. "No one does. You're the first Messenger to ever have someone like me, as far as we know. So we'll have to work it out together."

"Work what out?"

"How I help ease the load for you." Inside I'm flinching from the words, already dreading the possibility of more pain. But I keep my voice firm and even. Businesslike. "Just now you zapped some of that power into me, and it was enough for you to wake up. On the docks, same thing. If the storm is overwhelming, then I need to ease the wind for you, calm the seas. Maybe I do that by taking some of your magic."

"I don't want to hurt you," he says softly, eyes still closed.

"Well, you'll hurt me if it burns you up," I tell him. "We're talking about something that will kill you if you don't find a way to lessen it. Leander, I'm right here, and I'm willing to do it, but please don't make me argue with you about it."

He shifts his weight, and I can feel it in him, the urge to reach for me. When I reach out to brush his fingers with mine, sparks jump between us. His lashes lift, and those beautiful eyes of his—will I ever stop missing their mahogany brown?—meet mine.

Rather than speaking, I lift our joined hands, and press a kiss to his fingertips. My eyes never leave his. It's impossibly intimate, so much more than anything we've done before, and even as I tamp down my fear of what's coming next, some part of me revels in the fact that I'm the one who gets to do it.

I see the moment he capitulates, and closes his eyes.

When I lower my own lashes, the dark helps me focus, and I can feel the magic, the sheer power of it, building up inside him. I can feel the dangerous edge that belongs to his goddess.

Then, like he's opening the tap that fills up his stupidly big bath in the next room, he begins to let a trickle of the magic flow into me. It's a strange sort of warmth, a tingling, like my whole body's fallen asleep and circulation is just coming back. Which means it's going to hurt in a minute.

"More," I tell him, and his breath catches as he opens the floodgates a little more. I feel the hurt now—it's as though my bones are too big for my body, as though my sinews are stretching.

There's anger there, too—a righteous anger that makes me a sword for a moment, a spear, a weapon desperate for a target. I feel Barrica the Warrior in me, roaring for a fight.

Fire runs through my veins, burning a path from our joined hands up to my shoulders, and as it sears my body, my eyes fly open—I'm sure I'll see flames. I hear myself gasp, and as I start to curl over, a wave of terror washes through me.

Is it going to stop before I fly apart?

And then, in the very instant I despair, it's suddenly over, and I'm left with a dizzying ache, a thumping pain at my temples, my body trembling. I'm collapsed on the bed, still gripping Leander's hand, my palms sweaty, my body too weak to move.

I can't do that again.

My thoughts are scattered—I'm trying to stop shaking, I'm trying to find words, but before all of them comes a terrified, animalistic instinct to *run*. To get myself as far from him as I know how, to put any barrier I can between that pain and me.

But I can't leave him.

We both know what will happen if I do.

"That wasn't . . . so bad," I croak, but his mind is tangled up in mine, and he knows it's a lie.

"I'm so sorry," he whispers.

"Don't be," I reply, forcing my eyes open. "It worked, didn't it?"

For now.

But I make myself inject a little *I told you so* into my voice, because even as the last of the shakes run through my body, I know I've made my choice. I need him to do this again. And again. Whenever the magic is too much for him, I need to help him carry the load. And I need him to know it's okay to let me. I need him to live.

There are still layers of tiredness and strain shadowing his face, but I can also see *my* Leander again—the boy who wanted to dance with me, who licked his plate clean at the night market, who made me a paper boat as a promise.

It's worth any amount of pain, to keep that boy here.

"Oh, Selly," he whispers, brushing my hair back from my face. When his fingertips touch my temples, I realize I must have been crying. "All you've ever done is try to help me—"

"Occasionally while insulting you," I add, trying to break the mood, but he presses on.

"—and now you're far from home, trapped here with me." I can feel his pain through our bond, emerald-green tendrils of it curling around my mind until I feel it as my own.

I prop myself up on my elbow, and for a long moment, I let myself simply gaze at him. It's strange, to be able to just look at him, drink in his handsome face without pretending I'm not staring.

He has long lashes, strong brows, and a mouth that makes me lose my train of thought. When we first met, he was just a handsome prince. Now, familiarity makes him even more beautiful. He's not an idea anymore. He's a person.

A person I'll sleep beside every night, a person I'm bound up in and bound *to*. A person I can feel slowly relaxing under my touch, his pain fading away, if only for a moment. We're so closely connected that I can tell the moment his attention drifts to my lips.

I feel myself flush, and pray it's not creeping up my neck to my cheeks.

"Not trapped," I whisper. "Staying at your side was my choice."

He reaches up to catch my hand with his, and I watch as our fingers twine together—the complex loops and whorls of his magician's marks cover his skin, all the way down to the back of his hand. Beside them sit the geometric lines of my own unique marks. A perfect copy of a design carved into a temple more than five centuries before I was born.

Our minds are entwined as closely as our hands, and he catches the shimmer of uncertainty as it flickers through me, just for a moment.

"Selly?"

"Mmm?" I put on a smile and lift my eyes to his again, but he's waiting for an honest answer. "It's nothing. I was just looking at my marks. Still not used to seeing anything but the old stripe there."

"And now the mark of the goddess is on you," he says quietly.

"Maybe it always was."

Staying at your side was my choice.

My own words ring in my ears. It *was* my choice . . . wasn't it?

"Selly," he says again slowly, cautious now.

"What we feel for each other," I say, and it's like I'm listening to someone else speak the words, distant, detached. "It's us, isn't it? Or is it her?"

Leander's lips part, the breath going out of him.

But before he can answer, there's a sharp knock at the door.

LEANDER

◆

The Royal Palace
Kirkpool, Alinor

I'm still reeling from Selly's question, and for a moment I don't understand the sound I've just heard. But it comes again, and Selly bites her lip, then raises her voice.

"Come in."

The door to the antechamber opens immediately, and two servants bustle in, carrying trays of breakfast. The first stops short for a moment at the carnage all around us—furniture overturned, a vase of flowers smashed across the rug, debris everywhere. Then she picks her way through it, along with her companion, so they can set their trays down on a low table.

If they're trying hard not to notice the mess, they're positively vibrating with how hard they're ignoring the girl beside me in bed.

"Selly," I begin, once the servants withdraw, though I have no idea where that sentence leads. Suddenly I'm remembering the way she cut me off, before I could tell Augusta she kissed me. I can't believe that what we have—

Keegan's voice rings out from the antechamber. "I really don't mean to impose, but I assure you that His Highness— What? Well, nor do I wish to outrage anyone's sensibilities, but if they're in their nightclothes, then they'll be considerably more put together than—"

Keegan abruptly pops through the door, then closes it behind him with the air of a man who's gone through a trial. "Good morning. What a—" He stops short as his gaze travels across the broken bits of vase and tumbled furniture. "Uh . . . commotion, out there. But I see you have your own commotion in here." His eyes lift and flick between us, concerned.

"Leander's working on controlling his Messenger's powers," Selly says, carefully not looking at me.

"Good morning," I manage. "They've brought enough breakfast to feed an army, help yourself." As Keegan turns his attention to the trays the servants brought, I'm reaching for Selly's hand so I can squeeze it, and promise her we're going to continue our conversation.

She swallows, and nods silent acknowledgment. And after a moment I let her go. She's off the bed in an instant, picking her way through the broken dishes to join Keegan by the breakfast.

"It's a mess in here," she concedes, sounding just like her usual self. "I'm sure the palace servants are used to it. The stories about Leander—I expect he's done more damage throwing afternoon tea parties."

"I'm insulted." A lifetime of training waits for me just

beneath the surface, and I dredge up a normal tone of voice. "I would never disrespect a cake like that. Are you all right, Keegan?"

He nods, swallowing a mouthful of toast before he replies. "I sent for Kiki last night, before I went to bed."

Relief flows through me. "Brilliant news. Where is she?"

Keegan pulls a face. "They covered up my disappearance by bundling her off to an aunt in the countryside. If neither of us were in sight, nobody would ask questions."

"Wait—Kiki, is that the name of the girl you were engaged to? You're still engaged?" Selly asks, her brows shooting up. "You mean you ran away from home, stowed away, survived a shipwreck, survived an assassination attempt in a foreign port, sailed to the Isles and witnessed the work of an actual goddess, and you didn't actually . . ."

"Achieve the one thing I set out to do," he agrees, rueful.

"I'm afraid this friendship won't make it easier to dodge the marriage," I say, apologetic. "You're even more of a catch for her family now."

"Well, what was it the papers called you last month?" he asks, leaning over the tray to check whether the tea has brewed. "The most eligible bachelor on the Crescent Sea? Could be worse."

Things must really be grim if Keegan's cracking jokes to cheer me up.

"What other news?" I ask, and that's sufficient to shift the smile off his face.

"A great deal. First, there's a collection of priests, ah, *requesting* a chance to meet with you both, by which I take it they mean *poke and prod at*. With the greatest of respect, no doubt."

"Later," I murmur, closing my eyes. "What else?"

"The queen is eager to . . ." And now he hesitates.

"To what?" Selly asks, wary.

"To understand the extent of Leander's abilities," Keegan says carefully. And then, in that same considered tone: "She emphasizes that the quickest route to peace is to demonstrate our power to our neighbors, so that Mellacea finds herself confronted with a wall of allies."

I crack open one eye to study him, finding him suddenly busy with his toast. "You don't think that's what she has in mind."

"I am not well acquainted with your sister," Keegan says slowly. "Nor am I in any way suited to the sorts of decisions that come with not just running a country but potentially protecting the safety of an entire continent. I cannot imagine the pressure."

Selly leans in and steals his piece of toast, which has the effect of drawing his gaze directly to her face. Once she has eye contact, she speaks. "We were there, Keegan. We saw the way she acted when we used the word *power*."

A new tension knots itself just under my ribs. I remember the way my sister looked at me. The words she used.

Learn how best you can wield this gift.

What it means for your country.

Keegan lets out a breath. "She asked again, after you had left. She wanted specific information on Leander's capabilities."

"Well, she can have that information when we figure it out ourselves," I say, pushing that unease down deep, where it can join the roiling mass of fears and worries that live permanently in my gut. "And anyway, knowing what I can do isn't the same as commanding me to do it."

"Nobody's commanding you to do anything," Selly says immediately.

Neither Keegan nor I contradict her. As he and Selly eat, she and I tell him about my dream—about the feeling that Barrica is looking for a way through me to our world.

"I have the full run of the palace library, and couriers ready to bring me copies of anything I request from the Bibliotek," he replies. "The gods have only left our world once, and never returned—so the mechanism by which they might come back is a mystery. Perhaps there's something about it in the records created at the time of their departure."

"We don't want anyone getting any ideas about making it happen," Selly says quietly. "Not the queen, not the priesthood."

"Indeed," he agrees. "And I'll have to be careful, because I won't be the only one in the palace library. There'll be plenty of priests, and I don't want to show them how to bring back their goddess. The world has done very well without a Warrior, all these centuries."

And there we leave it, cut off by the arrival of a stream of servants to tidy up the chaos I created while I slept, and then a whole stream of personal staff, who have arrived to do their worst to Selly.

Keegan and I retreat across the room to the safety of a window seat, as half a dozen attendants cluster around her, grabbing at locks of her hair, holding her hands out to show off the *disasters* that are her nails, arguing with each other without any apparent need for input from Selly herself.

I ache with the need to protect her—this girl who's so out of her element, and yet still somehow holding her own. Who isn't even sure whether we chose each other, or were chosen *for* each other by our goddess, and yet is still by my side.

"I keep thinking of that night at the Salthouse Inn, in Port Naranda." The words surprise me with their arrival. "When you and I played Fates, and talked."

"I remember."

"I said then that I'd never want to keep her from what she loves."

"I remember that, too."

"That's exactly what I'm doing though. And to you."

"It's what's needed," Keegan says gently. "We must serve the greater good."

"But how do we do that? What if my sister asks . . ."

"She may not," Keegan replies, in a voice that sounds anything but certain.

A particularly difficult whirl of spirits catches me off guard before I can reply, the light coming through the window gleaming too bright, stinging my eyes. The world is too much, and all I can do is grip the edge of the window seat and make myself hold still.

"We'll address the wardrobe issue first," the woman who seems to be in charge is saying. She's *almost* talking to me, but she refuses to look in my direction and keeps bobbing up and down, addressing me from the other side of the room. "That's the most visible problem. Then, following that logic, deportment—everyone will see her walk, after all—followed by court etiquette." She turns to pick a man out of her crew. "Otto, put together a who's who board, would you, so you can drill her on faces?"

I try to catch Selly's eye, but she's got her head down, busy inspecting her fingernails—I can tell from the brush of her mind against mine that she's bewildered by the attention they're being paid.

"There's not much we can do about elocution," the woman continues, apparently addressing her companions now. "That accent is going to stand out. We'll say she's shy. Are you shy?"

Selly blinks up at her, so surprised to be actually addressed that she's rendered speechless.

"Perfect," the woman says, with an approving nod. "Now, where are the seamstresses? They'll need the longest lead time, so we'd better measure."

It's when she reaches for the top button on Selly's silk pajama shirt that my girl finally comes to life, slapping her hand away.

"What's your cleavage like?" asks another woman, striding forward with a tape measure as the one in charge gapes at Selly.

Selly blushes all the way from her cheeks down to the relevant area, and shoots me a look of mute appeal.

I look at Keegan, and he inclines his head, rising wordlessly to leave the room.

I wait a moment, pushing away the echoes that rattle around my head, forcing myself to ignore the way the light refracts around the room, then speak once I'm sure my voice will be even. "Thank you all for the excellent start you've made. We're going to try a different approach. If you'd be so kind as to step out to the antechamber for a moment?"

"We don't have that kind of time!" the woman in charge protests. Who *is* she? One of my sisters' dressers, perhaps? They're so used to me being the playboy, the one nobody takes seriously, that sometimes they forget my rank. I used to let them.

That was before they started treating Selly like an object.

I arch one brow and tilt my head, like a patient teacher prompting a slow student. "Have you perhaps mistaken my words for a request, Madame . . . ?"

She doesn't supply her name, but takes a step back, mouth falling open. "Apologies, Your Holiness. Your Highness. I wasn't—" She breaks off to flap her arms at her assistants, sending them scuttling toward the door. They all keep their distance from me, but the last to go—Otto, I think—takes an awed peek back at me before the door shuts.

"I'm sorry about them," I say, in the echoing silence that follows their departure. "I should have seen it coming. You took care of me, when I was in your world. I should have watched out for you."

"Does that mean you're on the case now?" Selly asks.

"I am. And for the record, because that lot are enough to make anyone doubt it, you look beautiful right now. Without changing a single thing."

"I'm wearing a pair of pajamas."

"And looking dashing doing it. Now, Keegan will be back in a moment, and you'll meet his fiancée, Lady Carrie Dastenholtz. Kiki, to her friends."

"Oh." Selly is immediately wary.

I shake my head. "She's a force of nature, but she'll be on our side. Keegan and I have both known her since we were children."

"She won't be . . . you know? A little irritated that he literally ran away to sea rather than marrying her?"

I can't help but laugh. "He told me that she helped him climb out the window. She would like to marry someone who fancies her, and fancying anybody is simply not for him. They get on very well when nobody's trying to walk them to the altar."

"Huh." She squints at me suspiciously. "She's coming to transform me?"

"It's going to work, trust me." I raise my voice and shout in the direction of the door. "Keegan, you out there?"

The doors burst open immediately, sending up a swirl of air, the spirits cavorting on the newly made currents like a puff of golden glitter, creating a fabulous entrance for the brunette striding through them. Judging by the way Selly's eyes widen, she sees it too.

Kiki has wide brown eyes and hair that falls in artful curls around her shoulders, and she's wearing a lavender dress tailored within an inch of its life. She's all curves, and she moves like she's not afraid to take up space. Which is fair, because she never has been.

She makes a curtsy so elaborate that she's clearly teasing, and I feel Selly unwind, where her mind brushes against mine. I'm going to protect her while she learns this place. I'm going to find a way to show her that my care for her is very real, and all my own.

"You summoned me, my prince?" Kiki asks, looking up with a grin.

My relief that she's not awestruck like the servants makes me laugh out loud. "Selly, this is Kiki. Kiki, meet Selly Walker."

Kiki turns those big brown eyes on Selly, all warmth and conspiratorial friendship. "I don't know what either of them have told you," she says. "But ignore it, unless it was wonderful. I'm here to save the day."

SELLY

The Royal Palace
Kirkpool, Alinor

In her own way, Kiki is as overwhelming as the army of beauticians that Leander just kicked out into the antechamber—the difference is that she actually meets my eyes. And because she does, I'm remembering that I'm the girl who spent a year sharing a room with our first mate—with my *friend*. With Kyri, who joked that she was the sweet to my sour. That not long ago I was a girl who knew how to have a friend like that. Kiki makes me want to be that girl again, though I don't know if there's any way back to her, after all the distance I've come.

"Pleased to meet you, Your Ladyship," I say slowly, and even though I've only known her half a minute, I already suspect that's going to be more than true.

"Just Kiki, please. And the pleasure is entirely mine," she says, walking across the room to reach for my hands. "About time someone pulled His Highness into line." Only now do I see the way her gaze flicks to Leander just a little too often—she's treating him like a normal human being, as Keegan no doubt told her to, but it hasn't escaped her that she's in the presence of the goddess's chosen Messenger. She's working hard to keep it together.

She clasps my hands, and leans in to speak in a low voice. "I know this must be overwhelming. Keegan has told me just a fraction of what's been happening, and I saw a long line of deeply offended seamstresses marching away just now."

"They were talking straight over her," Leander offers from the sidelines. "As if she couldn't hear them."

Kiki releases me to flap a hand at him without turning her head, and he falls silent. "I know you're as far from home as you can imagine being," she continues. "But, Selly Walker, there is *nothing* in this place you can't handle. You're standing at their prince's side. It's *their* job to impress *you,* so don't you let a single one of them make you feel less than."

"Oh," I say quietly. Leander was right. This *is* different.

"Do you want to know what I think?" she asks, and then tells me anyway—which is quite obviously how she handles most situations. "I think, what if nobody's better than anyone else? I happen to like fashion. Keegan likes books. Leander likes casually causing riots by showing up and looking handsome. You, I'm told, like sailing. So what if you haven't practiced your curtsies lately?"

"Not . . . lately," I manage. It's impossible to do anything but let her sweep me along.

"I suppose in some circles I should think that's uncouth," Kiki replies with a shrug. "But you know what? I don't know how to . . . hoist a deck mast, or whatever marvelous things you all do on ships. Keegan tells me you've been a guide for the boys through your world. I hope you'll allow me to be your guide through mine."

She feels like a hurricane, but she feels like a life raft too. And I want to cling to her. "Yes, please."

"Wonderful!" She claps her hands. "This will be fun. I'm thinking sea-themed dresses; let's really lean into your mystique. And you'll want trousers, I'm guessing—I can't imagine you get around in skirts on your lovely boats. Blues and greens will go with your eyes, and we'll tailor your sleeves to show off those extraordinary magician's marks."

"I don't really know how to choose . . . ," I begin, then trail off, because that much is completely obvious.

"That's what I'm here for," she promises. "Listen, you can't give up on what you want and who you are, and pretend it doesn't matter just to serve others. Keegan and I worked that out together. It makes you miserable. But for now, because we must, I can help you speak their language."

"What?" It's all I can manage.

"Your clothes are your key to this world," she replies. "You have to pass as one of them, if you want to influence them. Which is ridiculous, but we can only upend so many traditions at one time, and we're already doing quite a bit on the religious front."

I hear a snort from the direction of the boys, though I'm not sure which one of them it came from.

"I really just need something to wear," I say. "I don't need to start a revolution."

"You say that now," she replies cheerfully. "Give it time."

Her good mood is infectious, and I like this girl—but I don't need lessons in the intricacies of court etiquette. I don't need to learn what dress to wear to maximize my influence. I just need a pair of trousers so I can figure out if Queen Augusta is planning on using Leander to invade Mellacea.

"I'd love some help with all my clothes," is all I say. "Thank you."

Her smile is luminous. "Brilliant. I'm about to make your freckles the must-have accessory of the season."

The boys cram themselves onto the window seat and stay out of the way as Hurricane Kiki takes over the suite. She's all big gestures and bold colors and throaty laughs, and she's slowly easing the tension out of me as we talk.

Queen Augusta should consider putting Kiki to work as an interrogator—no matter how I try to hurry her through the process, she keeps drawing more information out of me, nodding as though she's committing every word to memory. She probably is.

When she summons the beauty army once more, she runs a tight ship, and has the tailors and seamstresses scuttling back and forth with the kind of urgency usually required for firefighters, living and dying by her nod of approval.

Kiki seems to be watching everything at once—every time my shoulders begin to lift, she's there to murmur something in my ear, to make me laugh. Every time one of them lays hands on me to turn me, she's at their side, asking me a question with the exaggerated courtesy that cues them to straighten up.

As she examines a bolt of blue-green silk, and I pretend to look at it too, my father pops into my head unbidden. What would Stanton Walker make of all this, if he could see me now?

But he can't, of course. He's far away, up north in Holbard, thinking only of his winter negotiations. He has no idea that the *Lizabetta* was lost, that I'm bound to a prince, that I'm standing here in his private chambers as Kiki orders up a dress worth more than I am.

Make the most of it, he'd say. That's his motto.

And it's good advice. I will make the most of every chance at my disposal. I'll need to, if I'm going to navigate this place, and protect Leander while I'm at it.

I can still see the hurt on his face when I let those words slip.

What we feel for each other. It's us, isn't it? Or is it her?

I risked my life for him, and I'd make that choice again. I just wish I was sure how much of the path we've been following was our own.

There's no time to think about such things, not while his sister wants to know his capacity. His stamina.

She wants to know what he can do for her.

If she thinks she's going to put him on the front lines of a war, then she's going to have to get through me first.

It's a couple of hours later when Kiki gives me a moment to breathe—her team is pinning together pieces of a dress in a patchwork that looks nothing like clothing, and I manage to sidle away to talk to the boys.

"There are half a dozen priests still waiting to see you," Keegan is saying thoughtfully to Leander. "To think that I considered that a large number. They fade into nothing before this effort." He tilts his head as I draw near, nodding a greeting and studying the group clustered around the dress as it comes together. "I have no wish to sound naïve, but are that many of them really required to outfit you? I don't see how they could all even reach you at once."

"I think some are for moral support," Leander supplies.

"Listen," I say quietly. "While we're here doing this, there are other conversations happening. What are we going to do about them?"

"You mean my sister," Leander says quietly.

Keegan grimaces. "I think we should try to determine her intentions. All three of us independently felt we had reason to doubt her commitment to a peaceful solution."

"I trust her," Leander protests, but it's weak, and I know he can hear it.

"Well then," Keegan says, more firmly than usual. "The sooner we confirm that, the less time any doubts will have to fester. What would you do, if you wanted to know what was on her mind? What she'd been thinking about while you were away?"

"I'd get into her private study," Leander says. "But—"

"Selly!" Kiki appears by my side and takes hold of my arm. "Do excuse us," she says to the boys, and hauls me behind a screen, where half a dozen pairs of hands are waiting to stuff me into this ridiculous dress, the pieces still held together with pins.

"What a masterpiece," she crows, reaching forward to pull my hair out of its rough knot and drape it over my shoulders. "And," she continues, with an outrageous wink, "the dress isn't bad either."

"I can't stay for much—"

"Gentlemen!" she calls out, grinning. "Brace yourselves!"

And then she pushes me out from behind the screen, where I catch sight of myself in a full-length mirror, just as Leander and Keegan catch sight of me. Leander makes a totally undignified noise, and I can see why.

The dress is . . . incredible. Pinned together it may be, but it's a truly beautiful, intricate mosaic of blue and green silk, accented by silver sequins that instantly remind me of sea-foam. The sleeves end at my elbows, showcasing my magician's marks. Kyri would have sold her soul for a dress like this.

"You look like a vision," Leander manages. "Like you were born from the sea."

There's a pleased murmur going round among the dressmakers, but I tear my gaze away from the mirror, and refocus on the real issue at hand.

"It's beautiful, Kiki, thank you. I saw some ready-made dresses back there, simpler ones. Can I put one of them on? There's something we need to do."

"Of course," Kiki agrees. "Soon, I promise. This is only the first dress. We'll need to—"

"I'll come back later," I tell her, ducking back behind the screen. The pair of seamstresses waiting there are forced to help me get the silk dress off, before any of the pins break.

"Your Highness," Kiki's saying, making Leander's title sound like a reprimand. "You of all people, the boy with a wardrobe more impressive than the rest of the top ten in Alinor combined, really should know—"

"I'm sorry," Leander says as I pull a plain blue dress on over my head and slip my feet into the most impractical pair of soft leather shoes. "There really is something we need to do."

"Curse you," Kiki mutters, as I appear from behind the screen. She doesn't sound annoyed, though. "Go on, then. I'll be here, making unappreciated artistic decisions."

I barely catch her words—Leander and Keegan are already on their way out the door, and I'm hurrying to catch them.

LASKIA

The Gem Cutter
Port Naranda, Mellacea

One of Ruby's lackeys tiptoes into the room, her footsteps too loud—it's like she's *inside* my ears, every sound echoing and vibrating.

"No!" I snap, startling her into stillness. "Go!"

"Laskia." It's Dasriel. He's the only one who just *talks* to me now—everyone else whispers, apologizes, cringes. I have no particular care for Dasriel, but no interest in hurting him either, and he seems to know it.

"Too loud," I rasp, and Ruby whimpers. We're side by side on her red velvet couch, where she's always held court at the Gem Cutter. She's curled over with her hands wrapped around the back of her head.

I reach out and rest a hand on her shoulder, and she flinches. So I tighten my grip to hold her still as I pour some of my power into her, my fingers digging into her skin. She tries again to pull away, her eyes unseeing, a low, frightening noise coming from her throat. I can *feel* her pain.

For a moment, my head is clearer, my body lighter—and then the magic surges back in. I can't tell if she can't hold it or if she's pushing it back—it's like I'm viewing the world again through thick, warped glass.

"Give that to me," Dasriel mutters, reaching for a cup of water carried by the cringing girl by the door. "You might not need to eat or drink," he continues to me, "but your sister's going to die if she doesn't, I assume."

Ruby doesn't respond as he approaches. With a growl of frustration he crouches in front of her, pushing her upright so he can hold the glass to her lips. Just a few days ago, he was keeping his eyes cast down when he spoke to her. Now he's manhandling her.

I watch the spirits drift around the pair of them, like tiny fireworks I can glimpse out the corner of my eye. I can see them now, command them, but only roughly—it's like trying to thread a needle wearing boxing gloves. I can tell how much easier all this would be if I were a magician already.

But Macean didn't have a magician ready to show him such faith, did he?

He had me.

I am his chosen, whatever that turns out to mean. Even now, I can feel him pushing on me, trying to batter down a door I don't know how to open. I can feel tendrils of his thoughts twining through mine, making me wild, making me a gambler just like him. Making me sure of things that some tiny part of me thinks perhaps I shouldn't be.

Ruby coughs and chokes beside me, but manages to get some of the water down.

Dasriel is studying her, but then directs his frown at me. "She's no use if you kill her, you know."

"And you care, do you?"

"*You* should care." He keeps his voice to a low rumble. "I saw what you were, before you chained her to you."

"Are you afraid I'll try you next?" I snap, my head ringing with the volume of my own voice. One of the bulbs in the chandeliers shatters, sprinkling glass on the floor.

Dasriel ignores the question, rubbing one hand along his square jaw. There's stubble showing—he looks frayed around the edges as well. "Laskia," he rumbles. "Everything you did, you did to impress her. Her and the green sister. Now you're the closest any of us can be to a god. Ruby's terrified, and Beris doesn't care if you drain yourself dry, as long as you fuel her crusade as you burn."

"What's your point?" The pressure in my head is building already, and again I push a little of the power into Ruby, pausing only when I feel her dance on the edge of consciousness. My sight clearer, my voice stronger, I repeat the words: "What's your point, Dasriel?"

"You've got their attention," he says simply. "Feel as good as you thought it would?"

Anger licks through me, as hot as one of Dasriel's flames, and I press my lips together, force my expression into something neutral. Was I so transparent? It doesn't matter now.

"Why would I care what they think," I make myself say evenly, "when I have a *god* at my side?"

"A god who's taking care of you as well as she did," he mutters, rising to stand, still holding Ruby's empty water glass.

I raise my hand, and it doesn't even have to connect to send him staggering back. He fixes me with a long look, but falls silent.

His feet scrape too loudly on the carpet when he moves. I can hear his heartbeat.

"Where in seven hells is Beris?" I snap. "How long does it take her to run an errand?"

"I am here," she says from the doorway. I wonder how long she's been there. There's a boy standing beside her—he wears a newsie's cap and holds a bundle of papers under one arm.

"Him?" I ask, hunger rising in me.

"He wishes to roll the dice," she replies. "And there are many more besides."

I push up from the couch and walk over to the boy—beyond him, through the open door, are more of them. A man in a suit. Another in a butcher's apron, still bloody. A woman in sailor's clothes.

Ruby can't take all my magic, not if I want her to live—and I do, very much. She's the closest thing I have to the prince's sailor girl. The only one who can stand up to the strain of easing my burden again and again.

And so, this. I will lay my hands on them. If they live, they will be paid enough to live off for ten years or more.

If they don't . . . well, that's the gamble.

My god wants his freedom. He wants the war he was never allowed to finish. And I will give it to him. I will prove that my faith is greater than any in five centuries.

I will give him *everything*.

Ruby gasps for breath behind me, and I force myself to focus as Dasriel leaves the room. His words echo in my ears.

You've got their attention. Feel as good as you thought it would?

Give me time, Dasriel. It will.

This is what I have fought for. And every one of them will see that I am worthy of all that I desire.

Beris closes the door behind the boy with a click, and he looks up at me with dark eyes.

Then I reach out, and touch him.

KEEGAN

Queen's Private Study
Kirkpool, Alinor

"Just how many secret passages are there in this place?" I whisper, as Leander reaches a crossroads and turns left.

"I could travel the length of the palace without setting foot in a public hallway," he replies, just as soft, forging ahead as Selly stops to look through a peephole that's probably set into a portrait. "Meant for the servants, of course, but useful for misbehaving princes."

"And you're telling me there's a secret doorway in your sister's personal study that she doesn't know about?" I press. "That seems like the most concerning of national security issues."

"She knows," Leander replies over his shoulder. "She just doesn't know I copied the key when I was nine."

He's as cheerful as I've seen him in days, but there's a strain to it—beneath that grin, and those easy words, he's as taut as a bowstring. I know his senses are pulling him in a thousand directions at once—he can't hide the way he flinches at loud noises or bright lights. And when I arrived in his apartments this morning, it was as though a hurricane had gone through them. Only a lifetime of schooling my expression allowed me to keep a straight face.

I fear the next few minutes aren't going to improve Leander's peace of mind.

He doesn't hesitate, though, when he peeks through a tiny grille to check the room and then swings open a door disguised as an ornate wooden panel, so the three of us can step into his sister's private sanctum.

It's a strange mix of fancy architecture and small touches that bespeak a personal space, and a level of informality. A sideboard runs the length of the room, made of dark wood with little clawed feet and delicately shaped iron handles. Atop it sits a radio playing soft music, and a stack of today's newspapers.

There are sofas facing each other, one covered with a rumpled blanket, a sheaf of papers dumped on top, as if the queen had lain there reading until a few moments ago. Her desk reminds me of the state of Leander's rooms this morning, with towering stacks of paper topped by makeshift paperweights: a glass ornament, a rock that looks like a fossil, a blue-and-white cup full of cold tea.

"Welcome to the inner sanctum, where all Alinor's secrets will be revealed," Leander says softly, gesturing like a ringmaster as Selly and I spread out to start looking around. I can hear the false cheer in his voice, though. He's worried.

"Your sister's as messy as you are," Selly observes, leaning over the papers dumped on the sofa.

"Clearly not my fault, then," he returns. "Runs in the family."

"We simply want to know what she's thinking," I say, trying

to look over the desk without sending papers cascading everywhere. "What intelligence she has that she's not sharing. If she's hiding nothing, then no harm done."

But the truth is, I know there's something Augusta isn't telling us. I saw her face. The way she looked at her brother. The calculations taking place behind her eyes.

I've never wanted so badly to be wrong, but I know I'm not. I can imagine her speech already—I can hear her voice as it'll sound through the radio on the sideboard.

Swift action is our only choice, she'll say. *With the power of a Messenger at our back, we can avoid the sort of long, drawn-out war that would cause a far greater loss of life. We must attack so decisively that Mellacea sees the only option is to lay down their arms.*

And then she'll send her people to kill, and to die. Leander will be one of them, and Selly too.

With a warrior goddess whispering in her ear, what other choice would she make? And what kind of destruction will satisfy her, once she begins?

I carefully lift up the fossil paperweight, resisting the urge to examine it more closely, and then pause when I get a better look at the top sheet.

It's a map of the Crescent Sea. As I run my gaze over it, the back of my neck starts to prickle.

"What are those?" Selly asks, appearing beside me and leaning in to study the series of red *X*'s inked onto the map in a sure hand.

"I don't know what they signify," I murmur. "Targets?"

She runs a finger in a line across the sea, thoughtful. "These would be good places to attack a ship," she says slowly. "No visibility from land, off the main shipping lanes."

Leander joins us. "Who would you attack?" he asks, frowning. "If these are places nobody would be?"

"Lure them there with a distress signal," Selly says, grimacing. "It's what pirates do."

"The targets aren't just on the sea," I say slowly, tapping the left-hand side of the continent. "There's one right here, directly over Port Naranda."

My words land like a lead weight.

"There are letters beside each *X*," Selly says, leaning in until her nose almost touches the map. "Tiny, but they're there. They must mean something."

I continue my way through the stack of other papers as she bows her head over the map.

Leander's the one who sees my expression, and takes a step toward me. "Keegan?"

Numb, I hold out the page I've stopped on. It's a list of Alinorish battalions. Where they're stationed. Their readiness. A list of naval ships, and merchants available for conscription.

I grew up in a military family. I know how to read lists like this.

"Gus, no," Leander whispers, leafing through them. "What are you doing?"

I feel like I've swallowed a rock.

I knew what I was going to find. And yet some part of me desperately hoped I wouldn't.

This is why she looked at Leander like someone had handed her a weapon. She was already planning a fight.

"These are invasion plans," Leander breathes, working his way through the papers. "She has them all drawn up. She had them before we even got back."

"But there's one thing she didn't count on, until yesterday," I whisper, as he reaches the final page.

And there it is, down at the bottom, written in red ink in her bold hand and circled.

(LEANDER.)

SELLY

The Queen's Council Chamber
Kirkpool, Alinor

"Leander, please just wait a—" I'm gasping as I chase my prince, Keegan at my heels as Leander storms down a hallway toward the council chamber. I don't even have time to properly marvel that *I'm* the one arguing we shouldn't rush into things, because I'm too busy trying to keep up.

It's like he's towing a hurricane in his wake—air spirits dance madly on the wind, and portraits rattle on their hooks, frames clattering against the wall. Tapestries twist and blow, and the small tables lining the hallway go flying, ornaments crashing to the ground. I feel like I'm trying to force my way along the deck in the face of a gale.

"Leander," I try again. "We should think about what we're going to—"

But he's reached a pair of double doors, and a pair of Queensguard who are too awed to stop him—they jump to the side as he throws the doors open and storms into the room.

When Keegan and I arrive panting in Leander's wake, they seem to think the damage has been done, and let us rush through after him.

Queen Augusta is seated at the head of a table lined with dignitaries—I see Princess Coria and the Princess Consort Delphine, as well as priests in their military robes, and other nobles who must be Augusta's councilors, richly dressed and wearing identical expressions of shock and concern.

"Leander?" Augusta manages, before her brother walks forward to slam the map we found down on the table. The table shudders with the impact, a crack running along the beautifully inlaid wood, and the nearest council members push their chairs back and away from their furious prince.

No . . . from their furious *Messenger.* I can see actual fear flickering across their faces.

A buzz of magic goes through the air like the discordant note of a badly tuned violin. I see the magicians up and down the table wince in discomfort, and Coria makes a soft noise of distress.

"How could you?" Leander demands, already at full volume. "You've been planning a war since before you sent me. All that talk of peace, and you've been marshaling your forces all along. You used me, used the progress fleet—my friends, who *died*—as a distraction, while you planned to start a damned war, and now you're going to use me again to win it!"

Augusta doesn't try to interrupt. She doesn't stand. She simply holds still, watching her brother until he pauses, and the way she looks at him makes the hair on the back of my neck stand up. She's measuring something in him, her head tilted a little to one side.

"Are you finished?" she asks. Her voice is quiet, but the words are clearly audible, dropping into the perfect silence of the room.

"Don't you—" Leander begins, but this time she does cut him off.

"Those aren't attack plans," she says simply. "Each of those *X*'s is an attack, yes. But on us, not *by* us. Did you think we were only dealing with taxes, with seizures of our ships in Port Naranda?" *You foolish boy,* says her tone, cold as ice.

"What do you mean?"

"The Mellaceans have been taking jabs at us for months, brother. That red *X* over Port Naranda is our ambassador's assassination. You witnessed it yourself less than a week ago."

Leander stares at her, chest heaving. I can sense it in him—he's lost his momentum, and just as those around him have been trying to reconcile their laughing, smiling prince with this powerful Messenger, now he's trying to see the sister he loves in the queen who stares, calculating, down the table at him.

Months of skirmishes with Mellacea, and he had no idea. Because she didn't tell him.

Keegan clears his throat, and all eyes turn to him. He looks like he'd prefer to crawl under the table and hide, but when he speaks, his voice is even. "Your Majesty, the attack on the *Lizabetta,* and those on the progress fleet and the ambassador, were not acts of the Mellacean government. We learned when we were in Port Naranda that the assassination attempt on the prince was driven by private interests. By one of the criminal gangs there."

"That does not account for the attacks that went before," Augusta says, cutting through Keegan's words like a knife.

"Those *were* the government in Port Naranda. And regardless, we now have an opportunity to bring them to their knees, and to secure another five centuries of peace. I can guarantee you that if our positions were reversed, they would show us no mercy."

The three of us stand silent, facing the long table of nobles. I realize nobody here cares who's responsible for any of the attacks. All they see is an opportunity to neutralize a foe, and that's what they intend on doing.

"So you weren't planning a war?" I step up to take my place at Leander's side. "Your desk was covered in battalion lists, conscription plans for the merchant fleets."

"Of course I was," Augusta replies calmly. "When I sent Leander to the Isles, I also considered the resources at our disposal, should we be forced into conflict. And you're beyond naïve if you don't think I should have been."

"You didn't even give peace a—"

She cuts me off. "None of that matters now." She turns to the woman seated next to her, and suddenly I see the woman doesn't match the nobles around the table.

She has skin of the deepest brown, and her clothes are the same shade, but now I see that the dark fabric has concealed their state. She's travel-worn, with bags beneath her eyes and her curls a windblown tangle. She looks like she hasn't slept in a while.

"This is—" Augusta stops herself as the woman's gaze snaps up. "One of my intelligence agents," she substitutes, in place of the name she had clearly been about to reveal. "She reports only to my chief spymaster, and to me. Please tell my advisers what you've just told me."

"That I am fresh from Port Naranda, Your Majesty," the woman replies. "I came as quickly as I could. I was near the Temple of Macean when the crowd began to gather. Once I saw what happened, I ran straight from there to the port, and boarded a ship we keep waiting. I stopped for nothing."

"And the news you bring?" Augusta prompts.

"That Barrica is not the only one to have created a Messenger, my queen," the woman says grimly. "The Gambler has done the same."

The air goes out of the room.

"That's not possible," I breathe, suddenly cold.

We saw her fall. We saw her lie there, still.

But we left her body behind. . . .

"I have seen her with my own eyes," the spy replies. "They say her name is Laskia. She spoke with a voice we could hear blocks away, and she was lit by the light of her god. Macean has his own Messenger. And she is calling for war."

PART TWO

SWIMMING WITH SHARKS

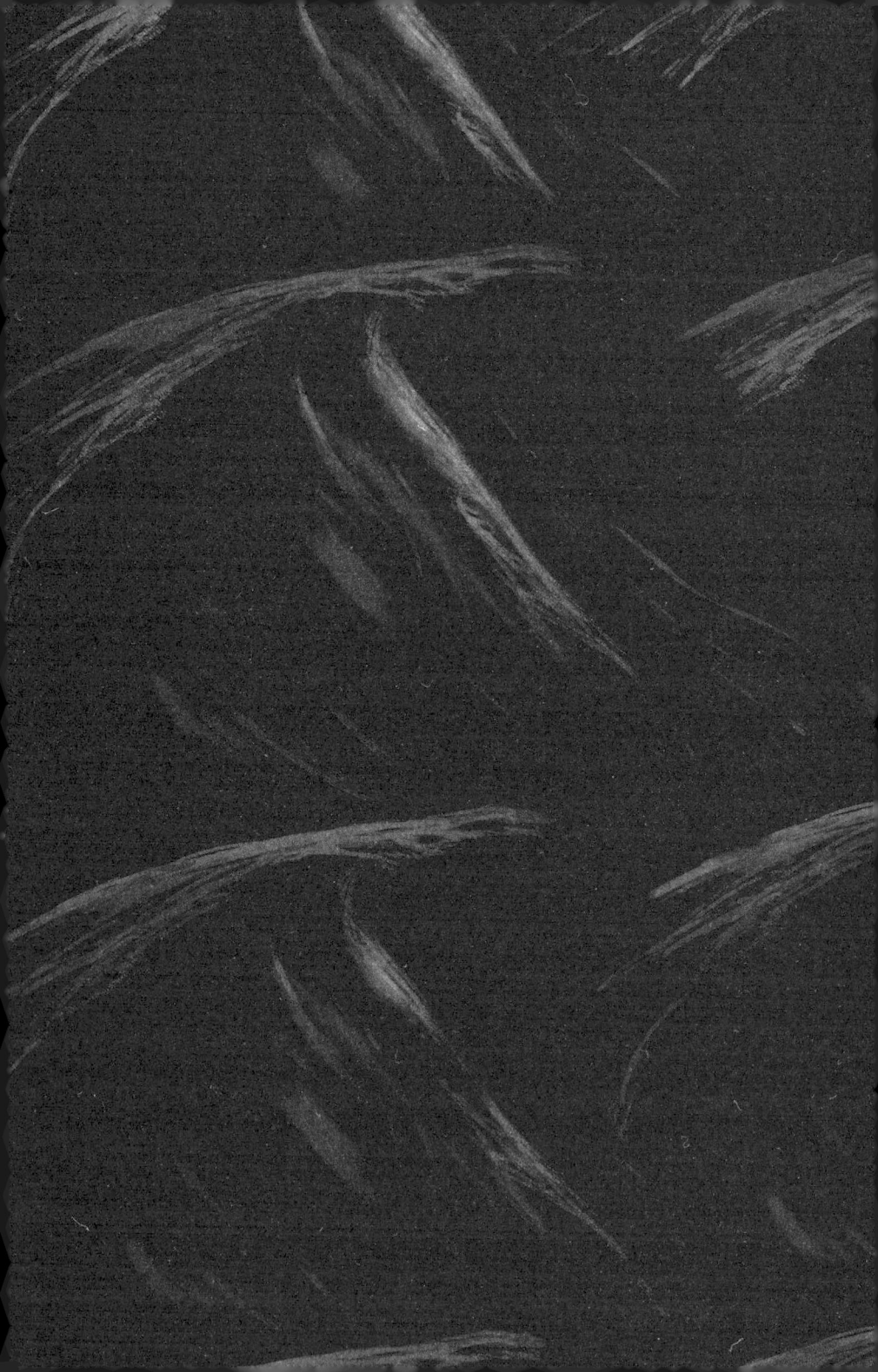

SELLY

The Queen's Council Chamber
Kirkpool, Alinor

I want to throw up.

"That can't be," Keegan murmurs beside me, sounding as dazed as I am.

"No," I manage, hands curling into fists. We saw her die. We did everything—*everything*—anyone could have asked of us.

A small, helpless part of me wants to scream that this isn't *fair*.

But fair or not, it's true. This spy didn't cut her morning shopping short and run all the way to another country without grabbing so much as a change of clothes for anything less than a mortal threat to her people.

"It cannot be," Augusta agrees. "And yet it is."

"I can be ready," Leander says quietly, and my heart drops.

"Leander, no!" I reach for his hand, hissing as his magic vents into me when we touch, sending a jolt up my arm like an electric shock. "You can't—"

"No," says Augusta crisply. "You can't. I don't know what the fallout would be if two Messengers met in battle, but I see no reason to find out. It was for moments such as this that assassins were made."

"What?" I think that was me.

"Gus, you can't—" Leander begins, and she cuts him off with a gesture.

"I can't what? Have her killed from afar? I should send you, the greatest gift our goddess has given us in the five centuries since she left us? So you can fight her hand to hand, and see if you can level a city? When the gods last met, they destroyed a whole *country*." Augusta's voice has been rising, and now she's on her feet. "I don't know what Messengers will do, but I don't plan to find out. I want a fight where Mellacea has a knife and we have a gun. This is how we get it."

Nobody says a word.

And having made her point, the queen turns back to the woman at her side. "Return to Port Naranda," she says simply. "And see it is done."

Without another word, her spy—her killer—rises to her feet, bows, and turns for the door.

Leander's the one who breaks the silence, speaking slowly, as if he's still trying to understand what just happened. "And what do we do now?"

"We will discuss our next steps when we receive word of our success," Augusta says, and her tone is only a fraction of an inch away from *let the grown-ups handle this*.

"Are you planning on sending Leander to war?" I press, standing straighter when her gaze swivels to me.

"We will discuss our next steps," she repeats. "And form a plan with which Barrica's holy Messenger can agree."

Keegan reaches forward to take my arm. "Then, for now, please excuse us, Your Majesty," he says, as politely as if we'd been invited to attend this meeting, rather than Leander nearly breaking down the doors on his way into the room.

I glance at Keegan, and he flicks his eyes toward the door in a silent but absolutely clear instruction that we should leave. And I trust Keegan, so I let him keep his hold on my arm, and lead me away. I feel all their eyes follow us to the door.

"Well, that was a brush-off," I say, once we're safely some distance away. "'We will discuss our next steps.' Could she have been any vaguer? Any more condescending?"

"Oh, she's a royal of the House of Alinor," Leander replies, ignoring the way the tapestries unravel as he walks past them. "Trust me, she could be more condescending."

"He said, proving the point," I mutter, and he almost laughs.

"We'll talk to her, Selly. She's trying to figure out where I fit into things. And yes, what I can do for her. But that doesn't mean I'm going to agree."

"I hope you have more luck getting her to listen than I did."

"I will," he says firmly. "And given some time, she'll learn to listen to you, too. She doesn't understand what you've done, who you are. She will."

"So we just sit here?" I ask, as we approach his apartments. "And wait for someone to murder Laskia?"

"I'm not—" He hesitates. "I don't want *anyone* killed. But Laskia is beyond reason. We know that. We saw it, at the temple. We need to trust my sister on something like this. She's the queen. She has a whole country at her disposal, a dedicated intelligence network, and a decade's experience dealing with international relations."

"I don't trust her," I say simply. "She hadn't told you about all those attacks before the progress fleet was sent off, had she?"

"What of it?" he shoots back, a glimmer of irritation showing.

"You say we should trust her judgment, but where was her judgment when our merchants were being attacked? She let it get this bad, Leander, and now she wants a fight that will distract everyone from the fact that she could have prevented all of this. She could have sent you on the pilgrimage earlier. She could have done something more about those first Mellacean attacks than recording them on a chart. If she wins a war, nobody asks those questions."

"She's told you she doesn't want a fight," he replies, ignoring most of what I've said. "She just wants a strong negotiating position."

Spirits save me. He's as naïve as she thinks *I* am if he believes that.

"She wants a war," I tell him again. "And she's going to have one. And it'll be you on the front lines when it happens."

"You don't have to trust her," he replies. "On this, I do."

It feels like I'm falling, and nobody's reaching out to catch me as I cry for help.

Queen Augusta's going to start her war as soon as she thinks Laskia is out of the way.

Am I going to be the only one who tries to stop it?

JUDE

The Tenements
Port Naranda, Mellacea

I need to find our good clothes.

I don't know what I'm supposed to be feeling, but my mind is eerily clear. The air is electric, like that strange, warm calm that comes before a storm, when the sky turns a sickly green, and everything seems to be holding itself in readiness.

Soon, the lashing rain and howling winds of my grief will arrive. But just now I'm unnervingly calm.

A few of our neighbors have laid out my mother in Mrs. Tevner's apartment down the hall, where there's more room for visitors, and less squalor. They've sent for Mrs. Kan, who'll know the Cánh Dōese traditions my mother would want them to follow. I wasn't here for my grandmother's funeral, but I remember my mother saying something about candles. About a silk dress.

Why didn't I listen? Why didn't I ask, knowing this was coming? Every day I watched her breathing grow more labored, watched her skin seem to grow thinner and more delicate, as though she might tear into pieces right in front of me. I watched the shadows under her eyes bloom, and I trudged off on another errand for Ruby, or signed on for another prize fight, as though a big enough purse was all I needed to rescue my mother from this place.

She was never leaving this apartment any way except the way she just has.

That's what you do, though. You kid yourself. Or it's what I did, anyway.

Because you don't speak death's name, when you know how close it's hovering. You don't want to draw its attention.

I push up to stand, glancing helplessly around our cramped apartment. The tiny table, the stove, the sagging sofa I use for a bed. I know every inch of this place—it's been my prison. And I know our good clothes can't have left it. Mum's been—Mum *was*—too sick to go out and sell anything, and I didn't do it. So where are they?

I make my way through to the bedroom, where the sheets are still rumpled on Mum's bed. Then my gaze slides down to the space below the bed.

There's a trunk there that we haven't opened since we lugged it off the boat down at the docks. That's where her dress will be. Probably my old suit from school, too.

I push aside the sheets where they hang off the edge of the bed to half hide the trunk. There's a sickly smell to them, but for all I hate it, it's familiar. I want to bury my face in them, and breathe the smell in and try to fix it in my memory.

The trunk is wedged tightly under the bed, and I have to

edge it out. I used to take it on the train to school, and as I run my fingers over the worn wood, the memories come, and my throat thickens.

As I touch it, I'm another version of myself. I'm so young, so at ease. I'm hauling this trunk off the train, and jostling with my friends for room on one of the porter's carts. I'm helping Leander heave his trunk up, teasing him about what he's got in it.

I trace my fingertip over a label pasted on for our voyage from Kirkpool to Port Naranda. It only half covers the one that was stuck on for my last year at school.

Then I flip the latches and push open the lid. I expect a musty smell, but it's clean inside. My riding boots are sitting on top of a racquet—*What did I ever think I was going to do with that, here in Mellacea?*—and then I find my old school suit. I carefully lift it from the trunk and shake the wrinkles out, then set it on top of the bed. It'll do for a funeral.

Packed beneath the suit, I see the silk of my mother's dress, a rich forest green with delicate vines embroidered around the collar and cuffs. I slip my hands underneath it to lift it up like it's some sort of ceremonial item.

There's something at the center of it, a little too much weight, and when I peel back the silk folds, I find a bundle of letters bound up with string in one of my mother's neat bows.

I know what they are before I reach for them. I know she left them here, where she knew I'd find them after she was gone. Are they supposed to be an explanation? An apology?

I set the dress on the bed and thump back to sit on the floor beside the trunk, the letters in my hands, my legs suddenly too weak to support me. When I pull the little bow undone, I feel something come undone inside me, as well.

My breath catches as I slip open the first letter and pull out a sheet of expensive, gold-edged notepaper.

> *Jude,*
> *I need to get in touch with you. I came by, but nobody answered the door. I sent a messenger, and she said the neighbors told her you're still there, but she couldn't find you or your mother.*
> *I heard your father didn't leave what you need for your schooling, and of course I'll . . .*

I reach for another letter.

> *Jude—please just answer me. . . .*

Another.

> *Jude, whatever it is, we can fix it. I went to your father's wife's house, and . . .*

A sob finally escapes me, grief and anger welling up like some kind of unstoppable tide.

What I'm holding in my hands is the loss of everything I knew. It's the evidence that I never *had* to lose any of it.

When my father died, he left no money for his mistress and her son. No more neat little house in Kirkpool, no more crowding on the train to boarding school with Leander and his friends.

I was so sure help was coming, but my prince vanished on me.

My mother said we needed a fresh start. Over my protests, she sold our furniture before we were evicted, and used the money to buy tickets to Port Naranda. She uprooted me from my home and brought me back to hers, only to fall ill just weeks later. The place she'd thought would be familiar was foreign to both of us. She'd been gone decades—there were no old friends to track down, no old haunts to visit. Not in the time she had left.

And as I tried in vain to nurse her, as I sank further down into the gutter, took on the humiliation of becoming a gangster's errand boy, let myself be beaten bloody in the boxing ring, all to try and find a way through this for us, I cursed Leander for abandoning me.

Except he never had.

I knew it somewhere inside, when I saw him at Ruby Red. I saw his face, saw the shock, the way he reached for me, and I knew he was telling the truth when he said he'd tried to find me.

But now I know it all the way down to my bones. And I know that every time I leaned over my mother while I nursed her, these letters lay beneath us. My way out of this was always right here. If I'd known, I could have written to him anytime. He would have helped. He would have been overjoyed to find me.

But now I'm lost. I can no more walk into the Alinorish embassy than walk across the water to Alinor itself.

I helped hunt their prince down. I stood and watched while the young nobles of Alinor were murdered. I'm as tangled up with Laskia as anyone could be.

I'm a part of everything she's done, my soul as black as hers, or Ruby's, or the green sisters'.

I should have died, before I let it come to this.

A sob breaks free from me, and I curl over on myself, lacing my hands together behind my head as I huddle on the floor.

My mother's gone.

And I'm so angry at her.

And I don't understand why she did this to me.

And I'll never get the chance to ask her, because she's dead.

I don't know where I'm going until I find myself at the staff entrance to Ruby Red. This isn't the door that leads in from the beautiful little arcade with its fancy gold lettering and its jewelry and fashion.

This is the stout wooden door off an alleyway, at the bottom of a set of narrow steps, a ramp running beside them for barrels to roll down.

There's a broad-shouldered woman with a broken nose on security back there. She nods at my pin—she knows my face anyway, I think—but raises one hand.

"Kid, you been hearing what I'm hearing? They're saying the boss's sister knocked down half the harbor, walked clean through a wall, left a city block in ruins. They're saying she was preaching on the steps of the temple. What in seven hells—"

"Later," I manage, shoving the door open and shouldering past her. Now I've nearly reached Tom, I'm suddenly desperate, like there's a hook sunk into my chest, pulling me toward him. I break into a run down the narrow passageways, fumble with the lock on the storeroom, and finally burst into the main bar.

It's empty—it's only afternoon and not time for the nightclub to start up yet. The mirror ball on the ceiling is still, and my footsteps echo on the dance floor, instead of being drowned out by the thump of music.

And there's Tom in his usual place behind the bar, polishing glasses and setting up for the night ahead.

I clatter to a halt, and he looks up at the sound, and we stare at each other. He's taller and broader than me, but gentler by far. His dark copper hair is always a little askew, and even in the dim light of the shut-down club, his freckles stand out against his fair skin.

He flips up the gate from behind the bar and steps out—and when I don't close the distance between us, he does instead.

Before, I couldn't stop moving toward him. Forget Laskia demolishing buildings—I could have done it myself, if they were between Tom and me. I barely remember the journey from the apartment to the club. My suit and my mother's dress are still on the bed, the letters still on the floor. I doubt I even closed the door.

Now, I stand helpless, and let him close the last few yards between us. I let him wrap me up in his arms, and I close my eyes, burying my face in the warmth of his shoulder.

"Jude, what's happened?" He sounds bewildered, and I don't blame him. For every night we've spent together, every time he's tried to get me to confide in him, to talk to him, to let him close in any way that's not physical, he's never once succeeded. And now I'm . . . His shirt is wet. I'm crying.

I'm crying all over Tom.

He doesn't ask again, just holds me closer, one hand coming up to cup the back of my head. He makes the kind of shushing noise you'd use to settle a child, but I don't mind. Just hearing him, feeling his heartbeat where I'm pressed against his chest, is enough.

"We'll fix it," he murmurs eventually, stroking my hair softly. And then, in a gentle tease, trying to draw me out a little: "You look and smell like you were dumped in the harbor, and came home via the gutter. We should get you cleaned up."

I pull back immediately—seven hells, he's right. I'm still covered in the sweat and dirt of the Isle of the Mother itself, in the salt spray on the way home that washed away not one ounce of my sins. I'm probably covered in flecks of Dasriel's blood from his ruined hand.

And when I pull back, I see the ruby pin stuck through his lapel, a match for mine. And it's not that I doubt his loyalty to me—he's always offered that, and I've offered him nothing, too busy scraping together enough money to live, chasing down another prize fight to drown my anger in the clean pain of someone else's punches.

It's not that I doubt his loyalty. It's that I can't drag him into this. I can't ask him to keep things from Ruby, or from Laskia, since she's in charge now. I've already endangered everyone I care about—everyone who's left alive.

They're saying that people disappear into Laskia's office, and never come out. I can't stop thinking about the crew of our fishing boat, shriveled to nothing as she drained them of life. I can't bear to think of Tom that way, and if Laskia thought he was against her, she wouldn't hesitate.

The ruby pin he wears means I could put him in danger with anything I say.

"I should go," I murmur, and his arms tighten around me.

"Jude, please. You look—tell me what's happened. Were you at the temple when Laskia was there? I heard—"

"My mother died." It's not what I'm expecting to say. My mind's caught up in what I can't tell him, what I mustn't say about Laskia, about what she's had me do these past days. And while I'm shying away from those words, my other wound breaks open and bleeds all over him.

Tom's lips part, and he searches for the right words. "Oh, Jude. I'm so sorry. How can I help? Come and stay at mine, will you? You shouldn't be alone."

I blink at him, searching his open, honest face. He might be a gangster's barman, but really he's just a nice guy who makes a great cocktail, and happens to make it here. He's not like me.

"I can't do that," I murmur. "I have to get back to work."

With a sinking horror, I realize that the bouncer saw me run in here to Tom. If I vanish now, they'll come looking for me via him.

I've made a new trap for myself, and the chain holding me there is this boy who's only ever tried to care for me.

"They'll understand if you need some time off," Tom counters. "I mean, who'd even be looking for you? Things are wild out there."

A strangled sound escapes me. I think maybe it wanted to be a laugh. I shake my head. "I think I came . . . I think I came to say goodbye, actually."

"You're leaving Port Naranda?" Hurt flashes across his

face, and surprise. His broad hands grip my shoulders. "You don't have to do that, Jude."

"Not leaving," I reply. "But Laskia will have work for me."

"And that means we can't see each other?" I can see it in him as we speak—the breaking of a dream. I suppose he always thought I'd cave in the end. That we'd get a happy ending. That all his waiting would pay off. And now he thinks this is just me breaking up with him, like couples do every day.

I'm trying to keep you safe, Tom.

"It means we shouldn't see each other. I'm going to be doing things I don't want you near. That someone like you shouldn't be near."

"Someone like me?"

"Someone good."

"And you're not?"

"I'm anything but good. The things I've done—they're even worse than I knew, and I knew they were bad."

"Then now can be the moment you change," he says, his fingers tightening on my shoulders again.

"I can't. I'm not like that."

"So you're not even going to try? You're just going to accept that you're terrible because you did terrible things?"

"Aren't I?" I demand, closing my eyes, and surrendering to the tears that want to run down my cheeks, over the dirt and sweat, the bruises and the blood.

"No!" he shoots back. "If you'd just trust me, Jude—if you'd let me help you. Let me be here for you. Let me *in*, for once."

But I can't, and I don't know why I came here, except to finally see that for myself.

I'm not like Tom, and what I've done has put me beyond him, beyond Leander, beyond any of the ones who've reached out a hand to try and help me.

I'm lost, and there's no way back.

I don't know how to be helped, and it's too late now to wish.

LASKIA

◆

The Gem Cutter
Port Naranda, Mellacea

First Councilor Tariden is smaller than I thought he'd be. I'd only seen his picture in the newspapers before today, and in person he reminds me of a bespectacled little tortoise. If someone knocked him over onto his back, he'd probably just rock to and fro trying to right himself. The head of our government is an old man.

He's sitting on the velvet couch in Ruby's receiving room with one of his ministers beside him—she's a mousy woman with hard eyes, and I haven't bothered to learn her name.

Dasriel and Beris—the first sister now—loom behind them, and Tariden has made the mistake of sliding too far back on the couch, instead of perching on the edge. If he's not careful, his feet will leave the floor, and he really will have to rock himself upright like a tortoise.

"We are honored to meet with Macean's Messenger," the first councilor begins. He speaks in a fussy tone, smacking his lips together on the letter *m*. *Meet. Macean's. Messenger.* I try to focus on that, to keep my attention with him, but the buzzing is rising within me again, the feeling that every part of the world is too loud, right down to the scrape of Tariden's clothes against the couch as he tries to discreetly haul himself forward a little.

"Of course you are," I reply, my gaze flicking up to Beris for a moment. *This is who was in charge all this time?* Her expression is blank.

"We would like to appoint you as an honored adviser to the government," he continues.

"A what?" I yank my attention back to him, reaching for Ruby's hand to drain a little power into her. She's slumped beside me, staring dully into space.

"An honored adviser," he repeats, speaking more clearly. "Touched by our god as you have been, we must—"

"Councilor." I cut him off with a huff of a laugh. "You've misunderstood. You're not in charge. You never were. We all saw you crawling to the church these past months, asking the green sisters to prop you up."

"I think you'll find—"

"I think *you'll* find, if you look around, that you're the one who's come to me."

Sister Beris speaks, her cool voice cutting through the start of Tariden's dithering reply. "Our god has created a Messenger for us. All previous ideas must be set aside, in the face of this new turn of events."

I send another surge of power into Ruby, and she groans, curling in on herself, trying to tug her hand free of mine.

"My dear Sister," Tariden protests, trying to twist around to look at Beris. "We have an *elected*—"

"Enough!" As my voice rises, every light bulb in the room flares to incandescent brightness, and then they shatter as one, shards of glass falling to the floor as the wires fade into nothingness, and we're left in the dark.

Then a flame appears, cupped in Dasriel's hand and casting dancing shadows over all our faces. My guests are silent as my fire magician walks across the room to open a drawer and pull out one of the candles Ruby keeps there in case of a blackout. He lights it and then carries it over and sets it down on the low table between the two couches.

"I speak for our god," I say quietly, my voice grating—there's a strange, dissonant undercurrent to my tone as the power surges up inside me again, and I wrestle it under control.

Nobody replies.

"I speak for our god," I repeat. "And I speak for Mellacea."

I can feel Macean in me, his power flooding through my veins. I can feel him pushing against his bonds, trying desperately to wake. I can feel the wild, heady gambler that he is, urging me to take control of the board, to throw the dice.

"Now see here," Tariden says, finally managing to rock himself forward on the couch, and reaching out one hand to point a finger at me, like I'm a small child who needs a telling-off.

My patience snaps, and I lean forward to grab him by the wrist. His eyes bulge as I drain my power into him, and the feeling of sweet relief is like taking off a pair of uncomfortable shoes after hours on my feet.

The first councilor makes a strangled, gargling sound, his already pale skin turning paler still, then bright white, then luminous, until he's glowing with the divine magic I'm desperately pouring into him.

And then I release my hold, and he's a crumpled heap on the ground, moaning softly. I narrow my eyes at him in irritation and will him to go . . . elsewhere. He blinks out of sight, and the other politician—who's been silent until now—cries out.

"What have you done to him?"

"He's in the alleyway," I reply, turning my gaze on her. She comes to her feet and stumbles back, until Beris catches her by the arm. Not to push her toward me, but to make clear that she could. And she would.

"Is he . . . ?"

I shrug. "He's not dead. But he's probably not much use, either. You will go pick him up, and you'll go back to your offices, and you'll send me his top military advisers and his head of intelligence."

"You want the spymaster?" she whispers, trying to pull her arm free of Beris's grip, but only so she can run for it.

"The Alinorish must know about me by now," I say. "I want to hear what they plan to do about it. I want the reports the first councilor was getting."

She stares at me, and swallows hard, her lips pressed together in a thin line. And then she nods.

It's some time after she's gone that I notice Ruby has passed out beside me—I only realize when Dasriel steps in to arrange her on the couch so she can doze without rolling off it.

I think it's the care he takes that annoys me. "Go," I mutter, irritation fizzing through me, and he silently steadies Ruby in place before slipping out the door. He moves quietly, for such a big man.

I lean back against the arm of the couch, pulling my knees up to hug them as I study Ruby. She's in a different dress—plain black, untailored, no sequins. She's not wearing her gold headband anymore, and without her almost-tiara, she looks younger. Her brown skin is dull, her lips chapped.

She's barely holding together—I can sense her fragility—and I'm not sure I'm close enough to anyone else to form this kind of bond with them. Certainly not Dasriel, or Beris.

I have to make sure she doesn't break.

I'm doing my best to keep the load from killing her—draining the magic like poison from a wound, pouring it into the volunteers who line up to roll the dice and see if they'll win a fortune, or lose their lives. Those who die, die quickly at least. Those who live . . . I can feel some of them, out in the city. Shells of what they used to be, with fragments of a god's power lodged within them. Still connected to me.

All of this, and it's still barely enough.

"Why is this so hard?" I whisper, gazing down at Ruby, as her lashes flutter in her sleep—I can feel that she's dreaming—and a lock of hair tumbles across her eyes as she shifts. "That sailor with the prince, she walked out of the Temple of the Mother. She wasn't like you. Is it because the two of them are magicians? Are they used to this?"

There's a smaller voice in my head, one I don't want to hear, that has a different question: *Was it easier for the sailor because she was willing?*

Gusting a slow breath out, I let myself fall into a trance, and reach out for the now-familiar texture of Ruby's dream. My lashes lower, and a moment later, I'm in it alongside her.

We're in one of her nightclubs, surrounded by a screaming press of bodies, dancers on the verge on hysteria. Lights spin across their bodies, reflecting off the mirror ball on the ceiling, and the band plays louder and louder, trumpets blaring, the singer screeching words I can't make out. It's an overblown, too-loud, too-close, too-everything version of a place we both know.

Ruby's there, buffeted by the crowd, staggering in place as they press past her, as they half fight, half dance, pushing and pulling at each other's bodies.

I shove a hand past a couple locked together and grab hold of my sister's wrist. She startles, and tries to yank herself free, but I tow her with me as I forge a path toward the wall. I point at a blank space on the wall, and the next moment there's a semicircular booth with a red velvet bench seat for us to slip into. It's just big enough for the two of us, with a tiny table for us to set down our drinks, if we had any. It's a place for lovers to crowd in close, to press their knees together, to take the chance to whisper in each other's ears.

"They came to the club," I say, letting her pull her arm free of my grip. "The first councilor and one of his sidekicks."

Her lip curls in contempt. "Are you proud of yourself?"

Someone in the crowd screams, the noise sharp and jagged. I make myself keep my voice even. "They never came to pay court to you, Sister."

"And they're not there for you, either," she snaps. "They don't bow to *you*, Laskia."

I see it then, the contempt in the twist of her mouth. In the way her eyes flick over me, then dismiss me. Perhaps I always knew it. But for the first time, it's right there on the surface, in front of me.

"You were never going to give me any of it," I say slowly. "You sent me out to kill in your name. You let me give myself away, piece by piece. Bleed myself dry. I would have done anything for you, Ruby."

"Exactly," she sneers. "Your desperation was written all over you, little sister."

Jude told me, the night he and I set sail to destroy the prince's fleet. *It won't get you what you want. Your big sister knows there's only so much room at the top.*

I didn't believe him. I didn't want to.

But if I can read Ruby now, then she can read me through our bond as well. She can feel the way the knife twists inside me.

"That's the difference between us," she says, shaking her head slowly. "You wanted me to tell you that you were good enough. I already knew I was."

Fury burns through me like fire. "How *dare* you! I stand with a *god*!"

All around us, the dancers shatter just as the light bulbs did, every one of them disintegrating into a spray of shards, glittering like the mirror ball above us, and then it's raining silver, and there's glass slicing our arms as we use them to shield our heads, and beside me Ruby's sobbing, making raw sounds that come from somewhere deep inside.

When silence falls, there's a sound from outside the big

double doors of the club. Someone's knocking on them, slow and deliberate.

Bang. Bang. Bang.

"Don't let him open them," Ruby gasps, and suddenly we're working together again, scrambling across the glass-strewn floor to throw ourselves against the doors, to brace them with our bodies.

Cracks begin to form in the wood, blinding light shining through from the other side.

"Wait!" I shout, voice high and raw with fear. "Wait, please! I'll find a way!"

A way that doesn't kill me.

"He doesn't care what it does to you," Ruby rasps beside me. "He's the Gambler. He'll use you up and throw you away."

Am I to him what she is to me? A means to an end?

Abruptly I snap out of the trance, and Ruby gasps awake beside me. We're slumped on the couch, Dasriel's candle nearly burned all the way down to the table. Just a small flame in a slowly spreading pool of hot wax. I stare at the flame, watching it flicker.

There's a part of me that *wants* to open the doors. That's all him, though—that's the god of risk feeding straight into me, giving me the urge to throw the dice, to spin the wheel, to see what comes. To start a war, just to see how it plays out.

And I will. I'll give him everything he wants. But not yet.

First, I have other problems to deal with.

KEEGAN

◆

The Royal Library
Kirkpool, Alinor

I am seated in the royal family's personal library, at a table otherwise occupied entirely by priests. Augusta has sent her scholars to the Bibliotek and elsewhere in search of information and archives. Her religious advisers have stayed here, which means I'll be working with them.

We are here to delve into the distant past, and as I look around, the knowledge we've lost could not be more starkly underlined.

The priests wear a uniform that's an almost theatrical imitation of the armor Barrica's priests must have once worn, during the war. The silver threads that run through the fabric hint at a chest plate, lines of stitches where the joints in the armor should be, but these soft robes wouldn't stop a weapon.

What would King Anselm have made of them? They're about as close to the warrior priests he fought alongside as a lapdog is to a wolf.

Father Marsen, the head priest from the temple in the city, sits at the head of the table, and though his face is made for smiling, his expression is grave.

"You know the work we are here to do," he says simply, nodding at the stacks of books and old papers running down the length of the table. "We have assembled what we can. We have whole teams digging through our libraries and repositories, and we have recruited archivists from the palace as well.

"We have sent agents to the Bibliotek, but they will need to operate very carefully—any evidence that they are seeking information on how to raise Barrica would see them ejected from the university."

I nearly choke on my glass of water. "I'm sorry, Father, we're seeking to *what*?"

He raises a hand, as though to fend me off. "Be easy, my son. We have no plan to raise the goddess, but it is as well to have the option now that she is close to us."

"She did, after all, leave the door ajar," a priestess points out, already reaching for the nearest stack of books. "When the other gods closed it entirely. To me, it seems she *meant* to return, one day. It may be she relies on us to make it happen."

"She wanted the *option* to return, if and when Macean woke," I counter. "Which he has not done. The prince saw to that with his sacrifice."

Father Marsen shoots me a look—he knows about Laskia, unlike the others at this table. The equation is not as simple as I make it sound.

"It is as well to know what we can and cannot do, before we chart our course," he says simply.

"The Messenger will chart our course," I insist. "And the queen."

Beneath my firm tone is a chill of fear. Would Leander even survive the return of Barrica, given how badly a touch of her power is harming him already? I'm fervently grateful I haven't told any of these people about his dreams. About the goddess who bangs at the door as he sleeps.

"Of course," Father Marsen agrees gently. "It is our role to provide counsel to our leaders. And it may be that our researchers will find something that will help the prince. We've instructed them to look for anything at all that might be useful." Gentle or not, it's hard not to hear his words as an excuse for what they're doing.

Most of the priests at the table are now regarding me with flat expressions, as though I'm a brass band preparing to rehearse in the middle of a silent library. Deeply unwelcome, extremely inconvenient, and entirely failing to read the mood of the room.

I don't mind that. They should have seen me at school. I've got a world of experience with not being wanted, and I am confident I can weather it.

Father Marsen gestures to the stack of books, and silently, we set to work.

The weight of responsibility is pressing down on me, though, and my foot taps a restless, worried rhythm as I scan the first table of contents. Leander asked me to do this. And it couldn't be clearer that nobody else at the table is doing it for *him*.

They've come to find a way to raise their goddess. I've come to find a way to stop it.

I need to understand *how* Leander could act as her doorway—if we know that, we can find a way to keep it locked.

I need to think like a scholar, not a priest. What can I do to take advantage of my difference?

I wonder if there are any records from the days around the time the gods departed—Macean to his enchanted sleep, and all his siblings to some other realm, save for Barrica, who left the door ajar and changed from Barrica the Warrior to Barrica the Sentinel.

I'm beginning to suspect she changed in name only, not in nature.

The question is how I can focus on those records without anyone noticing. Whether, if I find them, I can hide them so none of the priests can follow the same path I have.

My head is spinning with possibilities. I need letters, perhaps diaries. I need to find talk of the gods' return, of Messengers.

I need to research something that's never happened before.

We're a couple of hours in, everybody lost in their work, when I suddenly realize there's a palace librarian standing beside me. She's a small, slight woman with a shock of curly brown hair, and eyes that are unusually large for her pale face, rendering her permanently slightly surprised.

"Sorry," she whispers, grimacing as I jump. "Didn't mean to startle you. I'm told I need louder footsteps."

"I'm sure that on the whole, quiet movement is an asset in your line of work," I say, nodding at her uniform.

"I'm sorry to interrupt," she continues, tugging anxiously

at her shirt, her fingers brushing the white embroidered spear that's the symbol of the House of Alinor. Her uniform doesn't fit very well, and she keeps trying to tug it straight. "Just doing the rounds, checking if anyone needs any help."

A priestess looks up at us, narrows her eyes, and clears her throat ostentatiously. The librarian seems to shrink in on herself, mouthing an apology for—for what? Whispering?

That moment, and the pang of pity I feel for her in it, decides me. I have to trust somebody, and if not a librarian, then who? At the very least, she doesn't *definitely* have an agenda opposing mine, as the priests do. So I decide to risk it.

I lower my voice to the softest of whispers. "I'm looking for contemporary accounts of the departure of the gods. The kinds of documents that record conversations. Everyone else seems to be looking at formal histories and religious analyses. I'm wondering if anyone said anything in a letter or a diary about how they were to return. Perhaps it was known at the time, and we've lost it since then."

She nods slowly, considering this. She glances around at the priests. Then she looks back at me, and manages a timid smile. "Let's see what we can turn up," she whispers. "If I were you, I'd start with the correspondence archive of the monarchs of Alinor."

And *that's* what you get for being the only one intelligent enough to ask a librarian. They know where to find everything.

An hour later, I have it. It's just a scrap of a reference—one that makes me think the writer *did* know how the gods could return, and expected her reader would, too.

I've still got far more questions than answers, but one

phrase in an ancient, faded letter gives me the first breadcrumb of what I'm desperately hoping will be a trail.

And it's a hint, written in an impossibly curly script, of *where* we might need to be, to achieve the return of the gods.

What I would give, to be in the Temple of the Mother on the day this exile ends. . . .

SELLY

The Grand Ballroom
Kirkpool, Alinor

After Augusta's council broke up, Leander and I almost made it to his apartments before we were pounced on by palace officials. They didn't overhear our argument, at least. They clearly have no idea anything's amiss and are interested only in a grand ball they're organizing, to show Leander off to as many people as they can possibly cram into the ballroom.

I'm beginning to realize that's a lot of people, as I trail along behind a woman with a long list and a group of lackeys. She's pointing at things with her pen, as decisive as any ship's captain I've ever met, and she's been doing it for nearly half an hour.

"Someone will have to do something about the light fittings," she says firmly, gazing around to make sure her underlings understand the importance of this.

My jaw aches from clenching it—the queen is planning a *war,* and this is what they're thinking about?

I have to talk to Kiki, and soon. I understand now what she was trying to offer me—the clothes, the chance to put on a mask and pretend to be one of them. If I'm going to get a hearing by the time Augusta's ready to talk—if I want anyone in this place to listen to me—I have to learn to speak their language.

For now, though . . . I slow my pace, and Leander matches it, letting the group draw ahead a little.

"How long do you think it would take her to notice?" I ask softly. "If we just . . . weren't here?"

He nods, and reaches for my hand—I hate the tentativeness in that gesture, the uncertainty. He doesn't know whether I'll let him take it.

I wish I could stuff my words back into my mouth.

What we feel for each other. It's us, isn't it?

Or is it her?

Leander's power is building inside his body again—I can feel it fizzing and transferring through his grip, setting my muscles aching, but it's not too bad yet. It feels like the morning after a storm, when everything hurts a little, but it starts to loosen up as you get to work.

He steps back from the group as they bustle along, and turns to lead me away from them. It takes until we're halfway across the ballroom before I realize that the guards at the door and the officials poking at every corner of the room aren't just politely looking away—it's almost as if they don't see us.

When Leander stops in front of a huge tapestry of Anselm and Barrica's battle for Vostain, the footman standing beside it doesn't even turn his head as his prince and holy Messenger yanks the fabric aside and slips through a hidden door behind it.

"Are you doing that?" I whisper. "Making him not notice?"

"I can do anything." The words don't sound like a celebration.

We climb a narrow flight of stairs that spirals tightly upward, and passes through a little wooden door, to find ourselves on a balcony. There are cushions strewn on the ground, and the air is a little dusty. Green streaks accent the marble and gold finishes of this little space, and with a jolt, I realize I've been here before.

My heartbeat quickens, my entire being suddenly all too aware of Leander's hand enclosing mine. "This is where . . ."

"This is where I was hiding," he says quietly, his head bowed and his expression unreadable. "When you came to save me, in my mind."

"I didn't know it was real." Just like in the dream, I can't see what's over the edge of the balcony, but I can see the ceiling beyond it—it's high and wide, and when we walk over to the railing, I realize it's the ballroom below us. The huge, empty space is silent—the woman and her lackeys must have gone, and now it lies quiet, waiting for a sudden rush of bodies, of musicians, of movement.

I glance at Leander, whose face is turned away a fraction. My fingers tighten a little around his, and I murmur, "It's a good hiding spot."

"Generations of my family have lurked up here," Leander says, his frame relaxing, a smile touching his lips. "Best place to watch the proceedings below without being seen. It used to be my favorite hiding spot. I'd sit here and eavesdrop on the court, listen to my sister performing her queenly duties. I haven't been back in a long time."

"Why did you stop coming?"

"I realized I was never going to be a part of it. I was never going to be needed."

And so he became the playboy instead, the party boy, distractible and distracting, the despair of all his teachers, never trying, and so never failing.

I see that about him now. And I ache for the ways he tried to protect himself. My tongue feels tangled, too clumsy to form the words I wish I could speak—except I barely know what those words would be. That I see him? That I feel for that painful isolation? That, in my own way, I know what it's like to yearn to be seen by your family, and trusted to pull your weight?

Instead I say nothing, and after a few moments he pulls his hand away and sinks on the cushions, leaving room for me to sit next to him. I settle down and fold my hands behind my head, staring up at the gilt scrollwork on the ceiling. "Leander, what are we going to do about your sister?"

"We wait," he says quietly. "Augusta wants a war, yes. That doesn't mean she's going to get one."

"How can we stop her?" I press. "We can tell her that you—that we—refuse to fight. And we have to do that. But that won't be enough."

"It will," he says. "She won't go ahead without me if I refuse to join her."

"She'd already made the plans before she knew you were transformed. Of course she'll go ahead without you. And then when she commits her entire army and navy, will you really just sit there and watch them die, and refuse to wade in?"

His silence expands to swallow us both.

"The people we met in Port Naranda, they don't deserve this. There was a girl, Hallie—you never met her, but she sold me my dress and showed me how to do my hair. She was sweet, and she was kinder than she needed to be, especially after she heard my accent. Is that who we're supposed to fight?"

"I know how this place works," he says after a pause that goes on too long. "We wait until after . . . after we hear about Laskia. And then, when Gus feels less threatened, I talk to her."

"You just *talk*? That worked so well today."

"Yes," he replies, frustration rising. "You have to let me handle this."

"And you really think—"

"How did you persuade Captain Rensa to do what you wanted?" he asks, in a tone that says he already knows the answer.

"I didn't," I admit, flushing.

"Right, because trying to force her hand got you nowhere," he presses. "She and Augusta have a lot in common. I know how to do this."

"But if you're wrong, we're not just stuck on the dawn watch for a month. We're in a *war*, Leander!" I jab a finger at the closed door. "And there's a goddess who wants to come through there, who wants to use you as her doorway—"

"Do you think that's escaped me?" he snaps, propping himself up on one elbow. "This is *my* sister, Selly. I can make her listen."

I feel the pain that lances through his head—our voices have risen, and it's too loud for him, too much. The need to shout back at him, to make him hear me and feel my fear, vanishes in an instant. I prop myself up on one elbow too, facing him, and reach out to press my fingertips to his temple. He half flinches, but I persist, trying not to notice how warm his skin feels beneath my fingers.

A shiver of magic runs through me, twinging all the way up my arm and zipping down my spine. I focus on that sensation, even as my anger shimmers into something else, and my fingers begin to trail down to his cheek, his jawline.

Leander's eyes meet mine as we both feel the power within him settling.

As my fingers pause against his pulse, something else flares—a sudden catch of my breath, a shiver from him that's different altogether—and I drop my hand, suddenly self-conscious.

"I'm scared," I blurt in a whisper, half hoping to distract him from that flicker of shared feeling, half wanting to reach up and touch him again. "I want to do something to stop this, and I don't know how."

"I know," he murmurs.

"I thought you were so sheltered, when we met. I thought you had no idea how the world worked. But now I see it—it's different here. You're the one who knows how to swim with sharks, and I'm the one who's drowning."

Leander swallows hard, his eyes dropping and then lifting again, as if he's not quite sure that my face is a safe place to rest his gaze. "You're a strong swimmer," he whispers finally. "I won't let you go under. I promise."

LEANDER

◆

The Grand Ballroom
Kirkpool, Alinor

I'm desperately trying to find a safe place to rest my eyes, my pulse speeding to a roar in my ears that has nothing to do with the magic Selly just siphoned off. I can still feel the echo of her fingertips against my skin. She dropped her hand like the touch had burned her.

I'm not sure I've ever seen Selly blush before.

I settle for watching as her fingers pick idly at a snagged thread on her cushion, and take a deep breath. "You're worth more than anyone in this place, Selly. They'll learn to listen to you, just like I did."

"That's not the way they see it," she replies, and I can feel the hurt of that truth weaving through her thoughts. "The tailors' idea of a discreet conversation is pretty loud. Half of them think I'm an opportunist who took my chance to get my claws into a prince of my very own."

"Please," I sniff. "You'd have pushed me overboard if you thought you could get away with it."

"The other half think I'm a country bumpkin who has no idea what's going on," she continues. "And the rest think I'm a Mellacean spy, because I had glass magician's stones in my pockets when I arrived, instead of candles for my magic."

"Well, firstly, that's two halves plus some more, so you're counting more enemies than there actually are. And secondly . . . none of them know you," I say quietly, willing her to listen to me. "I do. Whose opinion are you going to listen to?"

"My own," she replies, reaching for a joke, and falling short.

I lift my hand, ready to brush her cheek with my fingertips, but then let it drop back onto the cushions. I don't know if she'd welcome my touch right now, not after the way she jerked away from me.

There are so many divisions between us.
Her mistrust of my sister.
Her mistrust of her own feelings.
Her distance from everything she knows.
What we feel for each other. It's us, isn't it?
Or is it her?

Did she touch my face because she was compelled to, to fulfill her role as my anchor? Or was that lingering caress along my jaw her own impulse? I can tell she's wondering.

I sit up, digging in my pocket for one of the documents I swiped from Augusta's office. I tear off a corner, making it as square as I can. Selly watches in silence as I fold and fold again, the action so automatic that my fingers move faster than I can think through the steps.

I'm done with uncertainty. My heart knows what's real, even if my head doesn't. My heart is as sure as my fingers creasing and folding the paper.

In a few moments, a paper boat sits on my palm, and I offer it to Selly in silence.

She takes it as gently as if it might crumble into nothing.

There's so much we don't know, but of this I'm sure.

"I loved you before I ever became Barrica's Messenger," I whisper, letting the words tumble out of me. "The first boat I made you was a promise, and so is this one. You asked me if this—if what we feel—is us, or Barrica."

Her gaze snaps up from inspecting the little boat, and fixes on mine. The mossy green of her eyes is soft and shining, that flush still brightening her freckles. I can see her in that moment we shared on the dance floor in the nightclub in Port Naranda, her head tipped back, her face so utterly irresistible—and the soft regret in her eyes when she told me not to kiss her.

I swallow hard. "I know what's real," I manage. "And I think you do too. You were afraid, back in Port Naranda. You said it would make things worse, make it harder to part, if . . ."

Her gaze drops to my lips, and my heart gives a painful lurch.

"I've wished . . . gods, I've wished I hadn't said that," Selly admits slowly, her voice uncharacteristically soft, almost shy, her long fair lashes half-veiling her eyes.

Hope flares within me, and I fight the impulse to reach for her. Of everyone I've ever met, Selly Walker has to make up her own mind—I can't try to make it up for her. I hold my breath, restraining myself with an iron will.

"Aren't you saying the same thing now?" I murmur, not

wanting to jolt her from this moment. "Wasn't your question this morning just another way of saying it would be safer not to leap?"

Her lashes lift, and this time she doesn't try to hide her longing.

I bite my lip to keep from leaning toward her. "I'm not going anywhere, Selly."

Her eyes search mine for what feels like an eternity. Then she exhales in a rush, a little huff of a breath that's almost a laugh, and nods. Just a tiny inclination of her head before she leans forward, fingertips stroking my jaw again, only this time . . . this time she leans in the rest of the way, cradling my face in her palm, and brushes her lips against mine.

The kiss is gentle at first, as though we're testing the waters together. Then she tilts up her chin, and her lips part, and I'm lost.

After everything we've been through, it's so strange—it's outrageous—that this is our first true kiss. That other time was nothing like this.

This is just us, even the goddess in my head quiet for a moment.

And for the first time since I set foot on the *Lizabetta* down at the docks, I feel like I'm home.

SELLY

The Docks
Kirkpool, Alinor

I don't know what happens if you punch a priest, but there's a non-zero chance I'm going to find out this afternoon.

Leander and I drifted back to his quarters as though we were in a dream, fingers twined together, pausing in empty hallways to exchange another kiss or three, smiling through each one. The rasp of his stubble against my cheek, the slow smile with none of his usual teasing in it. The way his throat shifted, and he made the softest of sounds when I kissed the tender skin there. The sensation of resting my hand over his heart and feeling it start to beat faster.

I don't know what might have happened, when we made it back to his quarters. I'm prickly enough that not many people have been brave enough to kiss me, let alone go further. I'm suddenly very interested in being a quick learner, though.

But the moment we made it back to his apartments, a maid showed up like magic—seriously, I need to figure out if opening the door rings a bell somewhere—to bob a curtsy and let us know we were urgently wanted.

I'm standing in the middle of one of the palace's million and one receiving rooms, wearing a shift dress that bares my arms to the shoulder. I'm surrounded by priests and magicians, all examining my geometric magician's marks. They walk around me, pointing at me, discussing me like I'm a particularly fascinating scientific specimen, and treating me as though I can't understand a word they say.

I'm not a person to them. I'm a puzzle, and they want to figure me out.

Leander sits at the edge of the room in quiet conversation with Kiki. Keegan's still off buried in the library, lucky thing.

Then one of the scholars actually *grabs* my hand, lifting it up so a cluster of them can get a better look at my arm.

Instinctively, I yank my hand from his clammy grasp and take a step back. The scholars blink at me like a bunch of surprised owls, startled to discover I have a mind of my own.

This is *such* a waste of time. There's a war in the offing, and they want to discuss the best way to analyze my magician's marks?

I make myself keep my tone even, though I'm speaking through gritted teeth. "Please don't manhandle me. If you'd like to look at my marks more closely, you can ask."

One of the men opens his mouth to protest, and then Father Marsen's voice rings out from the doorway, where he's standing with an apologetic expression. "You're right, of course, Miss Walker. Apologies." That last word is clearly an admonishment for the crowd around me, and they subside a little. "May we see your arm?" Father Marsen asks, polite as can be, as he walks in to join the group.

I let out a slow breath, and raise my arm. This feeling of being constantly surrounded is going to send me over the edge. I'm never, *ever* alone. Courtiers and servants and Leander's family are everywhere.

I'm used to standing on the deck of a ship, seeing all the way to the horizon. I'm used to climbing up to the crow's nest, feeling like I'm the only one in the world.

I can feel the little paper boat in my pocket once more, and I cast my mind back to the first promise Leander made me, what seems like a lifetime ago. He promised to get me back to the sea, but I don't see how I'll ever make that happen now. Not unless—and I can only even think this from a distance, acknowledging the idea without letting it get its claws into me—not unless Leander isn't around to keep me here anymore. And I'm not going to let that happen.

I need some space, even if only for a minute.

I gaze across at my prince, willing him to look up, to understand. And then, to my surprise, he does. Even though he doesn't lift his head, I know he can tell what I need. He's as attuned to me as I am to him.

He stands abruptly. "I hope your examination has been helpful, my friends. Unfortunately, we now have another appointment."

A magician looks up with a blink of outrage. "But we were told—"

Leander silences her with a look. "Whoever made that undertaking on behalf of Selly should have consulted with her first."

Kiki's already at the door, holding it open. In mutinous silence the priests and magicians all file out, and when Kiki closes the door with a click, she's also on the other side of it. Leander and I are alone again.

"I'm sorry," he says, rueful. "I should have realized how that was going to be." He takes a breath, as if bracing himself before plunging underwater. Then he reaches for my hand, and the familiar tingle passes between us. It's the magic, but now it's . . . more. What happens next? Do we pick up where we left off? "You know what?" he says. "You *should* take some time to yourself."

"Where?" I ask, trying not to sound like I was hoping he'd say something else. "There's nowhere in the palace I can hide away. Your balcony, I suppose."

"That's *my* safe place," he points out. "Yours is the water."

I snort. "I might as well dream about sailing to the other side of the Crescent Sea, my prince."

"You can at least go down to the docks. Breathe in some salty air. Remember yourself, a little."

"What?" I blink at him. "I can't leave you."

"I can do it," he replies, squaring his shoulders. The two of us can't lie to each other—I can sense that he's not certain, feel his uneasiness seeping into my own mind. But I can also feel his stubborn determination. "If Barrica wants a Messenger, then she'll have to contribute to keeping me alive."

"Don't say that," I murmur. I don't want a reminder that keeping him alive is something we have to concentrate on.

He doesn't reply, but tugs on our joined hands, pulling me in to brush his lips against mine. He tilts his head to find my neck, and my breath catches as every nerve in my body seems to concentrate on that place. *Oh, yes please. Why did we wait so long?*

Only when I'm breathless and scrambled does he speak. "I can handle it. You take my magic when I need to vent. But you need to vent too, Selly. So let's get you something sensible to wear, and I'll show you how I used to sneak out of the palace."

Leander's idea of *something sensible to wear* isn't quite the same as mine, but with the kind of ingenuity that I'm learning made him a legend at school, it takes him no time at all to kit me out in plain trousers and a shirt. The cut is simple, if the fabric is fine, and when I slip out a gate in the palace garden's wall, I find I can merge with the foot traffic in the street easily enough.

I let my feet carry me down Royal Hill toward the docks, the sounds of the city filling my ears. Merchants hawk their wares, music rings out from a radio on an upper floor, a priest stands on the steps of the temple, proclaiming the arrival of Barrica's Messenger. I pull the sleeves of the shirt down to cover the green marks on the backs of my hands, and keep my head down as I pass the temple, which is mobbed by worshippers.

The vines that Leander sent snaking along the buildings on our route from the harbor are still flowering, and there's a new hum to the city. Not the worried anxiety I felt in the air before the *Lizabetta* left port. Now, there's a certainty in everyone's step, a hint of something that's not quite aggression, but on the way to it. They have a Messenger on their side. They have a goddess who's paying attention.

They have no idea that Macean has a Messenger, too.

If the queen's plan works, and Laskia is *removed* from the political equation, then these people will never have to know how close they came to witnessing a war between gods.

If? My mind, uneasy at leaving anything so important to Augusta's machinations, shies away. *Don't waste these few moments to yourself fretting about things you can't change.*

It doesn't take long to reach the docks, and something inside me releases as the scent of salt tickles my nose. I draw in the deepest breath I've managed in days, and the familiarity—the sense of *home*—brings with it an ache behind my eyes.

Leander was right. I needed this.

I pass the harbormaster's office, slowing my pace to soak up the shouts of the sailors inside. I wonder what the gossip is, what they're saying now about the Mellaceans.

I don't realize where my footsteps are taking me, though, until I'm well out on the docks. I keep my gaze averted from where the *Lizabetta* was last moored—I don't want to see another ship there, as if she never was. I don't look at the mooring that held the *Freya*, either—if I'd managed to stow away on her, I'd be north in Holbard now. I wouldn't have been there on the Isle of the Mother, when Leander made his leap. *He* wouldn't have been there.

If I'd managed to stow away on the *Freya*, so much would be different now.

I look up from my thoughts to find I've walked out to where our little *Emma* is still moored.

The sturdy Mellacean fishing boat is out of place among the big trade ships, and I'm pleased to see she's neatly packed away, her sails stowed, her deck clean. The Queensguard took good care of her. I glance left and right, and then hop down onto her deck, landing lightly.

I'll just check everything's in its proper place below.

The hatch is unlocked and moves easily when I lift it, and I'm at the bottom of the companionway before I turn to look at the cabin.

Keegan's stretched out full length in the one bunk, looking at me in mild surprise over the top of a book.

"I see you've escaped," he says, by way of greeting. "That's unexpected."

"I see you have, too. What are you doing here?"

He shrugs, carefully marking his place before swinging his long legs over the edge of the bunk. "She's my ship, the way I see it. We bought her with my gold necklace, after all."

"Didn't you steal that necklace?"

He waves the book at me. "Details."

"You're a scholar, details are all you ever talk about."

"Fine time you've picked to take an interest," he replies. "Do you want to hide here with me or not?"

"I want to hide," I reply, taking a seat on a crate.

"Then welcome to my domain. I needed to get away from the priesthood and do some reading in peace."

"Hey, same. Well, escaping the priests, anyway. Are those bags all books?"

Keegan's smile turns a little sheepish. "I brought a few other things with me. It seems my father went running off toward the Bibliotek to try and head me off—I suppose figuring out my destination didn't require a huge stretch—and I'm guessing he'll have seen the newspapers and will know I'm back. I'm anticipating needing a hideout on an ongoing basis."

"She's your boat. Ironic that your father's hunting you down, and you'd do anything to dodge him. Mine's trapped up north for the winter, and I'd give anything to have him here. How did you get on with the research?"

His smile drops away. "I'm going to have to work hard. They're all looking for a way to bring the goddess through into our world. 'Just in case.' I'm the only one looking for a way to keep Leander safe—to keep her at bay."

My heart thumps harder in my chest. "Please find it, Keegan. We're just sitting here, trusting the queen to make sure Laskia isn't a threat, and I'm still not convinced that *Augusta* isn't the threat we should be worrying about."

"I will." There's determination in his voice. "I've made a librarian ally. Her name's Elga, and she's no more impressed with the rest of them than we are."

I grimace. "Speaking of not impressed, Leander sent me away to get a lungful of salt air before I snapped at someone."

"I can sympathize. The court is full of people who bullied me at school and are now trying to ingratiate themselves. Either they think I'm going to pretend it didn't happen, or they think I don't remember. I don't know whether it's more insulting to be thought spineless or stupid."

"You definitely think it's more insulting to be thought stupid."

We're both quiet for a while, although I nearly speak again. Left to itself, my mind inevitably spins back to Leander.

I should be fixated on Laskia, on Augusta, on the ongoing problem of keeping my prince grounded, and yet my thoughts rebelliously, relentlessly, foolishly snap back to the feel of his lips on mine. I nearly say *I kissed Leander* out loud, just to see how it sounds. To see how the only person who really knows us both reacts.

But it's something new, something private. Something that makes my stomach swoop in a way I don't mind at all. And so I stay quiet.

Then my stomach swoops again, and I realize there's a creeping sense of uneasiness moving through me. Like the jangling warning in the back of your mind that starts when a part of you wonders if you remembered to secure a hatch or stow a sail properly.

Then a bolt of pain lances through my head.

"Selly?" Keegan sounds like he's talking from far away—and at the same time the fragments of his voice are like knives, stabbing into my brain. I double over, hands pressed to my temples, a wave of nausea sweeping through me.

"Leander," I gasp. It's as though there's a string connecting us, and the goddess has just pulled it taut, yanking straight on my soul, demanding it return to Leander's once more.

Keegan gets me up on deck, and pushes me from behind as I scramble up onto the dock, flopping on my back like a freshly caught fish. He's beside me in one jump, pulling me to my feet and slinging my arm around his shoulders.

There are sailors, I think. There are people. I hear a shout from someone.

It's as though my head is in a vise, and any minute the pressure will crush my skull. All I can feel is a terrible, mindless urge to get back to Leander—a sense of utter *wrongness* that we're apart. I have to reach the palace. I have to find him.

I'm inside an auto, I don't know whose. The leather seats are smooth, the world is a blur outside. I'm pressing my head to my knees, my body swaying with every bump. Keegan's hands are on my back, helpless to do anything but tell me he's there.

The palace gates. The sapphire-blue uniforms of the Queensguard. Startled questions—*What are you doing outside?*—and then Keegan's pushing past them, calling out, "Quick, where's the prince?"

But I know. I could find Leander in the pitch-dark, in a howling gale.

I tear through the palace, and feet pound behind me, but I don't know who it is, and I can't stop for them. Air spirits fly ahead of me, pinpricks of light that dance in my vision—I don't know if they're leading me or clearing the way, but I reach out to them, connect myself to them, let them tow me along even faster.

I swing around a corner and then another, down hallways I've never seen before, coming closer and closer. The urgency is burning me up—I *have* to find him. I have to reach him, before it's too late.

I burst through a pair of wooden doors, letting them swing shut with a crash behind me. I'm in a chapel, and at the front is a statue of Barrica with her sword and her shield, both marked with the same patterns I wear down my forearms.

Light streams in through stained glass windows in magician's green and Alinorish blue, illuminating Leander, huddled on the ground before the statue. He's heaving for breath, and I throw myself to my knees beside him, pulling him up, wrapping my arms around his neck.

He clings to me with a ragged sound, and I brace myself just an instant before he releases his magic into me. My veins sizzle and my bones ache, my head spinning with the power of it.

Every time I take this load from him, there's a price to pay. I can feel it, deep inside.

In the old days, Messengers were consumed by the power of their gods. Now I—the first anchor—can help carry my Messenger's load. But even with two of us, we can't bear it forever.

As if the hour away from him has cast everything in a new, clearer light, I can see it now.

I can help him last longer. I can't help him do this forever.

"Selly," he whispers, hoarse. "I'm sorry, I'm so sorry. I thought I could do it."

"It's all right," I murmur, pressing a kiss to his temple, finding it wet with his tears. "It's all right, I'm here. Leander . . . I'm not going anywhere."

I echo the promise he made to me just hours earlier on the balcony without an instant's hesitation. Because that's the truth of it. I've bound myself to him. And whatever that means, I can't change it.

For a moment, it's as if I can feel the weight of the little paper boat in my pocket—a promise he can't possibly keep.

"She didn't want—" he manages, and pauses for a shaky breath. "I shouldn't have come to the chapel. She wanted you close to me."

"I'm not going anywhere," I whisper, kissing his temple, kissing his cheek, holding him tight. I think there are people at the door to the chapel. Keegan. The Queensguard. I don't care.

This is our path, Leander's and mine. The whole country—the world—needs this from us, and there's nobody else who can help shoulder the burden.

The last thing Rensa said to me was that she'd been trying to teach me to be a captain. To take care of my people before myself. To make sure they knew that I'd die for them. *The world's bigger than you, Selly Walker,* she said. *Bigger than me. That's what I've been trying to teach you all this time.*

I understand, I tell her silently, as Leander shudders in my arms. *I've learned the last lesson you had for me.*

"Let's get you back to your quarters," I say softly, smoothing back Leander's hair, my breath catching as another wave of magic passes through me and sends my nerves jangling. I glance up at the statue of Barrica above us, her sword and shield at the ready, her stone face implacable. "I'm here, Leander. I promise I won't leave."

JUDE

*The Tenements
Port Naranda, Mellacea*

My mother's funeral is going to be heartbreakingly small. It's just me and a few neighbors from our floor straggling along behind the cart that's transporting her coffin. The horse is taking its time, and we have to go the long way around—two buildings near the port collapsed after Laskia's rampage off the ship, and now they've closed down several roads. So we're all shuffling after the horse for longer than we expected, nobody knowing what to say, or where to look.

Mum got sick so soon after we arrived in Port Naranda that she never really made any friends, and the people she'd known here from decades before were hard to track down. Mrs. Tevner and a few of the other ladies from our building have shown up out of politeness, but I think they realize that trying to pretend this is something it's not will only make it worse.

I can't help but wonder what they make of me. They've all

seen my ruby pin, and now I have the black eye Dasriel gave me. A week ago, they might have been worried about going to the funeral of a gangster's mother. Now, they're probably trying to figure out what it means to walk with one of Laskia's companions. They're not sure, but I know there are whispers that I was on the ship with her. Out of the corner of my eye, I can see a couple of them making eye contact with each other, but never with me. Is what they're doing dutiful, or dangerous?

There's no green sister present—I'm not aware of my mother ever praying to Macean, and I didn't want to ask for one. It would have felt too close to inviting Sister Beris into my life, and I'd rather cut out my own heart with a blunt knife. I will never forget standing beside her as a whole ship of sailors died from the poison she fed them.

I grew up with the priests of Alinor, but my connection to Barrica died when I left her lands—when I prayed for help, and none came. And anyway, if there are any priests of Barrica in Port Naranda right now, I can only imagine they're keeping incredibly low profiles, and hunting for a way out.

Still, it's only now that I realize having no priest of any sort means there's no form or structure to follow. I don't know what we're supposed to do once we get to the crematorium.

That's what they do here. In the rolling green hills of Alinor we had plenty of room for burials, but in Mellacea every inch of farmland is needed—the mountains crowd the city against the sea, and they can't spare the earth for the dead. So they'll burn my mother. Normal to them, but strange to me. I'm trying not to think about it, but after months of feeling her hands as cold as ice, a part of me doesn't mind the idea that at last she'll be warm.

The undertaker's cart pauses at a crossroads to let a couple of autos go by, one blaring its horn. I stare down at the cobblestones beneath my feet, then crane my neck back to look up at the dark, crowded buildings. I'd give anything for the golden sandstone of Kirkpool right now. For the bright flowers in window baskets. For home.

We arrive to find a drab, faded sort of man holding his hand out for payment. It's most of the money I have left, and once he's counted it out they carry the coffin into a stuffy little room and set it up on two sawhorses in the corner.

Mrs. Tevner's brought a plate of sandwiches, and she sets it down on the little table before carefully peeling the cloth covering away. I set out the three candles Mrs. Kan said we'd need for a Cánh Dōese funeral and light them on my second attempt, my hands shaking. Technically, that's it. Candles and food.

After that, the awkwardness descends.

Suddenly I have to press my lips together, to keep them from trembling. There's an ache behind my eyes that won't go away.

Nobody has any stories to tell, any words to speak. None of these women knew my mother. They're just decent people who thought someone should do something, or that it would be safer if they did.

I should be the one to speak. I should tell them stories about cooking with Mum when I was small, both of us ending up covered in flour and laughing uncontrollably. Or about the letters she wrote me when I first went to school, full of pictures of her daily trials and tribulations, to make me laugh. I should tell them she used to be a person, before she was here, in this box.

But I can't seem to open my mouth. I'm afraid that what will come pouring out is my anger. My litany of complaints, accusations I'll never get the chance to make. That she brought me here when my friends wanted to save us. That she let me think they abandoned me.

That *she* abandoned me, that she got sick, that she became a shadow of herself, and stranded me in this place I know nothing about.

That she left me so alone, so desperate to find a way to at least feed us, that I fell in with Ruby. That I hunted the boy who was once my friend. That I abandoned any part of myself that was once good, and now I'm just . . . this.

And she's left me alone.

"Did your mother have any siblings in Cánh Dō?" The question jolts me from my thoughts. It's one of the ladies from down the hall, trying to make conversation.

I blink at her. "No. She was born here, in Port Naranda."

Silence descends once more, thick and choking.

I don't know how long we're meant to stay, and I'm desperate for this to be over. And at the same time, I don't know how I'm ever going to walk out the door, and leave her here alone.

I glance around the room, looking for anything at all that can distract me, and my gaze alights on the sandwiches. To my dull surprise, my stomach rumbles. I can't remember the last time I felt hungry.

It feels disrespectful to stand here eating sandwiches beside my mother's coffin. But at the same time, Mrs. Tevner did go to the trouble of making them. I don't want her to think I don't appreciate that.

There's a dangerous sort of laugh bubbling up inside my throat—I'm standing at my mother's funeral, or what should be her funeral, debating etiquette. I have a feeling that if I let that laugh escape, I won't be able to stop. Not until I'm howling.

A sound from the doorway makes me stiffen. It's no more than the scrape of a sole against the stone floor, but in the isolated silence of this room, it echoes like a shout. I turn, half hoping for some unknown friend of my mother's to have come to pay their respects, half indignant that anyone should have dared to violate the privacy of this moment.

Tom is standing in the doorway.

He's in the same clothes he wears to tend bar: black trousers, white shirt, and beneath the dark gray coat he's found, no doubt suspenders across his broad shoulders. He's made himself somber enough for a funeral. The gray of the coat makes his pale skin even paler, and his dark copper hair is neatly combed but already trying to escape into its usual tousle.

My first reaction is a flush of pure relief, a lightness sweeping through me. I take an involuntary step toward him, one hand lifting.

Our eyes meet, and on the heels of that flush of relief comes a humiliation that brings me crashing back down to the ground—that makes my knees want to buckle, that makes me want to back up, away from him.

I can just imagine him getting himself ready, dressing in his dark clothes, picturing a proper funeral. He would have been expecting mourners, a eulogy. And instead it's just me and a bunch of women I hardly know, and sandwiches nobody is sure they should eat.

When I don't move, Tom slips into the room and walks over

to take his place at my side. His hand reaches for mine, and his fingers thread through my own—they're so warm, and mine are so cold my knuckles hurt. And with his easy barman's charm, he takes over.

I stand there numb as he introduces himself, and somehow, impossibly, makes small talk. He never met my mother, but he eases around this fact without telling a lie. He's not here for her, after all.

He's here for me.

Relief travels through the room like a ripple, like Tom's a stone thrown into a pond and waves of reassurance are spreading out from him. This nice boy is here to take responsibility for me, and that means nobody else has to.

In just a few minutes, the women start to drift away. Mrs. Tevner is last, and she takes the plate with her. And then it's just Tom and me, standing alone—standing *together*—in the room.

I look at the coffin one more time. This is it. When I walk out the door, I'll truly have left her behind.

But with Tom's hand in mine, with his quiet, steady presence beside me, I find that I think I can leave. Because that's not her lying there. She's somewhere long ago, covered in flour, black hair turned gray with it, laughing at my jokes.

The drab little man peers around the doorway, and nods when he finds the two of us still here, as though this was to be expected. "My condolences," he says, not sounding particularly sorry about anything. "Your mother's ashes will be available for pickup in three days."

I have no idea what to say, so after the silence draws out, Tom handles that, too. "Thank you," he says simply, and wrapping an arm around my shoulders, he leads me away.

The two of us emerge into the bustle of the street, the crisp morning sunlight catching me by surprise.

Tom keeps hold of me, and I let him lead me a couple of blocks away, past these people just carrying on with their lives, until we reach a little café. I'd never noticed it before—it's tucked in between a grocer and a block of apartments, both several stories taller than it. Through the arched front window I can see a cozy space crowded with tables for two, the lighting low, the menu written up on big chalkboards.

The front door has a little stained glass window depicting a bowl and a spoon, and when we push through, we're greeted with the kind of warmth that soaks into your bones, and the most delicious savory smells.

Neither of us speaks as Tom guides me over to a small table by the wall and settles in opposite me, still keeping hold of my hand. A waiter glides up, and Tom greets him with one of his usual smiles.

"Don't suppose you've got any of the potato dumpling soup hiding back there?" he asks, making his eyes wide and hopeful.

The waiter, stern a moment before, finds a smile. "Let me see," he says. And then the two of us are alone, and I'm meeting Tom's gaze.

"I don't know what to do with her ashes," I say finally.

He grimaces. "Is there somewhere special to her you could scatter them, maybe?"

"I'm not sure. It used to be here. She thought all the answers were waiting for her in Port Naranda. But nothing about this place was happy for her in the end."

We fall silent again as the waiter sets down glasses of water and gives Tom a nod that I suspect promises potato dumplings in our future.

Tom squeezes my hand. "You didn't tell me it was her funeral today," he says. There's no accusation in the words, no ego. It's just a very gentle statement of fact.

"It was . . . you saw. It wasn't anything."

"I still wanted to be there."

"How *did* you get there?"

"I went to your building to look for you, and an exceptionally nosy old man from up the hall told me where you'd gone. He seemed kind of annoyed his wife was off gallivanting with such a handsome young man." Tom says it with a small smile, and somehow, impossibly, he draws one from me.

Our waiter returns one more time and sets down two big ceramic bowls of soup. Little round dumplings of potato bob among thick noodles, and the smell of chicken stock and herbs wafting up sets my mouth watering.

"Eat," says Tom, still gentle. "I bet you haven't."

I obediently scoop up a spoonful, and I don't know if it's just my hunger speaking, but this might well be the most extraordinary thing I've ever tasted. It feels as though the soup chases the very last of the chill out of my body, and the chewy dumplings taste like potatoes and butter and everything good. It's a little while before I manage to speak.

"You know a lot about how I'm doing, what I need."

He shrugs. "I'm on my own too."

I pause. He's never talked about his family. I've never asked.

"My parents died when I was small," he says quietly, and wards off my reply by lifting a hand. "No, don't say sorry, or anything like that. It was a long time ago. My aunts did their duty, then set me free."

"I didn't know," I say, aware of how weak that sounds.

"Well, I didn't tell you," he replies. "But the thing is—look, I don't know if I should wait to say this, or if it's what you need to hear as soon as possible. But it's what I want to say, so I'm just going to plunge in." He sets down his spoon, and again he reaches across the table for my hand. "Neither of us has to be alone."

My food turns to lead in my gut.

"I have savings," he presses on, though he must feel the deadweight of my hand, unresponsive, in his. "There's nothing in this city to hold me here, except you. I can read the signs as well as anyone. The church is chasing a war, Laskia will be at the head of it, and everyone will be hurt. Even Port Naranda won't be safe, Jude. She's insane, and she's *powerful*."

I shake my head. "You don't know the half of it. It's so much worse than that."

I've done so much worse than that.

"Then now sounds like a good time for me to leave," he says simply. "For us to leave. Together, I hope."

I blink at him. "And go where?"

"Fontesque," he says. "I have residency papers through my father. I speak the language well enough, and it's not that different—I can teach you. You probably learned it at that fancy school of yours."

"A little," I manage.

He nods. "A barman never has trouble finding work, and once I'm used to the city, well, I've always wanted to start a little place of my own. That's always been the dream."

Has it? I'd have known that if I hadn't cut him off all those times he tried to talk to me. If I hadn't pressed my lips to his every time he wanted to confide.

"I don't know how to pour a drink," I say, which is the most ridiculous objection to anything I've ever heard in my life. But I can't think straight.

Half an hour ago I was at my mother's funeral.

Not even two weeks ago I was watching a fleet of Alinorish nobles sunk, as Laskia tried to start the very war we're running from.

Just days ago I was standing in the Temple of the Mother, watching two Messengers created.

And now I'm talking to Tom about running away to Fontesque to start a cocktail bar?

This is insanity.

Except slowly, the strangest sense of madness is overtaking me. I mean, why not? What *does* hold me here? I have no ties to Port Naranda. I can't go back to Kirkpool, not after what I've done.

But that doesn't mean I have to be a part of what Laskia has planned.

Slowly, Tom starts to smile. "You're thinking about it."

"I don't have any money," I point out. "I just spent it all on a funeral. I can't even afford my rent. I'll have to get out by the end of the week."

"I have money," he replies. "Enough for a train fare for me, and we can get one for you. We'll sell our things. And once we get to Fontesque, we'll be fine. I'm employable, and so are you, in plenty of ways that don't involve being beaten to a pulp."

His eyes are on my face. He thinks my black eye is from a prize fight. Of course he does.

For an instant I'm back on the Isle of the Mother, screaming my desperate warning. *Leander, look out!* For an instant I'm making a leap as surely as he and Laskia did, certain that Dasriel will kill me for stopping his shot from killing the prince.

But he just sent me reeling, my vision dancing with stars, and raced after Leander. And after that, his hand ruined, he needed me, and so I lived.

And just like that, trickles of cold reality are running through the dream. Dasriel will never let me leave. Nor will Laskia, if she thinks I can be useful.

"No," says Tom firmly. "No, I can see your doubts kicking in. But Jude, we can make our own choices. Whatever's about to happen here, it's not our fight. We can be somewhere else, making a home for ourselves." He squeezes my hand, his gaze intent. "Let's run for the hills together. You have to be out of your apartment anyway. Give me a couple of days to sell my things, and we could be on a train up through Nusraya and the principalities before the end of the week. They can't stop us if they can't find us."

They can't stop us if they can't find us.

He's right.

Hope prickles inside me, as this wild, incredible feeling begins to seep through my veins.

I think I'm about to make another leap.

Tom sees my answer in my eyes, and he breaks into a smile like sunshine. Abruptly he comes to his feet, and reaches across the table to grab the lapels of my old school jacket, pulling me up too, so he can lean across our two bowls of soup and kiss me. It's like he's anchoring me in place—the press of his lips against mine, the rasp of stubble on his jaw, the warmth of his skin. He feels like certainty. Like safety.

Distantly I can hear the other diners clapping, and Tom's laughing against my mouth, and I'm sure I'm so light that if he wasn't holding on to me, I would float away like a puff of smoke.

I've found my way home after all. Everything's going to change.

I'm getting out.

SELLY

The Palace Greenhouses
Kirkpool, Alinor

When I wake up the next morning, my mouth tastes like I've been licking the carpet, and my body aches from my mad dash through the city to get back to Leander. But for the first time in days, I feel calm.

"I feel like I have a hangover," Leander murmurs beside me, rolling over in bed to lie facedown. "But I don't remember having any of the right kind of fun."

"Well, a goddess tried to scoop your brain out yesterday," I point out, squinting from the light streaming in the windows and fumbling around on the nightstand for a glass of water.

I see the words land more heavily than I'd intended. His body goes still, but he turns his head to look at me, shadows still dark under his eyes, concern in his gaze. "Are you all right?" he asks.

My head's full of barely remembered dreams, and I know he shared them—or maybe they were his and *I* shared them, I don't know. I remember a man I was sure was King Anselm. A woman I didn't know, but I could tell was another of Barrica's Messengers of old. She wore a rough tunic, and had lines of rich red earth daubed across her cheeks, and she carried a spear.

I don't know why the other Messengers visit our dreams, or even if that's what's happening. Perhaps Barrica just remembers them, and so we do, too. It's a sobering reminder that they're no longer here, though. That they didn't survive what Leander's doing now.

"I'm all right," I say quietly, and it's true. Yesterday was awful, unbearable. And yesterday also gave me the gift of clarity.

It's time to stop wishing things were different. It's time to stop looking for ways out, or wondering if there's any way I can change this path I'm on.

I'm here. The work ahead of me is clear, and Leander and I will do it for as long as we last. And it's that simple. It's strangely freeing, having all those decisions taken away.

The first thing I need to do is speak to Kiki. I don't trust Augusta not to start a war the moment she gets the chance, whatever Leander says. If I'm going to stop her, I've already realized I need to speak her language. And for *that,* I need an ally.

Leander's still watching me with those newly green eyes of his. I miss the deep brown they were before, but they're as easy to read as ever. I know he's picking up most of what I'm feeling, even though he says nothing.

I'm hit with a wave of self-consciousness. Between my headlong dash to reach Leander yesterday, and the agonized crawl back to his quarters, there wasn't exactly time for us to discuss our sleeping arrangements. Most notably, that it feels quite a bit different now that we've kissed, and admitted what we mean to each other.

I must've fallen asleep where I lay last night, stroking his hair until his breathing evened out. And now . . . now I'm stuck gazing into those green eyes, uncomfortably aware that the bond between us probably means he knows exactly where my thoughts have gone.

His lips quirk and shift, a gleam coming to his eyes. He draws breath to speak, and I sit up and roll out of bed before he can see my furious blush. "I'll see about breakfast."

Kiki is there when I open the door to Leander's quarters, saving me the effort of going to look for her. She might not have Leander's gift for reading my mind, but she must see something in my expression, some need for a confidante, because she winks at me and crosses over to Leander and hauls him out of bed. Ruffling his hair and turning him around, she gives him a shove toward the bathing chamber.

"Go wash, Your Royal Handsomeness," she instructs him in a tone that brooks no opposition. "And if you need us, *absolutely* do not hesitate to call out."

I can see just a hint of the tension she's hiding so well. She's known Leander since they were children—seen him make a fool of himself dozens of times, and laughed at him dozens more. And now he's something different, something holy. Every time she goes near him, she's working hard to be what we need.

She gestures for me to sit, and relieves a servant of his tray of breakfast, setting it out herself, and pausing to pop a strawberry into her mouth. "Well," she says as the door closes behind Leander, "you look determined this morning."

I let out a slow breath. "I've been thinking about how I ended up here. Perhaps other people would kill to be where I am, but I never asked for any of this. The things that impress them . . . I'd rather be at sea."

"That's true," she agrees, her voice quiet, her brown eyes full of sympathy.

"But you know what I thought next? I realized that Leander didn't ask me to do it, either. I had so many chances to leave him, and I never did. This is where I chose to be."

"And all of Alinor is grateful," she replies.

"I only partly did it for Alinor," I admit. "But still. I didn't know exactly what I was choosing, but I knew I was risking my life. And here I am. My life is very much on the line. I may as well do something with it."

"I like this line of thinking."

"I need you to teach me, Kiki. Not just make things happen for me, or tell me what to do next. I need you to help me *understand* this place. I can't keep being tossed around by the tides."

Kiki's face lights up, and she leans toward me, about to burst into animated speech. I give a little shake of my head, and she hesitates, waiting for me to go on.

"I think the queen wants a war, and she'll take it any way she can get it." I glance over at the door to the washroom, though Leander certainly wouldn't be able to hear us over the sound of running water. "The word isn't out here yet, but it's known everywhere in Mellacea, so I don't see why I shouldn't tell you. Mellacea has a Messenger too."

Kiki gasps, one hand lifting to press to her mouth.

"Exactly." I grimace. "It's not just my life on the line. It's all of our lives." I choose to stay silent for now on the problem of the goddess who wishes to return to our realm. "If I want to chart my own course—one that takes us *away* from war—then I need to know how to operate in this world."

I watch in something like wonder as Kiki packs away her worry and fear at the news I've just given her, and assumes her usual expression. "My child," she pronounces, leaning forward to pour us each a cup of steaming tea, "you have come to the right place."

"I have no doubt."

I need to do that, too—stow my worries for now and focus on the present moment. For better or worse, assassins are on their way to deal with Laskia. And after they're done, it will be time to talk to Augusta about what comes next. The best thing I can do right now is be ready for that.

"I'm going to start with the prince," Kiki says, reaching for a Fontesquan pastry, and pausing to nibble on it. "You'll see why in a moment. The thing about Leander is that he's the very personification of the phrase *poor little rich boy*. Everyone he's ever met has wanted something from him. Or at the very least, they knew they *could* get something from him. By rights, he should be suspicious of everyone around him, but somehow he's managed to keep himself open enough that he can still trust. These are the waters he swims in, though."

"And then he met me." I can't help smiling at the memory of it. "I told him he'd ruined my life, and I wanted him off my ship."

"You didn't!" Kiki is delighted. "No wonder he fell in love with you."

"I'm sure that was the moment," I agree, trying to sound wry—but there's a thrill of something in me at the possibility, a stutter in my heart.

"It makes sense that he would," Kiki replies with a shrug. "I mean, it's why I was nearly willing to marry Keegan, despite the fact that the only spine he wants to run his fingers down is a book's. He had no reason to pretend that he liked me—quite the opposite—so when he said he did, I knew he meant it. We schemed together beautifully to put off the marriage, and we very nearly managed it. We became good friends in the process."

"He told me yesterday that his father's on the way home to try and get you married all over again," I say.

"Oh, I know." She grimaces. "But one challenge at a time. So, Leander. He knows that everyone around him sees him as a ticket to whatever they want, even if they don't take advantage of that. And I've always thought his secret to getting by in this kind of world is to simply not mind. For the ones you like, accept that it's possible for them to know you're a meal ticket *and* to simply want to be your friend. For the ones you don't like, let them want, or let them expect, then do as you please. You should be doing as he does."

"What do you mean?"

She hands me a pastry. "I stand by my words. You think you need to impress them. Get the etiquette right. But you're the anchor to the first Messenger in half a millennium. You stand by the side of their prince. You simply don't *have* to care,

Selly. I don't mean to say you should be rude to everyone, but I do think it's time we shook up the power dynamic a little. Let *them* impress *you*."

"Do any of them have any practical skills?" I ask, unable to hide my smile. "I'm not that easy to impress."

"That's the spirit. Soon enough, every one of them will start to work out you're not going anywhere. Which means it's their turn to fit in with you, rather than the other way around. You've heard there's a grand ball planned to celebrate Leander's . . . what's the word? Transformation?"

"That'll do. And yes." I'm pretty sure I look like I've swallowed something unpleasant.

"That'll be the scene of your triumph," she announces. "We'll bowl them over, and you'll see how quickly they crowd around you." Her lips quirk. "It also helps to see the riches as ridiculous rather than overwhelming."

I consider this. "Are you very rich, Kiki?"

"Very," she replies. "But it's the least interesting thing about me."

"You know, I think you might be right."

I'm about to say more when a pair of servants bustle in to begin tidying up the room, straightening and tucking in the bedclothes and opening the curtains. Kiki's glance slides toward me when my mouth shuts with a little pop, and her own lips curve to a faint smile.

"I think we should plan a little outing today," she says, after a moment's thought. "Just the four of us—you and your beau, and me and mine." Her eyes gleam with amusement, but the arch of her eyebrow betrays the cleverness behind her suggestion.

Let's go somewhere without the constant eyes and ears of the palace following our every move.

Not long after, the four of us slip out through the door the servants use, avoiding the long line of officials waiting for Leander, and head toward our escape into the palace gardens. I'm free, and I'm wearing trousers again.

The relief of being able to walk without a dress swishing around my legs, of being able to take a proper step in proper boots—my whole body feels lighter. It's not that trousers are never worn here. Some women do, but most of them are in dresses, and the royals are more conservative than most when it comes to these things.

Still, it turns out that it was mainly a case of applying pressure on the right tailor, and trousers were available after all. Kiki says I look like a country gentleman in my light tweed—not a bad thing, to judge by her tone—but I don't care what I look like as long as I can move the way I want.

"If I'm going to forge my own path," I told her, "then I'm going to walk it wearing what I like." She responded with a crisp salute that, if Leander's laughter was anything to go by, wasn't entirely accurate.

The hallways we follow to the gardens are like a maze, but Leander seems to know every passageway well enough to navigate them all in the dark.

"Comes from being the youngest," he says, with an easy shrug, as we emerge into the pale sunlight of the winter morning. Now that I've seen Leander and his sisters together, I'm realizing the age gap between them is bigger than I'd understood.

Augusta and Coria are more than a decade older than he is, and they seem like part of another generation. I can't help wondering how much time Leander spent on his own growing up, and how much that distance from the other two contributed to his sense of uselessness.

The gardens wrap around the whole of the palace, a high sandstone wall protecting them from the hustle and bustle of the city. They've been bedded down for winter, and much of the greenery is gone, so it's as if the skeleton of the place is showing. The outlines of the flower beds are clear, and the rosebushes are like spiky fingers jabbing up at the sky. Bright red berries adorn glossy green shrubs, and carefully manicured trees spread their bare branches above us like the frames of broken umbrellas.

There's a stark beauty to it, but with the trappings of summer gone, it's easier to see that the palace gardens—which might seem overwhelming at the right time of year—aren't magical.

This is just a place, like any other. Which means it's somewhere I can learn to belong.

Leander walks a few steps ahead, leading the way, and the rosebushes bud when he passes them, then burst into bloom by the time Kiki and I reach them, white petals unfolding, their sweet scent filling the cold, crisp air.

"If only there were a way to keep them alive," I murmur.

Leander turns his head to tilt a glance back at me, and then reaches for my hand so he can pull me up alongside him and wrap his arm around my shoulders. "Their kind can live perfectly well here," he replies. "They just need a few allies. Come on, I'll show you."

We approach the towering greenhouses, and when we walk through the glass doors, it's like another world inside.

The air is thick: warm and damp and easy on the lungs. Life crowds every corner—there are huge ferns reaching for us, dark green vines climbing up columns, slender palms nearly brushing the ceiling. Condensation beads on the glass panels, which stretch three stories high. Flowers in pink and red and summer yellows burst from hanging pots and jostle for space in crowded beds. I can hear water flowing somewhere.

The day I met him on the docks, I told Leander this place was a waste—all this space devoted to growing flowers in winter. But I was wrong. Beauty like this is never wasted.

It's a place of work, too—I see shelves crammed with stacks of pots waiting to be filled, sacks of rich dark earth, a pair of gloves abandoned on top of a small pair of shears.

This is a place of beauty and practicality, and a reminder that Leander was right—survival is always possible.

The optimism of this morning's breakfast with Kiki flows through me again. I can learn to survive in this unfamiliar place, with the right allies.

And perhaps I'm not the only one.

We have priests, and we have scholars. And Leander's already defied expectations. Already he's different from every other Messenger in history.

Perhaps we just have to find the right kind of greenhouse, and *he* can keep growing.

Keegan and Kiki disappear around a bend, following the path, and I stop, turning inside the circle of Leander's arm and curving one hand up around the back of his neck. He lets me bring him to a halt, smiles as he obediently ducks his head.

"Fancy meeting you here," he murmurs, and a spark zips down my spine as his lips brush mine.

"Get used to it," I whisper, and his arm tightens around me. "And since we're going to be spending a lot of time together, we might as well enjoy the parts we like."

"Oh yes?"

I curl my fingers through his hair, and his breath catches as my grip tightens and my lips find his again. It's a little while before either of us speaks.

"Like that," I breathe, eventually.

His answering smile is brilliant.

This feels like a turning point. Yesterday was terrible. I'll see him huddled on the altar in my nightmares, I'm sure. But today we have a greenhouse. Today, we're remembering that anything—anyone—can flower, under the right conditions. With a little care.

"Selly, come up high with me!" Kiki's voice rings out from up ahead, and Leander releases me reluctantly so we can continue down the pathway.

Kiki is climbing a zigzag metal staircase that rises to the full height of the greenhouse, pausing every so often at a viewing platform. It's no higher than a crow's nest atop a mast, and though it's a little slippery from the moisture in the air, it doesn't sway as you climb. It's easy to jog up after her—easier in my trousers than in her skirts, I expect. Still, by the time I get to the top, I can pretend my flushed cheeks are caused by the climb, and not by the prince below us.

"You could be anywhere in the world up here," she says, when I reach her. We're at the very tops of the palm trees. The air feels denser and warmer, and water drips from the glass. Kiki has a piece from one of the palm fronds and is tearing it into long, thin strips. "You must have been so many places. I've always wanted to travel."

"I saw trees like this when I was very small. I sailed south, with my father. He was after spices, I think."

"One day I'll do that," she says, with a fierceness that tells me she's not resigned to marriage just yet. Not to Keegan, or to anyone else. Her quick fingers are braiding the palm fronds, and she ties them off to make a little bracelet, then slips it onto my wrist.

Together we lean over the railing, looking down at the ground below. Keegan is pointing something out and talking solemnly, and Leander appears to be listening, presumably learning about plants.

But then my focus shifts, and I see the mosaic tiles they're walking on. My voice rises in pitch as I grab for Kiki's hand. "Kiki, look at the floor."

It takes her a moment to understand. Then her gaze flicks to my arm, and I stretch it out so we can both look at my magician's marks.

Though the tiles below are scuffed with dirt, and in some places hidden beneath leaf litter, there can be no mistaking it: the pattern is the same. These are the markings of Barrica's sword and shield.

"This place was built over a century ago," Kiki says quietly. "Perhaps whoever designed the floor saw the markings at the temple, and copied them."

"She's everywhere," I murmur.

"We're her people," Kiki replies simply. "For all we know, she gave this pattern to the greenhouse's designer over a century ago, just so it would be here for us to see today."

"I can't help wondering how much she does preordain," I admit. "When I think about how I came to be Leander's anchor—what would have happened if I hadn't been there, how different the world would be now . . . I don't think it was luck. She *told* him it wasn't luck, in a dream. That she saw, after her other Messengers were consumed by their own power, how it was needed."

"He spoke to her?" Kiki whispers.

"He hears her voice often, I think. I wonder, though. Could *anyone* have been his anchor, if they'd been there? Or did it have to be a magician? Or a magician who'd never come of age? Who still had a child's plain marks? Mine shifted into these when I found the way to the Isles for the first time."

"You think she prepared you for it?" Kiki asks, her eyes on the bold geometric patterns tracing my forearms. "All those years earlier?"

"I don't know. I know that I grew up hating my magic for never showing up. My father must have dragged me to every teacher on the Crescent Sea, trying to help me. *Make the most of it.* That's his motto. And he was so sure he could help me to make the most of what I had—magician's marks. When I think of all those years of misery, of humiliation . . ."

I trail off, to find Kiki studying me thoughtfully. "Your father never stopped?" she asks.

"No, he never gave up on me."

"I'm not talking about giving up," she replies. "I'm talking about . . . when something's *humiliating* your child, perhaps there's a point at which *making the most of it* isn't . . ."

"It wasn't like that," I reply. The words set something squirming inside me, and I shove it away. I've spent my life trying to find my magic for my father. Trying to be the air magician his fleet needed. That experience shaped my life, shaped who I *am*. "He wanted the best for me," I say eventually, after the pause has gone on too long. "But perhaps the lack of magic was also what meant I could help Leander, when he needed me."

"If she was preparing you to be an anchor, then I suppose those hard years were the road you had to walk," Kiki says quietly.

"If she was preparing me for an anchor, then . . ." I study my arms resting on the railing. The floor far below, set in place a century before, marked with the same lines and patterns. "Then what else did she do?"

"How do you mean?"

"Well, if the *Lizabetta*'s voyage had gone as planned, Leander would only have offered the usual sacrifice," I say. "A cut on his palm. She'd never have had a Messenger, capable of opening the door back into our world for her. And he'd never have needed an anchor. I only did it because we were at the Temple of the Mother. Because he had no choice but to make a far, far greater offering. Because we were desperate. Did she make *that* happen?"

"You mean, did she sink your ship?" Kiki whispers.

"Laskia sank my ship. But could Barrica have had a hand in that somehow? And if Barrica *was* involved, that means she killed my crew. And everyone aboard the progress fleet."

Kiki lets out a slow breath. "Over the course of her existence—so many thousands upon thousands of years—I suppose we must seem so small to her."

"They weren't small to me," I whisper, my throat tightening.

"Nor was your love for them," she replies, leaning against the railing beside me and pressing her shoulder to mine.

It's dizzying, thinking about how far back it might all go. It's like watching the world from far above, as we're doing now, and seeing all the pieces fit together. Did she keep me from boarding the *Freya,* to make sure I was on Leander's crew? Did she keep my father in Holbard, to trap me aboard the *Lizabetta*? Did she send him there in the first place?

Is she why my mother gave me to him, and never looked back? Is she why they *met*?

Perhaps every moment of my life has been guided by the hand of a goddess, I don't know. And there's no way to find out—but I have to believe that at least one part of it is my own. That what I feel for Leander—every charming, frustrating, vulnerable part of him—is real.

She may have brought us together, but my heart is my own.

KEEGAN

◆

The Royal Palace
Kirkpool, Alinor

Leander has disappeared down a leafy path to pick strawberries for the girls, leaving a wave of newly growing and blooming plants and vines in his wake. I'm standing alone at the bottom of the large metal staircase as they descend.

It isn't my intention to eavesdrop, but as soon as I hear the first few words, I'm frozen in place. Kiki's using the bright tone she always used with me to distract me from my gloom—I've had plenty of chances to learn to recognize it.

"The thing about marriage to Keegan," she's saying, "is—well, there are so many things about marriage to Keegan. It's complicated."

"Do you think there's any hope you two can wriggle out of it?" Selly asks.

"We'll certainly try, but no, not much hope," Kiki replies. "We both just got all the more desirable, thanks to our proximity to your boyfriend."

"I could probably help you run away to sea," Selly offers, only mostly sounding like she's joking.

"That hardly worked out for Keegan, did it?" Kiki replies with a laugh. She's trying to keep her voice down, but she's just not very good at it.

She must have betrayed something, in her expression or her body language, because Selly's voice is quiet when she asks, "Kiki, what is it?"

Kiki lets out a sigh. "I'm not the one who needs to run away, you see. I was willing to do it. Marry him, I mean."

My brain is shouting at me to move, to get out of here before they discover me listening—but the rest of me is rooted to the spot.

She wanted to marry me?

Kiki's still talking. "I understood he wouldn't love me, or at least not the way I grew up dreaming someone might one day. Keegan loves deeply and loyally—look at him with you and Leander—but not in a romantic, sweep-you-off-your-feet, ravish-you-until-you-need-a-rest kind of way. Those things aren't part of the way he's made, which is perfectly fine, but different from me. I thought we could be friends, though. Make our own sort of life together."

"Then why didn't you?" Selly asks, so soft I nearly miss it.

"He desperately didn't want to," Kiki replies. "He simply couldn't. And once I realized that, I helped him climb out the window and get away, because I'm not a monster."

"What was it like, after he went?" Selly asks.

"Oh, frightful," Kiki replies, her voice wry, but carrying a weariness I'm not used to hearing in it. "Both sets of parents absolutely furious, me gazing at them with big eyes and making woefully inaccurate guesses about what he might have done, to try and send them in the wrong direction."

"That sounds awful."

"Oh no, darling. Awful would have been when the whole royal court found out about it. I wasn't particularly looking forward to being the girl whose would-be husband literally ran away from her. But you know what's even worse than that?"

"I hate to think." Selly's voice is closer now, and I'm standing like a statue at the bottom of the stairs, my skin feeling strangely stretched across my ribs, the back of my neck hot.

"Worse," says Kiki, as she rounds the bend, "is that I tried to give up my future for him, and it didn't even work." She stops short when she spots me, and Selly bangs into her back. And then both of them are staring at me.

"Hello there," says Kiki after an agonizing pause, never one to shy away from a social challenge.

I manage to drag in some air, but when I try to speak, discover I'm not sure what I want to say. "Kiki, I—"

"Yes, I know," she agrees, walking forward. "Come on, I'll walk you to your meeting. Selly, Leander will be just along that path. I expect you can find him without anyone's help."

Selly's already looking in the direction the prince disappeared, uneasy at being separated from him. With a nod and a grimace, she trots off in pursuit, leaving Kiki and me alone.

Kiki links her arm through mine, and stays silent as we walk. She always lets me gather my thoughts—yet another of the things I've taken for granted.

"I can't believe I've been so selfish," I say eventually. "I've thought so many times about what *I* needed. I never once asked what you needed."

"Well, it's all academic now," she points out, with a sigh. "I'm sorry you overheard that. Even if I had wanted to say it to you, I wouldn't have done it so bluntly."

"I don't mind blunt," I murmur. "Kiki, I'm the one who owes an apology. I consider you a friend. I should have been a better friend to you. I'm sorry. I shall do better from now on."

We both know I'll have plenty of chances—our fates are bound back together once more, and my duty to Leander will hold me here far more effectively than our watchful families.

I've spent so much time thinking about what my life would have been like if I had boarded any other ship, that day at the docks. I'd be at the Bibliotek now, losing myself in a book, hiding from the world.

Now, I could not be more squarely eye to eye with reality if I tried. I'm facing down a whole priesthood. I'm facing down marriage, which is just as terrifying. But I see it clearly: Kiki was willing to sacrifice herself for me. Now it's my turn.

I'll stay here, and I'll help my friends as best I can, and I'll be a good husband to the girl with her arm curled through mine.

She deserves more, and I certainly won't give her less.

No matter what it costs.

An hour later, I'm listening to a priest with a round, cheerful face and an unsettlingly intense expression. "We'll have half a dozen ambassadors here within a week," he says. I'm in the royal library again—Kiki has disappeared to find Selly and take her away for some sort of tailoring or tutoring, and I'm on my own.

It's strange, watching the priest's brows draw together, his fist thump down on the table. It doesn't suit him. "There are faith revivals under way all around the Crescent Sea. Every church and temple is suddenly full to the brim—everyone wants to prop their god up too, just in case they can summon their own Messenger."

For a moment it's hard to believe what I'm hearing—that he, or anyone, could treat what happened to us at the Isle of the Mother so casually. But they don't understand, of course.

"All of them will want to meet the Messenger," the priest continues. "And once they understand the extent of his power, the queen will want to start pushing forward with mutual protection treaties. They'll be scrambling to hide under our wing, and when Mellacea understands that everyone's allied against them—"

"He has a name," I break in, making my voice firm.

All up and down the table, heads swivel to study me. They each look some version of either surprised or irritated to find I'm still showing up, except for Princess Coria, who leans back in her chair and—if I'm not mistaken—raises one hand to conceal a hint of a smile. She nods discreetly, bidding me continue. She dropped in a few minutes ago, and has been watching without saying much.

"His Highness is the Messenger of Barrica," I say, pressing on. "It is not appropriate to treat him as something to be wheeled out and shown off. As a tool to pursue our own agenda."

The priest blinks at me. "I'm sorry, Mr. . . . ." He pauses and tilts his head as if to suggest he's forgotten my name again. It's a clumsy trick—in the short time we've know each other, I've already learned the senior priests are far too savvy not to know everyone at this table's middle name, favorite food, and childhood comfort toy. Truth be told, if I knew where Buzzy had got to, I'd probably be cuddling him every night. These are trying times.

"Wollesley," I supply. "But *my* name is immaterial. It is Prince Leander's we should recall, and use."

Father Marsen leans in and takes over, raising a hand to silence his sputtering offsider. "Mr. Wollesley, nobody is suggesting that Prince Leander is anyone's tool. It is simply a fact that when confronted with the reality of his power, other nations will be more willing to help us maintain the peace."

"I'm interested, though," the round-faced priest says, glancing up from his notes. "You say he's not to be used in pursuing Alinor's agenda. What is it you propose instead?"

I blink at him for a moment, trying to decide whether he's serious. Then, reluctantly concluding that he is, I elaborate. "He is the Messenger of the goddess we all serve," I say simply. "Has it occurred to anyone that it is *we* who should be answering to *him*?"

There's a moment of stunned silence in the wake of my words.

I can still see the smoke on the horizon as the decoy fleet went down. I can see the first mate of the *Lizabetta* crumpled by the mast, killed by shrapnel. I can see fire blooming in the dockside square as the ambassador's auto went up in flames.

The price we paid for our Messenger is beyond these people's smug comprehension.

* * *

Elga the librarian doesn't show herself until we've broken into groups to continue our research. I find myself alone, which saves me the trouble of driving off any would-be companions.

Then she appears, eyes as large as ever, curly hair perhaps even larger, as though she's been running one hand through it.

"I found the letters you wanted," she whispers, tugging at that ill-fitting uniform of hers. "At least, I think I did."

"Be more confident," I reply, gathering up my things and preparing to follow her. "I'm sure we'll get somewhere this time."

And so we do. So we do indeed.

The Royal House of Alinor has the most extraordinary archives—I can't believe I've lived here all my life and never known. Their preservation techniques are top-notch as well.

Any decent historian will tell you that you can rely on the analysis of others only up to a point. After that, you must go to the original documents yourself and draw your own conclusions.

And here are those documents. Letters to and from the nobles, rulers, and priests of several different countries and principalities, written with the sort of casual intimacy that suggests the bonds they'd built during the war were deep indeed.

Their shared history means they don't always spell out exactly the things that must have been common knowledge, but together, the letters start to form a picture. And this much is clear:

Valus, the laughing god of Vostain, was mired so deep in his grief that none could reach him.

Macean was asleep.

Barrica had retreated from our realm but—as we have always phrased it—left the door ajar that she might keep watch over her brother and ensure he never returned to wage war again.

And as for their siblings? Dylo, Kyion, Sutista, and Oldite had retreated as well, and they were *most* insistent that none of their number should ever return to our realm again.

They did not, I am beginning to realize, trust that Barrica the Warrior had entirely transformed herself into Barrica the Sentinel. And so they left themselves a fail-safe.

"They still have some influence here, in our realm," I whisper to Elga, our heads bent over the page. "There is one place where they can act, if only a little."

"But where?" she whispers, her eyes sweeping the page.

"For that, I believe we must go back to the letter we looked at last time," I say. "Do you recall what it said? *'What I would give, to be in the Temple of the Mother on the day this exile ends. . . .'* If the person who wrote that letter was talking about the exile of their god, then we know where it was supposed to end. In the place the gods still have a way to touch our world. The Temple of the Mother."

Our eyes meet, and I see my excitement reflected in hers. "What does this mean, Keegan? What will you do?"

"I don't know," I say slowly. "But it might mean the other gods will be willing to help us."

JUDE

The Tenements
Port Naranda, Mellacea

I'm dozing when Tom slips back into his apartment, closing the door behind him.

"I thought you went to work," I mumble, cracking open one eye to be sure it's him.

"I wanted to show you this." He keeps his coat on, sinking down to sit on the edge of the bed. He's holding a newspaper.

Tom's place is in a cramped but clean boardinghouse, with easy access via the fire escape, which makes it simple for me to get in and out without his landlady noticing. I couldn't make rent on my apartment, so I packed up a small bag and sold everything else.

I've spent the night here before—I could hardly bring him back to my place, not with my mother there—but it's strange to be living here. As though I could still go back home anytime I wanted, and she'd be waiting.

I hold out my hand, and he deposits the newspaper in it.

New Leadership! the headlines scream above a picture of Laskia on the church steps, huge columns rising behind her. Church to Head State!

All down one side of the front page is a list of service times at every church in the city, reminding people there'll be multiple services a day and that they can return if the building is at capacity. After her arrival in town, the way she demolished a path to the temple, then preached from the steps, Laskia *owns* this city.

I don't know how she's handling the magic, but they're saying around the tenements that if you want to roll the dice, you can head to the Gem Cutter, and something will happen. If you survive it, you're rich—but changed, they say, different. If you don't . . . well, that was the gamble.

In this poor part of town, and with religion sweeping through the masses, there's no shortage of takers. If I were to make my own bet, I'd say Laskia's using them like she used the sailors, and dumping her power into them.

What I'm really wondering about are the ones that survive having a portion of a god's power poured into them. What's happening to *them*?

"Second page," says Tom, and I realize I'm still staring at the list of church services. When I flip the page, he reaches across to tap a smaller article with his fingertip.

> *. . . and with war on the horizon, it is rumored there will soon be an announcement regarding a military national service model, conscripting citizens of appropriate ages and allocating them to brigades in an effort to hasten mobilization . . .*

"Seven hells." A high-pitched laugh that has nothing to do with humor escapes me. "We can't join the army."

"I'd really rather not," Tom agrees, and when I glance up at him, I can see the fear behind his light words. What little afternoon sunlight we get in here makes him look like a sketch in the newspaper, his dark copper hair turned charcoal, his pale skin too white.

"The plan is the same," I say. "We get the money for train tickets, we go. Nusraya is still letting people over the border, provided they're just transiting through. They can't conscript us if we're not here."

"You're right," he says quietly. I straighten his coat—avoiding touching the ruby pin stuck in the collar—and then take hold of his lapels and pull him in for a kiss. His lips are cold from the outside air, but after a moment, he smiles.

"Go to work," I say, releasing him. "Get paid. I'll keep working on the list."

And so he goes. But it feels like we're trying to run up a mountain made of quicksand—the price of train tickets keeps going up as those who don't want to be caught up in Mellacea's war scramble to leave. Whatever we earn, it's never enough.

There's no getting back to sleep now, so I roll out of bed and get dressed, pulling my flat cap down over my face and turning up the collar of my coat. Picking up the box of books he's left packed up in the corner, I head down the fire escape.

There's a sense of hurry in the streets outside, but that's not unusual. Everyone in the tenements is always hustling for something, finding a way to put together next week's rent, searching for that impossible thing: a pathway out of here.

The streets grow brighter as I leave our territory behind and head into a better part of town with the box of books. The buildings aren't huddled over me anymore, but the hurry I sense in the crowd is still the same.

Tom thought it would be smart to walk to a richer neighborhood to sell his books—there's only a market for his old furniture in the tenements, where people are willing to accept something as shabby as he's selling, but people read everywhere, right?

I didn't even know until yesterday that Tom liked to read. Novels, by the look of it. Some full of action, some full of romance. It feels like such a waste now. I could have known this all along—I could have been getting to know *him*—if I hadn't kept him at arm's length.

It's only a twenty-minute walk to the place he told me about—the little bookstore has a brick frontage and offices above it, and I can see the piles and piles of secondhand books through the arched windows on the ground floor. *Jacob's Books and Papers,* says the sign hanging outside, and I duck in through the door with the box of books held in front of me. It's warm inside, and it smells like a library.

"Ah," says the old man behind the counter, peering at me through round gold-rimmed glasses. "I spy a young man with a box full of new worlds. Have you come to sell or to exchange, my boy?"

"Sell." I make my way forward to set the box on the counter, bracing for the inevitable withdrawal when he spots my scraped knuckles, my black eye.

Instead, he only winces. "Inspired by this one, I see," he says, tapping the spine of one of the books. I glance down at the title. *A Thousand Battles.*

Without meaning to, I huff a laugh. "Something like that. Will you take these?"

"Yes, indeed," he says, studying the titles properly, running a finger along them as he reads each in turn. "Nothing particularly rare here, but most of them are in reasonable condition. I can give you two dollars for the box."

I bite my lip. "That's all?"

"I'm afraid that's generous," he says. "I understand if you'd prefer not to part with them, of course."

"No." I push the box across the counter. "I'll take the two dollars."

He carefully stows the box away and then hands over two gold coins, placing them carefully in my palm. "You know, I have something else," he says, holding up a hand to keep me in place.

I wait as he bends down to search the packed shelves beneath the counter, and then he straightens up to offer me a battered little paperback, so slim it's more a booklet than a novel. *Alinorish Children's Tales,* reads the cover.

"I don't think there'll be a market for this one anytime soon," he says, rueful. "And I do hate to see a book left alone. Perhaps, with your accent, you might find a use for it."

I walk the long way back to Tom's room. We need the two dollars just to feed ourselves today. How are we ever going to catch up with the price of a ticket?

It was so easy to say yes when he came to the funeral, like a knight showing up to rescue me. When he told me we were both alone, it made sense.

But Tom is a good guy. All we ever had before now was an occasional—and only ever physical—relationship, for all that he wanted more. For all that a part of me—buried under anger, fear, and shame—wanted more too. And he has no idea what I've done. No idea I was at Laskia's side when all this began. That I helped make it happen.

We have enough for one ticket right now, and it's getting harder and harder to see why I shouldn't just put him on a train to somewhere safe. By now, Leander and the government of Alinor must have heard about Laskia's return. Is Port Naranda about to become a war zone? I can't anticipate their response, but I know they *will* respond. And Laskia will escalate whatever that response is, and if I don't get Tom away from here—away from *me*—then he and his copper curls and his easy smile will be caught right in the center of the hurricane.

It feels as though the little book tucked in my back pocket is a message. That my brief dream of escaping this life was only ever that: a flimsy dream, bound to dissolve in the harsh light of reality.

LEANDER

The Grand Ballroom
Kirkpool, Alinor

"You look like the sea itself," Kiki tells Selly, with an apologetic glance for the fact that she's reaching up underneath Selly's dress to tug at her slip until the wrinkles smooth out. "Beautiful, unknowable, and capable of disappearing your enemies without a trace."

"I should take notes on the way you give compliments," I say, watching from a safe distance as she puts on the finishing touches.

"Many aspire to match me, but few succeed," Kiki replies loftily, shooting me a wink over her shoulder.

The fashion here is to be willowy, all straight up and down, and neither Selly nor Kiki is. Kiki is all curves, unapologetically daring in the way she dresses, unabashed about taking up space. Selly's shoulders are broad, and her muscles show when she moves.

I love that Kiki has had the tailors create a dress that celebrates Selly, rather than apologizes for her.

Selly would say it's blue and green, and show ponies like Kiki and I would say it's teal and jade and sapphire and emerald. The silk sections are pieced together flawlessly, the colors curving around each other and melding like they do in the sea itself. It's the perfect dress for a saltblood like Selly—a part of who she is, not a disguise for it.

The fabric is covered with crystal beads sewn on to echo the pattern on Selly's arms, and small green crystals wink at me from the corners of her eyes. A half cape is draped across her shoulders, leaving her upper arms bare, and green ribbons are braided through her hair. She looks like magic made human, and I can't take my eyes off her.

She's beautiful in the way that flawless tailoring can make you, but she's more beautiful still in her strength, and the jut of her jaw, and the direct gaze she trains on each of us in turn.

I hate that I've taken her from her world and put her into these clothes, among these people, learning to pretend how to be something else, and all for me.

"There," says Kiki, stepping back to study Selly. "Like a water spirit come to life."

"You look incredible," I manage, but Selly's gaze is on me, and I know the image in my mind is coming from hers. We're both back in Port Naranda, and she's showing me the green dress she bought for a few dollars and asking if I prefer this version of her. I remember exactly what I said.

I like you best with salt on your skin.

It's still true.

Kiki starts to rub a shimmery golden oil onto Selly's arms,

so her marks will seem to sparkle when she moves. Everyone who comes near her looks at them—I'd be surprised if half of the staff here could describe her face at all.

I wait until she's released to step forward, and she instinctively reaches out to brush her fingertips against mine. Sparks jump between us, and she almost hides her wince.

"All right?" I whisper, as pages and officials swirl around us, readying everything for our procession.

"Now I've seen you all dressed up, I realize that what you were wearing on the ship was your idea of going incognito," she teases, looking me up and down.

Tonight I'm in the sapphire blue of Alinor's flag, trimmed in gold. Fitted trousers are tucked into my boots, and my dark blue vest is buttoned over a white shirt, the sleeves rolled up to show off my own marks, as intricate as any on the Crescent Sea.

Kiki slips a black band up Selly's arm in silence, and a servant edges up to me, bowing low and averting his eyes as he offers me my own mourning band on his open palm. I take it carefully, without letting my fingertips brush his skin.

Here we are, dressing up while half the court is still grieving family lost on the progress fleet. Friends of mine, people I grew up with, went to school with. I haven't really let myself think about it, not yet. The only way I can honor them is to make sure we secure a new peace treaty, and others don't die.

Selly doesn't trust my sister to do that. I do—or at least, I want to.

"You remember the curtsy?" Kiki says to Selly, as we line up. "Just keep it simple. Don't get carried away—that's how disasters happen."

"Our aim today," my sister's pompous private secretary is saying, "is to reintroduce His Highness not only as the prince of Alinor but also as the Messenger of Barrica. This show of unity, and of confidence, is of the utmost importance." He pauses, glancing down at his notes and clearing his throat. "The blooms in the streets as His Highness made his way from the Temple of Barrica to the palace were extremely well received," he continues. "If there is the possibility of his producing some effect at the ball . . ." He trails off into silence when none of us respond.

It's Keegan who takes up the challenge, his grave voice coming from behind me. "Thank you for the suggestion," he says. "But I am sure we are all mindful of asking the greatest magician in Alinor, and the instrument of our goddess herself, to perform party tricks."

I almost snort, and I let my amusement distract me, at least for now. Given he saw me more or less constantly perform party tricks all through school, Keegan's rebuke is a bit rich, and I'm sure everyone around us knows this too.

"I seek only to ensure that word of the Messenger's powers spreads far and wide," the man says, gathering his dignity. "That is how we keep Alinor safe."

"That is how we keep every country around the Crescent Sea safe," I correct him quietly.

He blinks at me. "Of course, Your Highness," he agrees after a moment, though—*spirits save me*—he might as well say out loud that he has no idea why I'm concerned about the fate of anywhere else. "Ultimately, what matters is that the goddess Barrica has a Messenger. We will remind them of the power we wield."

And it will be all the more potent when Mellacea loses theirs, is the unspoken end of that sentence.

"We will be ready to proceed in two minutes," the man concludes, disappearing to inflict his clipboard on someone else.

I back up against the wall, closing my eyes and trying to tune out the power humming through me.

The barrier between my goddess and me feels thinner than ever. I don't want to fight her—I want to serve her—but I can feel the way she's pushing at my mental boundaries, testing them.

Her thoughts are preoccupied with Macean, and her urgent wish to return here more fully. It sends a shiver through me—I can't help wondering if she knows something I don't. If she can see what Laskia's up to.

Then Selly's at my side, her hand warm as she takes mine.

"Quickly, let me take a little of Barrica's power before we go out," she murmurs.

I balk, trying to stand up a little straighter. "I'm all right."

"Better here than in the middle of the dance floor," Selly replies, her voice low. "Come on, let's not argue in front of the children." When I look up, I see Keegan's gaze flicking between the two of us, but he doesn't speak. The officials ready to shepherd us out are watching from a safer distance.

Swallowing hard, I tighten my hand around hers. I let out a breath, and as I do, I let some of the power that's built up inside me flow into her. The relief is immediate—the light a little less bright, the buzz a little less loud, the pain a little less sharp. It's like I was being crushed inside a clamp, and someone has loosened the screws just a little.

Her breath catches and she tenses, her hand squeezing mine

in return. I can sense her pain, a sharp lance through her body, feel the pulse of it inside her as her veins turn to fire. Then the light on her marks flares bright—visible only to me—and settles as the power disperses through her and into the world around us.

Her breath is still coming quickly, and I can feel the effort it takes her to pretend nothing is happening. She has her knees locked, and now she's leaning against the wall beside me.

"I'm so sorry," I whisper, keeping my hand curled around hers.

She evens out her ragged breathing. "Be sorry about the shoes they want me to wear," she whispers. "That's the only thing I'm blaming you for, my prince."

She almost hides the strain of it—and I love her for the way she tries.

I make myself laugh, because that's what she's chasing with her teasing. But deep inside, like something lurking in the shadows, my fear is still there, the questions it asks still drumming through my body.

How long can we possibly keep doing this? I can feel the way it tests her body, wearing her down more every time, taking her closer to the day something breaks.

What will happen to her, when we reach that limit?

She releases my hand, and neither of us speaks as we're ushered down a hallway to wait behind a set of velvet curtains. Voices murmur on the other side of it—lots of them. They swell and give like waves, building in volume, then hushing again. Somewhere musicians are playing, their strings weaving through the conversations of the crowd.

Suddenly my mouth is dry—but no, it's not *my* mouth, it's

Selly's, our thoughts tangled together. Her hands are fists, and I gently reach out to straighten her fingers, swiping a thumb across her damp palms to stop her from rubbing them absently on her dress.

A woman with a clipboard counts down silently, holding up a hand so we can see her folding down her fingers.

Selly jumps as a fanfare begins, brassy trumpets rippling through the air. Then the curtains part, letting in a light so bright we can't see what's in front of us. The trumpets reach their peak, and walking into the light, toward the noise and the voices and the eyes of the court, Selly and I step out together.

The press of bodies around us draws back to give us room as we walk forward. Lights glint off the chandeliers and off sequins and sparkling jewelry. The murmur of voices washes over me.

Selly's steps falter, and I tuck her hand through my elbow, folding my own over it to keep her moving.

People are packed in around us, and now that I can focus, I see they're not just nobles. There are merchants too, and other professionals, all in their best clothes. There are priests in their military uniforms, standing at attention.

They're so different from the crowd we walked through just a few days ago, in Port Naranda. There, the colors were vibrant, dresses and waistcoats and scarves and ties like a box of bright jewels. Here, our royal family is in the sapphire blue of our flag, and our court is dressed in rich earth tones, in reds and golds, in browns and the sandstone of the city itself.

Augusta and Delphine sit on their thrones at the other end of the room, and to Gus's left stands Coria, arm in arm with her husband.

The crowd parts to form a path to the queen, and slowly Selly and I make our way forward. I've been in the ballroom a thousand times, but Selly makes everything new for me, and suddenly I see it as she must.

The vaulted ceiling rises high above us, its beams and pillars carved to look like they're trees and vines. Suits of armor stand on pedestals around the room, holding the hilts of their swords, the points resting on the ground.

We stop when we reach Augusta and Delphine. I bow, and Selly executes the curtsy Kiki taught her with all her natural grace.

Augusta inclines her head, her expression solemn. She's not my sister tonight, but my queen. I warned Selly it would be like this.

"I understand," she replied. "My father's a different captain in public from the man he is in private."

I wonder how she found it, taking orders from that public man after a raging argument in private. The fact that I stormed into Augusta's meeting and demanded to know her plans is simmering between my sister and me, unspoken, but clear in her level gaze.

I don't know whether I do it to relieve the tension, or to support her with a show of power, or to remind her what I have to offer, but I raise a hand, giving the crowd a moment's warning that something is going to happen. Then I set my intention, and let my power flow from me. With a barely audible creaking noise, each suit of armor decorating the room raises its sword.

The crowd gasps and presses into the middle of the ballroom, spinning around to face the empty suits. But the party guests are ignored. Each of the suits turns toward Queen Augusta and raises its sword in salute, then lowers it to bow at the waist. Having completed their homage, they return to their resting position, looking once more like they haven't moved in centuries.

A whisper of awe goes through the crowd, but Selly and I ignore it. I'm actually feeling a touch better—releasing a flicker of my power always helps.

We walk up the steps to take our place, standing on the other side of Augusta and Delphine from Coria, and gaze out across the sea of faces.

Two men step forward from the crowd, and together they bow to the queen and then walk across to do the same for me. This moment has been carefully choreographed—it's about them bowing *first* to Augusta and *then* to me. No matter our disagreements on what should happen next, my sister and I agree that there should be no confusion in the public eye about who's in charge.

A court official's voice rings out from behind us. "Sir James Tillek and the Honorable Mr. Walter Radcliffe," the herald booms, as the two gentlemen complete their bow.

And so it goes. They all gaze up at us in fascination—they're certainly looking at Selly's face now, that's for sure.

Eventually we're permitted to process to the high table. There's a brief pause as a footman tries to pull out Selly's chair and push it in for her—he gives way with relative grace once it's clear she'd rather do it herself. I reach across to fold my hand over hers once we're seated, letting our fingers weave together on the tabletop, where others can see.

I know what this place can be like—the way they look for the smallest weakness—and I'm determined to protect her from what she can hardly know is coming. I'm the reason she's here.

Someone has made an effort with the seating plan—my sisters are at the high table with us, but it's not all stuffy dignitaries. As the servants appear, reaching in to set a plate in front of each of us at exactly the same instant, my scan of our table companions reaches a cluster of younger nobles, faces I know from school.

Dana de Treval tucks a blond curl behind her ear and tilts her head, and just a moment too late, I see the way her eyes narrow. "What do you make of your meal, Miss Walker? There must be a great deal of food here that's unfamiliar to you. Some of it is certainly an acquired taste."

She delivers the question so sweetly, but she and I used to play doubles on the escanno court, and her eyes narrowed exactly the same way before she slammed a ball into an opponent's face. She always wanted to be a pair off the court, and she's clearly annoyed to see me clutching at Selly like a security blanket.

As my gaze runs further around the table, I realize we're sitting with half a dozen different people I've dated. *Spirits save me.*

Selly glances down at her plate as though she's only just noticing it. There are four little mouthfuls there, styled to look like the flowers that grow at the temple. I think there's some kind of seafood hiding beneath the petals?

"Very nice," she says, and Dana's lips part, but before she can reply, Selly continues. "The Kethosi vinefish isn't as robust when you're not eating it in port, directly off the boat, but I do like it."

Dana blinks at her, and only years of practice mean I duck my head in time to hide my smirk. Selly just smashed the ball right back across the net to Dana without missing a beat.

It's like a switch flicks inside me. Perhaps it's our bond giving me a dose of what's inside her mind, or perhaps it's just my time away from court, but suddenly I'm seeing all of this as she must see it. The money, the ceremony, the excess. The light glinting off the crystal goblets in front of us. The layers of servants, all silently ferrying dishes around. The dresses that half the women are sewn into. And it all seems so unnecessary.

It feels like everyone is playing an elaborate game, taking the ridiculousness so very seriously. And Selly is learning the rules because that's what she has to do, if she wants to make headway here—but she sees it for what it is.

What must she have thought of me, when I arrived on the *Lizabetta*?

"Tell me, Selly." It's my sister Coria, leaning around Augusta to bestow a smile on my sailor. "Do you have a favorite port? I've been lucky enough to travel a little, but of course we're so constrained. We never see anything properly, as you must."

I flash her a quick look of gratitude, and shove down the noise that's humming in my head, trying to clear my thoughts. That's what I should have done—signaled royal favor, made clear which side I expect everyone to take. But I'm having trouble focusing. With the power inside me I could upend this whole room like an earthquake, send everyone scattering like toys, but I can't focus on a single conversation.

I squeeze Selly's hand and then reach for my drink. "There's a lot that we indoor pets don't know," I agree.

And that sets the tone. Coria and I demonstrate that we're aligned with Selly. Kiki feeds her the odd question. And slowly the tide turns in her favor.

I have to duck my head to hide a laugh when one of the candles falls over during the dessert course, splattering wax on Dana's dress and nearly setting the tablecloth on fire. The air spirits are so thick around us that Selly probably didn't have to feed them more than a scrap of her supper. By this point, she's having fun, fielding questions on sailing life with ease.

"But how do you wash your hair?" Sanna—one of my more benevolent exes—asks.

"Oh, we just wait for it to rain," Selly says casually. "Then everyone strips naked and runs up on deck. There's no time for modesty, if you want a decent curl."

Sanna stares at her for a moment, head tilted in confusion, and then Selly gives way to laughter. A moment later, the rest of the table does too. Augusta preserves her queenly dignity by pretending she was talking to Delphine and missed the whole thing.

"Can I eat that?" Selly asks me, nodding to some sort of sugary mousse sitting untouched in front of me.

"All yours," I murmur, pushing it across to her. I know how it looks—sharing dessert, holding hands. These careful social calculations are second nature to me. But Selly's luminous, and I'm hers, and I want them all to see it.

Our happy little bubble lasts all the way up to the dancing.

"The what?" Selly mutters to me, her tone low and urgent.

"The dancing," I reply distractedly. "We . . ." My words

die out as I rapidly sort through all the tutoring Selly pushed through in preparation for this moment. "Nobody told you."

"Would I have this look on my face if somebody told me?" she hisses. "Of all the things to fall through the cracks, Leander. . . ."

"Ah," I say weakly. "Then you're really going to love this. The royal family kicks everything off."

Selly keeps her expression more or less under control, but when she smiles at me, I can see her teeth. "I am going to kill you," she murmurs. "With this small and useless fork I have left over because I forgot to use it to eat a single pea or something."

I reach for her hand, and together we rise to our feet as the musicians switch their tune and heads turn toward us. Augusta and Coria are already on their way down to the dance floor. "You're right," I say quietly. "This is completely my fault. You should carve me up with that fork. Slowly, because it's very small."

I'm babbling, because suddenly a part of me is back in that nightclub in Port Naranda. Lights are spinning across my face, music is throbbing in my bones, and I'm holding my hand out to Selly, asking if I can teach her to dance.

Asking if I can kiss her.

And she's saying no, because she can't imagine how we'll leave each other after that kiss.

And I'm back in the Temple of the Mother, gazing at her, knowing I'm about to die. Saying, *I wanted to teach you to dance.*

In that moment, I wanted with all my heart to go back to those few minutes in the nightclub. To dance with her and to kiss her, to tell her that we'd *find* a way to be together, we'd *make* a way.

We should have had that first dance together, for each other. Not like this.

"Everybody's looking at us," she whispers, as we approach the dance floor. "Help."

Somehow, somewhere, I dig deep inside to find one of the lazy grins that used to come so easily. "They're just admiring my outfit," I tell her. My voice softens. "Ignore them, Selly. It's just you and me."

Her eyes start to slide to one side, where a particularly keen-eyed group of nobles are staring at us. I reach out and catch her chin between my fingers, gently drawing her gaze back my way. "Eyes on me, sailor."

I can see the moment when the look in her eyes shifts—when that paralyzed fear gives way to something else. And I can feel it, in the strange, tangled space we share between our minds and hearts, when she finally sees me again, and not our audience.

"There you are," I murmur, feeling my heart give a lopsided thud in my chest. "Imagine we're back in Port Naranda, with no one the wiser as to who we are."

Her lips glint in the light—Kiki must've added shimmer there, too—as they curve into a little smile. "I'd rather imagine we're up in that balcony."

Half of me is tempted to glance up at the balcony where she kissed me, but the rest of me can't take my eyes off her face.

"Hold that thought," I whisper, just to watch her smile deepen and her eyes dance.

The musicians kick into high gear, the strings first. This isn't one of the fun, swinging songs my friends and I play on our gramophones in private, but something more stately, and that's good news. It means I can hold on to Selly the whole time, guide her.

Augusta and Delphine step out together first. My sister's always a little softer when she's dancing with her wife, and the pair of them fit together perfectly. The crowd forms a border for the dance floor, light glinting off sequins and beads, bodies shifting. Everything about it is familiar, and yet nerves—maybe Selly's nerves—are fluttering in my belly.

Then it's our turn, and there's no more time to think. Taking hold of Selly's hand, I lead her out, and we turn in to face each other. I take one of her hands, curl my other around the small of her back, and lean in to whisper to her. "I know this is against every instinct you have, but just follow my lead. I trusted you to steer the ship. This is what I know how to do. I won't let you stumble."

We're so close we can both feel the magic tingling and zipping between us as my body tries to vent into hers. And there's something more—a prickle at the base of my spine that zips up between my shoulder blades, that makes my breath catch in my throat. An awareness not of my anchor, but of *her*.

The musicians turn a corner, and then we're moving. For a moment Selly's unsure, and then I feel her understand and relax into my touch, and we're together. She's so light on her feet, her balance perfect; she makes this effortless.

The dance comes easily to me, thanks to a lifetime of lessons, and I gaze down at her as I guide us around the square the crowd have left for us. I could count every freckle across her nose and cheeks, and I can see the glint in her moss-green eyes as she gazes up at me. I can see the pulse in her throat.

She watches me watching her, and slowly, her lips curve

into another smile. I return it. I don't care how foolish I look—I can't take my eyes off her.

This is the girl I saw soaked in salt water, who huddled with me in a boat, who hid with me in alleyways. This is my Selly.

The music shifts again, and suddenly everyone is whirling onto the dance floor around us.

"Selly," I whisper, as the crowd turns into one of those perfectly spinning fractals that I always loved to watch from the balcony as a child. "How much trouble would I be in if I kissed you here, in front of everyone? Can it get worse than disemboweling me with that tiny fork?"

She laughs, and her eyes spark and hold mine. The music seems to fade away, along with the babble of conversation and the swishing of skirts and clatter of heels; the crowd seems to melt into a hazy background collage of meaningless colors and shapes. All I can see is her face, her lips as they part, about to tell me to do exactly as I want, and kiss her here, in front of everyone.

And then a scream splits the air. For a horrified moment, my mind thinks the sound is coming from Selly's parted lips—and then we're staring at each other, confused and shocked, as more screams break out in the ballroom, not far from where we stand frozen.

A terrible pressure erupts in my head, somewhere behind my temples, as a massive surge of power explodes above us. *Divine power. And not Barrica's.*

Something heavy drops down to the floor with a sickening, meaty thump.

The crowd scatters, and we're buffeted by bodies as people shove past us, trying to get away from the center of the dance floor. As each of them touches me, my magic tries to vent into them, and they recoil as if from an electric shock, ricocheting off each other and adding to the chaos.

Selly starts to shove her way *against* the current, pushing toward the source of the danger, because of course she does, and I duck my head and force my way after her.

We stumble free of the crowd to find Augusta has done the same, and the three of us stagger to a halt, frozen in place by the sight before us.

A body lies motionless on the ground, sprawled with its limbs at the kind of profoundly wrong angles that tell me immediately this person is dead.

She has deep brown skin, a shock of dark curls, and dark clothes. *My sister's spy.* This is the woman she sent to kill Laskia.

"She just appeared!" someone shrieks. "Out of thin air!"

"She just blinked out of nothing!"

The babble of voices around us rises to fever pitch, and I block them out, moving with Selly to crouch by the broken body. She keeps her hand on my arm, tightening her fingers when she feels me beginning to tremble.

Augusta is still frozen, her face ashen, with Coria now whispering urgently in her ear.

Selly manages to speak first, and her voice is miraculously steady. "It was probably too much to hope for that Laskia could be so easily . . ." I feel her eyes on me, her fear bubbling away at the bond between us. "Could you do that? Send someone all the way to Mellacea with your power?"

I swallow and nod, distracted by the fragmented thoughts rampaging around my head. "Yes. Yes, I could."

Behind me, the guards have staggered into action, falling

into their roles like damaged cogs in a bit of machinery, holding back the crowds pressing in for a better look at the carnage. I can hear them shouting orders, funneling people out of the ballroom, setting up a perimeter.

"She couldn't have chosen a better moment for maximum carnage," Selly whispers. "Are you all right?"

I force myself to get a grip, shaking my head and commanding my lungs to work again, and suck in a breath with effort. "I could feel it," I reply. "Feel her. Laskia. Selly . . . this is a message."

I finally tear my eyes away from the horrific sight of my sister's dead spy and meet Selly's gaze. Her eyes are wide and fearful, but stubborn, too, in that way she has of bracing herself, battening down her defenses in the face of an oncoming storm.

"What's the message?" she asks.

I shiver. "She's coming for us."

LASKIA

The Gem Cutter
Port Naranda, Mellacea

I collapse on the red velvet couch, exhausted, but more clear-headed than I've been since . . . since.

That effort took enough of my magic that for a glorious moment I feel almost free of it—no buzzing clouding my mind, no restlessness moving my limbs. I can think clearly, see clearly. It feels incredible, like being able to breathe through my nose after a terrible cold, only a thousand—ten thousand—times better.

A gulp of near-hysterical laughter tries to bubble up my throat, and I lift both hands to cover my face, trying to keep my composure.

I can't believe I did that. I can't believe it worked.

But also, I *can*. More and more, I'm realizing just how far my power goes. And I know it's Macean in my head, flowing through my veins, pushing me beyond the risks I dreamed of. I just don't care.

"Pleased with yourself?" Dasriel rumbles, looking down at the place where the dead spy lay at his feet a moment before.

"What does it take to impress you?" I ask, lowering my hands and gazing up at him. "All the way across the *continent*, Dasriel. I even caught an echo of the screaming. I wasn't fair to First Councilor Tariden. His spy network was actually very capable. Too late to tell him now."

Dasriel's injured hand is cradled against his chest in a sling, and because it's his dominant hand, his head and jaw are still dark with stubble. He looks tired.

"Every time you do something like that, you roll the dice," he says quietly.

I can't help laughing. "Dasriel, look at the god I worship. What else should I do?"

He simply shakes his head. "You should remember that no matter how many times you roll the dice and come out ahead, eventually the house always wins."

SELLY

The Royal Palace
Kirkpool, Alinor

Augusta called an emergency meeting, and we're not invited. She's in a room with her top advisers, and she doesn't want Leander and me there, arguing against a war.

"We'll talk before dawn," she said, immaculate in her ball gown, but at that moment looking every inch the queen of a warrior goddess.

Being left out suits us fine. Leander, Keegan, and I rushed back to Leander's quarters, kicked out every attendant, and now we're huddled in the center of the room, heads down and whispering, because Leander can't guarantee there aren't spies in the walls. Panic courses through me, and my hands are cold—I ball them into fists and then open them again, trying to push feeling into fingers.

This is like the moment we realized the *Lizabetta* was being chased. A moment when you desperately want to be somewhere else, anywhere else—but there's no option to walk away.

"We have until dawn to do something," Leander says softly. "When we talk to Augusta, she'll tell us we're mobilizing. And once she orders me to go with the army, I'll be faced with either obeying her or telling my queen I refuse, and either one of those ends badly."

Keegan raises his hand as though he's in class. Our gazes snap across to him, and after a moment, he speaks. "I have a plan so badly formed that I honestly can't even call it a plan. It's more like a collection of ideas loitering in the same general vicinity."

"This isn't the moment to hold back," I whisper. "Whatever you have, tell us."

"It's from the old letters I've been reading," he begins. "In the palace library. The way I see it, the gods need a doorway to come through, to return to our world. Barrica clearly needs one, or she wouldn't be trying so hard to push Leander to make it happen."

Leander nods slowly, his shoulders round with tension.

"There's a line in one of the old texts I was going through," Keegan says, digging in his pockets and producing a scrap of paper. "Here. *And when the gods travel between our place and their own, they must do so through a gateway. The gateway must be guarded zealously, for should it be destroyed, the god's way into our world would be lost.*"

"Leander's the gateway for Barrica," I say softly.

"And Laskia will be for Macean," Keegan agrees. "I think it was a safety measure the other gods created, or insisted on. A way to control them if they did try to return here."

"An emergency measure."

"So what we need is a way to stop Laskia from *being* a

Messenger," I suggest. "If we do that, we solve two problems at once. There's no longer any chance of our two Messengers meeting in battle, and there's no way for Macean to awaken and return."

"Can't fault your logic," Leander murmurs. "Please tell me this is the part where you have an idea for how to do it."

"I . . ." Keegan pauses. "This is the part where it really isn't a plan. An assassination probably would have done the trick, but I don't think we can assume future efforts will work any better than tonight's attempt."

"But what else can we do from here?" Leander asks, helpless. "There are limits to my power, Keegan. I know she just transported someone across the continent, but I can't do that to Laskia. She's as powerful as I am."

"I know. But what I also know from the letters is that the other gods were very much against anyone returning to our realm in the future. They left themselves a small, limited influence in the Temple of the Mother, just in case they needed to act somehow."

"In *any* Temple of the Mother?" I ask. "Or just the one on the Isles?"

"Any, I'm fairly sure. Those writing the letters hadn't been to the Isles, so they must have been referring to the temples in their city. Perhaps even the one here in Kirkpool. All I can think to do is go to the temple and appeal for their help."

There's a short silence as Leander and I consider the many barriers between us and the Temple of the Mother—which is outside the palace, in the city—and the many blank spaces in our plan.

"I don't have a better idea," I say eventually. "If they're

truly against their siblings returning, then if they can help us, surely they will."

"They may grant us some wisdom, some aid," Keegan agrees. His blue eyes meet mine, and I'm sure he's thinking the same thing I am.

If we can find a way to turn Laskia back from a Messenger to just a human, could we do that for Leander? A part of me isn't entirely sure he'd want it—for all the pain he's in, I can sense the bond between him and Barrica, and sense it growing deeper each day.

But perhaps Keegan and I can rescue him from this, with or without his cooperation.

"This feels like a terrible night to slip out of the palace," I mutter, glancing at the servants' door that Leander snuck us out of when we went to the greenhouse. My body is singing with tension at the prospect of weaving our way among the palace officials, Queensguard, and nobles who'll all be turning toward their Messenger tonight. And that's before we head into the city itself. "This is where your knowledge of secret passages comes in, though, right?"

"No need," Leander says quietly, distracted. "Nobody will see us."

"What do you—"

Leander doesn't reply, but crosses to the main door to his quarters and simply walks out, looking neither right nor left.

Keegan and I lunge after him as one.

"Leander!" I whisper, grabbing his arm. "We can't just—"

He doesn't respond—doesn't turn his head or acknowledge that he's heard me. He just keeps walking, dragging me with him. And after a few steps I realize he's doing it again, just as he did in the ballroom, when we crept away to the balcony.

Nobody's looking at us, nobody's making eye contact . . . but everyone is subtly shifting course to veer around us. My skin prickles, a chill running through me. It's as if they know we're here, but not enough to really register who we are, or whether we should be walking down the hallway toward the forecourt.

"Should we try the garden gate?" Keegan asks quietly. "The one Selly and I took to get to the port?"

Leander doesn't reply, doesn't look back. He simply walks toward the huge double doors that lead outside. They're propped open, Queensguard coming and going, and at just the moment we want to pass through them, they're suddenly clear.

My prince is crackling with magic—I'm surprised I can't see sparks jumping off him.

We emerge into the palace forecourt, a huge space paved with cobblestones and hemmed in by golden sandstone buildings on all sides, though the moonlight has turned everything silver tonight.

The place is a hive of activity—Queensguard and regular military are rushing back and forth, clearly preparing to mobilize, and it feels like walking through a hail of gunfire without a single bullet hitting us, the way the three of us walk through the chaos untouched.

"The gates, though," I murmur to Keegan. "The guards might not notice *us,* but they really won't see them opening?" The palace gates are easily three times my height—they're made of wrought iron with a pattern so intricate that only pinpricks of light show through. During the daytime they're often open, the rabble kept out by the Queensguard, but tonight they're firmly shut.

Leander stops when he reaches them and holds out a hand to each side. Keegan and I walk forward to take them—Keegan hisses through his teeth at the unfamiliar bite of Leander's magic pushing its way into him—and then the three of us walk toward the gate . . .

. . . and through the gate.

It feels as though every ounce of blood in my veins has turned icy—like I can feel cold liquid pushing through me—and then we're stepping onto the street outside the palace. I drag in a breath of what suddenly feels like warm air, though it was the crisp coolness of early winter just a moment ago. Keegan's eyes are wide and wild, and when Leander releases his grip on us, Keegan holds up his hands to stare at them, like they might not actually be there.

Word of what happened tonight has clearly left the palace—not a surprise, I suppose, given how many guests saw Laskia dump a dead body in the middle of the party. I'd have expected panic out here, but these are Barrica's people, and that's more true every day.

They're gathering weapons. They want a fight.

Are we the only ones left in the city who want to avoid a war?

We make our way down Royal Hill, and none of us speak as we wind our way through the streets to the Temple of Barrica. The last time we were here, it was after our ecstatic arrival into the harbor—the streets were lined with cheering citizens, and Leander was only just restored to himself. It's only been a few days since then, but it feels like a lifetime.

The temple faces a large, circular open space. There's a fountain at the center, glimmering in the moonlight, and around the edge of the open space are smaller temples. They're devoted to the other gods and visited by sailors, merchants, and travelers from different countries.

There's no temple for Macean—he's unwelcome in Alinor—and the temple for Valus has been converted into a garden and memorial, but five still stand for Dylo, Kyion, Sutista, Oldite, and the Mother.

As we make our way toward the Temple of the Mother, I can't help thinking about what happened the last time we set foot in her space, back on the Isles.

That was the moment everything changed. The moment we lost Leander, and got him back.

What will happen this time?

KEEGAN

The Temple of the Mother
Kirkpool, Alinor

The altar is at the center of the temple, with rows of pews ringing the open space in concentric circles. Aisles cut through them like spokes on a wheel, and at the end of each of them, closest to the altar, is a statue of one of the gods. I've never been here before, but the temple feels strangely familiar—the soaring architecture should intimidate me, but instead I feel almost at home.

As we walk toward the space around the altar, my mind is still on what we just saw outside. On the garden that marks the place where the Temple of Valus once stood.

The youngest of the gods, his domain was merriment and tricks. He was worshipped in Vostain, the country that is no more. It was destroyed in the last great clash between Barrica and Macean, and the wastelands where it stood are called the Barren Reaches.

What was once his homeland is now home to the Bibliotek—

the greatest repository of knowledge in the world, built on a place that reminds us to act with great care, lest we end up like the people of Vostain.

The Mother is worshipped at the Bibliotek, for more than one reason. First, knowledge is her domain. But beyond that, she is the only one powerful enough to hold sway in the place her son's people were obliterated.

Valus's people are gone, dead for centuries, and his temples were reduced to rubble in the same moment his country died. Why didn't I think of what that would mean for tonight's attempt?

I make myself speak the words, though they stick in my throat, trying to choke me. "They're not all here."

"What do you mean?" Selly asks, swinging around to inspect the statues. They stand about twice our height, and it's not quite the dark of the night that makes it hard to see their faces—or perhaps just to remember what their faces look like, after you glance away.

"Valus," I say slowly. "He's not here."

"He's right there," she insists, pointing at his youthful figure posed with one hand on his hip.

"That's a statue."

"Keegan, they're all—"

"No, I mean he has no worshippers left. He's in mourning for his people; he has been for centuries. He's no longer tethered to our realm, not without his people. He won't be able to answer us. He probably wouldn't want to anyway."

There's silence for a moment as Selly absorbs that. Leander doesn't appear to be listening.

"Well, it's still the best idea we have," she says eventually.

"And we're here. We've still got four gods, or maybe even five, if Barrica can join us too—she'd want to help disempower Macean's Messenger, right? Close the door to him?"

"One can hope," I agree. "I think we should press on."

A voice rings out from the shadows between the statues of Sutista and Oldite. "I'm not so sure that's a good idea."

I recognize the voice, but for a moment I can't place it. Then, as I swing toward the source, just before I see her, it clicks.

"E-Elga," I stammer, the strangest feeling sweeping through my limbs. It's as though my body has heard something in her tone that my brain can't quite understand yet. I scramble for an explanation. "What are you doing here? Did you have the same idea?"

She has her arms folded across her chest, and I see her clearly now. She's dressed in black, her librarian's uniform gone. "If I were capable of having the same ideas as you, I wouldn't have had to follow you along all your winding paths."

"Keegan?" says Selly slowly, wariness in her tone.

I'm cold all over. "This is Elga," I say, still trying to put the pieces together. "She's been helping me find my research materials. She's a . . . librarian."

But the word nearly chokes me. The ill-fitting uniform. The way she asked me what I wanted, never venturing an opinion of her own.

"Or at least, she was *posing* as a librarian," I manage, hoarse with anger. "To assume the mantle of one of those sacred guardians of knowledge is the most heinous breach of trust."

Elga grimaces, but keeps her distance. "I actually felt kind of bad about it," she confides. "You're sweet."

"I'm stupid. I can't believe I told you to be more *confident*." My initial outrage is already boiling away, leaving a clear-eyed fury in its wake. She's betrayed me. She's here for a reason. I need to find out what it is. "You're Mellacean," I say, trying the idea out loud, the words bitter on my tongue.

She shrugs, as if to say, *What can you do?*

"Was it all fake?" I demand, a new, horrifying thought lancing through me. "Were the letters real?"

"Oh yes," she replies. "Like I said, if I could have figured this out myself, I would have. I wasn't trying to lure you off the trail. I needed you to sniff out answers for me. I made sure you had everything you needed, Keegan." She sounds as though she actually thinks she's done me some sort of favor.

I glance at the others. Selly looks like she wants to physically attack Elga. Leander, on the other hand, is expressionless. He's gazing at the Mellacean, assessing her, but his mind is at least half elsewhere.

"Who's your friend?" Selly asks.

For a moment, I'm about to reply—*Elga, I told you*—and then Elga turns her head, and I see the shadowy figure behind her.

"That . . . is complicated," Elga replies. "I assume you're here to appeal for help in dealing with the Messenger of Macean? I was thinking the same thing, after the letters. I sent word home for instructions, but I've been staking this place out, just in case you made a move before I heard." Her forehead creases, and she glances at the door. "Strangest thing, actually. I didn't see you come in."

"Who's your friend?" Selly grits out, her expression growing

more murderous as Elga continues in her conversational tone.

"My boss sent him over," Elga replies, which isn't really an answer.

Finally, Leander speaks. "He has Laskia's power in him," he says softly.

Selly gapes. "That's her anchor? How is he so far from her?"

"No, not her anchor," Leander replies. "Just some of her power."

I get a better look at the boy's face when he walks forward. His expression is frighteningly blank, and he's so white he looks bloodless. His newsie's cap is askew, his shirt filthy. Lips slightly parted, eyes staring, unblinking.

There are small lines of light crackling between his fingertips—raw power. It feels like the air is full of static.

Like something's about to happen.

Then Leander's shouting and surging forward. "Watch out!"

LEANDER

*The Temple of the Mother
Kirkpool, Alinor*

T he boy hurls a bolt of pure magic at me, blunt and brutal, meant to be a weapon and nothing else.

I raise my hands, creating a shield half a heartbeat before it strikes—his volley ricochets off and lands on the ground between two statues, leaving a long scorch mark on the stone floor.

"Get behind me!" I gasp, and I sense rather than see Selly and Keegan move. I can feel it rolling off the boy—the urge to leap, to throw himself at me without a care for his own safety. The undeniable, unquenchable pull of *risk*.

His god is in him now, and my goddess is barreling through my mind with the deafening roar of a train in a tunnel—with the battle cry of a thousand armies, of swords banging against shields, all furious, all calling for blood.

I can throw an attack at him in return, I know this—I can

do *anything*. I need only think it, and my magic surges to make it so, desperate for the outlet.

Barrica roars in the distant place of her exile, and when I hold out my hand, a spear appears—that same spear that glows white on the flag of Alinor. I feel her rejoice, feel her carry me forward like a wave sweeping a ship before it, and I start toward the boy.

He raises his hands once more, and I see the power spark there, and I know what he is.

He hasn't the power of Laskia—he's just like an arrow nocked in a bowstring. She's filled him with magic, she's pulled him taut, and she's sent him flying in my direction. He'll spend all the power he has, and then there'll be nothing left of him.

He hurls another bolt of magic at me, and I catch it and throw it back in his direction, stalking toward him for the kill. I'm Leander, and I'm Barrica, and I'm a thousand warriors who've fought by her side, every one of them reveling as they lift their arms for the killing blow.

Somewhere far away, someone is screaming my name.

I heft the spear, and drive it down toward him.

He lifts his hands, and magic blooms between us.

And then it explodes.

Time slows so perfectly that I can see the moment his eyes glaze, and feel the moment his heart stops. I watch him drop toward the floor at what feels like a fraction of the speed he should.

Someone is screaming my name.

I watch the magic, the force of our meeting, start to ripple out from both of us.

Selly!

I turn, twisting my body and launching myself back toward her. I have time only to throw up a shield, to curve it around the three of us, so Selly, Keegan, and I can kneel inside, my body sheltering theirs, as the world turns white around us.

Silence.

And then a ringing in my ears. I lift my head, and the white is no longer light, but dust falling from the sky, catching the moonlight that streams in where the roof of the temple used to be.

The pews are matchsticks, the statues are rubble, the pillars have collapsed to the floor. The whole, massive structure is in ruins.

The boy in the cap is simply *gone,* and I can see what's left of the Mellacean spy crushed beneath a chunk of rock.

And then *she* comes for me.

A wave of Barrica's ferocity sweeps through me, and I am larger than my body, bigger than myself. I am invincible. I know that she was *never* Barrica the Sentinel.

She has always been Barrica the Warrior.

She has seen a thousand battlefields, and now I see them before me. I hear the cries of pain, the scream of beasts. I hear the clash of swords and shields. I am at war. I am standing on the deck of a ship, and I am crawling through the mud. I am charging across a meadow. I am in a brawl, the fight itself a living creature that pushes and swells around me.

I am standing opposite my opponent—just the two of us,

knowing only one can walk away. I am a part of every battle, large and small, my goddess has seen since time began. I am blood, and sweat, and pain, and I am *determination*. I will die before I surrender.

Leander!

It takes me a moment to realize that I'm hearing my name.

Leander!

It's Selly—forcing her way into my mind, heaving for breath, *making* a place for herself beside me on the battlefield. All around us, swords ring out, and the cries of the dying echo in the air. I look across at her and try to understand what she wants. I can't hear what she's saying, only read it on her lips:

Come home.

She holds out her hand, and without thought, without hesitation, I reach for her, my fingers curling tightly around hers.

And then the chaos is gone, and I am snapped back to my place, where I kneel in the ruins of the Temple of the Mother. I am human again, every part of my body in pain, gasping for the breath my body still needs.

And my goddess herself stands before me.

She is here, and she is real.

She has returned.

LASKIA

*The Temple of Macean
Port Naranda, Mellacea*

His rage sears me. I am on fire.
Macean comes at me in quick flashes. Each is no longer than a single heartbeat, but in those moments, I know the vastness of my god.

He is awakening.

I grab Ruby by one arm, yanking her to her feet, and stagger toward the main room of the Gem Cutter.

The door is in my way—with one gesture, I break it into splinters. The jagged edges catch at my clothes as I stumble through.

There's a meeting under way at one of the tables, where groups of diners used to eat and gossip before they took to the dance floor. Now it's surrounded by green sisters and government officials.

Every head snaps around to take me in as I stagger to a halt.

"He is awakening," I rasp, nearly choking on the words. "She has returned, and he is awakening. I need more strength. I need *prayer*."

The deepest of instincts tells me this is true. He must fight his way from sleep, and for that, he needs all our strength.

I need prayer.

While the others gape at me, Beris shoots to her feet and turns to scan the novices nearby. "Ashara, go!" she snaps at one. "Run like your life depends on it—tell them to ring the bells, to summon the sisters."

The girl only stares at her, as though she's said something outrageous.

"This is our life's work in the balance, you stupid girl," Beris snaps. "Go!"

As if the word releases her from a slingshot, the novice is gone, the front door to the nightclub rebounding and slamming in her wake.

"She will summon green sisters from all over the city," Beris says urgently, moving toward me. "They will come to the church, and we must join them there."

I can't reply. I am splitting at the seams. I will come apart with the power that is in me. My god will tear me apart on his way through to our world.

Unless I am stronger.

I press into Ruby's mind, bind her to me anew. Make her understand that she must follow me—I cannot keep hold of her, cannot drag her with me.

And then, my sister following unwillingly in my wake, I stagger toward the door. I lift my hand to twist my fingers into a fist and bring down the wall before me, walking straight out into the alleyway.

I turn toward New Street, in the direction of the temple. I prepare myself to walk through anything in my way until I reach it.

I stumble forward, nearly tripping on the cobblestones. Then Beris catches up with me, panting, hair askew for the first time in all the years I've known her. There's a layer of dust across the shoulders of her green robe from the hole I left in the club's wall.

"An auto," she gasps. "An auto will be faster."

I blink at her, but she simply strides into the middle of New Street and holds up her hand. The line of autos heading toward us screech to a halt, and I hear a series of bangs and the shattering of glass as one after another rear-ends the auto in front. A chorus of angry horns rises, but the front auto, nearest us, is still intact.

Beris strides toward it and climbs in beside the protesting driver. I follow and somehow get myself into the back seat, where I sprawl on the cool leather. Ruby lands beside me.

Beris says something. The auto takes off with a jerk. I know nothing except pain, except the looming presence of Macean. His sister has returned, and he will roll any dice, take any risk, to match what she has done.

Wait, I beg him. *Wait, and I will make a door.*

By the time we reach the church, the green sisters are arriving. They have bundled up their robes above their knees and they are *running* toward us from all directions, pouring in from across the city in answer to the signal the bells have sent them.

Onlookers stop to stare as the women elbow their way past them, nearly tripping in their haste to climb the steps.

They are past the great columns outside the church and pouring through the huge double doors, but then they stop, and they make a space for me.

Their faces are ecstatic as I cross the threshold.

The urge of the Gambler is growing. The god of risk is in me, and I no longer care if his coming will tear me apart. The Gambler and I are one—we will throw the dice, and come what may, we will laugh at the result.

I drop to my hands and knees before the altar.

At first, I think I am unsteady—I think I'm swaying, that I can no longer control my body. And then I realize the very earth is shaking beneath me, the stained glass windows above are shattering and raining shards onto the ground.

Behind me the sisters raise their voices in prayer, chanting as one, and the whole world builds to an unbearable peak.

Everything is pain.

Somewhere there is Ruby, and she screams as I ground myself through her like lightning, pouring this magic into her.

And then I am in my body again, and I hear his laughter, and all is still around us.

I sit back on my heels and gaze up, then up, then *up* into his green eyes, and take in his cruel, beautiful smile.

"*At last,*" says the god of risk, in a voice like velvet. He stretches, the movement exaggerated, soaking up the response of the adoring sisters around us. "*That was far too long a sleep. Now tell me, my faithful Messenger: What did I miss?*"

PART THREE

ROLL OF THE DICE

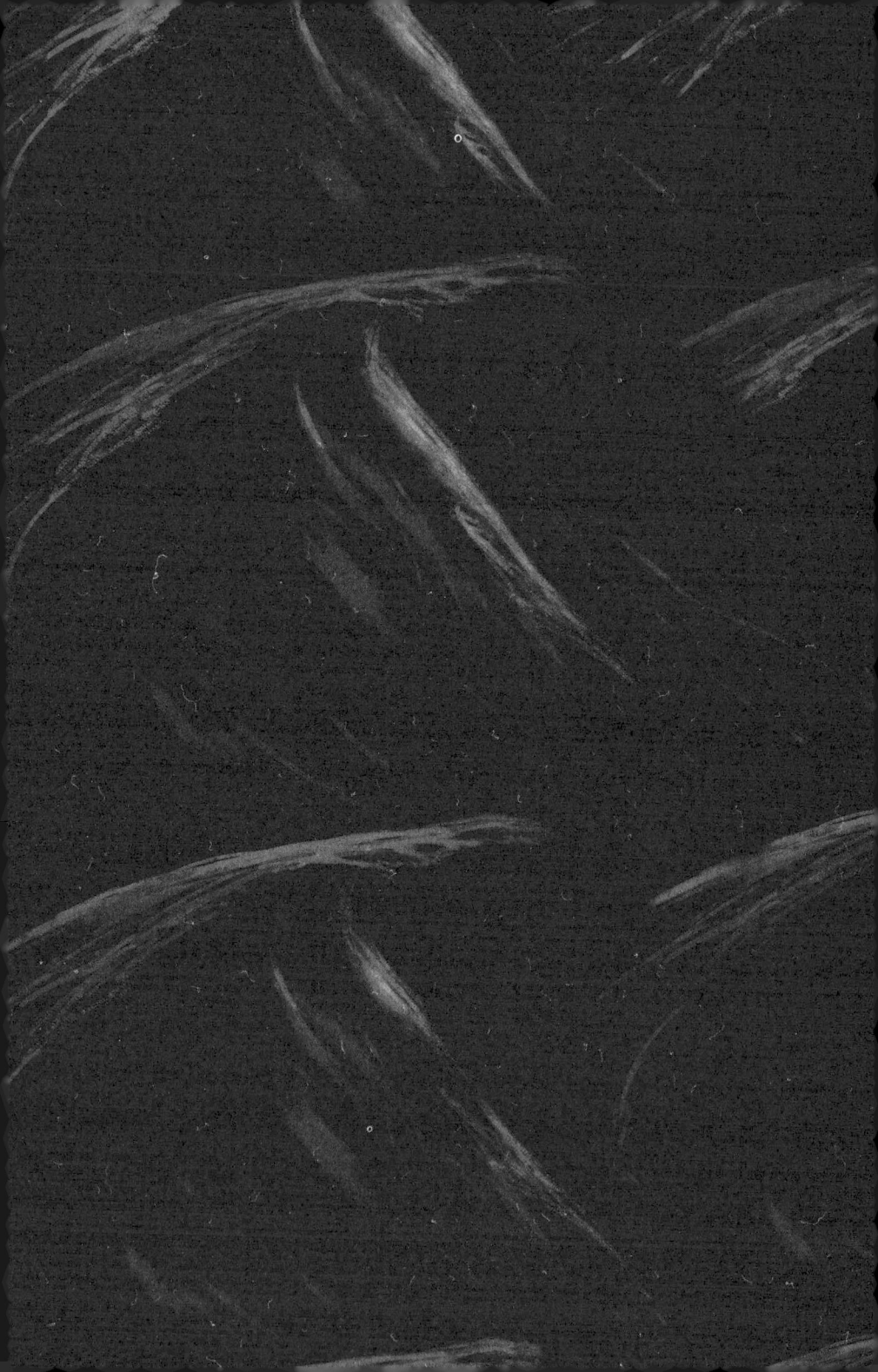

JUDE

Central Station
Port Naranda, Mellacea

"What do you mean, you stole a watch?" Tom's staring at me with worried gray eyes, half-awake, and sitting bare-chested in a pile of the blankets we've been using to save on heating.

"I mean I stole a watch," I lie, from my place in the doorway. "And fenced it for the ticket money. I'm not proud, but I promise you this man was wealthy. He'll have another half a dozen pocket watches just like it. This was *not* a man who needed the money—we're not stopping him from leaving the city by doing this. When we get to Fontesque, I'll donate twice as much to charity, I swear it."

"Jude . . ." For a guy who works for a gangster, Tom has an odd set of morals, but that's one of the things I like most about him. He still has a compass. He follows it.

"It's done," I say gently. "The tickets are bought. Tom, it's time to go. If we don't, I don't think we're getting out of the city at all."

He gazes at me for a long moment, and I see the moment he concedes in the softening of his shoulders, the slow release of his breath.

"Get dressed," I say, relief washing through me like a wave up a beach, erasing all the marks of guilt and deceit that were etched in the sand. "We don't have long." I have to get him moving before he asks to see the tickets.

I pack up a bag for each of us as Tom pulls on his clothes, and I glance sidelong at him, watching the way he moves. He's graceful, for someone as tall and broad-shouldered as he is.

I told him what I've done, last night. We sat in the dark, and he held me, and I told him all of it—Laskia, the prince's fleet, the journey to the Isles themselves. I told him where I was born, and who my friends were at school, and that I'd hunted them.

I poured all that darkness out of me, and he sat quietly, holding my hands, calm and open. It felt like I was bleeding, like I was cutting myself open, showing him all the worst parts of what I am. But he had to know.

I was braced for the revulsion to finally arrive on his face. For him to pull his hands away, for his lip to curl. For him to turn his head, and look at something—anything—that wasn't me. I was waiting for him to understand.

But when it was done, and he'd dried my tears, he kissed me.

"You chose none of that, Jude," he whispered. "Your choices are what make you who you are. And now you're choosing to leave it all behind."

And that was when I knew I'd do far worse than steal a pocket watch to get this boy out of Port Naranda, and to safety.

The station is crammed with bodies, and there's a frantic note in the air—an edge to the shouts that ring out as people search for each other, a sharpness to the whistles the guards blow as they try to bring order. Everyone's pushing and shoving as though the great clock that ticks above the tracks is counting down to disaster.

The city is divided into two groups right now: Macean's people, who laugh and celebrate and welcome the uncertainty of our future with open arms—and everyone else. Everyone who looks to another god, or no god, is running for their lives.

I grab Tom's hand as we approach our platform—number five—and pull him out of the flow of bodies for a moment. "The train's going to be packed," I say, raising my voice above the noise around us. "There's no chance we'll be able to get off at any of the stops for anything to eat. I'm going to get us some food."

He shakes his head and reaches for my arm. "We should stay together."

I can feel something cracking inside me, and I tug him in for a quick kiss to hide it, curving my hand around the back of his neck, tangling it in his hair for just a moment. When I draw back, I'm composed again. "I have time, and if you faint on me, how am I supposed to carry you? I'll be right behind you."

He hesitates, cupping my face and running a thumb over my cheekbone. He's so careful to avoid the edge of my black eye.

"Go," I say again, handing him my bag. "Get these stowed."

And though he wants to argue—I can see it on his face—we're out of time, and so he grabs my bag and turns to join the line of passengers.

I force myself to drag air into my lungs, force myself to push it out again, because my work isn't done, not yet. Tom waits to present his ticket to the guard at the gate, and I walk back along it, letting the crowd hide me from his view as I scan the people behind him.

I choose a Nusrayan couple. She's round-faced with warm brown skin and a kind smile, her head shaved to the soft fuzz the Nusrayans prefer. He's tall and watchful, one arm curled around his wife to keep her from being jostled.

"Excuse me." I slip into place alongside them, pulling out the best version of a smile I can muster, to try and counterbalance the fact that I look like a thug who lost a fight. "I'm sorry to bother you. That's my boyfriend up there—the tall one, the redhead."

The woman starts to shuffle to one side, thinking I want to jump into the line and making space, and her husband cranes his neck, nodding when he spots Tom.

I take a deep breath. "He thinks I'm coming to join him," I say. "But we only had enough money for one ticket."

There was no stolen pocket watch, no fence, no lucky eleventh-hour ticket money. There was just a lie I'd tell a thousand times, to keep Tom safe.

The woman softens, her lips parting, and she reaches out to take my hand. "Oh, sweet boy. I'm so sorry, we don't have anything to give you. If I could buy you a ticket—"

"No." My voice is too sharp as I cut her off, and I stop,

make myself moderate my tone. "No, I don't need money. I'm just asking—I'm begging—please, follow him. Get into the same carriage. When he realizes I'm not coming, stop him from getting off the train." My voice threatens to break; my throat tightens, and I try to swallow. "I need to know he's safe. He has to get out of here."

Her eyes fill with the tears that I can't allow myself, and that almost undoes me. "Oh, sweet boy," she says again, and it's the care in her tone that kills me. It's so much more than I deserve—if only she knew. "Of course. Amos will keep him on the train."

The big man's jaw clenches, and with a pained expression, he nods. "We'll see him over the border, son," he says quietly. "I'd do the same in your place. I'll act for you on this."

"Thank you," I manage—and then I have to whirl away, force a path through the crowd, get away from both of them, from Tom, to whom the last thing I said was *Get these stowed.* Such stupid, nothing words. Because if I'd said anything important, he would have seen my lie in my face.

He has both our bags, full of everything I could fit that might help build a new life in Fontesque.

I have a battered book of children's bedtime tales tucked into my back pocket. I stuffed it in there as a reminder to myself never to be so foolish again. Because that book is full of the same things my dreams of Fontesque were. Stories, made up and impossible.

I stand there until the guard blows his whistle, my heart thumping in my chest, my lungs too tight, desperately wishing for another glimpse of Tom, and desperately hoping Amos keeps him pinned to his seat.

And I don't see him. But I hear him, as the train pulls out. My heart's so attuned to his voice that I can pick it out of the chorus of yells and shouts, whistles and engines.

"Jude!" His scream is raw, his voice breaking, and in my mind's eye I can see him fighting against Amos, desperate to find a way off, to find a way back to me.

Amos wins, though, strong enough to keep him safe. The train disappears from view, curving away into a tunnel, and just like that, Tom is gone.

He's so much more than I ever deserved. But I'll always be glad I had him, if only for a few days.

I stumble out into the sunlight, blinking against the sudden brightness and at the change in the noise around me. Gone are the roar of train engines, replaced by the quick chatter of the daytime crowd. I pick a direction and start to walk, letting my feet carry me back toward the tenements.

This is what I had to do. One day, I know Tom will see that. He held me last night as I poured my heart out to him—but over time, he'll come to see what I did for what it truly is. He'll see the blood on my hands, and he'll understand I'm a killer, as surely as if I gave those orders myself.

And then he'll be glad he left me behind.

I walk, pushing my way past people without lifting my head, and eventually I realize that time is passing—that by now the train will be near the border. That I'm truly alone—and this time, nobody's coming to save me.

All I need to do now is decide what to do with the time I have left—before Laskia scoops me up once more, before I'm conscripted and sent to fight, before I find myself too cold and too hungry to make it through a winter night.

Then, like the faintest of lights twinkling on the horizon, I realize that I *do* know what I want. I've done everything I can for Tom. Now, I'm going to clear my debt to the only other person in my life who truly deserves my loyalty.

Leander doesn't know I'm here, and he doesn't know I'm his.

But he has a double agent in Laskia's court, all the same.

LEANDER

The Royal Palace
Kirkpool, Alinor

My sisters and I were raised with the most complex etiquette classes on the Crescent Sea. I might be a layabout, but I know how to greet an earl, what to wear to an afternoon tea thrown by a duke in late summer, and how to make small talk with the curator of a country museum.

I have no idea what to say to my goddess.

She's tall—taller than me by at least a head, built on a slightly larger scale than the rest of us. She has brown hair braided in businesslike fashion, and her eyes are the blue of Selly's beloved sea. She wears a golden circlet on her brow, a tunic of the same sapphire blue as our flag, and sandals.

She's impossibly beautiful, but I can't remember any more than these vague details unless I'm gazing at her. I can't seem to look at her for any length of time, but it's even harder to look away. Her features blur whenever I'm not with her, as though my mind can't quite hold on to her.

She led us back through the city on foot, the whole population of Kirkpool lining the streets and gazing at her in absolute silence. You could have heard a whisper—I could hear our footfalls on the road, the soft scuff of each step unnaturally loud. It was there in every face gazing up at her: absolute faith.

I feel it too. She's been here less than a day, and already it's hard to imagine how we ever felt whole without her. There's a sense of rightness about her presence. There's a sense that a part of us—as individuals, and as a whole—was missing, and we never knew it. And now, held safe in the arms of Barrica, we're complete.

She stands at the head of the table in my sister's council chamber, Augusta at her right hand, and gazes at each of us in turn. We're a small group—both my sisters are here, and Selly's at my side. Father Marsen looks exactly as you'd expect the head of the church to look when he finds himself at a meeting with his goddess. Adoring. Overwhelmed. Like his brain is melting as he tries to wrap his head around the idea that he's standing with Barrica herself.

"You have served me well," Barrica says, her musical voice sounding like it holds only one note, but *feeling* like an orchestra. She turns her gaze on Augusta, who looks up at her with rapt attention. *"Your family have been worthy stewards of Alinor. You have guided my people through the centuries as I would have wished. I am proud to have you at my right hand."*

Augusta swallows before she speaks—it's the first time I've seen my sister gather her nerve since I was six, and she was taking the throne. "Thank you, Goddess. We all wish only to serve." There's a tremor in her voice, a sort of incredulity to it. There can be absolutely no question as to what's going on and who stands here with us. And at the same time, there's a note of *is this actually happening?* humming through the room.

Selly reaches out to take my hand, squeezing as she senses the power building up inside me, and I nod to tell her I feel it too. But I don't release it just yet—I don't want either of us to miss a moment of this conversation.

"What next, Goddess?" I ask, breaking the silence. "You know about the Messenger of Macean." It's a statement, not a question. All my life, I've had a hint of a connection to her—a sense she was present when I prayed. A legacy of what King Anselm did for her.

Then, when I became her Messenger, I could sense her much more closely. Now, she's woven through me. Perhaps it should feel intrusive, but it feels like a blanket, like being held. Like strength, and safety, and sureness.

"I know of her," Barrica agrees. *"She does not thrive as you do, my prince. She is not a magician, and has not your touch for commanding power. She tries to bind herself to her sister, as you have done with your anchor, but the girl fights her with every breath. Still, she has an iron will and great ambition. My brother always admired that."*

"She poured some of her power into an assassin," I say, and Augusta's head snaps up. "I fought him tonight."

"She has done more than that," Barrica replies. *"She has done what she wished—she has woken my brother from his sleep."*

My stomach drops, and the shock of her words ripples around the room like a physical thing.

"We must prepare to fight," Augusta says immediately, ignoring the others, who raise their hands to their mouths, who still stare at Barrica with wide eyes. "We met them once. We will meet them again."

I can feel Selly gathering herself to burst out in protest, and I squeeze her hand gently. Her eyes fix on my face, like they want to burn a hole through my skin. But now is not the time to argue against war.

"Just so," Barrica agrees. *"The Gambler cannot be allowed to cast his dice, to make a play for the lands of others. His neighbors have no god to protect them, so we must."*

"Our armies are already assembling," Augusta reports. "We have plans for supplementing our navy with merchant ships. Give us two days, and—"

Barrica raises a hand, and my sister falls silent. *"First, my mother bids us speak, and search for a way to keep the peace,"* Barrica says solemnly. *"I cannot believe in my brother's good faith, but she has asserted her will, and I must bow to it, if only for now."*

"How do we . . . ?" Augusta begins, and then trails off.

"I have promised her six days," Barrica says. *"On the seventh, our peace will be suspended, and war will begin."*

"Where will we go?" I ask, as the magic buzzes in my ears, and Selly grips my hand in silent warning.

"To a place that will remind us of what is at stake—of what may happen if we clash again," Barrica says, the music of her voice dipping low. *"We will meet in the land that was once Vostain, where my brother Valus tended to his people. We will go to the Bibliotek."*

SIX DAYS OF PEACE REMAINING

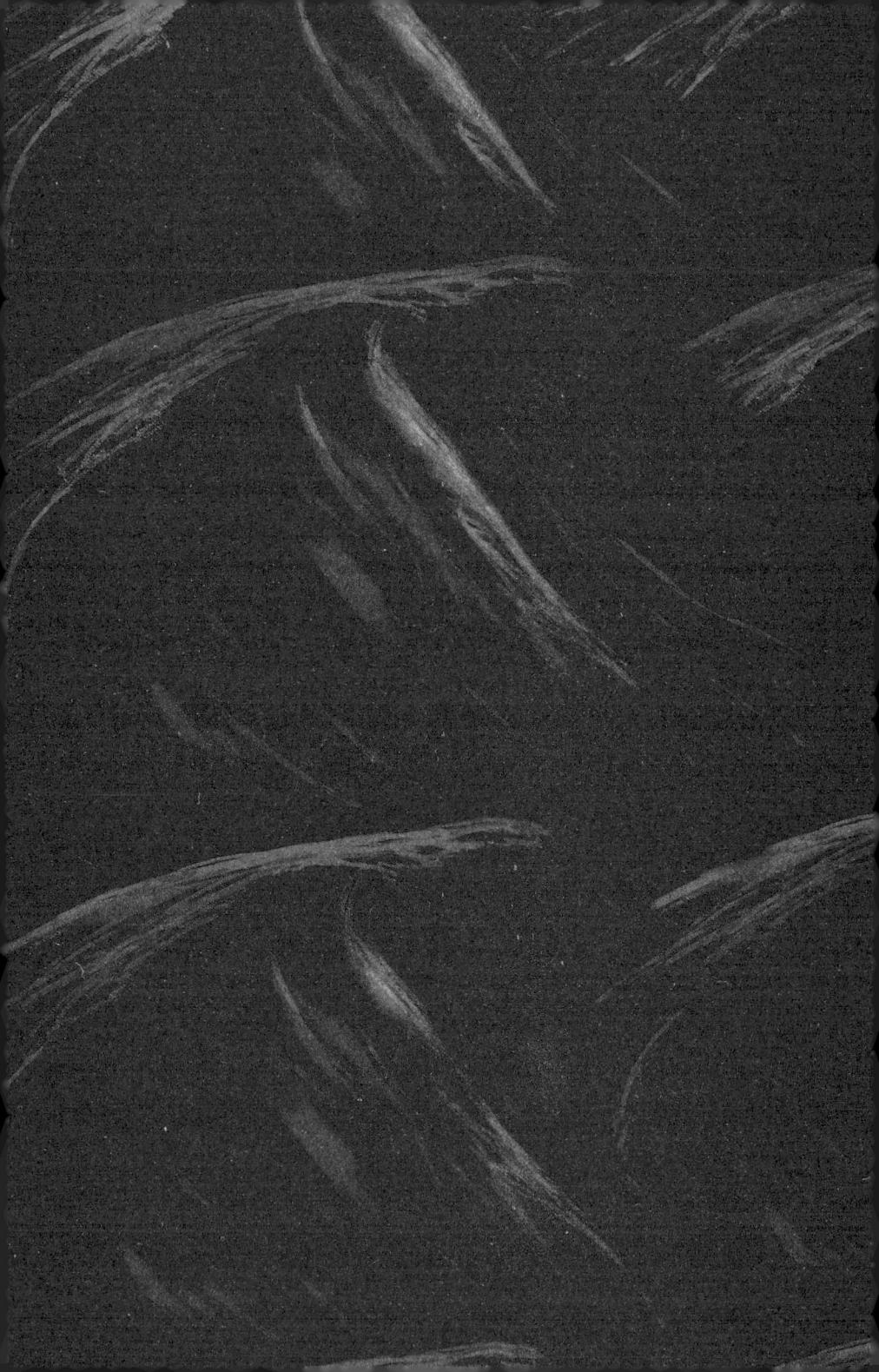

JUDE

The Temple of Macean
Port Naranda, Mellacea

I have to fight my way up the steps of the temple, toward the huge double doors, winged on either side by mighty columns. Even from a distance I can see that it's now covered in scaffolding, and workers in harnesses suspended on ropes are scrubbing and stripping away the black paint.

It's been painted black for centuries, to mark Macean's enforced slumber. Now he's returned, and this place is transforming to mark it.

The great building is set higher than street level, the stairs wrapping all the way around it, and it's *mobbed*. So are the streets for blocks in every direction, bodies pressed together in a heaving mass, everyone trying to get closer.

It's about halfway up the steps that I encounter the part of the crowd that really means business. The people who have forced their way past everyone else and are jammed in around the doors with a fervent energy that sends a ripple of fear through me.

Then I see Dasriel standing by the huge double doors. For a moment I'm frozen. The reality of inserting myself back into this horrifying mess hits me all at once, my stomach lurching uncomfortably, my skin prickling. I steel myself and lift one hand to wave, and bellow his name. "Dasriel! Over here!"

Slowly his gaze ranges over the crowd until he finds me. Then Laskia's fire magician detaches himself from a group by the door and wades down toward me, open flame dancing above his palm by way of threat. That and the ferocity of his scowl melt away even the most ardent objections, and he grabs me by the shoulder, so hard it feels like the bones are grinding together, then pushes me in front of him, stumbling up the steps toward the entrance.

I let him push me. Let him think I'm so weak that I've come crawling back to Laskia's side, not knowing where else to turn. That suits me fine.

Dasriel's silent as the roar of the crowd fades away behind us, and we make our way into the huge, echoing space of the church itself.

"*Again!*" someone bellows up at the altar, and the voice travels *through* me. I feel it in my bones. I feel it in my sinews. There's so much power in that one word, and the voice that speaks it.

Dasriel shoves me up the aisle ahead of him, and what's in front of me is like no church I've ever seen.

I've never been inside a church of Macean, large or small. I don't need to have seen this place before to know that it's changed, though.

They've turned it into a gambling den.

Bodies are crowded in around tables; people are talking, laughing, eating, sleeping here. Forgetting their own needs, driven to remain and keep playing their wild games. They look haggard, unwashed, and alive with energy. Curtains are drawn across the windows, and no surface is left untouched by this transformation.

Macean himself lounges on what I can only describe as a throne, up on the altar.

He has jet-black hair, marble-white skin, and green eyes that track my movements as I come closer. He's a predator, coiled and ready to spring, and for all his lazing in that chair, one leg slung over the arm, seemingly at rest, there's something in his green eyes that makes it almost impossible to look away. I nearly stumble over a girl sprawled in the aisle as I walk toward him.

He's utterly magnetic. Just being near him brings something out in me, makes me want to run a little faster, lean a little closer. He brings out the risk-taker that's slept so long, dormant inside me. I haven't been able to afford to take a risk since before we arrived here—I've only been able to do what was known, safe, what would protect me, what would protect Mum.

But now it's just me, isn't it? Me, and what I can win for Leander, before this place eats me alive.

My mouth is dry as I come closer to the altar, my steps dragging—I want to run toward him, and I want to run *away*.

I keep trying to make myself understand that I am walking up to an actual *god*. One part of me can't believe it. The other knows the truth of it right down to my bones.

There are two fire magicians standing before his throne, sweaty and bedraggled, chests heaving for breath, a wild light in their eyes.

"Again!" Macean shouts once more in that rich, rippling voice, and his laughter spreads through the crowd like flames.

The two magicians each conjure a handful of fire—I don't see either of them throw down a sacrifice first. Without a sacrifice, are they offering up *themselves*? I'm no magician, but even I know the first rule—the spirits demand a sacrifice, or they will take one from you that can never be restored. In their headlong drive to please their god, swept up in his risk-taking ways, are they . . . ?

Each magician raises a hand, showing the flame that burns above their palm. Now I see the two lengths of rope that hang from the rafters and end just above them.

The magicians each set a rope ablaze, and the fire races up the ropes at their urging—the crowd is cheering and laughing, their shouts deafening. Bets are changing hands, golden dollars dropped on the floor to roll away and disappear into the forest of legs.

The fire reaches the top of one rope. The winner raises both his hands in celebration, and the loser shrieks—at first I think it's in anger or frustration, but the noise keeps going. My gaze snaps down to him, and that's when I see the flames licking up his legs and racing along his arms.

I'm frozen in shock, and an instant later the man is completely alight and beating frantically at the flames, his wild flailing only fanning them higher.

Macean lifts one hand and then pinches his finger and

thumb together as though extinguishing a candle. In a blink the flames are gone. The man has been reduced to a pile of smoking ashes. I stand there, mouth open, hands half lifted.

And everyone else carries on like nothing has happened.

The winner simply turns and walks away. He's a redhead, like Tom, and for an instant my heart squeezes with grief.

Macean is staring at me. My body wants to tremble, even though I wish it wouldn't—it knows danger when it sees it. And this danger isn't like the boxing ring. It isn't like a fight—there's no chance I can punch back.

If he wanted to, he could bring his thumb and forefinger together again and extinguish *me*. And we both know it.

Laskia stands beside him, and Ruby behind her in the shadows. For once it's impossible to read Laskia's expression, and I can barely drag my eyes away from her god to try.

"*Ah, Jude,*" Macean says, and a shiver of unwelcome pleasure runs through me at the sound of my name on his lips.

Sister Beris stands on his other side. "You know Jude, honored Macean?"

The god shakes his head. "*No, my daughter, but you know him, and your minds are open books to me. What need have I of knowing, when you have worked so hard to learn it all for me?*"

I manage a glance at Beris, who's smiling at him, and then glance again at Laskia, who looks thoughtful.

In their own way, each of them has followed their god into risk. Laskia more obviously, perhaps—she killed over and over for the chance of power. Beris, though—she has devoted her whole life to a church that was in ruins. To a church that, when she joined it, had no worshippers left. To a sisterhood that begged for its next meal. This was the moment that *she* gambled on, and oh, how it has paid off.

"*Come here, Jude,*" says Macean slowly, and, legs shaking, I walk toward him. I'm caught helplessly in his green eyes, a fly in his web. "*You are not one of mine,*" he says, speculative.

I don't know what to say in reply. I've never been his worshipper, I can't lie. And worship—faith and sacrifice—is all any god seeks. How can I possibly account for my lack of it? The tension draws out, and his followers begin to fall silent, their games stilling, as they turn toward us.

And then he laughs, and everyone relaxes. "*Your mind,*" he says, "*is not an open book to me. But you are not my sister's either, and so you are still of use.*"

I don't want to be of use to the god of risk. But spirits save me, I don't want him to think I'm useless either.

Before me is a god who has rolled dice over lives—real people's lives—without thinking twice. Laskia has served him—Laskia was willing to give her *life* for him. And now he's not even glancing at her.

I walked in here to serve Leander—to try and find something I could use to help him—but now all I want to do is survive.

"*We're going on a trip, Jude,*" Macean says, his voice like silk.

"My lord?" I manage. It's a stupid thing to say—that's not his title—but it seems to please him.

"*Indeed,*" he agrees. "*You like books, don't you, Jude?*"

"B-books?" I stammer. A shot of panic goes through me—does he know about the book of children's tales in my back pocket? It's the only thing I really own now, and the bookseller gave it to me because it came from far away, and wasn't a part of this place—something we have in common. An hour ago, I was cursing it as a reminder of my own foolishness in believing in happy endings.

Why would I care if Macean took it? I don't know—except that I would.

"Yes, books," Macean agrees.

"He's not going to be any use unless he can stop repeating the last word he heard, honored Macean," snarks Laskia, "and start saying something original."

What do books have to do with a trip? Where are we going? Macean says he can't read the question in my mind, and if he sees it on my face, he doesn't reply. Instead, he lifts one hand and beckons me closer.

Legs still shaking, I climb the last few steps to stand before him. He leans in until those mesmerizing green eyes are just inches from mine, and with a flap of one hand, he shoos everyone else away.

I can't breathe. He's so close I can see the flecks of gold in his irises. The unearthly flawlessness of his skin. He's like a statue brought to life, and an insane part of me wonders if his skin would be warm, or cool.

"Your mind is difficult to read," he muses. *"It is your lack of faith. Faith can be learned, though, and your mind is strong. Suitable to hold a god."*

"I'm sure I'm not—" I try, but he silences me with just the faintest lift of one brow.

"You will stay close, Jude," he says, so soft that his words are no more than a breath between us. *"I cannot be without a*

Messenger, not if I wish to remain. And that, I very much do. So you will stay close in case the girl burns. I may have need of you yet."

I can't reply, can't make myself speak. All I can do is stare, trembling, into his green eyes, as though he's a snake and I'm a small, terrified mouse.

Then he leans back, and the spell is broken, and suddenly we're back in a church filled with games, filled with laughter and arguments, with howls of triumph as the dice fall someone's way, and with shouts of dismay when they don't.

"What's your favorite game, Jude?" he asks, conversational once more.

Unbidden, an image comes to mind of Leander and me at school, sitting up late in our dormitory over a game, pushing stones around a small board, talking earnestly about things that we thought mattered.

"Trallian Fates," I manage. "But I'm not very good at it."

"Well," he says, his low voice caressing me. *"That just makes it all the more exciting to play."*

A ripple of fear goes through me at the thought of being the subject of this god's excitement. At being his entertainment.

I don't want to be anywhere *near* what entertains him.

I don't want him looking at my mind, and deciding its strength might suit him.

But everyone near the god of risk ends up throwing the dice, and I've decided how I'll pitch mine. I'm going to find something for my prince, and repay the loyalty I never should have lost.

Even if it breaks me.

FIVE DAYS OF PEACE REMAINING

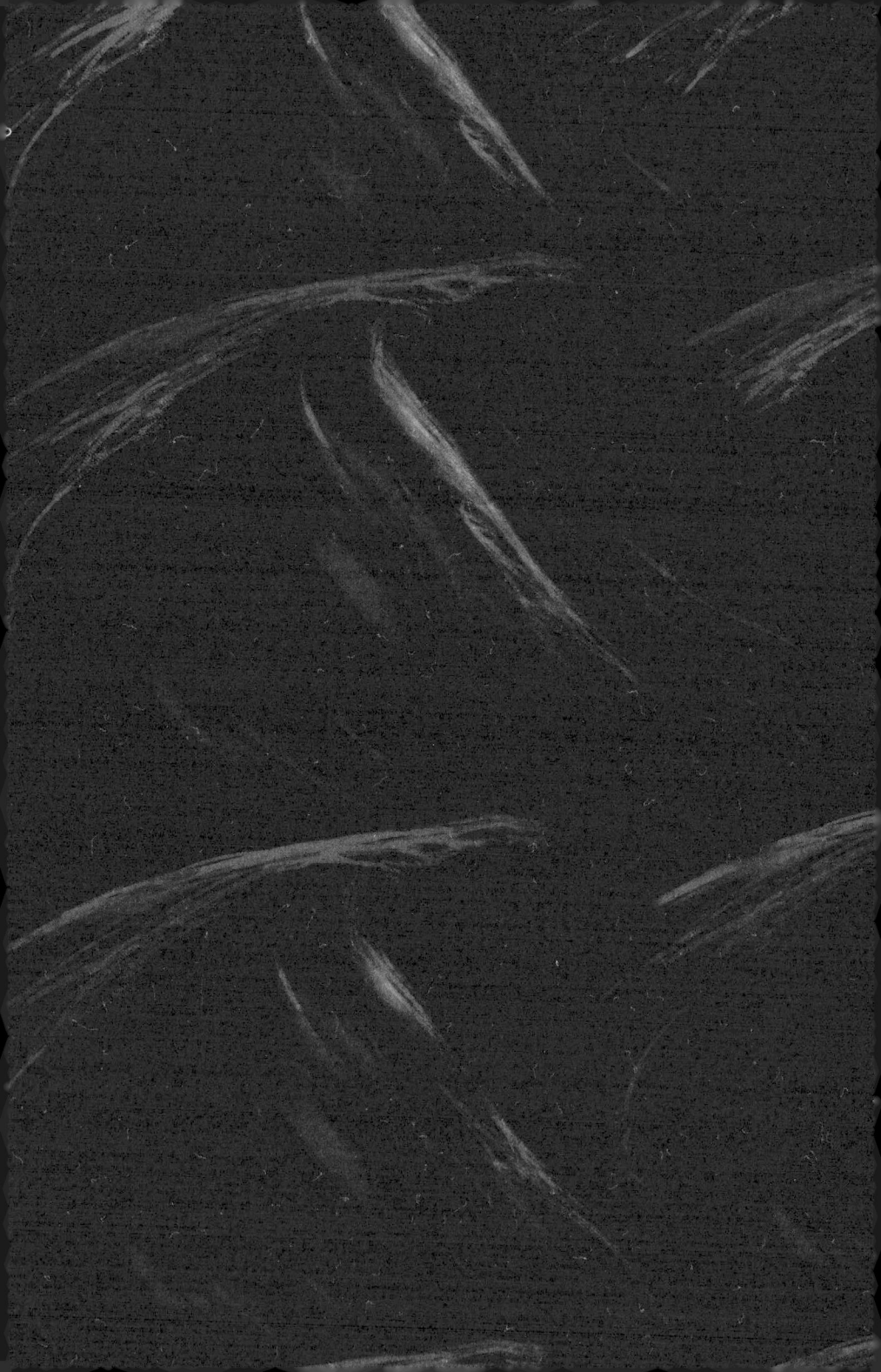

SELLY

The Goddess Blessed
Kirkpool, Alinor

The masts and rigging of the *Goddess Blessed* tower over us, decked out in spirit flags, the Alinorish standard at the head of the mainmast silhouetted against the sun.

At last, I'm about to set foot on one of my father's ships again.

The royal vessels were all lost with the decoy fleet, and a naval ship doesn't really send the right message at peace talks, however insincere Barrica clearly is about them. So we're aboard an honest merchant instead, with none of the flourishes of gold leaf, but built to last and with a crew we can trust. She usually flies the flag of Alinor—the white spear on a blue background—but it's strange not to see the Walker standard below it.

Most of the crew are out of sight when we board, though I glance up into the rigging, and see a deckhand I know— Tarrant always has a smile, always has a tease. Last time I saw him was at the harbormaster's office, making bad jokes about my search for my father, and about his ship, the *Fortune*. Now he's perched in the crosstrees, gazing down at me without a hint of a smile.

Captain Linnea is standing at what I'm sure she thinks is attention as she welcomes us aboard. Barrica leads the way, moving through the crowds with that impossible grace of hers. There must be thousands of people gathered to see us off, crowded onto balconies and roofs, leaning out of windows, crammed onto the docks until the timbers creak, but it's so perfectly silent that I can hear the waves lapping beneath us.

It took us most of yesterday to prepare to sail, and so today is the second of the six allotted for negotiations. On the seventh, there'll be nothing left to prevent a war. It feels frighteningly like the city is ready for it. These aren't the shopkeepers and citizens I've known all my life—they're taking on their goddess's aspect, subtly shifting, and it scares me.

The goddess is followed by the queen, who walks with Father Marsen. Then comes Leander, with Keegan, Kiki, and me close behind.

Kiki takes my arm to guide her as she glances back, checking that the endless chests of clothes she packed for us are still trundling along, part of the procession. In theory she's here as my companion, and the two of us are sticking together for whatever comfort familiarity can bring.

We've left behind Princess Coria—by far the more sympathetic of Leander's sisters—and the Princess Consort Delphine, who tends to act as the voice of reason for her wife. There's every reason to be afraid of what will happen when we reach the Bibliotek, but for now that worry is swept aside by the physical relief of making my way up the gangplank and setting foot on the deck of a ship once more.

Something releases inside my chest, and it feels like I can take a deeper breath of the sea air as we make our way aboard the *Goddess Blessed*. Everything around me is still strange, the deck populated with courtiers and royalty and a goddess herself, and I know we're headed to seven kinds of trouble.

But at least for a moment, I'm home.

Barrica walks up to the ship's bow, and without a word Leander reaches for my hand so we can follow together.

The goddess stands alone at the point where the port and starboard sides of the ship curve to meet, like a fearsome figurehead, and then raises her arms, as if she's beckoning someone, or something, far away.

In the next moment, the world shifts around us.

I gasp as an army of air spirits swings sharply to change the very direction of the wind itself, and power the ship. Her sails billow and strain, and slowly, silently, she begins to move.

It's like watching the wind lit on fire—millions of points of light follow every whirl and eddy, like a thousand small streams joining together to form a mighty river.

I glance at Leander, reminded vividly of the last time we stood in a place like this. We were aboard the *Lizabetta*, that first morning—I introduced him to the water spirits, and he charmed me as neatly as he charmed them.

Now all I can see is the strain on his face—the storm of magic around us is too much for him, the volume too loud, the sensation too much. When he draws in a breath it's ragged, and he sways. For a moment I'm seized with an urge to wrap my arms around him, rest my head against his shoulder, hold him.

I'd give everything to help him, but I don't know how to do anything but pump the brakes as he careens downhill, slowing his descent toward the fate every other Messenger has suffered. And moments like this, with millions of spirits wheeling around us like seabirds, make it so much worse.

I shove down a quick flash of dread, stuffing it deep inside me—Leander mustn't feel it—and then squeeze his hand.

"Leander, give some of it to me."

The look he shoots me is a mix of misery, apology, and relief. "I'm sorry," he whispers, almost inaudible.

"Don't be. Hurry up."

With an exhalation that sounds more like a sob, he lets his power vent into me, and the pain sears up my arm, spreading to every limb, inflaming every joint, until I feel like I'll combust if I so much as move. My nerves sing and scream, and I clench my jaw so hard that I'm sure my teeth will crack.

And then it's over, and the ripples of pain are dying down, and I force my eyes open, trying to shove away the reaction.

When I can focus again, I find Barrica studying me.

"I regret that it causes you pain, to provide such relief to my Messenger," she says.

"I don't mind," I manage, still ragged, and more than a little surprised she cares at all. Then it clicks—she senses there's a limit to the number of times we can do this before my body breaks. And she doesn't want me to fail him.

"You are very closely linked," she observes, thoughtful.

Leander's the one who replies. "We care for each other, Goddess."

"Indeed," she agrees, with a hint of a smile. *"But that was not what I meant. Have you each a sense of what the other is*

thinking? Feeling? One that goes beyond the empathy to be expected between two who—as you say—care for each other?"

"Yes," I say. It's more than that. I know exactly where Leander is at every moment. I could find him with my eyes closed, and lay my hand on his heart.

"*This worsens the pain,*" she says. "*You each experience the other's, as well as your own. I will teach you to separate yourselves.*"

I study her before I reply, and she meets my gaze squarely, with eyes as blue as the sea. In this moment we understand each other, my goddess and me.

She wants Leander to last for as long as possible, and for that to happen, he needs to be willing to hurt me when I help him. It'll be easier for him to do that if he doesn't experience my pain.

Thing is, that's what I want, too. That's the choice I made, when I bound myself to him. I stand by it. And I'd like a place to keep a few of my thoughts just for myself. To be alone, even if only for a moment.

"Show me," I say.

"*Stand and face each other,*" she says, and Leander and I turn in, still holding hands. "*Now, picture the other—do not see them with your eyes, but know their presence. Sense the part of them that is linked to you.*"

The two of us gaze at each other, and for all that the echoes of pain are still jangling through my limbs, I almost giggle, because at exactly the same moment we both narrow our eyes, trying to throw the world out of focus as we do when we look for the spirits. I can sense Leander's amusement, too, and then—

—then I'm a speck on the ocean, one tiny, ragged white sail, as the blue water—the color of Barrica's eyes—spreads out around me in every direction. I'm infinitely small, so small that I feel myself shrinking out of existence, a mote of dust, and panic wells up in me as I start to lose myself.

"*All is well.*" Barrica's voice sounds in my mind, and *she's* amused too, not at us, but with us, sharing in that hint of a giggle.

She's something more than I knew she was—she's Anselm's friend and companion, she's Leander's guide and mentor—and I see her clearly, the broad sweep of her power, and the outer limits of it, too.

Barrica's mind—just the smallest edge of it—touches mine and shows me how to sketch out Leander in green lines the color of his magician's marks, until he's a figure made of magic and our goddess's power, standing with his hands in mine.

"*Now,*" she says gently, "*you will create a barrier between the two of you. Not too strong—you must still be joined. Think of a fine cloth, not a steel plate.*"

Slowly, the green lines begin to etch a sort of mesh between us. I can still see Leander, still sense his thoughts, his emotions. But I can also lean into the barrier and strengthen it as I wish, to create a space between us, or a distance.

When I open my eyes, the world looks just as it did, but it's as though I've been carrying weights, and someone's lifted them from me.

"Thank you." I look across at the goddess, who only nods. We want different things, but we understand each other, she and I, at least in this moment.

She hungers for a fight with her brother, and I'd do anything to keep us from it—but we each wish this boy between us to continue, so on that we will work together.

Barrica turns away and walks back along the deck to where Augusta and her advisers are spreading out maps on a large table. The wind doesn't seem to snatch at the edges of the maps, and as I watch the spirits whirl around them, I'm reminded that all the Alinorish royals are magicians, though none as strong as Leander.

"Feel better?" Leander asks, stepping into the place at the very tip of the bow that Barrica has vacated, and pulling me with him.

"Much," I admit.

"Good." His smile is a little different, softer, and the corners of his eyes less strained. "You know what else it's good for? Makes it more of a surprise, when I do this." He uses our joined hands to tug me in against him, and as our bodies bump together he tilts his head to find my lips with his. A shiver runs through me, and as one of his hands curves around the small of my back, I arch against him.

Then I remember where we are, and cheeks burning, turn my head away. "Leander, your sister's right there! So's half of Alinor."

"They won't notice," he murmurs, nosing his way in to nibble on my neck and scattering my thoughts like a flock of birds wheeling away in every direction. I *do* like not knowing what's coming next—and I like the way I can still feel his wanting, and the way it warms the link between us.

"Leander, they—" But he's right. Nobody is looking at us.

He's hidden us again, as he did when we walked to the Temple of the Mother. Just for this moment, the world's attention is somewhere else.

"What are they doing back there?" I ask, as he nibbles my neck again, sending tingles zipping all the way to my fingertips.

"Strategizing," he replies, lifting his head to press his forehead against mine for a moment, then stealing a kiss. Then he makes a show of leering at me. "Just like me."

Augusta's jabbing at the map with one finger, and as the *Goddess Blessed* romps through the waves, she lifts her other hand to gesture at the coastline to the north of us, where Alinor curves up into the small province of Caspia, before the coast becomes Fontesque's, then Beinhof's, then fades into a faint line before reaching the Barren Reaches and the Bibliotek. She's speaking of alliances, that much is clear, and it's enough to sober us both.

"Hoping for the best," Leander says softly, wrapping his arms around me. "But preparing for the worst."

"Planning for a war on the way to peace talks?" I ask, resting my head on his shoulder.

"Planning to protect our people." There's a resolve in his tone, but there's something more, too—I can sense a hardness to his thoughts, an edge that reminds me of a weapon, even if it's still sheathed for now.

It doesn't feel like my Leander. But it *does* feel like the Messenger of a warrior goddess. Silently, I sketch in another couple of lines in the mesh between us, to keep that thought from him.

And to keep from him the sudden flicker of uneasiness in my mind.

I'm rescued from the need to reply when Kiki comes marching up the deck, Keegan in tow.

"This is so bracing!" Kiki cries, taking in the ship with a sweep of one hand. "The sea air! I might swab something at any minute."

Keegan eyes her sidelong. "What do you think swabbing is?" he asks, curious.

Their chatter fades out as my attention drifts from my friends. Kirkpool lies in our wake, the golden city lit by the morning sun. The coast stretches away from us, north toward the Bibliotek, south toward Kethos. The air smells of salt, and there's clear blue all around us.

I love this place—every part of me belongs here—but I can't shake that worry that lies in the back of my mind.

My gaze shifts to the group aft of us—the goddess, the queen, their advisers, all clustered around their maps.

And slowly, moving with infinite care, I sketch in the first lines of a barrier between my goddess and me.

FOUR DAYS OF PEACE REMAINING

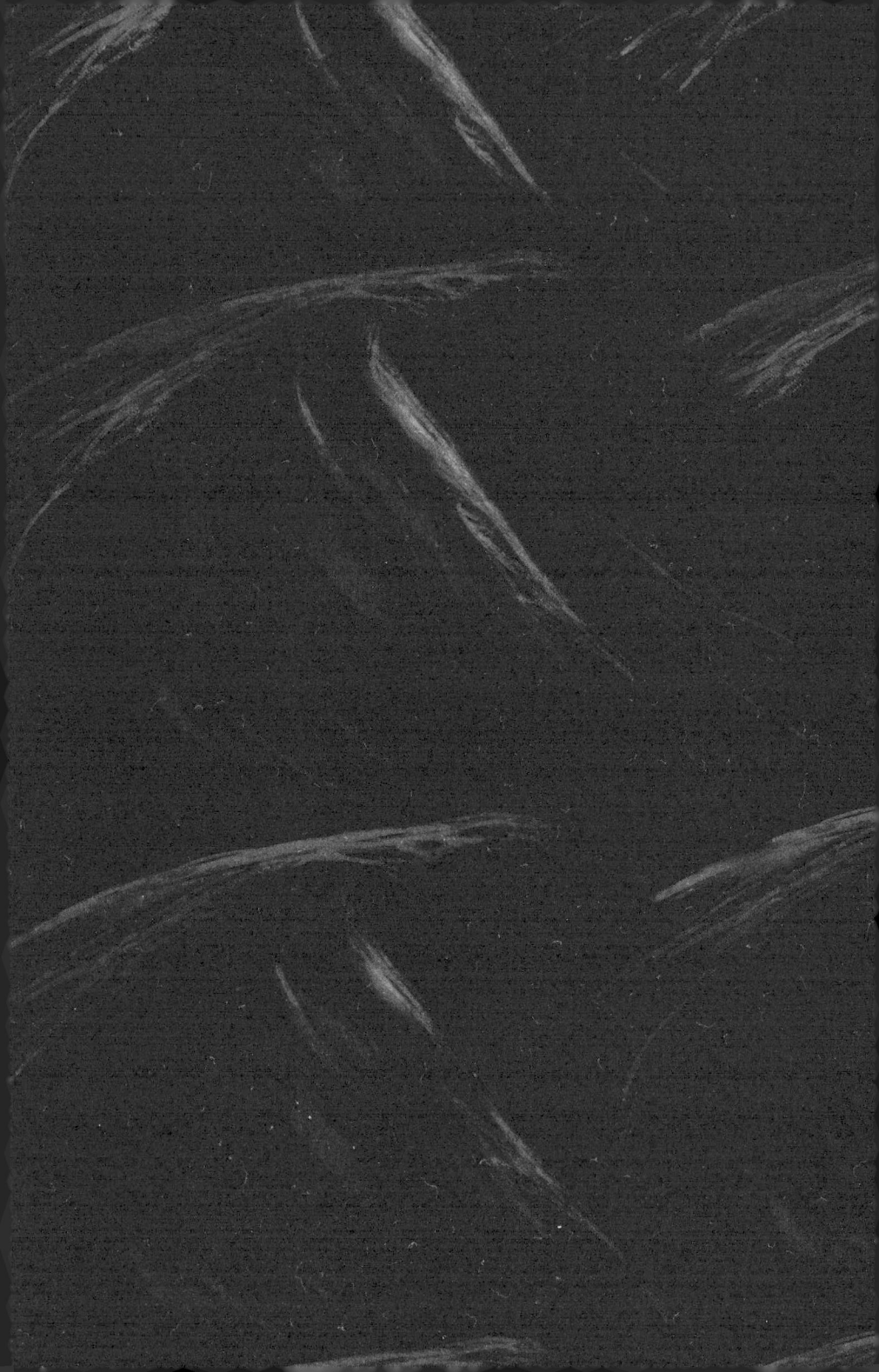

KEEGAN

◆

The Entrance Hall
The Bibliotek, the Barren Reaches

The Bibliotek is everything I dreamed it would be.

The entrance hall has soaring vaulted ceilings inlaid with intricate mosaics of wood and tile. The floor is carpeted with rich rugs woven in the vibrant colors of every nation on the Crescent Sea. Even here, before one reaches the libraries, there are display cases holding rare texts, as well as tapestries and paintings of the building of this great place. At the center of it all stands a statue of the Mother, in her aspect as the guardian of knowledge. It's comforting to think that perhaps she has a special place in her heart for bookworms.

The Alinorish negotiating party is assembled here, and scholars hurry around, taking down names and allocating rooms. They wear black, the collars and cuffs of their robes embroidered in thread of different colors to indicate their academic discipline and their progression through their studies.

Mine would have featured a single ring of red at the cuffs, to mark me as a first-year history student.

Six sets of double doors lead off the entrance hall, each to a different part of the Bibliotek. Beyond them lie grand vaults of priceless documents, student dormitories and classrooms, wood-paneled lecture theaters, and long dining halls, and over a hundred libraries devoted to knowledge both general and specific.

I have read so many accounts of the Bibliotek that I could walk it with my eyes closed. Many times, late at night, waiting for the indignities of the day to fade away and let me sleep, I have allowed myself that daydream.

"Wake up," one of the soldiers barks, clapping me on the shoulder and laughing when I jump. "Your bride-to-be has a dozen trunks packed. Aren't you going to carry them all to her quarters?"

Kiki arrives a few steps behind him, wincing apologetically for failing to intercept him. "Please, Captain," she replies, voice bland. "Pray do not diminish my strength. A girl ought always to be able to lift her own makeup kit."

"Indeed, Lady Dastenholtz?" he asks, one brow quirking.

She returns his gaze, unblinking. "Would you care to test my strength, Captain?" There's a restless energy to both of them—they're so much quicker to a confrontation than they'd ever be otherwise. He should be careful to mind his manners around someone of Kiki's rank, and she should be quick to defuse things with a laugh. Barrica's edge is showing in each of them.

He's the one who backs down this time, turning on his heel and marching away. Kiki rolls her eyes once the stalemate is over.

"Now, darling," she says, leaning down to hoist an impressively large makeup kit and stack it on top of a trunk. "Be a lamb and pick up the other end of that trunk, will you? It's impossibly heavy."

I pick up one end of the trunk obediently, stooping a little so that we're level when she takes the other. We work well together. That part was never the problem.

I make myself focus on the task of gripping the trunk, rather than taking in our surroundings. This place is my might-have-been. It's my almost-was. It's my never-will-be. And instead of studying here, instead of donning those scholar's robes, I'm trailing after the queen and her retinue, dully certain that nothing I say will sway anyone who even bothers to listen.

I thought Elga was like me. I thought she was someone who could become a friend. Instead, she played me like a violin, used me for what she wanted, and then reported it all back to Laskia.

I'm the reason that boy was able to attack Leander with Laskia's magic. I'm the reason we were even at the Temple of the Mother, to test my foolish theory that the other gods would care about what happened to us.

We sailed here overnight, and today is the third day since the gods reappeared. Including today, we have four days left before the truce ends, and war begins. We'll meet this afternoon to start negotiations.

I thought it would be more than I could take, to be shown my dream—to be here—without being permitted to have it. But now, I can't imagine ever deserving a scholar's robes. Elga fed me lies and I swallowed them whole, and all of us will pay the price.

We might have missed our chance to stop Laskia, to stop Macean reappearing, but I still hope there's something I can do for Leander. They call this place the heart of the world—the greatest collection of knowledge ever gathered. There must be *something* that can help him.

Kiki tugs on her end of the trunk, and we follow a patient scholar toward the room we've been assigned to share with Leander and Selly. There are no quarters for dignitaries here—everyone from the queen to the lowliest of her servants is housed in simple scholars' rooms.

As we leave the entrance hall and enter the Bibliotek itself, my chest tightens until it's hard to breathe. If I had made it this far—if I had stepped over the threshold of those double doors when I'd run away—I would have been beyond my father's reach forever.

We are all of us hemmed in now—by war, by the gods, and by the fates that have chosen us.

I only hope that our sacrifices will buy us the peace we've been willing to die for.

I only wish that was what our leaders wanted.

LASKIA

The West Dormitories
The Bibliotek, the Barren Reaches

Ruby and I are silent as we unpack our things in the little two-bed dormitory room we've been assigned by the scholars.

Macean showed us how to build a barrier between our minds, and now she feels more distant, but also much more coherent. I can feel her taking it all in, processing this place, the people who've come with us.

We're at the center of a very complex web right now, and Ruby's always been good at those.

"What kind of room do they call this?" I mutter, and then instantly feel my belly knot—I shouldn't be trying to start a conversation, and leaving myself vulnerable to her silence.

She doesn't reply.

Our quarters are small and neat, everything well-built. Two beds, two wardrobes, two desks, two chairs. Our door leads to a common room with sofas, bookshelves, and tables; off that are doors to the room shared by Sister Beris and one of her assistants, and the rooms of another few sisters, diplomats, intelligence staff, and military sorts.

Dasriel has Jude with him, to make sure he knows if Jude tries to vanish. He'll be useful later—he's familiar with all the players on the Alinorish side.

There's no room for Macean. I asked him what he required, and he just looked at me, and raised one brow. *"Do you think I sleep?"* he asked, and then turned away without waiting for a reply.

I don't sleep, I wanted to say. *I don't sleep, and I still have a room. I fall into strange trances and dreams, but my mind never properly falls asleep. Ruby fights me for every inch I need from her. I think I'm losing my mind. Do you care?*

But I said nothing. For a brief, panicked moment, I thought perhaps he was dipping into my thoughts, for his steps seemed to slow. But either he didn't care enough to look at my mind, or he did, but didn't care about the agony he found there.

Just now, Macean is in the common room, playing dice with Dasriel, of all people. My big, gruff bodyguard doesn't seem overawed in the least.

None of this is what I thought it would be.

Macean acts like the negotiations are all a game.

I think they're a waste of time. Four more days, and then we can fight. Then we *properly* roll the dice. That's what I want. I think.

For now, the green sisters and the diplomats talk and argue, and nobody's looking to me. I'm their Messenger. I should be second only to our god, and yet . . .

Ruby snorts as she pulls another dress out of her trunk, and

I realize she caught that last thought. She really *is* more coherent, since we learned to build that clumsy mental wall we've slapped up between our minds.

"Well," I snap, "say it."

"You shouldn't have killed Sister Petra," she says, and for a moment there's a flash in my mind of the moment I grabbed hold of the first sister, the moment I consumed her on the temple steps. "You should have gone for Beris."

"Beris has always believed in me," I reply, blinking at her.

"Beris *groomed* you," she snaps. "How can you be this stupid? She took you in when you thought I didn't give you enough godsdamned hugs, she flattered you, she fanned your faith, and she got what she wanted. She's first sister now, and her god has returned."

"It was what I wanted too," I shoot back.

"Beris will fight you for control every step of the way," Ruby replies, with a shake of her head. "You could have ruled over Petra with one hand tied behind your back."

"She was the *first sister.* You don't think she had steel in her?"

"She was nothing like Beris." Ruby's voice drips with disdain. "Petra saw risk as chance, as a reason to hope for something better. To her, planting crops was a throw of the dice, something we hoped for and believed, but could never know with certainty would bear fruit. Risk was training as a doctor, treating patients, placing your bets on the right diagnosis, on your own expertise. She saw risk as a gift, because it gives us a way to do things we only hope are possible."

I say nothing, trying to make my expression blank, trying to absorb her words. Beris never preached anything like this.

For Beris, her faith tells her to make her own luck. To take risks, the bigger, the better. For her, the outcome is less important than the action of stacking her chips on one number. It's about the way she flies, as she waits to see where the dice will land.

"Petra would have been easy to control," Ruby repeats. "Beris will fight you every step of the way. Perhaps that's what you wanted."

"What do you mean by that?"

She shrugs. "You always want to be second to someone," she replies, glancing at me as though I'm not worth a proper look. "First me, then her, now him."

I lower my voice. "You'd have me challenge him? Are you mad?"

"I'd have you rot in every one of the seven hells for what you've done to me," she hisses, and the hatred comes at me like a knife, sharp and unexpected, lodging straight in my gut.

When I was small, I was always trying to work out how people fit together. Ruby made me go to school while she earned our living, and every night I'd curl up in our little room, chatting to her while I did my homework. I'd tell her who sat together in the classroom, and where. Who played a game or wasn't invited. And she'd ask questions.

"You have to understand," she'd say, wrapping her arms around me. "How are we going to win the game if we don't know who's playing?"

We.

But it was never that. I tried to play her game. I would have stood by her side, but she was never, ever going to let me up onto the top step with her.

"What *I've* done to *you*," I echo, turning those words over in my mind. She doesn't see any part of what she did to me first. She doesn't see how she's the one who broke our trust. And yet . . . the very fact that I could tie myself to her like this means there is still something between us.

How could she treat me as she did if she loved me?

"What you've done to me," she repeats. Her words drip with venom, her eyes dark with hatred. "You made me into your puppet, took my mind from me, humiliated me."

"And you didn't humiliate *me*?" The words burst out of me. "Ruby! You made me dance to your tune for years, and I was only ever a tool for you. Now things are reversed, you see it for what it was!"

I can feel the power building in me again, pouring into me from that stream that never ends. Her steps are too loud. I can hear someone moving in the next room. My skin itches and seems to stretch, my bones aching.

Ruby feels it too. "No," she says, taking a step back. "Laskia, no."

"What use do you think you are?" I spit. "If you're not for me?"

I grab her by the shoulder and pour the magic into her before it overwhelms me. I feel her pain, feel the way her body rebels against this impossible load. The way her mind starts to unmoor itself once again, though she clings to her sanity.

But she clenches her teeth and stares at me.

And she refuses to scream.

SELLY

The Hall of Scholars
The Bibliotek, the Barren Reaches

A huge, round table dominates the room where the peace talks will take place. There's an extra ring of chairs around the outer edge, for observers, and the scholars have laid out a notebook and a glass of water for each of us. Everyone's place has been set up so it's exactly the same. No differences for rank or religion.

Nobody's looking at the table as we file in, though. One wall of the room is taken up with floor-to-ceiling windows, and beyond them are the Barren Reaches.

The blasted landscape is completely devoid of life—huge, melted slags of stone stretch across it, melted rivers destroyed when Barrica and Macean last clashed.

There are boulders, too, and piles of rubble—and then I realize, with a sudden pinch in the pit of my stomach, that those aren't rocks.

They're what's left of the city of Vostain. Every building was flattened, every soul killed in the blast.

Until now I'd been imagining a war filled with clashes, with battles and explosions, with whole buildings blown to pieces, as the Temple of the Mother in Kirkpool was when Leander protected us from Laskia's assassin.

But this isn't a battleground. It's simply been obliterated.

And in four days, it will begin again.

There's a scholar waiting in the room as well, and Keegan leans forward to whisper to us.

"That's Scholar Kel. They're the head of the Bibliotek. Not that scholars have ranks. But if they did, Kel would be in charge."

"First among equals," Leander murmurs, studying Kel. They must be in their seventies, though their walnut-brown skin isn't lined—I don't think the scholars here spend a lot of time outdoors. Their silver hair is neatly combed, their black robes don't have any colored thread on them, and there's no sign of their rank. This is the kind of power that doesn't need to announce itself.

"Good afternoon," Kel says quietly, and we move to take our places. I'm beside Leander. On his other side is Augusta, then Barrica herself. Across from us is Macean, with Laskia at his side, and the girl who must be her sister. Then comes a green sister who gazes at us like she's a snake who'd like to strike. The rest of the table is given over to officials and diplomats on both sides.

"Welcome to the Bibliotek," Scholar Kel continues. "My name is Kel. I am a scholar, and I am an acolyte of the Mother. I remind you that it is she who is worshipped here, though as in every temple of the Mother, all her children are present. Two of her children are welcome at our table today." Kel doesn't seem the slightest bit intimidated to be facing down Barrica and Macean—then again, the scholars worship their mother, so perhaps they feel protected. "This place is often called 'the heart of the world,' for the knowledge we keep here. That is the Mother's domain: knowledge. All we have learned is at your disposal. But I bid you look beyond our libraries, and gaze upon the lost land of Vostain outside our windows. I bid you think on your lost brother, Valus, and choose a path of wisdom and peace today."

I peek around the table—if any of us had been getting a little casual about having actual gods walking among us, the sight of the land they destroyed has put us right back where we started. Among the observers around the edge of the room are ambassadors from every country on the Crescent Sea, accompanied by priests of each religion. And every single one of them looks completely overwhelmed by the sight of the two huge figures at the table.

I linger on Laskia for a moment. This is the girl who hunted us, who tried to murder us. Who *did* murder all my crew, while I hid and watched, helpless. My nails bite into my palms as I gaze at her, my jaw tightening.

Then she turns her head to lean back and speak to her big fire magician, and I see it. A glint of gold at her neck.

Before she threw Keegan overboard, she took one of the gold necklaces he was going to use to pay his way into this very place. She took it, then had him tossed into the sea, and then she had my crew killed. And she's still wearing it.

Keegan is sitting behind us, at the edge of the room. I hope he hasn't seen it.

"Let us begin," says Queen Augusta. "I hope you have come in good faith, as our hosts have requested. Much is at stake for you, after all."

"For us?" spits Laskia. Beside her, Macean lounges in his chair, his beautiful mouth curving into a slow smile.

"Would you care to explain what you mean by that?" It's the green sister. I know her now. She's the one who stood on the boat while Laskia killed us.

Leander takes up the reply. "You destroyed our royal fleet. You killed the young people of our court." One hand slaps at the black mourning band he wears on his arm. "Let's not play games. You hunted me. You tried to kill me, and you failed."

"Let us remember," says the sister—Beris, I remember now—"what it is *you* were trying to do."

"And what was that?"

"You sought to bind our god in sleep," she replies archly. "To deprive us of the sacred connection you have always enjoyed with your own goddess."

Father Marsen pushes his way into the conversation from farther down the table. "As all agreed was the only safe way!" I glance at him, and for the first time I realize he's not wearing his usual robes, stylized to look like armor. He's wearing *actual* armor, polished to a gleam. Gone is the calm, friendly face we met in the temple.

"The list of your crimes goes on," Augusta says, cold and precise. "You murdered our ambassador in broad daylight. She was the living embodiment of Alinor on your shores."

"I suggest we discuss the future," Sister Beris says, just as cold. "If only because an accounting of the past does not cast you in the light you seem to think it does."

Macean shifts in his chair, and his movement draws my attention. He sprawls comfortably, coldly handsome with his marble-white skin and silky black hair. He's watching us like we're at a card game and he's deciding how many chips to push into the center of the table. It makes me shiver.

Then he turns his head to look straight at me, and I'm caught in his gaze. With a wave of nausea I wrench my attention away from him.

Arguments are breaking out all up and down the table, voices rising over each other.

Around the edges of the room, the foreign priests and ambassadors are talking urgently to each other. None of them seem to be aligned—I'd wondered where Caspia would sit, as they're a next-door neighbor to Alinor, but famous for their casinos. They're beside Nusraya, whose territory lies directly above Mellacea's, and the two women, priests of Kyion and Sutista, are whispering, their heads close together.

"Your insistence has never made it so, brother." Barrica's voice rises above the others, and Macean bares his teeth at her in a grin.

"And your self-righteousness has never made you right."

They sound like two children arguing over a toy, and the sudden pettiness of it jolts me out of my own growing anger. Was that Barrica's lust for war creeping into my mind, as I'm watching it creep into everyone else's?

I lean in to Leander to speak very quietly. "This isn't getting us anywhere."

"Perhaps because there's nowhere for us to go," he replies, just as soft.

"Can't they see what's going to happen if we don't do better than this? There's a land as big as Alinor, as big as Mellacea, completely ruined right outside that window," I murmur. But I stop when I sense a thread of something running through Leander again, like a golden seam of heat that's more his goddess than him.

Surreptitiously, I check the mental barrier between us—and between me and Barrica. There are flushed faces on both sides of the table as people lean forward, gesture in anger, raise their voices to be heard. There's a recklessness on the Mellacean side, an aggression on ours, and both of them scare me.

"If I may!" It's Scholar Kel, raising their voice in what's clearly not their first attempt to be heard. Finally, they get some traction. "There is much to discuss," they continue, and though their tone hasn't changed, they're less serene than they were before. "I am assembling notes—I understand both sides wish to lodge claims for compensation and also wish to discuss future plans. Let us break, and reconvene in half an hour with an agenda assembled by my scholars, based on what you have said."

There's a long pause where it seems like nobody will move. As though we'll simply stay here and shout and spin out all the time we have left until the Mother's deadline in this pointless argument.

So, ignoring the clenching in my gut, I stand, reaching for Leander's hand and pulling him with me. And somehow that breaks the tableau, and everyone around the table starts to move.

Keegan's just ahead of me as we file out into the antechamber on our side of the room, and I walk straight into the back of him when he suddenly stops. He stumbles, revealing a man with dark hair, strong cheekbones, and a stern expression.

I know who he is the moment I see him—he looks exactly like his son, though he doesn't have Keegan's unfortunate shaved head.

"Lord Wollesley," says Augusta crisply. "At last you have joined us."

Keegan takes a slow step back to my side, and when I look at him, his face is drained of color. "This," he mutters, "is why one should never say that things can't get any worse."

JUDE

The Mathematicians' Library
The Bibliotek, the Barren Reaches

It's late at night as I make my way into the Mathematicians' Library. The dark wooden shelves stretch all the way up to the ceiling, radiating from the center of the room, with ladders leaning against them at intervals. The room smells of old books and impossible equations.

When I found the note in my pocket after the first summit, I didn't think it could be from Leander. I was sitting back against the wall on the Mellacean side, and I never saw him spot me. But the handwriting was his, and the more I thought about it, the more I thought, *Well, if he had to choose somewhere he imagined nobody else would be, he'd certainly pick a mathematics library.*

Still, when I reach the center of the room and find the prince of Alinor sitting cross-legged on the librarian's desk, holding hands with the blond sailor I now know to be Selly, I stop short.

Their fingers are interlaced, their heads bowed toward each other's, their bodies turned inward. It's an intimate moment, and I don't know how to interrupt it, so I clear my throat softly.

Their heads snap up, and for a moment, Leander's eyes widen. He's not a Messenger, not even a prince—he's just my friend.

He nearly falls off the desk in his scramble to climb down from it, and comes running toward me. I have an instant to brace, and then he's knocking the air out of me, and his arms are around me, and he's hugging me so tightly I grunt a protest. My body tenses, but he doesn't let go—and in the end, I surrender. I soften and rest my forehead on his shoulder, and the hot ache behind my eyes that I've been fighting since I saw Tom onto the train threatens to overtake me completely. There's a strange, staticky feeling I know must be Leander's magic, and my skin prickles with it, but there's no way I'm letting go.

"Jude, I'm so sorry," Leander says in my ear. "I tried so many times to find you."

"I know," I choke. "I know that now. I should have known it then."

"You'd just lost everything," he replies. "How were you supposed to see clearly?"

"Of course you'd see it that way," I manage.

He's wrong, though. I hadn't just lost everything. *Now* is when I've lost everything. My honor. My home. Tom. My future. And there's no way to ever get any of it back.

My mother and I didn't grieve my father—whatever she had with him died long ago, and I'd never known him, except as someone to pay my school fees and the upkeep on our little house in Kirkpool.

It was her determination that bowled me over, after he died. Perhaps she didn't want to take money from Leander, to transfer her eternal debt to another rich man. I'll never know.

Finally he releases me, and I take hold of his hand, dropping to one knee, my head bowed.

"Jude, don't—"

"Let me swear myself to you," I whisper.

"You don't need to—"

"I broke faith," I cut in over him. "I am your man, Leander. I should have been all along. Please accept my oath."

There's a long pause, and then I hear Selly speak from where she sits on the desk, watching us. "Leander," she says softly.

He lets out a breath and lays his free hand on my head, which is still bowed. "Jude Kien," he says softly, "I accept your oath."

Something releases inside my chest at having bound myself to him once more. In a few days we'll be at war, and someone like me doesn't last long when that happens. And that's all right—I'm not looking for redemption. I'm not expecting it. I don't even think I want it. The lost land of Vostain is somewhere I understand—a place broken into too many pieces to ever put them back together.

I'm lost too—too lost to be found. But I want to go having tried to make this right.

Leander pulls me to my feet. When Selly comes up behind him, he turns toward her before she touches his arm, as though he already knew she was there. There's something in the way he looks at her—the way he's always a little angled toward her. This isn't one of Leander's crushes. This is different.

"Jude, meet Selly Walker."

"Good to meet you properly," she says with a soft smile. Of course—she was with him when we met at the club in Port Naranda. I'd hardly noticed her. They say in the Mellacean camp that she anchors Leander, tied to him in the same way Ruby is to Laskia, though I can already tell there's something very different about these two. She looks tired around the eyes, but nowhere near as ruined as Ruby.

"What I want to know is what you were doing there," Leander says, wrapping one arm around her shoulders. "What happened?"

I know what he means by *there*. Port Naranda, not the nightclub where I ran from him.

"It's a long story," I reply, weary. "My mother wanted to go home. She fell ill when we got there. Working for Ruby was . . . a way to make a living. To give my mother some kind of life."

"How is she now?" Leander asks—always so generous of heart, despite my mother being the one who took me away in the first place. Then he sees the answer on my face, and his smile falls away. "Oh, Jude, I'm sorry."

"Why did Laskia bring you here?" Selly asks gently.

I swallow down a sick feeling. "To give her intelligence on the royal family and their advisers. I'm not, of course."

"Of course," Leander agrees. "You needn't stay with them. We'll find a room for you in our dormitories. You should be with your friends."

I look at the dark wooden shelves, crammed with leather-bound books in blues, greens, and reds. Mathematics. Everything in those books adds up, makes sense. I'm more like the little book of bedtime stories tucked into my pocket, full of wishes and impossibilities.

How do I tell him I can't come back?

"Leander, we can't just . . . ," Selly says softly, and he turns his head to look at her. A pang hits me as I think of Tom. It's so stupid of me—I never had this with him, so why should I mourn it now?

Because, says a small voice inside me, *he tried to offer it to you.*

"Selly's right," I say, forcing the words out. "I'm not leaving them. I worked my way back in there on purpose. I'm there to gather intelligence, to be your man in the Mellacean camp. Anyway, you saw how it was today. If I defected, the war would start tomorrow."

"So what?" Leander asks, his tone too light for the question he's asking.

Selly flashes me a look of concern, brow creased, and I understand without words what she's thinking. Leander has always been a peacekeeper. To simply shrug off the prospect of a war . . .

The gods are changing people. Barrica has her hand on him, as surely as Macean is driving Laskia toward the edge of madness.

"I'm not going to be the one who causes it," I say firmly, and as I speak the words, I realize it's true. One hand slips to my back pocket, to my book of bedtime stories.

My heart clenches as I realize that some part of me brought

it with me for just this invitation, desperately hoping to be told I should come home. It's the only thing I wouldn't want to leave behind.

But I can't do it. Not when everything around us is kindling, just waiting for a spark to start a fire.

I won't be that spark.

I might be lost, but I have to hope our world isn't.

LASKIA

◆

The West Dormitories
The Bibliotek, the Barren Reaches

There's a common room we share, with doors leading to each of our sleeping quarters. Like everything else at the Bibliotek, it's simple but comfortable. Chairs are clustered around low tables to invite conversation, and shelves are stacked with books that I suspect the scholars rotate, depending on which diplomats or researchers have these rooms, and what they'd like to tell them. There's a lot of history on the shelves just now.

We've gathered here for our latest council of war—a few of the senior green sisters and a few of the diplomats and advisers I inherited when I took over the government. Ruby and me. And Macean, lounging full length on an oversized sofa, watching us like we're a second-rate show he's not quite energetic enough to walk away from.

"We are in a position of strength," a diplomat is saying earnestly. I can't remember her name—I'm not sure I bothered to learn it. "They cannot simply bind our god again. Barrica no longer has the strength advantage, which means they are forced to negotiate."

Sister Beris stares at the other woman as though she's speaking an unknown language. "What's wrong with you?" she asks, and all the attention in the room snaps to her.

"What's wrong with me?" the woman repeats, blinking.

"I've had enough," Beris snarls. "Ours is the god of risk. The Gambler. I am the head of his church, and my move will not be to simply *negotiate*. After five hundred years of labor to keep the flame of faith alive, fighting to awaken our god from his slumber, you want to *limit our losses?*" She swings around to Macean himself. "Honored Macean, I implore you," she tries. "This cannot be what we fought for."

She falls silent as he looks them over.

"*Negotiation.*" His drawl is as slow and easy as ever, the words spilling from his lips like silk. "*Doesn't sound very exciting, does it?*"

And then his gaze cuts to me. I understand him so clearly, it's as though he's spoken directly to me.

What are you doing, sitting here watching, waiting for them to decide what we'll do?

"*You can go,*" he says to the trembling diplomat. Then, glancing idly around his room, he flicks his fingers at the door. "*You can all go. This*"—and he tilts his head at Beris—"*is the more interesting option.*"

None of them says a word—they just rise and scuttle for the exits, taking their papers with them, leaving Macean with Beris, Ruby, and me.

Beris smirks, as though she's won some sort of victory, settling herself more comfortably in her chair. And I don't know what it is—that twist of her lips, the way she smooths out an invisible wrinkle in her robes—but a quick lance of pain runs through my jaw as I clench it.

She's a green sister. I'm the Messenger of my god.

Macean is right. What *am* I doing, sitting here, watching? Letting this woman who used me, who tried to undermine me with my own sister, who lied to me constantly, take over?

"Beris," I say slowly. "I don't think we need you, either."

Her gaze snaps across to me. "What?"

I can feel the way Macean's interest is stirring—the way he watches, to see if anything will come of this moment, as the tension sings through the air between me and the woman I used to trust. He revels in the feeling of anything hanging in the balance.

"I said," I repeat softly, "that we don't need you, either."

"I am the first sister," she snaps. "I am the leader of the church, child."

"No," I reply, coming to my feet, feeling as though I'm riding the crest of a wave, one that could dump me under at any moment, grind me to nothing against the rocks. Or it could push me along, faster than I've ever gone before. "No, Beris. *I* am the leader of the church."

"I was there when you came sniveling to your first service," she spits, her famous composure finally slipping. "If you think—"

Her words cut off with a strangled cry as I take a little of the power in me—the power Messengers have used to level mountains, to divert rivers—and do something much more difficult. I keep it all inside my skin, except for the smallest trickle. And that, I use to bear down on her will.

My heart pushes against my ribs, and the magic sings inside me, begging to be let out, to be allowed to pour into her, to consume her.

And slowly, she takes a step back.

"Honored Macean," Beris tries, her voice trembling, tearing her gaze from me. "All my life, I have served you. I am your first sister. I have led the church from the wilderness to become the power she is today. I have brought your people back to their worship. Please, you cannot—"

"Beris." My voice is a purr as I cut her off. My power is clamoring inside my head like a thousand church bells, shaking me from the inside out, but I'm utterly in control. "Beris, it's time for you to go."

"No." Her teeth are gritted now, her hands balled into fists. She's shaking where she stands, fighting to keep herself from running.

"Now!" I let my mind push against hers, show her just how small, how useless and how helpless she truly is. I curl my fist around her mind, and prepare to crush it.

I feel the moment she breaks, and then with a high, keening noise of fear, she scuttles for the door. A moment later it slams behind her.

"There," he drawls. *"Now we can have some fun. What took you so long?"*

"So long?"

"To claim your place. You pushed a whole government aside without batting a lash, but that woman . . ."

"She heads your church. I thought you'd want—"

"*You hold a part of my power in a way she cannot understand. You are the doorway through which I entered this world. She sensed it.*"

"She always wanted to be first sister," I say softly. "But then even that wasn't enough for her."

"*Mmm. Enough.*" He draws out the word as though he's trying it on, trying to imagine what *enough* might feel like. Then he shrugs, and his voice shifts to something firmer. "*I must go.*"

"What? Where?"

"*To my mother's temple,*" he replies, with a nod toward the heart of the Bibliotek. "*I must speak with her.*"

My lips part in surprise. "You can do that?"

He simply gazes at me until I feel my cheeks heat at my own stupidity.

"*My mother is strongest here,*" he says, his voice like velvet. "*Here, where she is worshipped above all others. That is why she has summoned us here.*"

There are so many things I could say, so many questions I could ask. But I stay silent, and I stand there, shaking, until he turns on his heel and walks away.

Only then do I let myself collapse on the couch beside Ruby, who's curled herself up there, and is hugging a cushion. The shadows under her eyes are darker than ever.

"This is going to end badly, isn't it?" I say quietly.

Ruby snorts, like I haven't heard her do since we were small. "You awakened a god, allied yourself with a woman who dreamed of overthrowing the head of her own church, now you've overthrown *her,* and you're locked in a negotiation nobody wants, with no chance of success by any definition. I don't know how it's going to end, but it's sure going to be interesting before it's over."

I want to ask her what I should do, but I can't. Not with Ruby's anger softly pulsing at me through our bond. So instead, I cast my mind back to a memory.

"When I came back from burning the prince's fleet, I came to tell you what I'd done. I dropped Beris off and went to shower first, to tidy up. We'd been at sea for days. By the time I reached you, Beris was already there. She must have left as soon as she was out of my sight, rushing to speak to you first."

I feel rather than see Ruby's shrug. "She's willing to take a risk. That makes sense."

I hesitate then, the words thick in my throat. But I force them out. "You let her in. You listened to her. And when I came, you dismissed me."

"That's true," Ruby agrees.

I want to stop there. I don't want to ask. But I do. "What did she have that I didn't? Why did you turn to her? It was my plan. I did that for you. She just came along to watch."

Ruby glances at me, and I look back. She glows softly in my vision, with the power I've poured into her. "You, I could always rely on," she says. "Beris, I could never trust. I had to keep her close, if I wanted to see the plan through to its end." She huffs a soft breath of what might be laughter. "Remember when the plan was to start a war so we could work the weapons market? Those were the days."

A flush of something far too close to pleasure goes through me at *You, I could always rely on,* a warmth spreading through my chest. "You never said that before. That you could rely on me."

"We're not the kind who say things like that," Ruby replies.

Was I wrong all along? Was Ruby always going to let me in, if I'd been patient?

"You're a funny match with Macean, really," she says, when I don't reply.

"How do you mean?"

"Well, you took risks, plenty of them. But it was never really because you loved the roll of the dice. You just wanted approval. You wanted certainty. And you wanted it so badly, you'd do anything to get it."

Her words sting. "You wanted power," I shoot back. "And you'd do anything to get it."

"At least I don't lie about who I am," she replies, unrepentant. And there it is, just like always—that hint of scorn in her voice.

Little Laskia. Just wanted someone to tell her she was a good girl. That she did a good job.

My magic swells inside me again, thumping at my temples with my heartbeat. I reach across to lock my hand onto her wrist, and she gasps in pain, trying desperately to pull away, as I drain it into her.

Who's in control now, Ruby?

I'm alone, perhaps an hour later, when Dasriel slips into the common room. He greets me with a nod and crosses to pour himself a drink from the pot that sits by the stove.

"Ruby asleep?" he asks, after a sip.

"No. She's trying, but her mind feels busy."

He doesn't seem unnerved by the fact that I can tell that

from out here. Instead, he just takes another sip, and eases down onto the edge of one of the sofas.

"Heard you sent Beris to bed without any dinner," he observes.

I cast him a sharp look. How did word get around so quickly?

He meets my eyes, and simply shrugs. His direct gaze isn't a challenge like hers is, though. He's seen me at my best. He's seen me at my worst. He's still here. Originally, Ruby assigned him to me as my muscle. Now, I'm not sure what he is. Has whatever's between Dasriel and me become true loyalty? Or is he just not stupid, and standing behind the most likely victor?

He's Mellacean, after all. Perhaps he's just gambling on me.

"I had to do something about Beris eventually," I say, making myself sound certain.

"True enough," he agrees.

"She and Ruby are different."

"What makes you say that?" he asks quietly.

The sound of the fire crackling in the hearth is the only thing that breaks the silence. What *did* make me say that? Did I want him to agree? To tell me that Ruby's still my sister and that means something?

"Where does this end, Dasriel?" I ask softly, instead of answering his question.

He snorts. "You know the answer to that."

"Do I?"

"You know who he is. You think the god of risk ever wanted to shake hands with his sister and go home? He's never a moment without dice in his hands, never alive unless he's tipping the balance on something, to see if it'll fall. There's just one thing he wants, and that's the biggest gamble of all. Only question is whether there'll be any historians left to write a book about it for the scholars to put on their shelves."

His words settle heavily between us, and with a sick feeling in my gut, I let myself press my face into my hands, just for a moment.

I think my bodyguard might be the only honest voice I have left.

THREE DAYS OF PEACE REMAINING

LEANDER

The Hall of Scholars
The Bibliotek, the Barren Reaches

The ambassadors are panicking, and I can understand why. They sit in a ring of chairs around the edge of the main table with their priests by their sides, and whispers travel along the row of them like ripples in water. They jab fingers as they softly make points and cast worried glances at us, and occasionally one gets up and leaves, presumably to send a report to their leaders.

Three days remain until the Mother's deadline. The wait feels interminable.

Father Marsen is speaking now—his chest plate gleams in the sun from the windows, and his faith seems to amplify his voice, which cuts through the noise around us.

"Last time," he bellows at Macean's delegation, "every country here united because of *you*. All other gods stepped back from this place, because of *you*. Our goddess devoted five centuries to her duties as a sentinel, because of *you*."

Laskia rises to her feet to speak over him, and her voice really *is* amplified, the air spirits puffing and swirling to carry it around the room. "And our god was bound in slumber, and all of us were left alone, because of *you*!"

Scholar Kel, who's standing at the head of the table, raises their voice, helplessly trying to cut in. "Both parties are—"

They're drowned out.

Kel stands in front of the huge window, and beyond them are the Barren Reaches, the ruins of the city of Vostain, the graves of every one of Valus's people.

I understand their desperation to find some sort of peace. But how much should we give, for something like that? Lines have to be drawn in the end.

As if echoing my thoughts, Augusta comes to her feet. "What are we to do, then, Messenger of Macean?" she asks, her voice thick with contempt as she gestures at the ring of ambassadors. "Should we choose which of our neighbors' lands you can have as your price for sparing the others?"

That causes a flurry of shouts from around the room, with ambassadors on their feet and priests trying to invoke the wrath of their own gods, as if they have a chance of raising them.

Barrica sits silent and unmoving beside Augusta, but I can read her thoughts behind her stern expression.

She's been here before.

For us, this is the first round of negotiations, our first attempt at peace talks. For her, this is a conversation she's had over and over again with people who've been dead for centuries. She understands the inevitability of every part of this conversation, the way each step has been laid out in advance.

And I'm starting to as well.

Ours is the warrior goddess. It will fall to us to make war, that we might keep the peace. It's a renewal that will serve us all—even those who suffer.

Sometimes, I can hear the cries of battle in my mind. Smell the sweat. See the flash of light on the metal of guns and knives. A dream of the past, a memory from Anselm . . . or a vision of the future? I'm not sure anymore that there's a difference.

"Leander." Selly leans in to whisper in my ear, jolting me back to the present. "We should take a break, before someone says something they can't take back."

I glance at her, and find her green eyes waiting for mine. I drink in her fair, freckled skin that I want to kiss, and her full lips, and when I reach up to tuck a strand of her blond hair behind her ear, I come back to myself and remember who I am.

I'm Leander, who made this girl a paper boat, and a promise to keep on caring for her. To remember who we are, together.

"Leander," she whispers again. "Someone's about to cross a line. We need to take a break."

"You think they can take back what they're saying now?" I ask softly. "You think they should?"

"Use your rank," she whispers urgently. "Call for a break. You're her Messenger, you can make them stop for a minute. Do this for me." She pauses, and I catch the flicker of recoil in her thoughts before she hides it. "And there's too much power in you. You need to give some of it to me to carry."

My gut drops, and there's a sour taste in the back of my mouth. I *hate* hurting her. I can barely stand to do it—except that in the end I always have no choice, and the longer I wait, the more pain it causes her.

I push abruptly to my feet, and all around the table, heads turn in surprise.

Augusta takes my cue—she's too seasoned a diplomat to let anything look accidental—and she stands as well.

Relieved, Scholar Kel jumps into the break I've created. "We will take a recess," they announce, as though it was their idea.

The rest of our party are waiting for us when we make our way out into the anteroom. Kiki starts to move toward Selly, then pauses when she sees the two of us move to the side, hands joined. She winces.

"I'm sorry," I whisper, as I do every time.

"Don't be," Selly replies, sticking her lower lip out, daring me to continue.

I will those around us not to notice we're here, and that's all it takes—they turn away, they speak to each other, and we're as good as invisible.

I lean Selly back against the wall, resting one hand by her head to keep my weight off her, letting our bodies meet as our lips do. A bolt of desire shivers through me, mixing with that full-to-bursting feeling of too much magic, too much power.

Would it be possible to vent it another way? To dismantle a city, instead of pouring it into my anchor, this girl who's stood with me through everything?

The tiniest trickle of temptation courses through my thoughts. In three days' time, if we're at war, then this power would have a place to go that *isn't* Selly. This power would have a purpose. *I* would have a purpose.

Then Selly jabs me in the ribs with one finger, and I break the kiss, forcing myself to smile. She reaches up to cup my face with one hand.

"Go on, Leander. Let me help you carry it."

And so I let it flow through her. It's like pouring water out of me and into her. Every muscle in my body releases, and the pain grows less as my skin stops prickling, my lungs no longer bound tight.

I feel the pain sing through her body, and fight the urge to take it all back from her—and then slowly it dissipates, and she's left breathing hard, pale in the wake of it.

I smooth her hair back from her forehead, which is damp with sweat. And for the first time, I see a few strands of silver in among the gold. My breath catches, and I turn cold. Every time we do this, it costs her more.

How many times can her body survive this?

When we gather ourselves enough to look up and rejoin the room, conversation is in full swing around us. Lord Wollesley stands beside my sister, his expression like a thundercloud. That's when I realize Keegan is nowhere in sight—he didn't show up to the negotiations.

"What I'm saying is that we need to accept that we *cannot* negotiate," Lord Wollesley's saying, jabbing a finger to make his point, though it's not clear anyone around him needs convincing. "That would require good faith from the Mellaceans."

"It would require good faith from *us*," Selly says beside me, her voice hoarse. "Are we showing it? We start the shouting as often as they do."

"We have something to shout about, at least," I point out. "They're the ones who upset the balance."

Her gaze snaps to mine, and I don't need our bond to read her expression: *What are you doing? Why are you undermining me?*

"We're not looking for a fight," I say, mostly to her, and a little to hear the words out loud. "But they're looking to take land from our neighbors around the Crescent Sea. From us! And we're the only ones with a god capable of meeting them. Do we wait until it's happening before we do something to prevent it?"

Selly's eyes widen, and abruptly I feel the barrier between us strengthen, as though she's physically recoiled from me.

Then Barrica speaks, and everyone falls silent. *"It is time to consider the idea that my brother will never concede. Risk, after all, is his domain. And what greater risk than this?"*

Selly's the one who replies, her voice a whisper now. "Then what do you want us to do, Goddess?"

Barrica's gaze sweeps over each of us in turn, and I wonder if I see regret in her blue eyes.

"Perhaps," she says, *"we are the ones who should be looking to new territory."*

SELLY

◆

The Memorial Library
The Bibliotek, the Barren Reaches

"Where are we going?" Leander asks, as I lead him along the hallway, our fingers twined together.

"I want to show you something."

I push open an ornate wooden door and pull him through it. The Bibliotek is like a labyrinth of small libraries all joined together, each with its own personality and purpose. The one I've chosen today is for historians, and that's deliberate. We need to talk.

"One of the scholars told me about this place," I say, as we make our way among the ancient bookshelves. "It's an archive."

"Of what?"

"The war."

The shelves are made of wood so old it almost seems like stone, crammed with texts I'm too scared to touch, some framed in glass cases.

A blue shield is mounted on one wall. It's nicked and battered—it's seen real combat—and has a faded white spear painted on it. Leander leans in to read the engraved plate beneath it.

"The shield of Princess Sammia," he murmurs.

"Do you know who she was?"

"Anselm's sister. She became queen after he died. She fought alongside him in the last campaign."

We make our way among the displays—there are battle maps and roughly drawn sketches and scratched and dented weapons that turn the long-ago war into a real battle, between real people. It's impossible to think of it as a story when we can see the hits they took.

One sketch stops both of us, and Leander's arm curls slowly around my shoulders as we gaze up at it. It's of a man. He's older than Leander, but despite the five centuries that separate them, they're clearly related. The lines of the drawing are still crisp on the yellowed paper, and we don't need to read the inscription to know who he is.

"Anselm," I whisper.

He's looking at some distant point on the horizon, his expression tired and sad, but resolute. The portrait is drawn with such attention to detail—it feels like it was made by someone who cared about him.

"It's strange to think that Barrica knew him," Leander says softly. "I mean, you know she's always been here, but . . ."

"But she was really there. For all of it. He looks sad, don't you think? Determined, but so sad."

"I wonder when it was drawn," Leander murmurs.

He doesn't say it, but the question is on both our minds. *Did he already know how it was going to end?*

And it's there, by Anselm's portrait, that I turn toward my prince, and the words come tumbling out.

"Leander, I don't want to lose you. I don't want you to be the next royal she costs us."

"I don't want to go anywhere," he replies, wrapping his arms around me. "But we can't just give in to what they demand."

"I feel like . . ." Even as I speak, the words are like water, slipping through my fingers as I try to hold them long enough for him to see sense, to understand. "Don't you see it? Nobody's even negotiating. The gods are here because the Mother told them to come, but Macean wants to throw the dice, and Barrica was made to fight."

Leander lets out a slow breath, his lashes lowering as he closes his eyes. "Selly, maybe she was made that way for a reason."

Something inside me hollows out. "Leander, no."

"We all act according to our nature," he says softly. "Birds nest, fish swim, and the warrior goddess . . . it's the same thing, I think. She was made as she is to keep the balance in the world. Sometimes war is what creates the space for something else to come next. Something good."

"How can it be good?" I whisper. "At that price? How are we even peacekeepers when we're the ones who want this? How are we not the aggressors?"

His eyes open, and his green-eyed gaze is steady—I've never missed his warm brown eyes more than in this moment.

"Selly, they're Mellacean. They were made to grasp. We were made to break that grasp."

I gaze up at him, and there's not even a hint of softness in his face.

I'm trying so hard to fight Barrica for this boy I love. For the boy who made me a paper boat just days ago, and told me it was a new promise—a promise that he cared for me.

I'm fighting Barrica, as she tries to drain that part of him away. But I'm losing. Perhaps I've already lost.

Neither of us speaks on our way back to our quarters, where most of the Alinorish delegation is scattered in groups around the common room.

Neither of us reaches for the other's hand.

Leander can go a little without venting, and I need . . . I don't know what I need. Space. Time. A chance to *think*.

Leander lets me drift away, and I cross over to Kiki, who's flipping through a huge book she swears she got from a library devoted entirely to fashion.

"Hello, sunshine!" she begins, looking up. "I—oh my, that's a face."

I sink down beside her and she closes the book, turning her attention to me. "I don't know what to do," I whisper, swallowing hard against the way my throat wants to close.

"Auntie Kiki will help," she says solemnly, or as solemnly as Kiki gets. "Tell me everything."

I can't even make myself smile for her. "He's not thinking clearly, Kiki. His tie to the goddess is— He thinks war is inevitable, and we haven't even *tried* to avoid it. Is it because he's a prince? Does he not understand what that kind of fight would actually be, would actually *mean* for real people? But that can't be it. He was with me, I saw how it affected him when my crew died for him." The pressure behind my eyes is unbearable, and I lift my chin as if tipping my face up will stop tears from falling. "Where's that boy now, Kiki?"

She's looking at me strangely, her smile gone, and the silence between us stretches.

"Selly," she says eventually, her rich voice full of regret. "That boy, the one who could hardly stand to see your crew die for his pilgrimage? That boy grew up."

Something cold takes hold of me. "What do you mean?"

Kiki glances at the chair where Barrica so often sits, though the goddess isn't there now. "It's who we are," she says slowly. "Alinor's people. The kind of peace you're talking about . . . that's a child's dream. We all grow up, even Leander. Even me. That part of us was asleep for a long time, but . . . if war is where our goddess leads us, we'll follow."

The coldness inside me is spreading through my limbs, pinning me in place as though I've turned to stone.

One by one, they're all falling into line. They're all becoming the warriors she wants them to be. Soon, hiding behind the mental barricade that Barrica herself taught me to build, will I be the only one left who sees clearly?

Her nature is to want war.

And soon, she's going to have one.

SELLY

Vostain
The Barren Reaches

Barrica and I stand together, looking out over the ruined land of Vostain.

You can still see the outlines of the streets. The city itself has been reduced to piles of rubble that lie strewn around rivers of rock that melted and hardened again centuries ago.

Jagged pieces of stone point up at the sky in accusation, and not even a hint of green shows among the bones of the city, despite the five hundred years that have passed.

"What was your brother like?" I ask, the still air seeming to swallow my words.

"Valus?" Her voice is as rich and musical as ever, almost hypnotic, and the note of sorrow that weaves through it now brings the hot prickle of tears to my eyes.

"Valus."

She came here when I asked her to, walking with me in silence. It almost seemed she'd been expecting it.

"He was joyful. He made you happier when you were near him. He didn't seem to take anything seriously, but there was a depth to him most did not suspect."

I wipe my tears away with the back of my hand and fix my gaze on a broken tower before us. "You could be describing Leander."

"*I suppose I could.*"

There aren't even birds here, now that I look at the ruins properly. There are seabirds down by the port, but the air above the dead city is still.

"No green, no signs of life," I murmur. "Everything is gone."

"*His people are gone,*" she replies. "*And his grief is so great that nothing can live here. Nothing can grow from this loss.*"

"Nobody's ever tried to rebuild? Nobody's come to worship him? Couldn't he start again?"

Barrica shakes her head. "*He is too deep in his loss to be reached. And faith is harder to come by than last time I was here.*"

"It grew less when you went away?"

"*Perhaps,*" she replies. "*Or perhaps faith is just harder to find in a world with electric lights. With such proof of wonders, few need to believe.*"

We're both quiet for a little, standing vigil over the dead land before us, but eventually I speak again. I have questions, and it's past time to ask them.

"I want to know—and it's safe for you to tell me, because they're all where you wanted them now—was this always the plan?"

I feel her press against my mind to understand which *this* I mean. I strengthen my mental net against her a little, and she pulls back in response, leaving me alone.

"*Impressive,*" she murmurs.

"I meant all of it," I say. "The war. Leander as your Messenger. Me as his anchor. Summoning you back to our world. Was it always your plan, that we'd end up where we are?"

"*You credit me with the ability to see many, many moves ahead,*" she observes.

"You bet I do, Goddess of War."

She's quiet, and I make myself wait, though impatience surges in my veins and beats with my pulse. I want *answers*. Then she tilts her head to tell me to follow, and sets off down the broken steps in front of us, gravel crunching beneath her feet.

"My magician's marks," I press, as I climb down after her. "They never changed, not since I was a child. I never found the spirits, before Leander showed me how. Was that . . ." My fingernails press into my palms, my knuckles aching as I clench my fists. "Was that you? Were you keeping me ready for Leander? Did you stop me from finding my magic?"

"*Yes,*" she says simply.

Shock ripples through me, my breath sticking in my throat. But at the same time, some part of me isn't surprised at all. That part of me had already worked it out.

All that pain, that humiliation. Every time I was dragged to yet another teacher, to be told I was a failure. Every time I pulled my gloves on to hide the marks that showed I was a freak. The lack that shaped who I am in every way, that shaped my relationship with my father, that took over my life . . . she caused it.

Make the most of it. That's what my father always says—they're the words that should be on his headstone. And here was his daughter with this gift—these magician's marks—that she couldn't make *anything* of. Everything that failure cost me, she caused.

"And Leander?" I manage, feeling dizzy. "Did you make him a powerful magician so he could be your Messenger?"

"No, that was luck. It took many generations for a royal magician with such power to be born." She crouches down, the move sinuous and deliberate, to turn over a piece of rubble, revealing a little carved face on the other side. *"He did have to . . . make a place within himself, though. Somewhere for you to fit, as his anchor."*

I dread the answer, but I make myself ask anyway. "And how did you do that? Have him make a place inside himself?"

Barrica glances up at me. *"I can tell you think I revel in such things, Selly. I do not delight in war, or in loss. I simply understand it as a part of the cycle of your world. A necessary part."*

"What did you do?" I demand, nausea pushing its way up my throat. "How did you make a space inside Leander for me? What did you take away?"

She sighs. *"It was when he was aboard your ship. He conjured wind and waves to flee from your pursuers. It was as powerful an act of magic as any magician has ever performed. Only a few have even had the skill—only those gifted by their gods with the ability to summon more than one type of spirit, as I have gifted my royal family."*

I can picture Leander aboard the *Lizabetta,* standing with his arms outstretched, calling up the wind and waves of the storm that swept us along. That so nearly got us away from Laskia.

We said then that we didn't know what he was sacrificing to the spirits for that sort of power.

We wondered if it was a part of himself.

"So he . . . he made a space inside himself with that sacrifice?"

"*A place for his anchor to fit,*" Barrica agrees. "*My Messengers were always consumed by their power too quickly. I wished him to live.*"

The full meaning of what she's just said suddenly clicks into place. "So you killed my crew?" I manage, shock trickling through me and flickering into hot anger. "To force him to sacrifice himself, you put him in such a desperate situation—one my crew never would have been in. . . ."

"*Everything in nature kills something, in order to live,*" Barrica replies calmly.

I can see them still. Kyri, smiling, pulling me aside to whisper some gossip with Abri. Rensa, her jaw clenched, reaching for her patience yet again, but turning toward me every time, never away. Conor and Jonlon, side by side always, one wiry and quick, the other a gentle giant.

I can see each of them, sprawled on the deck, their life simply . . . gone. So quickly that it seemed impossible.

I can see Leander, his hands clamped over his mouth to stop himself from screaming.

And I can see him just now, in the library, telling me that somehow war is a natural part of the world.

I can see myself, a child, sobbing in the dark over the magician's marks that had ruined her life.

Barrica did all of this.

And I can't scream at her, I can't strike out. I have to force my anger down. I have to understand, especially if I'm the last sane person left at the Bibliotek.

There's one more thing I have to know.

"You planned our bond before we ever met," I say slowly. "Did you . . . did you make me feel the way I do, about Leander? And him about me?"

Barrica sets down the little piece of stone and pushes to her feet. *"No. I said to Anselm once that I am only the frame upon which the vine may grow."*

I squint at her. "Meaning?"

"I set the stage," she replies. *"But I cannot command the players in that respect."*

Deep in my own heart, something releases, and the relief of it rushes through my veins, spreading to every part of me.

I really do love him. He really does love me. Or . . . he did, once. Before all of this, before he began to hear those war drums and pull away from me.

Barrica begins to walk again, and I follow her, our shoes crunching in the silence as we make our way along what must have been a street, long ago.

"You remember what you said to Anselm?" I ask, as I shore up my mental shields against her once more.

"Of course. We fought side by side for many years in the last war." There's something in her voice—almost a catch. *Were they friends?*

"He died for you," I say. "You let him do that."

"Yes." Her voice is heavier still.

"I just can't help thinking . . ." The words want to tumble out, and after a moment, I let them. "He died to help you win the war. Because it was the only way to end the war. But did the war ever have to happen? Were you defending those who needed it, or were you the one who started it?"

Barrica pauses, looking across at a mess of wreckage. I can see carved columns among the debris. *"This used to be a concert hall,"* she says, half-lost in the memory. She lifts one hand, and as I stare in disbelief, the stones and rubble lift and dance through the air to rebuild themselves. They fit together seamlessly—I can't even see a hairline crack—the columns soaring as the building rises above us. It's as tall as the palace in Alinor, and carved all over its wide frontage are intricate reliefs that show people in all kinds of costumes, laughing and dancing.

In just a few heartbeats, a piece of Vostain is lost no more, but stands before us, breathtakingly lovely.

"I saw a play here," Barrica says, gazing up at the huge stone edifice. *"The boy who had the lead part was so beautiful, people used to turn and stare after him when he walked down the street."*

"Did he die, when you and Macean fought here?"

"Yes."

Again she lifts her hand, then curls it into a fist, and just like that the building collapses, stones crashing and sending up clouds of dust and debris as I skip backward, jumping over a broken piece of masonry to take shelter.

"It was beautiful!" I protest, staring at a chunk of stone that stares back at me, one carved eye still visible.

"Valus prefers to grieve," she replies. *"He will not rebuild. He cannot die, but he refuses to survive the loss of his people."*

"And do you . . . do you care at all about that?" My anger gets away from me in a quick, hot flush. "Do you feel anything at all, when you think about the loss of a boy so beautiful he stopped traffic? Of all the ordinary, everyday people who came here to see a show, to laugh or cry? Who had lives of their own, however small and petty you thought them?"

"My child." Her voice rings through me, and I have to brace myself to stay on my feet, to keep my knees from giving out. *"My feelings run deeper than yours, I assure you. I simply care for different things. I do not wish your prince to die. I do not wish you to die. You humans live for an instant, like fireflies flashing to life and then gone again, but still I grow fond of you."*

"And yet."

"And yet I am called to conflict. The leaves must fall in autumn, that the tree may bud again in spring. This is my part."

As I gaze at the ruined city, I can feel in my bones that there's no changing her mind. She won't consider any other way the world might work. Perhaps she truly can't.

"It is my hope," she says eventually, *"that you will come to understand why I must do as I do."*

I have to make sure she doesn't see me as a threat.

"I just want to stay alive a little longer," I say softly, letting my voice catch. It's not hard to let the emotion out. "I want a little more time with Leander."

"That, I hope you will have."

And so I bow and turn away to begin the hike back to the Bibliotek, leaving behind my goddess among the ruins she created.

What am I going to do?

The Mother demanded they speak for six days, before they fought on the seventh.

Today is the fourth.

What am I going to do?

TWO DAYS OF PEACE REMAINING

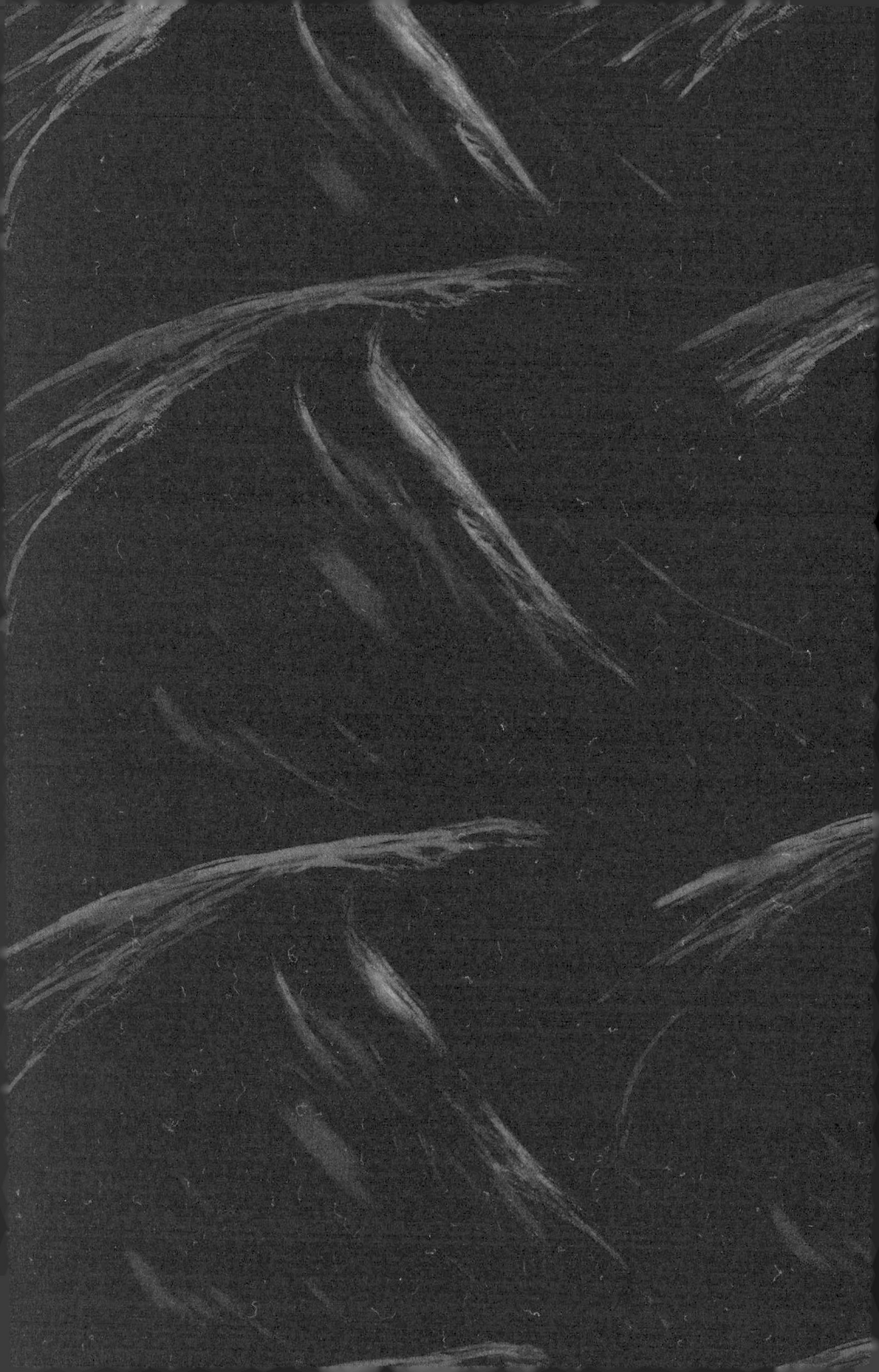

KEEGAN

The Theologians' Library
The Bibliotek, the Barren Reaches

I glance over my shoulder, then move deeper into the library, Jude close on my heels. This place is long and narrow, the shelves towering several stories above us. They're accessed by spindly wrought-iron spiral staircases at regular intervals, the symbols of the gods worked into the latticework—a spear, a pair of dice, a rose, an ear of wheat, and so on.

In one hand I hold an ancient book against my chest; with the other I carefully smooth my stolen scholar's robes.

Our hosts have been welcoming, but there was no chance they were going to let me into the Theologians' Library unsupervised, not when I might be looking for an advantage against the other side. What we need to do can't be seen by anyone, so I raided their laundry. Ordinarily I'd have enlisted Kiki for that, but even she has fallen to Barrica.

It physically hurt to pull the robes on over my head. This could have been my life, and I still yearn for it with the kind of desperation that manifests itself in my body. It feels like the ultimate cruelty, that I should be wearing these robes, but only pretending to have joined the scholars' ranks.

Instead, I have just come from a conversation with my father, which led me as far as I can go from the life of a scholar. I went to such lengths to escape him. I can still remember the way my heart was in my mouth as I lifted the gold necklaces that were supposed to pay my way to this very place. The way my pulse beat in my temples as I climbed out the window. Now, I have more pain to add to that tally—the knowledge that I hurt Kiki deeply, whether I meant to or not. And it was all for nothing.

"It may be that we can even make a better match than Kiki Dastenholtz, with you as a personal aide to the Messenger," my father mused this morning, as if he hadn't been screaming at me to be grateful for what I could get just a month ago.

"Father, I don't—"

"For now," he continued, as if I hadn't spoken, "we have other business to attend to." And then it was back to talk of war, as it always is.

They haven't even bothered to try and negotiate this morning. It's the fifth day of our six enforced days of peace, and now it feels as though everyone is just waiting out the clock.

That's why Jude and I are here. He sees it too—the way our people hunger for war, look for ways to squabble even with each other. The way the Mellaceans' fingers twitch to roll the dice. But none of them see it in themselves.

I spoke to Leander last night, and he scared me.

We've become friends, since that first day on the deck of

the *Lizabetta*. We speak frankly. We share trust, in the way that only those who have leaped and caught each other can.

"How do you think Anselm felt?" I asked, as we watched the queen and Father Marsen spread out great maps on the table in our Alinorish common room, marking out the territory we might need to protect. "He fought in a war. What do you think it was like for him?"

I know exactly what the old Leander would have said: *I imagine he was terrified, but looked great in his armor. It's a gift that runs in my family.*

The new Leander had a simple reply, his gaze never leaving the maps.

"Purpose. I think Anselm felt as we do, an overwhelming sense of purpose."

I'm losing my friend. I'd only just found him.

I have never worshipped, never gone to temple. I accepted the reality of the gods—the evidence is plentiful, of course—but I have always preferred a library to any other sense of certainty. I don't know if that's what protects me now—I find it hard to believe. There must be others who do not turn to the gods for guidance, so if that's what protects me, then where are they?

Selly tells us she has a way of protecting her mind from Barrica's influence, but why Jude and I have been spared, we don't know. It's impossible not to be awed by Barrica and Macean in their presence, and I can feel how easily my mind might slip from there into the place all my companions occupy. We have to do this work quickly, in case that happens.

I lead the way to a quiet corner, lean back against the wall, and bend my knees to slide down it until I can sit in the shadows, still cradling my book. Its worn leather cover once had a design etched on it in gold, but centuries of hands have worn it away.

Jude's carrying the other books, and he moves on silent feet to join me, dropping to a crouch.

The queen sent scholars here to search for information on summoning the gods, before Barrica rejoined us. The texts they consulted are recorded in the access lists, so I started there.

Next, I moved to archival materials—records from five centuries ago are surprisingly easy to find—and theoretical texts by religious scholars, who have spent quite a lot of time thinking about how to bring the gods back. That sort of thing is naturally interesting to them.

All the material I needed was far easier to locate than I had anticipated, but I've realized that it was never really intended to be hidden. This is a library, after all. Everything has its place. The knowledge was only ever obscured because, for the last five hundred years, there was no realistic prospect of using it.

Carefully I open the book's cover, minding the binding's ancient stitches, and turn the pages with reverence. This volume is a copy of a much, much older book, but even this version's more than two hundred years old.

I find an illuminated illustration of Barrica and two other gods—the colors are still bright, the thick black lines of ink outlining the portraits still fresh. And inside these pages, the gold leaf still gleams.

My breath catches in my throat at the likeness of it. Barrica stands tall, her shield in one hand, her sword in the other.

Beside her stands Kyion, tall and slender, with skin the same rich, warm brown as the fertile soil of Ladriana and Nusraya.

They hold a sheaf of wheat, to mark their affiliation with farming and fertility.

Then comes Sutista, clad in red and holding a flower, the symbol of her domain over matters of the heart. To this day, the Trallian, Fontesquan, and Caspian flags bear that flower, or versions of it.

What steals my breath, though, is the familiarity of the illustration. Barrica's head is tilted in just the same way as I saw this morning. Her feet are planted on the ground, one a little ahead of the other, just as she always stands.

Whoever drew her portrait in the original book, many centuries ago, had met her. And though I knew our goddess was eternal, this reminder that she was *here,* that she knew those who walked this place all those years ago . . . it's enough to shake one. Yet again, her age is brought home to me—the fact that she is playing this game on a board that spans centuries, even millennia.

"If only we hadn't missed our chance," I mutter, gazing down at the page.

"What do you mean?" Jude asks softly.

"We tried to appeal to the gods to take Laskia's power from her—my reading suggested that without a Messenger, Macean wouldn't be able to appear. But she anticipated us—she used a Mellacean spy—and we failed."

Jude blinks at me, wearing an expression I'm all too familiar with in those around me—he's trying to make sense of what I've just said. "How have we missed our chance?"

"Because Macean is here. He has used Laskia as his doorway. It is done."

Jude leans forward to press his hand to the book, to stop me from turning the page and to command my attention. "Keegan," he whispers urgently, "that's not what Macean said to me."

I go still. "What do you mean?"

"He told me to stay close to him," Jude says slowly. "He told me he couldn't be without a Messenger if he wished to remain. He wanted me as a backup, in case Laskia burned herself up with his power."

We stare at each other for a long moment before I speak. I try the words out, letting them sink in properly. "He spoke as if there was still a way he could be banished from our realm? If he lost Laskia?"

Jude nods.

I take a careful breath, but my hands are trembling. "The letters I read back in Alinor suggested the other gods would help us break the Messenger's bonds, if they could. But we don't know how to create that opportunity for them. I thought we had to do it before Macean returned, so I had abandoned my research."

Jude swallows hard. "The way he spoke to me, I'd say we can still do it. And you think they'd help us to banish . . . only Macean?"

"No, I . . . I think we need to banish them both. If we banish Macean and not Barrica, do you think anyone in that meeting room will hesitate to carry out their plans for war?"

Jude's jaw tightens, and wordlessly he shakes his head.

"Well then."

Jude closes his eyes. "But we don't have any idea how to . . . how to de-Messenger Laskia *or* Leander, unless it's by killing them. And even then, it sounds like Macean could just recruit me, probably whether I wanted to or not. I assume Barrica would try using someone for a Messenger."

"We're not killing Leander," I reply fiercely. "We're going to find something, Jude. This is what I do. I research. I find answers. What we need is somewhere in this place, and I'm going to track it down."

"I know you are," he murmurs, touching my hand in silent apology.

But the real question we can't answer rings out between us, as loudly as if it had been spoken: *Will I do it in time?*

The question settles on me like a weight.

There's a way to send the gods back—to banish them from our world and prevent this war from ever beginning.

But to do that, we have to destroy their gateways.

What will we do if we run out of time?

To stop Barrica's war, would I be prepared to take Leander's life?

ONE DAY
OF PEACE
REMAINING

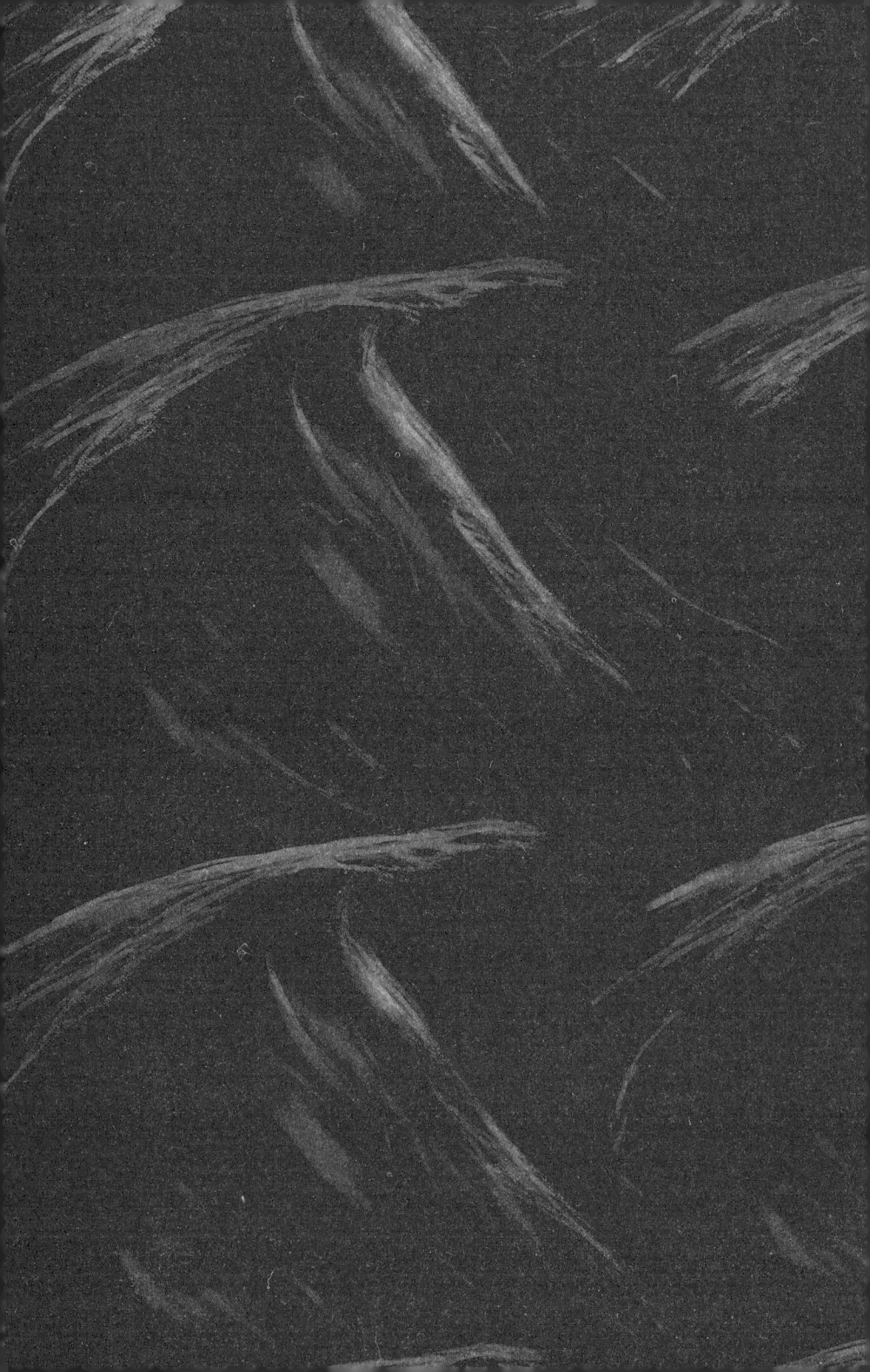

SELLY

The Harbor
The Bibliotek, the Barren Reaches

I'm sitting with Leander in our common room, our hands joined, as he slowly bleeds magic into me. The sensation spreads through my body, my tendons singing, my bones aching. It's getting harder to wake up each morning, and my body's starting to protest every time I try to climb stairs, my joints sending jolts of pain through my hips and down my legs.

Every time we do this, it costs me more, and I'm forced to tighten the mental net between us to prevent him from seeing just how much it hurts me.

Still, though, our minds are twined together enough that I can feel the way the burden lifts off him—and also the way it's not quite enough, not quite as much relief as it was the first time.

The gift of the goddess keeps pouring power into him, like a river into a dam that has to lift its gate, or else break. But every time I try to help him lift the gate, it's a little more difficult, and a little less helpful.

"You all right?" he asks, his voice hoarse.

I look at the shadows beneath his eyes. "Are *you*?"

"I'll be fine. Where's Keegan gone?"

"In the library again. I think he slept there last night."

And then the door to the common room bursts open, and Kiki comes flying through it, heaving for breath. She's been *running*. The whole room snaps to attention, conversations breaking off—the one thing everybody knows about Kiki is that she doesn't voluntarily run anywhere.

"Quick!" she gasps, flapping one hand behind her and bending over to brace her hands against her knees. "The—quick!" Giving up on words, she straightens up and wheels around to race back the way she came. I'm pretty sure I ricochet off the queen of Alinor herself as we cram ourselves through the doorway.

"It's only the sixth day!" Augusta shouts, tearing along beside me. "We have until tomorrow before they're allowed to—Lady Dastenholtz, what's happened?"

Kiki tears down the hallway, grabbing a doorframe to swing herself around to the left. We're right on her heels as she bursts onto a balcony that overlooks the Bibliotek's harbor.

Ships from around the world, carrying scholars and negotiators and diplomats, are moored side by side, and all looks quiet below us. I haven't been down to the docks since we arrived.

Why not? Why didn't I go to smell the salt and remember who I am?

I look at Kiki, who simply points out to sea, beyond the mouth of the harbor.

There's a fleet sailing toward us, ten ships in total, and there's an Alinorish flag at the top of every mast, sapphire blue cut through with a white spear. I look them over automatically, not expecting to recognize any, and then . . .

. . . then I'm pressing a hand to my mouth, my body suddenly lighter, as though I could float straight off this balcony and down to the ships as they begin to furl their sails.

"The *Fortune*," I whisper.

"What?" Leander crowds in beside me. "What do you see?"

Relief is running through me like a fire, hope in its wake.

"That's the *Fortune*," I manage. "Leander, that's my father's ship!"

Leander squints at the fleet as little pilot boats begin to gather around them, ready to pull them into place in the tight squeeze of the port. "But isn't he up north? In Holbard?"

"Yes." I'm staring at the ship, and even though I *know*, I can't help counting her masts, craning my neck for a look at the tiny figure at the wheel.

"I thought it was a suicide run down the North Passage, once winter set in. There are icebergs."

"Yes," I agree, barely hearing his words. But then slowly, a knot forms in my gut. "They're going to think we're readying ourselves for war. Before the talks have ended."

Augusta's the one who replies, her voice hard. "They're going to think that we're *strong*."

Leander just wraps his arm around my shoulders, laughing. "Like daughter, like father. Of course he'd do something mad—and of course he'd pull it off!"

"But how did he even know to try?" I whisper.

Then Barrica speaks. I didn't hear her arrive—I can't imagine she ran with the rest of us. *"In Kirkpool, my people knew* of the coming of my Messenger by my voice in the temple. So it was in every temple of mine. Even the smallest, in Holbard, to the north."

"They heard your voice," I say slowly. All my happiness is turning to horror, the joy inside me to ashes. "And you told them to come here?"

"I do not command."

"Oh, that's right." The words fly out of me. "You're just the frame upon which the vine may grow. You told them you were here, you told them war was brewing. How were you *possibly* supposed to know they'd risk their lives trying to get here for you? Not that you'd have cared if they died on the way."

"Selly!" Leander's shock is audible.

But Da is down there, and up here is a goddess who's just started a war, and more than anything in the world, I want the first person who ever felt like safety to me.

I pull free of Leander's hold and run for the stairs, hurtling down them, jumping from step to step as my momentum nearly overtakes me. My lungs are burning by the time I reach the bottom, and I hear someone calling out behind me, but I don't care.

I want my da.

Some small, foolish part of me wants to grab Leander, jump aboard the *Fortune*, and sail for the horizon, sail so far that he's free of her, that he won't hear her voice in his head anymore.

But the rest of me knows there's no longer any corner of the world where her voice could not reach him.

The docks are buzzing with activity—it's no small job, slowing down and mooring this many ships at once, especially with dozens already squeezed in. Scholars and workers are moving calmly, despite the chaos this fleet represents, and I dodge around them as I run toward the moorings.

I jump onto a Fontesquan schooner, and run along the deck on light feet, the voices of the crew ringing out behind me. Then, as the *Fortune* pulls in slowly beside her, I step up onto the railing and launch myself across the gap.

I hit the deck with a thump, and a shout goes up near me, but it's not the bellow I'm listening for.

"SELLY!"

I haul myself to my feet, and then Da is there. He's abandoned the wheel to his first mate, and he folds me up in his arms. He smells like salt and canvas, and his beard is rough against my cheek, and at last, after all this time, after all this way I've come, I'm where I'm meant to be. Heaving sobs escape me, and I bury my head against his jacket, clinging to him like an anchor in a storm.

"It's all right, my girl." He rubs my back, and his voice rumbles in my ear. "I'm here now, I'm here. We heard her voice, and we knew we were needed. What are you doing here? Where's Rensa?"

Cold water douses my happiness. I lift my face to look up at him, and he reads the news every sailor dreads in my expression. My lips trembling, I can't make myself speak.

He closes his eyes. "The *Lizabetta*?"

"Gone," I rasp. "And the crew."

He lets out a slow breath. "You're here. How?"

"It's—" My voice wobbles. "It's a long story. We had Lean— the prince. Prince Leander. He was aboard. We were on a mission for the royal family. He survived, and another boy called—"

"You saved the prince?" he asks, his eyes snapping open, his gaze fixing on me.

"I mean, we all . . ." I look at his face, and trail off. "It's complicated. Yes, sort of."

Slowly, he shakes his head. "I always knew you'd be worth something, my girl. A prince! How did the royal family take that?"

I blink up at him, caught in a hot tangle of contradictory feelings. I've spent a lifetime trying to prove I was worth something—but somewhere deep inside, a part of me thought he already believed it. And of course he did. I'm being foolish.

"Selly girl, speak," he urges me. "We haven't much time before we have to walk out there and speak to the queen herself. How do you stand with them?"

"I . . . I stand with the prince." I swallow, suddenly not wanting to say it. "At his side."

His face creases into a mix of disbelief and triumph. "That's my girl!" he crows, pulling me into a hug.

I let him fold me up in his arms and burrow into his embrace. Why are we talking about this? My whole crew . . . "Da, it's not like that. Leander and I are—"

"You know what we always say, Selly." He's grinning at me. I can hear the words before he speaks them. And I desperately don't want him to. "We have to make the most of it. This is our chance to raise the Walker fleet, the Walker name."

I stare at him, searching his face for . . . I don't know what. Some way to understand this. Is it Barrica's influence? *No.* This isn't him hungry for war.

This is him just plain hungry.

Make the most of it.

It always sounded like optimism to me, not ambition. But when I think of how far those words drove him, drove *me* . . .

I ease away from him, raising one hand to rub at my chest, where suddenly there's a pain.

"Da, we're on the edge of war, and you've just sailed in with ten ships to interrupt the peace talks. How do you think that looks?"

"It's not for me to deal with that," he replies simply. "I answered my goddess's call, and I'm here to serve my queen."

"Da, Rensa is dead. And Jonlon and Conor, Kyri and Abri. The *Lizabetta* is gone."

"And you're here."

I always thought he dragged me from tutor to tutor because he loved me too much to give up. Because he believed in my magic. Because even when I was almost broken by it, even when I was humiliated, failing over and over, he knew I was capable of more.

But he only ever wanted to extract the value he was sure was in me.

For the first time in my life, I'm coming back to him after being apart, and like something that's been dragged out into the daylight and is suddenly obvious, I can see that I was under his influence as surely as everyone else is under Barrica's.

I don't want to *make the most* of Leander. I don't want to *make the most* of being a part of the queen's court.

We're teetering on the verge of a war between the gods, and I think my father has just pushed us over the edge. And all he cares about is how he can *make the most* of the situation.

Da releases me and wheels around, calling out to his crew for clean clothes. He's ready to meet the queen.

And I'm left standing there, more alone than when he was on the other side of the continent.

I'm not the girl he left behind. And he's not the man I thought he was.

JUDE

The Hall of Scholars
The Bibliotek, the Barren Reaches

V oices are raised all around me, shouts echoing off the walls of the council chamber.

This is the moment it all disintegrates.

I know this, and I'm watching it happen, yet there's nothing I can do.

At the edges of the room, ambassadors and priests are whispering hurriedly to their aides and packing up their papers, whole delegations preparing to depart and tell their rulers to prepare for war.

Around the table, it's as though everyone has picked an opponent, and they're all shouting, trying to be heard over the din, fingers stabbing the air as they make their points.

Sister Beris is screaming something at Father Marsen—his smile has vanished as though it never existed, and he's bellowing in reply, slamming a fist into his palm to emphasize whatever he's saying.

One of the Mellacean officials has cracked and is either desperate enough or so emboldened by Macean's urge to gamble that he's trying to inject himself back into the game. He's snapping at Laskia, red-faced and furious, his glasses slipping down his nose.

"—and this is what happens when those unqualified to lead—when *children*—are allowed to—"

Laskia comes to her feet, and as she raises her hand, his voice abruptly cuts out. She tilts her head as she watches his mouth move, and then, as his eyes bulge in fear and horror, she laughs. The man bangs on the table in a frantic bid for her attention, but she turns to smirk at Ruby, who simply leans back in her chair and returns the smile.

As soon as Laskia turns away, Ruby's smile vanishes, giving way to an ugly, contemptuous twist of her mouth. If Laskia thinks her sister is on her side, she's wrong.

A door opens on the other side of the room and Selly slips in, looking sick. Her freckles stand out more against her skin these days as she loses the tan she had from a lifetime at sea.

Her gaze slides around the room, alighting on mine for a moment. She's not lost to this warmongering. She's like me, like Keegan. He's still buried in a library, desperately hunting for something that will save us.

I threw away my faith when I left Alinor, and I've been adrift ever since, as lost as the grieving god Valus, in my way. If I belong anywhere, it's here, in this land of ruins. I can only assume that's why Macean can't get the grip on me that he wants. And Keegan's always been more interested in reading a book than going to temple. How Selly protects herself from Barrica,

I don't know. But she does. And she sees what I see. And she looks as hopeless as I feel.

"I left this realm once before." Barrica's voice rings out above the others'. *"And yet here we find ourselves once again. This time, I will not make the same mistake. I will remain, and I will rule. Under my hand, there will be no dissent. There will be peace."*

"At what cost, sister?" Macean drawls. *"Eternal boredom?"*

"At any cost!" she thunders.

Macean doesn't flinch. Instead, he leans deliberately back in his chair and props both his feet on the table, folding his hands behind his head.

"Listen, please!" Selly's voice breaks through the noise—she has Leander by one arm. "Can't you hear what she's saying?"

Keegan's voice comes from the doorway, where he's appeared, clutching a bundle of his precious papers. "Leander, this peace we speak of—this is not the same peace as we have lived for five centuries. This is sacrifice, a whole country bent toward the power of a goddess. What she wants is the peace of brute force, not of prosperity!"

"Then that's what we will have, coward." Lord Wollesley is shouting at his son, nearly drowned out by the other arguments up and down the table. "What else can there be?"

Leander shakes his head and reaches up to rake his hair back from his face with an achingly familiar gesture. This Messenger isn't him anymore, but I knew this boy once. "Keegan," he says, letting out a slow breath. "How is it that your father understands, and you can't?"

I watch as all the air goes out of Keegan Wollesley. As all

the trust that had built between them is shattered—as Leander takes the side of every bully, of everyone who's ever told Keegan that he didn't fit, that he wasn't enough.

Slowly, Keegan sinks down into a chair, as though he doesn't remember how to stand.

"Leander!" Selly cries, reaching again for his arm.

He shakes her off. Eyes widening, she takes a step back from him.

"Selly," Leander snaps, his frustration showing, "this is my world, not yours. You couldn't possibly understand."

Laskia's watching them too, her lips parted, her head tilted, as though she's trying to understand what she sees. Then she shakes her head and looks around the room like she's just waking up.

I follow her gaze, and we both see Dasriel at the same moment. The big man who's always been by her side is at the door, in the act of opening it to slip out.

He pauses when Laskia catches his eye. I don't know how, but somehow I know with absolute certainty: Dasriel is leaving. He's measured the situation, and he's made his choice—it's time to go.

Laskia knows it too. And after a moment, she simply closes her eyes and turns away, not trying to stop him. For his service, here is his reward: she lets him leave.

I press my back against the wall, wishing I had the courage to follow him. Wishing I could melt into the stonework. I reach unthinkingly into my back pocket for the little book of stories I've been carrying around with me, and pull it out to press it against my chest.

I want bedtime stories to be true. I want to believe monsters can be vanquished. I want to believe bravery is its own reward. I want to believe Tom's out there somewhere, coming to rescue me from this tower where I'm besieged by enemies of my own making.

I want to believe in happy endings. But there's no help coming.

SELLY

◆

The Theologians' Library
The Bibliotek, the Barren Reaches

"We're all that's left," Keegan says quietly.

"You're right." I close the library door behind Jude as he joins us, and after a moment's consideration, I lock it. "Everyone else is in the grip of it."

The words I *don't* speak echo between us: we don't truly know how Keegan and Jude have protected themselves from the gods' influence for so long, or when they might fall.

I left the others in our quarters, packing up our belongings and still shouting at each other, reliving old arguments again and again.

Even Leander has turned—but I can't let myself think about that. I can't let myself crumple to the ground the way I wish I could. If I'm going to keep fighting for him, I have to stay standing.

Jude lets out a breath and closes his eyes. My own

desperation is etched in the exhausted lines of his face. "This is it. Something happens now—the three of us do something—or it's war."

"We'll be sailing back to Alinor to raise an army before nightfall." I walk toward the little cluster of leather armchairs where scholars are supposed to sit, sink down onto one, and pull up my knees so I can bury my face in them. "How do we beat the gods at their own game?"

I hear Keegan take the seat next to mine. "I don't think we do," he says slowly. "I don't think it's possible." But there's an odd note in his voice, and I lift my head. There's a flutter in my belly.

"Then why do you look like that?"

"I don't think *we* beat them at their own game," he says. "Maybe nobody does. I mean, nothing like this has been tried in recorded history."

"But you have an idea," I say slowly. I want to grab him and kiss him on the forehead. "That big, beautiful brain of yours has an idea. If we don't beat them, who does?"

"I've continued my research," he begins, with the air of a professor about to launch into an hour-long lecture.

"Spirits save me, Keegan, if *ever* there was a time to skip listing your sources and showing your work, and just tell us your conclusion . . ." I'm smiling, and he's not stopping me, and that means he *has* thought of something. And that small sliver of hope is like the first ray of sunshine arriving to warm you up when you're soaked through.

Keegan raises a hand, though, telling us to hold off on our smiles. "The Messengers are the key," he says gravely. "We guessed it when Barrica tried so hard to use Leander as her means of entering this world. We realized she couldn't return here without him. And we thought we'd missed our chance to stop the gods, when they both appeared."

I blink, trying to keep up. "But didn't we?"

"I don't think so," Keegan replies. "Macean told Jude . . ." He glances at the other boy.

"He told me he needs a Messenger if he wants to remain," Jude says. "He offered—threatened, I don't know—to make me his next Messenger, if Laskia burned up."

My lips part, but it takes me a moment to speak. "So you think we can still . . ."

Keegan nods. "This is what I've been buried in the library trying to work out. If Jude's right, then if we cut the connection between the gods and their Messengers, they'll have to return to whatever realm they've been in all this time."

This is what it feels like when the wind hits your sails and the boat begins to heel just a little, and suddenly you're under way.

"And have you worked out how to do that?" I ask, hardly daring to hope. "How to cut the connection Laskia and Leander have with the gods?"

"They have to stop being Messengers," he replies.

My hope vanishes as quickly as it came. "What does that mean? Do they have to . . . ?" I can't say it.

Die?

"I don't know," he admits. "Nobody's ever done anything like this before. But I haven't wasted my hours in the library. I think—I *hope*—we can create an opportunity for them to *choose* to step away from the gifts the gods offered them."

"How?"

"We were right, thinking the Temple of the Mother was the place. We'll need the priests from all the delegations to appeal to their own gods, to strengthen them enough to step through and take hold of Barrica and Macean. If they do, they'll create an opportunity . . . after that, it's up to Leander and Laskia."

"And if they can't go back to what they were?" Jude asks softly. "Or they won't?"

The silence stretches between us, dread stealing our words. My jaw clenches—I can't make myself speak.

I can't kill Leander. I won't. No matter what happens.

But even as I think it, an image of him flashes through my mind—he's laughing and reaching for my hand. His eyes are brown. He's the boy he used to be. I miss him so fiercely I feel a physical pain in my chest. And I know exactly what that boy would tell me right now.

If Leander the Messenger can't make that choice, what do I owe the boy I fell in love with?

"This is what it comes down to," Keegan says softly, with the sort of quiet neutrality so many people have thought meant he doesn't feel—though really it hides the depth of his feeling. "We have to be willing to act against everyone we know. And we have to trust that if we can gather all the right people in the right place at the right time, they'll find their way to peace."

Jude shakes his head slowly. "I don't know if Laskia can. Although . . . none of this is what she thought it would be. I don't know. Perhaps."

"We don't even know if we can trust Leander," Keegan admits. "He's deeply under Barrica's influence now."

"It's our only choice," I say as the certainty settles into me, filling me up slowly but surely. "If we don't, whole countries will be destroyed. We have to send the gods back, or die trying."

"You really know how to lift the spirits," Jude mutters.

"I want to be clear that dying trying is a very real possibility," Keegan says, with the faintest ghost of a dark smile.

"I . . . I think it's more than that." I'm shocked at how calmly I can say it. "I'm tied so closely to Leander, I don't know if I'll survive if he doesn't. I don't even know if I'll survive if he *does*."

I reach across to Keegan's hand, which is resting on the arm of his chair, and settle my own over it, squeezing hard. He's become the truest of friends as we've fought together, first to save Leander, and then the rest of the world. He's who I'd want to be with in this moment.

"Selly," he murmurs, his heart in his eyes.

"It's what I choose," I tell him. "If that's what it comes down to, it's what I choose."

"Then we'd better get started," he says. "We don't have much time."

PART FOUR

THE HEART OF THE WORLD

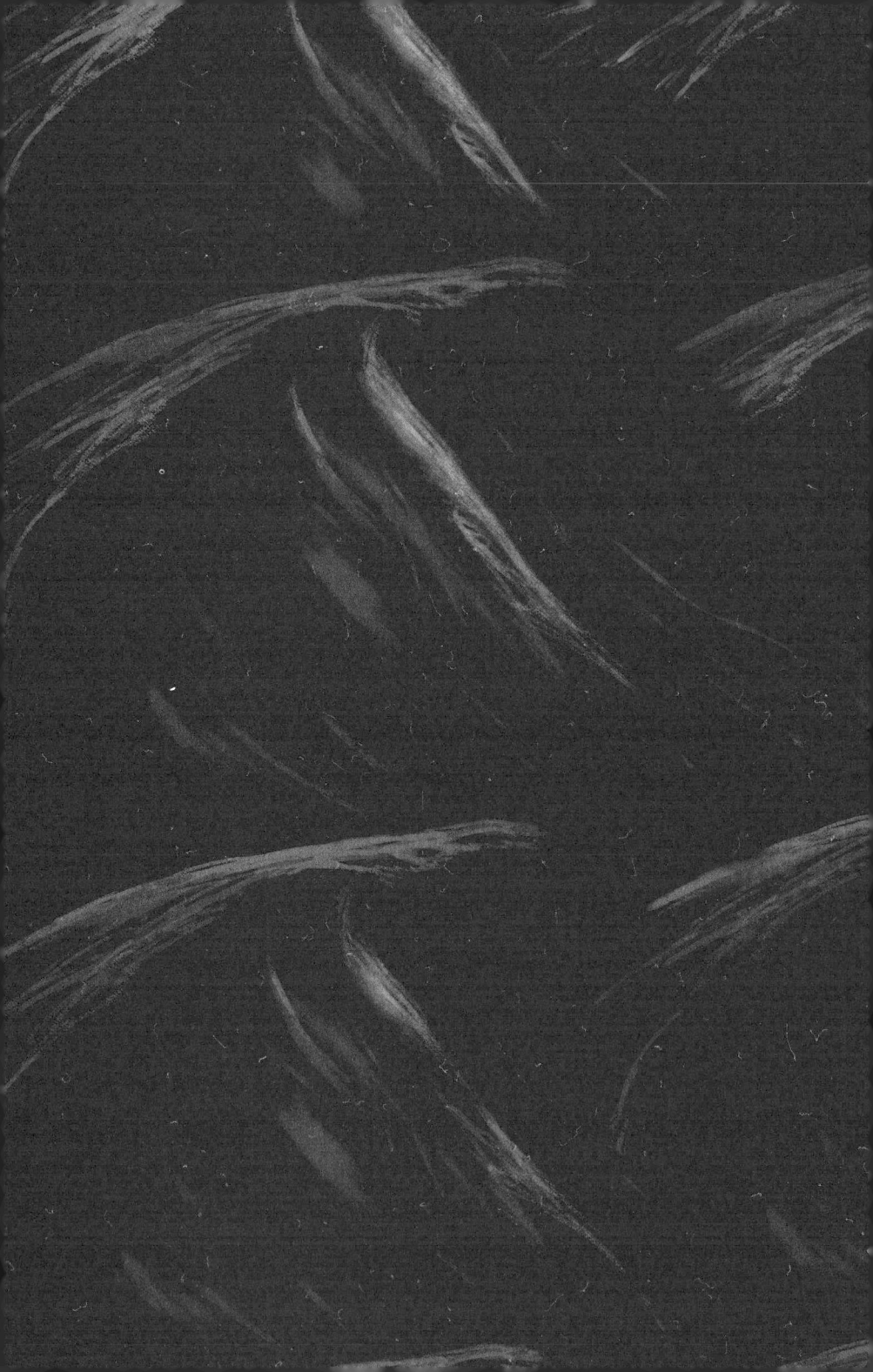

SELLY

The Astronomers' Library
The Bibliotek, the Barren Reaches

Macean likes high places. Of course he does.
My goal is the Astronomers' Library, which is at the top of the Bibliotek's tallest tower.

With the ground floor guarded by green sisters, there's only one way up, and even with a lifetime of climbing rigging behind me, I'm not wild about it.

"Just focus on that carving that runs alongside the windows," Kiki says again, making her hands into a stirrup so I can set one foot on them. "I got pretty good at architectural guesses when Keegan and I were plotting his escape. I think it'll be structural, and easy to grip."

"You *think*?" I squeak, as she gives me a boost—I have no choice but to grab at the rock as I rise into the air.

"You can do this," she stage-whispers after me. "Wish me luck!"

"Good—" Before I can finish, she's turned to run back the

way we came. I can only pray—no, I can only *hope*—she does everything else I've asked. She believes we're getting an advantage over the Mellaceans, and accepted that there's no time for questions. Everything depends on her trust in me, though. If she starts to wonder . . .

I heave myself up the stone carving, gripping with my fingertips, and bite off a curse as my boot slips and I scrabble to find another foothold.

By the time I slither in through the second-floor window and land in a heap on the ground, my fingers are bleeding and my mouth is dry with nerves. I pause to listen for the green sisters downstairs, but although there are shouts coming from the ground floor—it's as chaotic here as in the Alinorish camp—there's no sound of anyone coming up the stairs, so I rise to my feet and start to climb the staircase.

At the wooden door at the top, I pause and take a steadying breath. I'm shaking, and I make my hands into fists to try and still them.

I've never been afraid to sail into a storm, but this will need more than my old courage. This will need what I've learned in Leander's world, too.

If I want Macean to listen, I have to speak his language.

I tighten the weave of my mental barrier, then, before my nerve can break, I push open the door and stride inside.

Macean stands with Sister Beris in the center of the round tower. The shelves are lined with books, and there's a huge telescope in the middle of the room, pointed up at a window in the ceiling.

Macean turns his head and tilts it to study me, and instantly

I'm like a rabbit meeting a wolf, my heart thumping too fast, my body quivering with the desire to run away.

Beris looks like she's been dragged backward through a hedge—her once-perfect braid is askew, her eyes wide and shadowed. "What are you doing here?" she snaps.

I keep my movements slow and deliberate, looking her up and down before I turn back to Macean. "I've come to speak to you," I tell him. "Alone."

He pushes against my mind—his power is so vast, I feel like a single ship in the middle of the endless, rolling ocean. But I only have to sail the part of it that I'm in right now, and I force myself to keep up eye contact.

Slowly he smiles, lips curving, and then he bites his lower lip. My stomach flips, and I have to blink to break his spell. He's magnetic, compelling in a way that's utterly different from his sister. He likes that I'm willing to fight him.

"How did you get past the sisters downstairs?" Beris demands shrilly.

I'd already forgotten she's here. I give her my answer without ever taking my eyes off her god. "I took a risk, Sister Beris."

And that pleases him even more.

"You may go," he says.

It takes Sister Beris a moment to realize he's talking to her, not me. She gapes at him and catches her breath to speak—then cuts off with a gargling sound, as though she's choking. One hand at her throat, she stumbles past me and closes the door behind her.

Macean lifts one brow. *"She'll probably listen at the door. Not the first time she's found herself sent away recently."*

I make myself shrug. "I'll get to the point. I've come to offer you a deal."

"*Oh?*" he asks, idly interested at best. Or perhaps he just has a very good poker face.

I try to keep my own firmly in place. "Are you interested?"

He laughs. *"How did you get past the green sisters?"*

"I climbed up to the second story, then came in through the window."

His lips part a little, and his gaze turns more intent. He likes my answer. He likes single-mindedness. It drives you to take chances. And he likes *those* very much.

"You could have been one of mine, you know," he says. *"Sailors often are. The wise ones, anyway. They understand the risk of the sea."*

"Actually, I'm here because that's not off the table," I say evenly.

Now I truly have his interest, and he turns his whole body toward me, giving me his full attention. *"Go on."*

"I've never really been hers," I say. "Your sister's."

"Then whose are you?"

"Leander's," I say simply. "This is my offer: I'll help you defeat Barrica."

"And in return, your lover?" he asks.

"Yes." Finally I let a little of my emotion creep into my tone. Not too much. Enough to tell him I'll do something desperate, something foolish. Playing this game like Kiki taught me to—slowly, calculating, and thinking about how he'll interpret each moment. "I just want him back," I say, and finally I let my lashes lower, breaking eye contact.

This is the moment it all comes down to. All my bluffing,

the chances we've taken, the plans we've made. I keep my mental shields up as Macean presses close, trying to read me.

And then, because I have them to spare, I let a tear spill, waiting as it tracks down my cheek before I speak again. "If you want this deal, then you need to follow me right now. Otherwise, the two of us are on a ship, and your chance is gone. So come, or don't."

I turn on my heel, every nerve in my body screaming at me not to turn my back on anything as dangerous as him.

He laughs as I push the door open.

But as I start down the stairs, hurrying past a startled Beris, I hear his footsteps behind me.

KEEGAN

The Temple of the Mother
The Bibliotek, the Barren Reaches

"You are leading us to my mother's temple," Barrica says, as we make our way along the hallway.

"Yes." I'm speaking far too fast, nearly falling over my words. "Yes, there's a book I need, and the scholars won't let me in. But they'll let you in. Obviously. She's *your* mother. And you're a goddess. As you know."

"There are books in the Temple of the Mother?" Leander breaks in, possibly to spare me from myself.

"Knowledge is her domain," Barrica reminds him.

"I suppose there weren't any on the Isle of the Mother because, you know, sea air," I babble. "Terrible for paper." My heart's beating so hard, I think it's about to explode, and I don't care what the texts in the Physicians' Library say.

"What's in this book?" Leander asks.

"I think it will give us an advantage." That isn't an answer, but I accelerate, walking as fast as I can without breaking into a run, and he doesn't ask again.

I hope Selly's got Macean.

I hope Jude's got Laskia and Ruby.

I hope Kiki's got . . . No, I don't need to worry about Kiki. She's an incredible party planner. Rounding up a bunch of people and getting them where she wants them to be is like breathing for her.

I'm moving so fast that I burst through the doors of the temple and make it halfway to the center of the room before I slow to a halt, blinking.

It's a huge space, with a mosaic circle in the middle of the floor, surrounded by towering statues of each of the gods. High above are windows, positioned so light streams down to illuminate each statue.

There are bookshelves between the statues, crammed with volumes I'd usually kill to get my hands on. But right now all I care about are the clusters of bewildered diplomats, priests, and scholars standing in front of them.

Kiki's done it.

She swings around from where she's berating a group of assorted priests, and in the same moment, Leander and Barrica walk in, then stop short.

"What—" Leander manages, before Selly appears at the other side of the temple, striding in just ahead of Macean.

He stops too, lips instantly drawn back in a snarl.

And then comes Jude, hurrying along with Laskia and Ruby, talking rapidly, arms waving, spinning some sort of tale that's keeping them moving.

Laskia stops with a jerk when she sees the assembled crowd. "What are you doing here?" she snaps, and she's clearly speaking for everyone who's just arrived.

Selly's the one who answers as I back toward the edge of the room. My work is done—it's her turn now.

Selly strides forward to the middle of the mosaic circle, and stops there to turn slowly, taking in the priests assembled near the statues of their gods.

The beams of light from the windows high above us illuminate her, and she's magnificent in the sunlight.

"We have tried to find a path that leads us away from this war," she shouts—and she's not looking at the priests of Barrica, or the green sisters. She's looking at the others. Those who came here in the service of their siblings—of Sutista, and Kyion, and Dylo, and Oldite. She's looking at the scholars, protectors of knowledge, who serve the Mother.

"We could find no path," Selly continues, her voice rising louder still as chatter breaks out around us. "So we will *make* one. We will do it together, and all of you are needed."

Bewilderment buzzes around the room, but they're all watching her—every single one of them.

"Pray to your gods!" she shouts. "Bring them through so they can help the Messengers free themselves! That will send Barrica and Macean back to their own realm!"

For an instant, everyone's frozen in place. Priests and scholars and diplomats stare at her, their mouths open, caught between surprise and confusion.

I can't hear anything but my own breath, and it feels like someone's squeezing my heart.

Nobody's moving. Nobody's praying. Everybody looks like they think she's lost her mind.

"Do it!" she screams. "Raise your gods! You've been watching, you've been looking for a way to stop this. This is how you stop it. This is how you level the playing field. And if you want it to happen, you need to pray to your gods *right now*!"

They stare at her, and I'm riveted to the spot, watching helplessly as the whole thing spools out in front of me. I can see just how it will go.

First one will step back, and then another. And slowly they'll shuffle away, and we'll have just enough time to realize we've failed before Barrica and Macean strike.

Selly lowers her voice, and every pair of eyes in the room is on her, every breath held as she speaks. "The only way we come through this is together," she says. "By asking for help. So pray to your gods. *Please.*"

And then a woman wearing the deep red of Sutista slowly, hesitantly raises her hands. Her voice is shaking as she breaks the ringing silence that follows Selly's words. "Sutista, I reach for you . . ."

And then a man in the gold of Kyion joins her, beginning to chant softly, and his companions take up the words and join him, their voices weaving together in harmony.

Then the priests of Dylo and Oldite step forward, and I see Scholar Kel raise their hands in appeal to the Mother.

And all around us, the air begins to shimmer.

LEANDER & SELLY & LASKIA

◆

The Temple of the Mother
The Bibliotek, the Barren Reaches

LEANDER

The room fades away, the shouts around me muffled and then melding into a different kind of clamor.

I'm at a party, the room a swirl of colors and movement. The music is too loud, and everyone is moving too fast, paired off, dancing perfectly in time with the thumping beat, but I can't remember the steps. Everyone has their place, and I'm not needed.

Maybe I can fight my way up to the balcony. Maybe I can hide.

"Leander! Leander, listen to me!"

Wait. I know that voice.

LASKIA

I'm in a tiny, cramped room with no window except for a skylight. It's full of rickety furniture other people have thrown away; a sagging bed is jammed against one wall.

There's a mirror with a crack in it propped up beside the bed, but I can't see myself properly in the shattered surface.

This place is dimly lit because lamp oil's expensive. And I know that, because I know where I am. This is the room that Ruby and I had in the boardinghouse, after our mother left us.

I'm instantly small, instantly helpless, fear running through me in an involuntary shiver as I look around the most frightening place I've ever been. The place where I was nothing.

"She said she'd come back," I whisper.

"Oh, grow up," someone snarls behind me.

When I swing around, Ruby is sitting on the bed.

SELLY

I hate this party. Leander's pushing through the crowd, buffeted by the bodies of the dancers as he tries to get away.

This is the place he learned he didn't matter—the place he realized he wasn't invited to play the game, so he should sit back and stop trying to be needed. The pain of it is rolling off him in great waves.

"Leander!" I try again. "Listen to me!"

He turns his head, trying to find me, but his glazed eyes skate right past me as they desperately search the crowd.

I look down at the polished floor and find the geometric marks of Barrica's shield, of my magician's marks, right there.

"No." That's my voice, though I didn't mean to speak out loud. "I'm not going to fight for him here."

I'm not going to fight where he's weakest, and I'm an outsider.

I'm going to fight for him where I'm strong.

"What?" A woman in the crowd turns her head to look at me, and for a moment she's a goddess with eyes as blue as the sea. I wrench my gaze away before she can ensnare me.

And I choose a storm instead.

I reach for the fabric of this place, as I did when I rescued Leander from his mind once before. Taking hold of it, I make a fist and *pull.*

As the room comes to pieces around me, I use my hands to reshape it into a ship.

LEANDER

I'm on the deck of a sailing ship, and I can see Selly at the other end, fighting her way through the storm to reach me. Great waves rear up and dump floods of water on the deck, and it runs across the wooden boards, ankle-deep.

"Selly!" The wind rips away my words, but I work my way toward her.

Then there are hands steadying me, and when I look up, Barrica holds my shoulders. She braces me against the wind. She protects me.

LASKIA

"*What are you doing?*" Macean's by the door, looming tall enough to fill the room. His lips are stretched in a snarl, and his shadow dances against the walls.

"I didn't do anything! It was them, out there! The priests!"

"*Then get us out there!*" he roars, turning to grab for the door handle and wrenching at it. It twists and groans, but he can't move it further. "*Girl!*" His fury is terrifying, and I stumble back from him. "*Open it!*"

"You're a god! If you can't, how can I possibly—"

"*Open it!*"

I scramble across the room, dropping to my knees by the door to squint through the keyhole.

On the other side, I can see the Temple of the Mother—the priests chanting, the crowd gathered.

"*OPEN IT!*"

And that's when I realize. This is the door to the world. He *can't* open it. He needs me.

If I don't open it . . .

His hand grabs hold of my hair, and I scream as he yanks my head back.

SELLY

"*There!*" Barrica points at an island on the horizon when I reach her and Leander.

I squint, the salt stinging my eyes, and for a moment I can

make out a ring of huge statues. It's the Temple of the Mother. It's the Bibliotek.

"*Sail us there,*" Barrica snaps. "*There is a battle to be won.*"

"Selly, quick!" Leander shouts, reaching for my hand when I don't move.

"You need him to get you there," I say slowly, the wind howling around us as I start to smile. "We were right. You can't do it on your own."

Barrica seems to grow, looming over me, and now there's a sword in her hand. "*Do it!*" she screams, her neck corded with tension, her voice hoarse.

I plant my feet on the swaying deck, and when the cold spray hits me, the strength of the sea flows into my veins. This is where I'm meant to be. This is where I'll fight her for my prince. I look her in the eye, and give her my answer.

"No."

LEANDER

"Selly, what are you doing?" I shout, urgency beating in my temples like a drum. "We have to get to the island, the battle is already under way!"

She looks me dead in the eye, soaked to the skin by the waves, the wind pulling strands from her braid. "That's not the battle I'm here to fight, my prince."

SELLY

Barrica bellows her rage and launches herself up from the deck, dissolving into the wind. The next gust hits me like a body blow, and I stagger backward before regaining my balance.

She's become the storm, and in the shriek of the wind I can hear the clash of weapons.

"We're not taking you there!" I shout. "Your time in our world is over."

"Selly, what are you doing?" Leander gasps, grabbing for my shoulder. "She's our goddess!"

I let my gaze lose focus, and there are the air spirits, whirling around the sails, racing along with each gust.

I need your help, I tell them, reaching into my pocket for the little paper boat Leander made me.

This time, I don't mind sacrificing it. It was a promise, but I don't need the reminder.

I *am* the promise now.

I'm not going anywhere.

LASKIA

Macean has me by my hair, and I reach back and grab his wrist with both hands, digging my nails in. His magic is bursting through me at the direct contact, and I let it, let myself swell with it, until every part of my body is on fire.

He yanks me to my feet, and I push up, using the momentum to rise quickly and drive my head back. It connects with his chin, and he releases me, cursing.

I spin around to face him, balancing on the balls of my feet with my hands spread.

Ruby is behind him, standing by the mirror and sizing us both up.

"Ruby," I say softly, never taking my eyes off Macean. I don't have to tell her I want her help. She knows. She can read everything I don't say in my tone.

But she doesn't move, and after a moment, the pit of my stomach drops in disbelief.

She's waiting to see how this plays out.

My sister isn't on any side but her own.

She never has been.

SELLY

The storm that is Barrica rages around me. As the wind roars, I hear battle cries. As the rigging shudders, I hear the clash of swords on shields, the sharp retort of gunshots. In the ripping of canvas, I hear the cries of soldiers and horses.

Leander staggers for balance as I launch my air spirits to meet the goddess—she sends them scattering, wheeling away, helpless before her power.

"You cannot have him!" I scream into the furious raging of the wind. "We won't sail you back to our world!"

"Selly, we must!" my prince shouts, and I feel him reach for the water spirits, still so under his goddess's spell that he'll do anything to get to the fight.

Even this, the deck of a ship, isn't a safe place to fight.

I abandon my resistance and let her split my wind spirits

in every direction—I'm turning my mind instead to the ship herself.

I form a picture in my mind, starting at the prow and working my way back amidships, then past Leander and me toward the stern. I see crisp white folds above us, and clean lines all around us.

Barrica roars, but this she cannot stop.

A heartbeat later, it's done, and we're sailing on a paper boat.

LASKIA

I catch a glimpse of myself in the mirror beside my sister, and see that I'm a child. I'm the child I once was, here in this room, eyes huge in my face, skinny and scared.

My mother left that child, and never came back for her.

"Open the door!" Macean roars, stalking toward me.

I was so good for Mama, and she left and never came back.

I did terrible things for Ruby, and for Beris, and they never repaid me with the love, the respect that I wanted so badly.

I did horrifying things for my god, and still I'm only a tool to him. A doorway he happens to need.

I crouch, ready to spring at Macean, but he's so tall now, his black hair falling into his green eyes, his lips drawn back in a snarl over those perfect white teeth.

This room is the place where Ruby learned to grasp for more, and she's never changed. She never will.

This room is the place where I learned I wasn't good enough. Where I began to try and prove myself to someone, anyone, who could tell me I was.

But I'm not Ruby. I *will* change.

This is where I'll learn something new.

I pause for a moment in regret—in the sting of a life spent pleasing others, never once thinking that perhaps I could just please myself.

And that's when Ruby strikes. My sister charges past Macean, shoving me aside and sending me crashing into the wall as she lunges for the door.

The bonds of magic between us start to snap as she grabs the handle, and then the room starts to break apart. . . .

"Ruby, no!"

SELLY

"Selly," Leander gasps. "It's our boat, what's—"

"It's our promise!" I shout over the wind. "I'm not leaving you."

"But—"

I grab him by the lapels and haul him in against me, and my mouth finds his. His skin is cold, and there's spray soaking us, wind tugging at our clothes, and everything tastes like the sea, but he's solid and real and I cling to the boy I love like he's the only thing that can keep me afloat.

I like you best with salt on your skin.

His arms wrap me up, and as the waves crash around us, I tear down the mental barriers between us.

Instantly we're together—*truly together*—as we haven't been since the day Barrica taught us how to raise those shields.

The onslaught nearly overwhelms me, and my knees buckle as I'm torn away from Leander.

He grabs for me, but Barrica takes her chance, and a gust of wind like a physical force shoves me across the deck to the railing.

I hit it so hard the air's driven from my lungs as I half fall over it, grabbing frantically to try and pull myself back up. Terror comes at me in a wave as I realize I'm losing my balance—that in a moment I'll be over the railing, and lost to the sea. The water races past beneath me, so fast it's like we're flying.

Then Leander's there, and he abandons his own safety to reach for me, wrestling me back onto the deck until we collapse there in a tangle of limbs.

All the mental shields between us are gone now.

Our minds meet, and I'm him and he's me, and we see each other completely.

We're five and sitting on my father's shoulders, playing at being lookout.

We're six and watching Father Marsen lower a crown onto Augusta's head, awed by the way the jewels glint.

We're ten and climbing the rigging, a skinny girl with freckles and a braid flying behind us.

We're twelve and walking into our first day at boarding school, our new uniform itchy, our nerves jangling.

We *are* each other, and we know each other, inside and out. We see all of each other, and for the first time, we are *seen,* our minds woven together.

And what we see, we love. What we see, we pledge ourselves to.

And because he is me, and I am him, he knows what I know. Our goddess has no place in our world.

His eyes snap open in shock.

LASKIA

Ruby yanks at the door again as pieces of the room start to break apart. Chunks of plaster rain down from the ceiling, and the floorboards splinter beneath my feet.

Macean staggers, and I throw my hands up to try and *will* this place back together, his roar of fury and frustration echoing in my ears.

But as the ties between Ruby and me disintegrate one by one, I see what I need to do.

There's only one way to defeat him.

I need to let all the ties between Ruby and me break, cast off my anchor and stand alone.

And then I need to let the power swallow me completely.

LEANDER

"What do we do?" I gasp, looking around like I've just woken from a dream—though what kind of reality has a giant paper boat and a storm that's made of an angry goddess, I don't know.

I've been in a trance, I've been—I don't know.

But now I see clearly. I see this girl who fought for me, this girl I love.

And I see a goddess who tried to drag me to destruction.

"There's no way through this storm," Selly shouts over the wind, "except to surrender to it."

"What do you . . . ?" I start, but the words die.

I know what she means, and something drops inside me, and I feel like I'm falling.

We have to let the magic overwhelm us, until it consumes us and breaks our connection.

We have to sacrifice *ourselves,* to close Barrica's doorway to our world.

Selly's agony is there on her face, her heartbreak in her green eyes. She doesn't want to ask this of me. She doesn't want to lose me. She doesn't want to die. Tears stream down her cheeks, melding with her beloved salt water.

"I won't do it," I manage, dragging the words from somewhere deep inside.

I'm willing to die, but I can't let this kill Selly. I won't. There can't be a world without her in it.

The Temple of the Mother, where our bodies are—it's at the center of the Bibliotek. And they call the Bibliotek *the heart of the world*—the very center of it, where wisdom lies.

They're wrong. It's this girl's heart that's at the center of everything.

I cannot let her go.

She is the heart of the world—she's all the love and courage in it.

SELLY

"Do it!" I scream, the words torn from my throat. My heart is breaking, and the magic is coursing through my veins, the pain unbearable.

I can't bear to wait. I can't bear to lose him. I want this moment to last forever.

I want him to do it now, before she defeats us.

LASKIA

I've spent all my life trying to please the ones I looked up to. My mother, Ruby, Beris, Macean. To show them I'm enough.

Now, my mind is tangled with my god's, the urge to gamble running through me like an addiction, like a call I can't resist, like rocks I'll willingly wreck myself on.

Now, it seems to me that the greatest risk of all was always to believe that *I am enough.*

But I wish I could have stayed longer.

I wish I could have lived a little, without their shadows.

At least the way it ends will be my choice.

"Laskia!" Ruby screams.

I let go of my hold on this place, and the room flies into a million pieces.

Macean roars his fury as the doorway disintegrates.

The ties between Ruby and me snap, and for one glorious moment, I'm attached to no one. I'm wheeling away in the darkness, simply *me*.

And then everything goes black.

LEANDER

I gather my magic around me, and the moment I stop resisting it *rushes* into my body.

For years I've been the most powerful magician on the Crescent Sea.

For days I've been the Messenger of a goddess.

Never before have I commanded my power like this.

I could flatten a city with a thought.

No sooner does that idea strike me than Barrica is in my mind, whipping around me like a hurricane. *Do it, do it!*

I can feel her hunger for war howling through my veins. Soon it will overtake me again.

Selly's magician's marks—the ones that marked her as my anchor—are pulsing with a pure white light, as the magic begins to overwhelm her.

And as I gaze at them, I see the first hints of another way. Another road I could take.

Could I . . . ?

Barrica appears on the deck, and the paper begins to crumple beneath her weight. Her sword is in one hand, her shield in the other. *"What are you doing?"* she cries.

Selly is my anchor. Without her, I'll be devoured, and Barrica's doorway will close for good.

But without me . . . maybe Selly can live.

I need to cut the bonds that bind her to me, and set her free. Only I need to go, to close the doorway.

Every muscle in my body screaming, every joint straining, I turn my power inward, wrestling it under control by sheer will.

It's like bringing an axe down and severing a limb, and I try desperately to flinch away from it. But I hold my nerve—I hold on to my love—long enough.

Long enough to burn away my own magic, casting it out of my body.

The cords between us snap, and Selly screams, and then the storm takes me.

JUDE

The Temple of the Mother
The Bibliotek, the Barren Reaches

It's like a hurricane's raging through the temple—I'm sheltering against a bookcase with Keegan and Kiki, flinching as books and debris fly by.

All the priests are chanting. Kel is by the statue of the Mother, and the others are at the bases of the statues of Dylo, Kyion, Sutista, and Oldite.

Selly, Leander, Laskia, and Ruby stand in the middle of the circular space, the wind whipping around its edges, but leaving them as still as if they're in the eye of a hurricane—there's not even a breeze tugging at their clothes.

Selly and Leander are . . . glowing. No, their magician's marks are glowing—a bright white so dazzling I can't look at them directly.

"Please, stop!" cries Father Marsen, reaching out with both hands, his shout raw with desperation. "There is another way!"

Then Leander sways, and I'm scrambling to my feet as Keegan grabs for me, and misses.

Abruptly, all four figures in the center of the circle drop, like puppets with their strings cut.

I lunge forward, but Keegan has caught up, and he wraps his arms around me, holding me back with surprising strength. "Jude, it's not safe!"

The priests raise their voices above the wind, and a golden light begins to form at the edges of the circle.

"You can't do this!" Beris screams, her face contorted.

Keegan's speaking in my ear, his arms still around my body to keep me in place. "Seven hells," he murmurs. "I think Beris is right. We *can't* do this."

"What?" I gasp, and when he releases me, arms dropping to his sides, I whirl around.

There's pain in every line of his face. Everything he's done, every faded page he's read to get us here, and he's sure he's watching it fail—but why?

In answer to my question, he lifts one hand to point at the statue of Valus. There, the golden light forming in a circle around the temple fades into nothingness.

There is no priest for Valus. He has no people left. The god of laughter, the trickster, is now the god of loss, and he's too deep in his grief to answer the call.

"It's not going to work," I whisper, nausea sweeping through me.

"And if Messengers have severed the links, but the other gods can't bind them, they'll look for new . . ." Keegan's voice dies away, but I'm barely listening, even when he grabs my arm, his voice rising. "Jude, Macean will look for you if Laskia's gone—you have to run!"

But I'm staring at the statue of Valus. The youngest of the gods, caught in laughter, reaching out as if to share a joke.

And then I pull free of Keegan's grip and break into a run, shoving my way past ambassadors and officials, past priests and royals. I push through the crowd at the edge of the circle, and only at the base of Valus's statue do I stop.

"Jude!" It's Sister Beris, spitting in her fury. "Get away from that! You're not his!"

I rest one hand on the cool stone and look over my shoulder at her, feeling the smooth marble under my fingers. Calm.

"I am, Sister," I say quietly. "In the form he takes now, as the god of the lost, I am. And I have been for a long time."

Then, closing my eyes, I offer up my prayer.

Valus of Vostain, I call on you, grieving god of a lost land.

The world is humming with energy, and I don't know what I'm doing, but there's static in the air, a frisson of *something* that makes me keep going.

Valus! I know what loss is. My father turned away from me, and now he is dead. My mother ripped me from everything I knew, everyone who cared for me, and took me to a faraway place. Then she grew sick, and I gave up every part of who I was, to keep her alive.

And then she died.

I lost my home, twice.

I lost the friend who would have saved me.

I lost my happiness. I lost my honor.

A wave of sadness rolls through me, so intense that I drop to my knees, my body rounding over.

There was a boy who tried to care for me, and I lost him too.

My gut hurts, and my head aches. Tears spill down my cheeks.

I'm no longer of Alinor. I was never of Mellacea.

It's hard to swallow, my throat is so thick. There's no happy ending for me. Everything I've ever loved is lost to me.

I am *loss. And I pray to you.*

Everything is quiet. The world is nothing but silence for the longest moment.

Then, so slowly that at first I don't understand what's happening, something nudges at my mind.

Something so big that it takes me a moment to understand the scale of it. I was looking for a hill, and this is a mountain range.

Then abruptly I'm . . . somewhere else. I see the ruins of Vostain, the endless rubble, the destruction. Not a hint of green in this barren wasteland.

The voice that chimes in my thoughts is so beautiful, though, so musical, and so devastatingly sad that I weep afresh.

"There is loss in you that I understand. Why do you pray?"

And in the quiet that comes after his words, I see it.

This is why I kept my mind, when others were overwhelmed. I was truly no longer of Alinor, not Barrica's. I was never of Mellacea, not Macean's.

But my loss, and my solitude, had made me Valus's, whether I knew it or not. He's been with me ever since I set foot on this shore. Perhaps he's been with me all along.

"I pray because I need your help," I tell him.

"There is no help. Nothing can be saved." His words are a symphony in the saddest minor key I've ever heard.

"That's not true. Join with your siblings, and bind Barrica and Macean back to your realm."

"That will not return my people to me."

His solitude, the sheer loneliness, threatens to overwhelm me. I make myself speak, choking out the words.

"Your people are gone. But if you help us now, others can be saved. You can keep them from suffering as your people did." I gesture at the ruins before me, at the crumbling columns and flattened homes. "This need not happen again."

But Valus doesn't stir. He's beyond caring for the living, so caught up is he in the dead. His call is seductive. His mind is a dark pool I could glide out into. I could sink beneath the surface without leaving a ripple, immerse myself in his velvety sadness.

"*Join me,*" he says quietly. "*It is quiet here.*"

The temptation is almost overwhelming. I could walk out into the quiet, broken stone, the only sound my footsteps. I could sink into my solitude. I could soak up the sadness of losing my friends, my mother, my lover.

I shift, sliding one foot forward to take the first step.

But as I move, the little book of stories in my coat pocket digs into my ribs.

And just for a moment, I remember daydreams. I remember happy endings.

I remember that a storyteller can always lean in, just as you think all is lost, and say, *Ah, but that wasn't the end. . . .*

Two paths lie before me, I realize. Down one lies Valus, drowning in his grief.

Down the other . . . perhaps down the other is the next twist in the tale. Perhaps there is life. Perhaps . . . there is forgiveness.

A hint of warmth returns to my body, and I lift my head.

"Valus," I say slowly, "I can't go with you. But you can come with me instead. You could clear aside the ruins. You could raise a new temple. You could let people in who'll laugh again."

For a moment our minds meet, and I'm drenched in sadness.

My eyes burning with tears, I manage to give words to my thoughts one last time: "I am not the only one in this world to know suffering. You think you have no worshippers left . . . but there are many who would come to you, if only you would open your arms.

"And perhaps we could walk somewhere lighter together."

And then we part.

But as he pulls away, I feel him sifting through my mind—between one heartbeat and the next, he's a schoolboy, he's a bare-knuckled boxer, he's a son, he's a friend.

For a moment he kisses Tom, and he sees how Leander holds out his hand to us in friendship.

And as the ruins before me vanish, just for an instant—creeping out from between two broken pieces of rock—I think I catch sight of the smallest green shoot.

KEEGAN

◆

The Temple of the Mother
The Bibliotek, the Barren Reaches

We watch in awe as the statues around the circle animate, their huge stone bodies moving slowly but with perfect grace. They each reach out their hands and join them, linking together as one.

Even Valus.

Only Barrica and Macean remain frozen in place, standing on either side of the Mother, who turns her head to look first at her son, and then her daughter. The eldest, twins, in competition from the moment of their birth.

And then she turns to *me* and nods, and something inside me unlocks and responds.

This has been my protection. When I turned to knowledge, I turned to the Mother. *This* is why my mind was shielded from Barrica.

You were always mine, my son, a mighty voice says inside my head, all the music and all the beauty in the world in that tone.

And she's right. I was always hers. I always belonged here—I always *belonged*—even when they told me I didn't. With that knowledge comes a lightness, a sense of certainty that's always been missing, as something deep inside me untangles itself.

The storm whips around the room, books and papers flying. Kiki pulls me out of my reverie, yanking me down to the ground beside her before something decapitates me. She hunkers down with her hands over her head, trying to avoid the paper missiles, and we both duck as a book flies past and self-destructs against the floor, pages fluttering everywhere.

On the other side of the circle, Sister Beris is screaming something, but I can't make it out. Father Marsen has gone still and quiet.

Around the circle, the golden light starts to pulse, and then it grows brighter. And brighter. My vision swims with the tears forming in my eyes, but in the moment before I'm forced to close them, I see the statues of Barrica and Macean shift, and slowly, reluctantly, take the hands of their mother and complete the circle.

Then everything is still.

SELLY

◆

The Temple of the Mother
The Bibliotek, the Barren Reaches

I'm not sure how long I lie there trying to remember how to use my arms, but eventually it comes to me. With the greatest effort of my life I curl my fingers, and the movement seems to travel to my wrist and elbow, until I heave one arm in close and prop myself up.

"Spirits save us, she's alive!" someone shouts.

Leander, Laskia, and Ruby are sprawled on the floor near me. I can't do anything with my legs just yet, so I crawl over to Leander by pulling myself there, every movement sending jagged pains through my skull. He lies facedown, unmoving, one hand outflung like he's reaching for something.

I can't bring myself to touch him, to confirm what I'm heartbreakingly sure is true—but then he draws a great, shuddering breath, and my tears start to spill.

He's alive. He's alive. He's alive.

Carefully I roll him over, and he groans and blinks blearily. My breath catches in my throat as I gaze down at him.

His eyes are brown again.

"Are you real?" he croaks, squinting at me and reaching up with a wobbly hand to try and touch my face.

I catch it and lift his fingertips to my lips, then press his palm to my cheek so he can feel my tears.

"Selly . . . ," he whispers, his eyes widening.

I follow his gaze, and inhale sharply at the sight of his arm.

There are no magician's marks there. The warm brown skin is completely bare.

The greatest magician on the Crescent Sea is just an ordinary boy.

Our minds aren't joined anymore, our link severed—I can't tell what he's thinking. What must it be like, to wake up with that part of himself gone forever?

He moves carefully, tracing a finger down my forearm—it's only then that I realize my marks have changed too. They're no longer the straight lines and geometric shapes of Barrica's shield. Now, my freckled skin shows the ordinary loops and curves of an air magician's.

There's movement at the edge of my vision, and I look up to find Keegan, Jude, and Kiki cautiously creeping closer.

"I hope you were taking notes, Keegan," I rasp. "Because that's going to be some kind of historical record for you to write up."

And Keegan—always so measured, so thoughtful—*laughs.* One hand lifting to pinch the bridge of his nose, he drops to a crouch beside us. "I might have a lie-down before I begin work."

Kiki's as disarrayed as I've ever seen her, hair flying every which way and eyes wide. "Keegan, did you just save the world with *research*?" she demands.

Keegan is still chuckling, his face in his hands, and he doesn't reply.

Then Laskia stirs, and we all freeze.

Jude's the one who goes to her. He crouches between her and Ruby and checks Ruby's pulse. Slowly, he shakes his head.

Nobody speaks as he helps Laskia sit up. Nobody has any idea what to say.

Faced with the same choice, Leander chose love—he chose our promise; he chose not to leave me. All his life, this boy I love has been told his magic was the most impressive thing about him—and he chose to burn it away, to lose who he was, to save me. In making that choice, though, he showed exactly who he really is. He showed all the best parts of himself.

But Laskia and Ruby . . . There was no way out for them, except destruction. I don't know what happened in their fight, but I can't imagine them facing Macean side by side.

Laskia *did* make the choice, though—she didn't open the door again for Macean—and even if we can never forgive her for what she's done, in this moment, that earns her a truce.

There's a truce all around the room, it seems. I see Queen Augusta shaking her head like she's trying to dislodge something. Father Marsen's face is soft once more, his expression puzzled, as he sinks to the ground and sits. I don't see Sister Beris anywhere.

All around us, it's like people are coming out of a fog, and silently we watch as they look at each other and then their surroundings.

And then everyone starts to talk at once.

Scholar Kel strides across the room toward Augusta, towing one of the senior Mellacean officials by the arm and speaking firmly as they come face to face. Ambassadors and priests are comparing notes, voices rising to be heard over each other, and a few of the scholars are already trying to pick up the ruined books.

I roll over and collapse onto my back, and Leander thumps down beside me, his hand finding mine.

Nearby, I hear the rise of Kiki's voice. "Lord Wollesley, I'm not marrying your son! What? This is *exactly* the time for such a declaration."

"I'm not marrying her either," Keegan chimes in.

"Really, either one of us saying no is enough," Kiki points out.

"I'm trying to show solidarity," he protests.

"Ah yes, of course. Neither of us is marrying each other. Or anyone, presently. And your son is brilliant, by the way. I really think . . ."

I don't hear the end of that particular discussion. I don't need to.

"Now what?" I say to Leander, without turning my head.

"Now, they talk," he replies. "They go back to the negotiating table, with nobody more powerful than anyone else. With every country and principality around the Crescent Sea present and with a voice. Nobody's god is here to guide them to war. Nobody's god is bound in sleep, either. They're all on an equal footing for the first time in centuries. Perhaps they'll even get somewhere."

"But our part is over," I say, testing the words out loud.

"Our part is over."

I turn my head to study his profile—the familiar lines of his face, the slow curve of his lips as he begins to smile. "What do we do next?" I ask.

He meets my eyes, and then he grins. "We'll think of something."

KEEGAN

◆

The Entrance Hall
The Bibliotek, the Barren Reaches

I heft my bag onto my shoulder as I make my way into the entrance hall. It weighs almost nothing—I lost most of what I planned to bring to the Bibliotek aboard the *Lizabetta*.

I stop just inside, glancing up at the vaulted ceilings and soaking in the feel of the place. Scholars swirl around me, used to new arrivals without black robes, and for nearly a minute I stay where I am, reveling in my anonymity.

Then I make my way over to the students manning the desk, joining the short line for their attention. I listen as they dispatch each person in turn to the appropriate place—new students to find their quarters, researchers to meet with the scholars who will escort them to the particular collections they wish to access.

Then, suddenly—after all these years—I'm at the front of the line.

"Good morning," says the girl behind the desk, looking up, pen at the ready. "Purpose of your visit?"

"I'm enrolling." I can't help but smile around the words I've waited all my life to speak, and her grin in return tells me she understands.

The first time I tried to come here, it was to hide.

Now, I'm here to grow. To learn. To make my own contributions to the wealth of knowledge that lies at the heart of the world. I'm finally where I've always belonged.

"You'll want to start by collecting your robes," the girl says. "Through that door, first on the left. Welcome to the Bibliotek, Scholar."

JUDE

The Midnight Hour
Sèvrent, Fontesque

I make my way down the cobbled alleyway to where the painted blue door waits for me. Sèvrent is a big city, and finding this place has taken time. I started at the first cocktail bar I could find, and the staff there directed me to the next, and so I continued, asking the same question at each.

I don't knock. The bar is closed, and nobody will answer at this time of day. Instead, I just try the door.

It's unlocked.

It swings open when I turn the handle, revealing a sleek room with bronze accents and black-painted tables.

And there behind the bar, his copper head bent over the glass he's polishing, is Tom.

"We're not quite—" He looks up as he speaks in Fontesquan, and his words die midsentence.

I stand in the doorway, my little book of children's tales in my hand and my heart in my mouth. Hoping—praying—for my happy ending. For something that I finally realize might be mine after all.

Then Tom's vaulting the bar, and in three quick steps he's reached me, and I'm in his arms. And his mouth finds mine, and I cling to him, smiling through our kiss.

"I thought . . . ," he says eventually, pressing his forehead to mine, running his hands down my arms, as though checking I'm whole.

"Forgive me," I whisper.

"Already done. Does this mean . . . ?"

"If you'll have me. But before you answer, know that I can't stay here in Fontesque. I've made a promise somewhere else."

He draws back, brow creasing. "Where?"

"Vostain."

"The Barren Reaches? Jude, where have you *been*?"

"It'll take a while to answer that question, and tell you everything. And when I have, then you can decide whether you want to come help me clear some rubble. We'll need someone like you—someone who knows how to make people feel at home. Someone to help those who'll be coming to make a fresh start."

You could clear aside the ruins. You could raise a new temple. You could let people in who'll laugh again. That's what I said to him. And he listened, because I understood his loss.

Valus is distant—he retreated from our world with the others. But when I pray, I can tell he's there. And when I laugh, too. Like the first drops of water that signal the spring thaw, I can feel the changes in my lost god. And in myself.

Slowly, Tom's shaking his head. "I *really* want to hear this story," he says. "But the truth is, all I care about is the ending.

You and me, making a place in the world together. I don't care where it is. Vostain will do just fine."

And then he kisses me again, and I realize that I'm not living in the book of stories. I'm the storyteller, leaning in to say, *Ah, but that wasn't the end. . . .*

There's so much more to tell.

LASKIA

The Docks
Caspia

They're famous for their casinos in Caspia—just a little principality, tucked between Alinor and Fontesque. Some people say that this is where the first Mellaceans came from, centuries ago, and that's why they love to gamble here. Others say there's just not much else you can do with a tiny territory except set up favorable tax arrangements.

I've just learned all this from an extremely chatty woman at the docks, who's still yammering on about something as I study the map of the city pinned up to a large noticeboard. She delivered the part about the Mellaceans with a frown of disapproval at the very idea of being connected—but just a frown. No fear, no horror. The peace talks are continuing, and already balance is returning.

Caspia felt like the right place to come. My god is gone—and good riddance—but I felt like perhaps I might still have just a hint of luck clinging to me. And if I do, surely I'm owed something.

I managed to hide in my cabin for most of the voyage, but now I'm out in the world, and people are . . . talking to me. Looking at me. And every single one of them is treating me like I'm nobody in particular.

That's never happened to me before—I've always been *someone*. Ruby's sister. Beris's protégée. Macean's Messenger.

Now, for the first time, I'm on my own. And perhaps this is where everything truly begins.

"Oh, spirits save me," the woman scolds herself, after she's been monologuing at me for a while. "I never thought to ask. What brings you to Caspia, dear? Who are you?"

"Do you know," I say slowly, "I'm not sure I've ever really known. But I'm ready to find out."

KIKI

The Dastenholtz Residence
Kirkpool, Alinor

My father never calls me Kiki. He says it's a ridiculous name, and calls me Carrie, which is technically what's on my birth certificate. I tell him I'm a ridiculous person and go on using it anyway.

"I'm serious," I say, frustration rising. "I can do more. I want to try something bigger, Father, something better. Something like . . ." I trail off, well aware I'm undermining my own argument in doing so. "What you do," I conclude vaguely.

"Trading and commerce?" he asks, one brow rising. "Darling girl, you know we don't only trade in pretty dresses, don't you?"

"That's incredibly insulting," I snap. "Are you genuinely dismissing my intelligence on the basis that I happen to look the way I do? That's your fault, yours and Mother's."

He barks a laugh. "I am dismissing your sudden interest in my business on the basis that you once told me, and I quote, that you'd never be interested in crates and boxes when dresses and shoes existed in the world."

"Well, that was . . ." My voice cracks, and his expression softens. "That was before."

Before half my class at school died at sea. Before my friends worked together to save the world. Before I realized that I'd nearly let other people choose the rest of my life for me, and I wanted more. That I wasn't afraid of a little disapproval.

"You've been through a lot," he says soothingly. "The best thing for you to do now is rest, darling girl."

I can see it in his face—there's no talking him around. Not today. I have a lifetime of cultivating a flighty reputation to overcome. But that's what I'm going to do.

Watch out, world. Kiki Dastenholtz is coming for you.

LEANDER

The Paper Boat
The Crescent Sea

"I said heave! What are you using for muscles over there?"

I'm laughing too hard to obey Selly's orders, but I get the line tied off eventually and the little ship heels over onto her side, leaving the island behind us in our wake.

We thought about calling her the *Little Lizabetta II,* as a thank-you. But in the end, there was only one name for her: the *Paper Boat.*

We're romping down the Kethosi coast, ready for a little island-hopping at the bottom of the continent. We'll catch our dinner with a line over the side, and pull into little villages for water and supplies, and be quietly, delightfully anonymous.

Later, duty will call. I'm still a prince, and Selly still wants a trading fleet of her own someday, though she plans to build it without her father's help.

She'll enter my world with me when she must—she's become

terrifyingly good at negotiating the political waters of the palace. I think Kiki's tutoring her.

And sometimes, having already given enough to my country for one lifetime, I'll slip away to her world. I think I'm becoming a slightly less hopeless sailor, though Selly says compliments make me unbearable, so she's refused to confirm it.

Sometimes I glance up at the sails or out at the waves, and I find myself looking for spirits I can no longer see. Sometimes I see Selly's eyes lose focus, and I know she's reaching out to coax the air spirits into behaving. And sometimes it bothers me, but I wouldn't change my choice.

I know my worth, now.

I have everything that matters. And I wasn't afraid to fight for it.

SELLY

The Paper Boat
The Crescent Sea

My prince disappears belowdecks, and a minute later he's joining me at the wheel, a big slice of cake in each hand.

"Where in seven hells did that come from?" I ask, taking my slice from him and speaking around a mouthful of it. "I packed the hold myself. Oh, this is really good."

"One of the old ladies at the last village gave it to me," he replies, fitting himself in behind me so I can lean back against his chest, and he can rest his hand on the wheel beside mine.

"*Gave* it to you? Who just *gives* someone a cake like this?"

He shrugs. "People give me things. I'm charming."

"Huh. I've never noticed."

He presses a kiss to my temple, and then tries his luck working his way down my jaw, sending shivers down my spine.

"How long until we drop anchor for the night?" he asks, his breath tickling my ear, and my hand tightens its grip on the wheel.

"I could be persuaded to find a harbor sooner than later," I manage.

"What good news," he murmurs. "Let's do that. We're not in a hurry to get anywhere in particular."

And he's right.

We have a lifetime of voyages ahead of us.

Together.

ACKNOWLEDGMENTS

Acknowledgments are the place authors pause to thank all those who helped bring a book to life: agents, editors, family, friends.

This time, reader, I would like to start with you.

This is my twentieth published novel, and I am one of those people fortunate enough to do something they truly love each day. That's only possible because my readers show up for me time and time again. I lean in and say, *Do you want to hear a story?* And they—*you*—set aside daily life to come and spend some time in a new world with me.

Whether this series is the first time you've picked up one of my books, or whether you're one of the faces I recognize from more than a decade together, *thank you*. I've loved taking you to the Crescent Sea with me, and you're the reason the voyage was possible.

I'm deep in plans for my next stories, of course. If you'd like to hear about them, you can find my monthly newsletter at amiekaufman.com—it's my favorite way to stay in touch, and means you'll always know about new releases and what's happening behind the scenes.

Speaking of coming behind the scenes, if you've enjoyed

this series, you might also enjoy my podcast *Pub Dates,* which I host with Kate J. Armstrong. It's all about how publishing works, and we use our own books—including *The Isles of the Gods* and *The Heart of the World*—as examples.

And now, if you'll permit me, a few more quick thank-yous—for truly, no book is created by the author alone.

My team at Adams Literary are wonderful advocates and even better friends—Tracey, Josh, and Anna, thank you for all you do for me.

I am grateful, as always, to my editor, Melanie Nolan, for her insightful questions, editorial eye, and deft hand in steering my books through the publication process.

Many thanks as well to my wonderful teams at Random House in the US, Rock the Boat in the UK, Listening Library for audio, and Allen & Unwin in Australia for your efforts in sales and marketing, production, design, publicity, and beyond.

Thank you to the endlessly generous Virginia Allyn, for the beautiful map at the front of this story, and to Aykut Aydoğdu, for a second cover worthy of the first—the highest compliment I can offer.

I must also thank (and thank again) the many booksellers, librarians, and reviewers who help spread the word about my books—I am grateful for every time you've invited a reader to one of my worlds.

When writing, I am always guided by a series of readers who offer me insight on experiences different from my own. I am, as always, grateful for their time and care.

Many friends in the writing world shared their wisdom as well. Meg Spooner read every page of this book as it came together, and my work—as well as my life—is endlessly richer for her presence. Both C. S. Pacat and Sarah Rees Brennan helped shape the story and were so generous with their time and wisdom. Thank you as well to the many writers and creatives who provided all kinds of other support: Marie Lu, Kiersten White, Susan Dennard, Alex Bracken, Jay Kristoff, Leigh Bardugo, Johnathan McClain, Will Kostakis, Michelle Dennis, the Summer Fridays crew, Eliza Tiernan, Ellie Marney, Kate Armstrong, Lili Wilkinson, Liz Barr, Nicole Hayes, Pete Freestone, and Skye Melki-Wegner. Thank you, always, to the Roti Boti crew, Kat and Gaz, Dale and Zaida, Matt and Jack, Soraya, and Kacey.

My family—both the one I was born into and the one I was lucky enough to marry into—is always a place of calm, always ready to celebrate, always ready to help. Mum and Flic, thank you for the daily chats, especially through the hardest parts of writing this book.

My constant writing companion, my sweet dog, Jack, stayed for as much of the voyage as he could. Jackie, we miss you every day.

My husband, Brendan, has been my rock as I wrote this book through illness and recovery. Brendan, I'm so glad you're my person. I love you.

My daughter, Pip, is so wonderful that I could write pages just listing the things I love about her. Pip, the best part of each day is when you come running down through the garden to my office, bursting to tell me about your adventures. Here's to many, many more.